ROBERT LUDLUM'S
THE BOURNE SHADOW

THE BOURNE SERIES

ROBERT LUDLUM'S THE BOURNE DEFIANCE (*by Brian Freeman*)

ROBERT LUDLUM'S THE BOURNE SACRIFICE (*by Brian Freeman*)

ROBERT LUDLUM'S THE BOURNE TREACHERY (*by Brian Freeman*)

ROBERT LUDLUM'S THE BOURNE EVOLUTION (*by Brian Freeman*)

ROBERT LUDLUM'S THE BOURNE INITIATIVE (*by Eric Van Lustbader*)

ROBERT LUDLUM'S THE BOURNE ENIGMA (*by Eric Van Lustbader*)

ROBERT LUDLUM'S THE BOURNE ASCENDANCY (*by Eric Van Lustbader*)

ROBERT LUDLUM'S THE BOURNE RETRIBUTION (*by Eric Van Lustbader*)

ROBERT LUDLUM'S THE BOURNE IMPERATIVE (*by Eric Van Lustbader*)

ROBERT LUDLUM'S THE BOURNE DOMINION (*by Eric Van Lustbader*)

ROBERT LUDLUM'S THE BOURNE OBJECTIVE (*by Eric Van Lustbader*)

ROBERT LUDLUM'S THE BOURNE DECEPTION (*by Eric Van Lustbader*)

ROBERT LUDLUM'S THE BOURNE SANCTION (*by Eric Van Lustbader*)

ROBERT LUDLUM'S THE BOURNE BETRAYAL (*by Eric Van Lustbader*)

ROBERT LUDLUM'S THE BOURNE LEGACY (*by Eric Van Lustbader*)

THE BOURNE ULTIMATUM

THE BOURNE SUPREMACY

THE BOURNE IDENTITY

THE TREADSTONE SERIES

ROBERT LUDLUM'S THE TREADSTONE RENDITION (*by Joshua Hood*)

ROBERT LUDLUM'S THE TREADSTONE TRANSGRESSION (*by Joshua Hood*)

ROBERT LUDLUM'S THE TREADSTONE EXILE (*by Joshua Hood*)

ROBERT LUDLUM'S THE TREADSTONE RESURRECTION (*by Joshua Hood*)

THE BLACKBRIAR SERIES

ROBERT LUDLUM'S THE BLACKBRIAR GENESIS (*by Simon Gervais*)

ROBERT LUDLUM'S

THE

BOURNE
SHADOW

BRIAN FREEMAN

G. P. PUTNAM'S SONS
NEW YORK

PUTNAM
— EST. 1838 —
G. P. PUTNAM'S SONS
Publishers Since 1838
An imprint of Penguin Random House LLC

ISBN 9780593716458

Printed in the United States of America

This is a work of fiction. Names, characters, places, and incidents either are the product of the
author's imagination or are used fictitiously, and any resemblance to actual persons, living or
dead, businesses, companies, events, or locales is entirely coincidental.

ROBERT LUDLUM'S
THE BOURNE SHADOW

Ten Years Ago

THE YOUNG MAN IN THE RUSTED RENAULT BLAZED AROUND THE CURVES OF the Swiss mountain road. Shadows lengthened around him; it was almost dark. On one side of the car, the granite of the cliff face rose over his head like a craggy, pitted wall. On the other side, inches away from his squealing tires, the land plummeted sharply toward the black lake at the bottom of the valley. He swung the wheel back and forth as he climbed higher, and the old Renault gripped the road like a wild goat clinging to a rocky ledge.

He needed to slow down, but he was late, and he couldn't afford to be late. Not with these men. Not on his first mission.

His fears came in a rush, fueled by a spike of adrenaline. The road. The men. The meeting. And Monika.

Jesus, *where* was Monika? Her apartment near the college was empty, stripped of everything she owned, as if she'd never lived there at all, as if she'd never *existed*! He'd loved her. He'd wanted to marry her.

And she'd betrayed him.

Now she was gone.

Thinking about Monika was a mistake. Focus! Be in the moment! That was what an agent had to do.

But his mind drifted from the road, and he misjudged the next turn. One tire of the Renault scraped over the cliff's edge, and the car lurched. His stomach somersaulted with panic. He twisted the wheel, overcorrecting, and the vehicle slammed into rock with a screech of metal and a spray of broken glass as the left headlight shattered. He hit the brakes, jerking the car to a stop. His head sank forward, his heart pounding.

His handler, Nash Rollins, had warned him about moments like this. Despite all of his training, he wasn't ready. Reality was different in the field. He hadn't learned yet how to smoothly break down his thoughts, organize a plan of action, and tackle each threat one by one. Nash had said that his confidence would come with time, that he should be patient with himself while he gained experience.

You have unique skills. Unique intellect. But professionals are built, not born.

Until then, all he could do was close his eyes and breathe. Forget the distractions, and remember the mission.

The mission is everything.

Treadstone.

But *how* could he shut it all out? Everything was happening to him at once. A year ago, he'd left his home in Paris to become a teacher of language and physical fitness at a private college outside Zurich. He'd found himself in a small Swiss town in the mountains. In love with a beautiful woman. Then Nash Rollins had appeared, sent by David Abbott, the closest man he had to a father, the man after whom he'd been *named*. Nash had told him the real reason he'd been brought to the college and explained the rules of the agency that Abbott expected him to join.

That was how his Treadstone recruitment had begun.

Now there was a Glock in a holster in the small of his back and a knife strapped to his ankle.

Now Monika had vanished.

Now the life of David Webb was falling apart.

No! You are not David Webb! You are Cain!

He drove again. Ahead of him, the road leveled off at a meadow framed by jagged snowcapped peaks in the distance. He drove in and out of low clouds that blew across the fields. The cold made its way through the windows of the Renault and got under his skin. Up here, the road was nothing more than two rutted dirt tracks, and the car bumped forward over the emerald-colored hills.

He didn't have to go far. Not even a mile later, he spotted the chalet.

The meeting point.

It was built of wood and flagstone, with an A-frame roof and huge windows on all sides looking up toward the mountains and down toward the distant valley and lake. Three other vehicles were parked outside, two dark SUVs and a sleek Ferrari in a metallic color that looked like deep purple. One man stood in the tall grass, a semiautomatic rifle level at his waist. A man? No, he was barely more than a boy. Nineteen years old. David knew him as a student in his modern language class. His name was Gunther, from Mannheim, son of the number three executive at one of Germany's largest auto manufacturers. He was the kind of boy who would have money and power handed to him based on nothing more than his family pedigree. Someday he'd be CEO of that company.

Gunther. *Jesus*, Gunther was one of them?

But Nash had said *Le Renouveau* was a hungry spider, trapping the young European elite in its web and wrapping them up to use them in the future. That was why it had to be infiltrated. That was why it had to be destroyed.

The others were inside. They were waiting for him.

David parked his beat-up Renault next to the Ferrari. It was a 458 Italia hardtop model. As he got out, he noticed that the plum-colored sports car had no registration plate. That was the kind of detail Nash had told him to watch. Gunther met him as he got out of the car, with the rifle pointed at his chest.

"*Willkommen*," the boy said, but the welcome had no warmth.

"Hello, Gunther."

"*Bitte keine Namen. Nicht hier.*"

David nodded. No names. It didn't matter that they knew each other. Up here, no one had names.

"*Haben Sie Waffen?*"

"*Natürlich,*" David replied.

"*Gib mir alles.*"

David hesitated. If he declined to hand over his weapons, this rich kid would probably shoot him. He didn't like the idea of walking inside unarmed, but his goal wasn't to kill anyone. The people in the chalet were nothing but gatekeepers, just leaves on one branch of a larger tree. He needed them to accept him, to believe he shared their goals. Once they did, he could gather intelligence on the entire operation. Find their strengths and weaknesses. Find the men in power. *Le Renouveau*.

He moved slowly.

Never make sudden movements when a man is pointing a gun at you.

Treadstone.

He spread his fingers, opened the flap of his coat, and handed Gunther the loaded Glock. He thought about not disclosing the knife, but if they searched him and found it, they'd probably use it to cut his throat. So he pulled up the cuff of his slacks and removed the dagger from its scabbard and gave it to the boy.

Smart move.

The next thing Gunther did was sling his rifle over his shoulder, turn David around and force him against the Renault, and give him a pat-down from head to toe. The kid spent more time than was necessary between David's legs and grinned as he did so. But the search was thorough. Gunther definitely would have found the knife.

Then, rotating the rifle again, the young student gestured at the chalet door with the barrel. David headed that way.

Another student met him at the door, armed with the same kind of rifle. This one was Mario, from Madrid, son of two Spanish lawyers with political connections, the top student in David's fitness class. Whenever David had seen him outside class, Mario had a different girl on his arm. He always wore a grin, like a mask, and his teeth looked especially white against the gloomy shadows of the mountain estate.

"*Der Professor kommt,*" he announced cheerily from behind his smile. "*Was für ein Vergnügen.*"

Then his smile disappeared as he said to Gunther in accented German: "*Du hast ihn durchsucht?*"

"*Ja. Alles klar.*"

With a confirmation that David had been searched, Mario led him from the foyer and down a couple of steps into a vast great room with a high angled ceiling. Lush carpet sank under his feet. Tall windows on two sides looked toward the mountains and valley, but the windows had been swathed in heavy drapes, blocking out the view. A couple of sconces on the timber-sided walls, and a fire in the flagstone fireplace, threw strange shadows.

Two other men stood on either end of a four-paneled room divider, which had been painted with a mural of wildflowers. David couldn't see what was behind the divider. He recognized the two men, as he'd recognized the others. One was another student, an orphan and math prodigy from Prague named Lukas. The other was an economics professor at the college, in his midtwenties like David, a Cambridge Brit named Gavin Wright. They'd had drinks a few times in the year David had been here. Gavin was the one man David had expected to find at the chalet, because Gavin had been his first contact. According to Nash, Gavin Wright was the local field man for *Le Renouveau*, the one tasked with unearthing the political views of teachers and students and determining who might be potential recruits.

So, three months earlier, David had made a point of drinking too much and going on a rant about Muslim immigration in front of Gavin. Not long after, Gavin had floated the idea of introducing David to some people who shared his disgust with the leftist leadership of Europe and were committed to shaping a very different future for the continent. They were looking for men like David, Gavin told him, men who appreciated the hard choices that would have to be made.

Was David interested?

Yes, he was.

After that first meeting, David had worked his way up the chain, answering their questions, passing their tests, submitting to their background checks, all the way to the formal initiation ceremony on the mountainside. Here. Tonight.

He would finally be accepted as an official member of *Le Renouveau*.

Treadstone would have a mole inside the most poisonous neo-Nazi cell in Europe.

Gavin nodded at David from his position beside the painted divider, but he didn't move. He wasn't the man in charge. David realized there was a fifth person in the great room, a man seated in the corner near a staircase that led to the second floor of the chalet. His face was almost invisible in the shadows. All David could see was firelight glinting on silver-framed glasses and long legs ending in shiny black boots. A cloud of cigarette smoke blew out of his mouth toward the high ceiling.

Gunther nudged David with the point of the rifle, and David knew what to say. Gavin had already explained the protocol.

"Ich bin hier, um der Sache mein Leben und meine Treue zu versprechen," David announced.

A long silence followed.

David squinted, trying to see the man in the corner more clearly, but his face remained little more than a ghost hidden behind smoke and shadow. David had a sense of glittering eyes—were they blue?—but he couldn't be sure. He saw the man's arm move with languid slowness, stripping the cigarette from between his lips.

"Auf Englisch, bitte," the man said. *"Sie sind Amerikaner."*

That voice! David was sure he had heard it before. It was familiar to him. But he struggled to place it.

Who was this man?

But David couldn't stay silent any longer.

"I am here to swear my life and loyalty to the cause," he repeated in English.

"Yes, that is better," the man went on. "Americans sound so foolish when they speak anything but English. Ninety percent of Americans can't order a fucking cup of coffee in another language, but you amassed so much power that you made the rest of the world learn English in order to cater to your ignorance. Remarkable."

"I speak five languages fluently," David pointed out.

"Oh, yes, yes, don't misunderstand me. I'm not talking about you. And I say this with nothing but admiration for America. What's the point of having power if you don't use it?" He took another drag on his cigarette and offered up a nasty chuckle. "Of course, having made English the official language of the world, now you're doing your best to give it up for yourselves, aren't you?"

David listened to the man's voice, still trying to pinpoint why he knew it. The man obviously wasn't German or American himself, despite his perfect pronunciation. His raspy voice shifted easily between languages, but there was no obvious giveaway of his native tongue. If he'd been speaking Italian, or French, or Polish, he probably would have sounded different with each one.

It made David think the man was trying to hide his true identity. *We know each other, don't we? How?*

"America has forgotten the *unum*," David replied. "Now it's *e pluribus pluribus*."

"Indeed, but Europe is no better, letting heathens flood our borders."

"I agree."

"So I'm told," the man said, eyes shining in the firelight. "You come highly recommended, but our group searches for much more than philosophy in our members. Philosophy is cheap, easily put on, easily shrugged off. My people say you are blessed with a unique combination of brains and physical skills. That is the kind of man we need. The kind of man who can go far in our organization."

"I'm pleased to hear that," David said. "That's what I want. To make a difference."

"Excellent." The man's voice turned sharp, like the edge of a razor. "However, I'm sure you can appreciate that we need to be careful about whom we invite to join us. The oath you spoke about life and loyalty isn't just words. It must be backed up by action. That's the only way for us to trust that you are a friend and not an enemy. There are spies everywhere who seek to take us down."

"I understand."

"Then I have an assignment for you. From someone who intends to go far, much is expected."

"What is it?"

The man behind the cigarette smoke and the silver glasses gestured with a flutter of his hand at Gavin, who stood beside the elaborately painted screen. Gavin slowly slid the screen closed in accordion style, meeting his partner on the other end. The two men lifted the heavy screen and pulled it aside, revealing what was hidden behind.

A woman sat in a wooden armchair, wrists and legs tied, a black hood covering her head and neck.

Oh God, *no*!

She was unmistakable. He recognized her body, the shape of her torso, the wavy blond hair at her shoulders, the curve of her legs. He'd made love to her a hundred times. He was *in* love with her. This was the woman he was going to spend the rest of his life with.

Monika!

Gavin yanked off the hood, and there she was. That perfect face, oval and slim, tanned skin from sunny days on the ski slopes, dark, wickedly angled eyebrows, nose soft and small, deep red lips. Seeing that face made him want to touch her, kiss her, hold her, protect her.

But she was in danger *because* of him. Her luminous blue eyes were wide with terror, her mouth gagged into silence, her ears covered so she couldn't hear a word of what was happening around her. She stared back at him in shock and confusion, with no idea why she'd been kidnapped and taken here, why she was being held by men with guns, why David was in this room with them.

"I believe you know this woman," the man in the corner said from the darkness.

David had to drag the words from his chest. "I do."

"Fine. Then you will kill her, please."

David blinked, his mind going blank, the words not even registering in his head. "What?"

"Kill her."

"I have no weapon," he protested, hunting for excuses, stalling for time.

"A soldier needs no weapons to kill," the man snapped in an oily voice. "Are you our soldier? Then follow my orders. Do it now. Or I will instruct my men to fire, and they will kill you both."

David tried to remember his training.

He tried to hear Nash's voice in his head. What to do next. How to salvage the mission. How to save the woman he loved. But there was no middle ground left for him. The mission was already blown. He'd failed. He'd moved too fast, pushed too hard. They didn't trust him. They *knew*. Of course they did. They'd known from the beginning that he was a spy. This had always been a trap.

And now he and Monika would both die for his mistakes.

No!

David Webb might fail, David Webb might die, but not Cain, *never*

Cain! Cain was a survivor. He was the man David Abbott had raised him to be. He was a killer. He was Treadstone.

"As you wish," Cain said.

He marched toward the woman in the chair. The barrels of four rifles followed him, ready to fire. The closest was in the hands of Gavin, six feet away, just out of his reach. It would take two steps to reach him, but that was one step too far. If he tried, the bullets would riddle his body before he got there.

Cain stood behind Monika, who squirmed below him, struggling against her bonds, screaming into her gag. He wanted to comfort her, to tell her that everything would be okay, but he couldn't.

His boots snapped together. He came to attention.

"I am here to swear my life and loyalty to the cause," Cain announced loudly.

Then he placed his hands on either side of Monika's trembling head and prepared to break the neck of the woman he loved.

PART ONE

PART ONE

1

The Present

JASON BOURNE WATCHED THE HOT PARIS SUMMER GET EVEN HOTTER.

The protest in the Place de la Bastille began to descend from unrest into violence. Soon there would be rocks and bricks thrown. Fights in the square. Cars on fire. It had been happening that way for weeks. The young people, sweat pouring down their faces in the blazing August sun, hurled threats at the police in their riot gear. At least fifty students had stormed the plaza and the Colonne de Juillet, as if it were the year 1789 again and they were launching another French revolution. The rest of the crowd, hundreds strong, spilled into the surrounding streets. They chanted and marched and waved flags bearing the words *La Vraie*.

True.

As in True France. That was the name of the far-right political party that was threatening to shock the world by winning the next French election.

Bourne sat in an outdoor café on Boulevard Henri IV, directly across from the plaza. The restaurant had been crowded when he arrived, but the other tables were mostly empty now. As the protesters filled the square, the paying customers had scurried away to the nearby Métro station, leaving behind half-eaten cheese plates and cold cups of espresso. Everyone knew what was coming.

He studied the crowd with an analytical eye. Automatically, he looked for the instigators, the hidden hands directing the mayhem. These kinds of protests rarely turned into riots organically. Someone was always there to light the spark with a well-timed knife thrust or a Molotov cocktail. He spotted at least six of them working the crowd, dressed in black robes and wearing Guy Fawkes masks. Bourne could see the wires of radios leading to their ears as they fed instructions back and forth.

Fomenting chaos.

Maybe they were truly part of *La Vraie*, trying to unleash populist anger that would sweep them into power. Or maybe they were agents of the ruling party, hoping to stir a backlash against the violence spreading around the country.

Or maybe something else was at work.

Truth is what you can make people believe.

Treadstone.

It was Thursday afternoon. Bourne always came to this café on Thursdays. He sat at the same table, ordered *steak au poivre*, and left an hour later out of the Bastille station to return to his apartment on the north side of the city. He spent the hour watching the street to see if anyone was watching *him*, but most of all, he kept an eye on the Métro sign above the escalators. If there was a hashtag symbol on the sign in orange chalk, that meant he had a message waiting at a boutique hotel two blocks away off Rue Saint-Antoine.

A message from Abbey Laurent.

But no.

It had been seven months since Abbey had said goodbye to him in Quebec City, and there had been no message since then. Not that he expected one. Abbey had moved on with her life and left the world of Jason Bourne behind her. Their affair was over. And yet he kept coming back to the café.

Every week, as he sat over his fiery pepper steak and a cold bottle of Kronenbourg 1664, Jason thought about sending *her* a message. He'd set up the communications protocol—the back door—so that it worked in both directions. If he scrawled the hashtag on the Métro sign himself, then someone—a lawyer, but he didn't know who—would collect a note for Abbey at the same Rue Saint-Antoine hotel.

Jason rubbed his fingers over the orange chalk in his pocket. He always had it with him, but he'd never used it. The only thing he could say to Abbey was that he was still in love with her, but that was the worst thing he could tell her. He needed to let her get on with her life, and he needed to do the same thing.

Forget Abbey Laurent!

But he couldn't. That was the terrible irony for Jason. The things he wanted to forget were burned into his memory, and the things he wanted to remember were lost in the mists of his brain.

A few years earlier, he'd been shot in the waters off Marseilles. The injury had robbed him of his identity. His memories of who he was had been erased, and all that was left behind were the skills of a killer. His whole past was lost in shadow. Only a few fragments had begun to come back recently, isolated bits and pieces like snippets from a movie. Missions. Deaths. Places. People. For months, strange things had triggered him. Smells, sounds, and faces brought unexpected recollections. But none of it felt real; it felt as if those things had happened to someone else. He didn't know what to believe.

Bourne smelled smoke drifting his way. In the plaza, he saw an arc of fire as a police car erupted in flames. Paving bricks crashed through windows. From the opposite side of the square, where the police gathered, water cannons blew people off their feet. He heard a series of loud bangs, and tear gas rose like a cloud, blowing toward him and stinging his eyes.

Amid the bedlam, he saw the men in the bone-white Guy Fawkes masks calmly moving among the crowd, seeding pockets of disruption. Wherever they went, blood trailed in their wake.

It was time to go.

But before he could stand up, a voice interrupted him.

"Les enfants, eh?"

He glanced sideways. The table on his left was no longer empty. A man sat there, heavyset, about fifty years old. His age didn't make Bourne let down his guard. He wasn't Treadstone—Cain knew the look—but with a glance, Jason assessed the man's upper-body strength and realized he was formidable. The man made no attempt to hide the pistol that was holstered under his gray-checked sport coat. But he kept his hands on the table, fingers spread wide, an obvious signal that he intended no harm.

The man nodded at the chaos unfolding steps away from them. *"C'est toujours les enfants."*

"No, it's not the children," Bourne replied in English. "They're just the foot soldiers. Someone else is orchestrating this."

"You mean our friends in the Fawkes masks?" the man said, also switching to English, although his accent remained French. "Ah, well, they could be children, too, *n'est-ce pas?* It's hard to tell without faces. But I get what you're saying. The orders come from elsewhere."

Formidable and smart.

"Who are you?" Bourne asked.

"A woman who goes by the name Vandal sent me to find you," the man told him. "I'm supposed to give you a message."

Vandal.

That wasn't a name Bourne was expecting.

Unlike this man, Vandal *was* Treadstone. She was an attractive Black woman, tall, lean, and tough. They'd done a mission together in Barcelona three years earlier, and he'd crossed paths with her again the previous summer outside a house in Maryland.

The house where an agent named Nova had died.

Yes, Bourne knew Vandal. But *why* was she sending him a message? And why was she going outside the Treadstone network to do it?

"If Vandal sent you, she knows I'd ask for confirmation that the message came from her," Bourne said. "She'd also want to be sure you're talking to me."

Another firebomb in the Place de la Bastille rocked the street. Neither man flinched or took his eyes off the other.

"Yes, of course," the man replied. "She said I should ask to see the coin."

Jason knew what coin he meant. He kept it in his pocket—a Greek coin encased in a pendant that Nova had worn her whole life. He'd taken it from her body when he found her in Maryland. Vandal was the only person—other than Abbey Laurent—who knew he'd done that.

So asking about the coin was her way of letting Bourne know that the man in front of him was genuine.

Vandal was also smart enough to know that Bourne would have the coin with him. He always did. He dug for the chain inside his pocket and opened his palm long enough for the man to identify it.

When the man nodded his satisfaction, Jason tucked the coin away again.

"How did you find me?" Bourne asked. "Vandal doesn't know where I am."

"Not specifically, but everyone knows Cain's home base is Paris," the man replied. "I have my own sources. It only took a few days before someone spotted you. You're not as much of a ghost as you'd like to think."

Bourne frowned. "Why did Vandal want you to find me?"

"To deliver a warning. You're being hunted, Cain."

"By who?"

"She does not know. She also does not know why, although I imagine there could be any number of people who would like to track down Cain, yes? But it doesn't appear to be the usual suspects. Russia, for example. There's no chatter from that direction, despite what you did to their assassin Lennon last year. Oh, yes, my friend, I know about that, too."

"How did Vandal discover the threat?" Jason asked.

"By accident, it seems. She needed a cleaner for a particularly bloody scene—apparently a man you'd used yourself for similar services in the past. When she got there, she found him in his apartment, almost dead. He'd been tortured for information. She was able to save his life, and he told her that the men who'd done this to him were looking for *you*. He didn't know where you were, so he couldn't tell them anything. But they weren't going to leave him behind to talk."

"Who was this resource?"

"His name is Gabriel Wildhaber."

Bourne shook his head in puzzlement. "That makes no sense. I've never used a cleaner by that name. I don't know him."

"Are you sure?"

It took Jason only a moment to understand what the man meant. He didn't remember anyone named Gabriel Wildhaber, but his memory only went back as far as that moment in Marseilles that had stolen away his life. It was possible he'd used Wildhaber on a job in his forgotten past.

If that was true, then the hunters might be part of his past, too.

"Where is Wildhaber based?"

"Zurich," the man replied.

Zurich.

Jesus!

Yes, Zurich had been a part of his life before and after he'd lost his memory. It drew him like a magnet; it was the first place he'd gone after Marseilles to find his identity. But even years later, the time he'd spent in Zurich *before* his injury remained a mystery. And all he knew of Zurich afterward was death.

The Gemeinschaft Bank! A killer in an elevator! Wherever he'd gone in Zurich, assassins had been hunting for a man known as Jason Bourne.

Just like now.

Who are they?

Across the heat of the street, the violence of the protests crept closer. The riot spilled out of the square, young people screaming and running, the burn of the tear gas getting thicker. Bricks flew. He saw unconscious bodies in the street, blood pouring from head wounds. At the café, a window shattered inward, spraying them with glass. He spotted knives in the hands of people escaping toward the Seine.

And guns, too. Some of the masked men had guns.

"We should go," the man said. "Chaos can be a cover. The danger isn't just in Switzerland, Cain."

"What do you mean?"

"I believe men are looking for you in Paris, too. I told you, I have sources. One of them made the mistake of using your code name. Twenty-four hours later, the police pulled him out of the river."

"And Vandal has no idea what this is about?" Bourne asked.

"No, but Wildhaber mentioned a Zurich café. The Drei Alpen-häuser. She said that would mean something to you."

Jason felt a pounding in his head, a sharp pain exploding behind his eyes. The Drei Alpenhäuser! A restaurant only steps from the lake! The café had practically been his Treadstone headquarters when he'd operated in Zurich. He'd been there countless times; he'd used it for contacts and drops. He'd gone there after Marseilles, and they'd *recognized* him at a time when he didn't even recognize himself.

They knew him as Cain.

They knew him as Jason Bourne.

"Wildhaber said someone at the Drei Alpenhäuser had been asking about you," the man continued.

"One of the killers?"

"He didn't think so. He said a woman had been at the café several times looking for anyone who knew you. She said she needed your help. Vandal went to the café to see if the woman showed up again, but she got called away on a mission. That's when she reached out to me and asked me to find you."

"Did Vandal get a name for this woman? Or a description?"

"No name. Young, late twenties, blond hair—"

The man suddenly stopped talking.

He stopped because he was dead.

What looked like a fly landing on his forehead was the hole left by a bullet tunneling soundlessly into his brain. As the man slid off the chair, more bullets hit the windows behind Bourne and ricocheted off the metal table with sharp pings. He threw himself to the ground, drawing his Sig Sauer into his hand, and rolled onto his stomach, arms extended. Near the escalator leading down to the Bastille station, a killer in a Guy Fawkes mask fired his handgun, emptying his magazine at Bourne, bullets kicking up concrete shrapnel that flew like razor blades. Jason drew a bead on the man, but panicked people flooded the sidewalk between them, and he had no shot.

When the killer's gun was empty, Bourne scrambled to his feet and charged. The masked assassin jumped down the stairs toward the Métro. At the station escalator, Jason leaped the fence and landed hard on the moving stairs. He shouldered his way through a crush of people into the underground and swung left and right, trying to find the killer among hundreds of bodies.

But he was too late.

At his feet, he saw a black robe and cowl, like something a monk would wear, plus a white plastic Guy Fawkes mask being kicked and trampled by people running for the trains. The killer had shed his disguise. He was gone.

Bourne hiked back to the street. He wiped blood off his face where it had sprayed from the gunshot that killed the man. Outside the café, police had already begun to gather around the dead body.

The body of the man who'd come to deliver a warning.

You're being hunted, Cain.

Jason melted into the crowd. He needed to be gone before someone pointed him out to the police. He didn't bother heading to his Paris apartment. If that man could find him, then others could, too. His apartment was blown. Instead, he marched south on Boulevard Bourdon, leaving the madness behind him.

Fifteen minutes later, he was at Gare de Lyon, in the ticket line for an SNCF high-speed train to Switzerland.

Zurich.

Bourne had to go back to where everything was dark. He had to return to his past.

2

JASON STOOD IN THE SHADOWS OF A HOTEL LOCATED ON A SIDE STREET off the bustling Falkenstrasse. He could see the twilight waters of the Zürichsee one block away. A taxi passed in front of him, and a middle-aged couple got out on the far side of Dufourstrasse. They were elegantly dressed, as if they'd come for a late dinner after an evening at the symphony. The man paid the driver, and then he and his wife strolled inside the café on the corner, passing below its distinctive logo of three wooden triangles set against white stone.

Three Swiss chalets.

The Drei Alpenhäuser.

Jason felt his chest tighten, choking off his breath. Sweat gathered on his neck. Years ago, after Marseilles, he'd been drawn to this place by nothing but instinct, remembering those strange triangles. He'd known that this restaurant was important to him—he could recall exactly how it looked inside, with heavy crossbeams along the ceiling and romantic candlelit booths—but he hadn't known *why*.

God, he'd been young then. It may as well have been a lifetime ago.

He tugged up the collar on his jacket. Cool air blew off the lake, rustling his close-cropped brown hair. He reminded himself to be in the moment. A man named Gabriel Wildhaber had been tortured and nearly killed by people hunting for Bourne. If the killers knew about Wildhaber, then one way or another, they knew about the Drei Alpen-häuser. So it stood to reason that the café would be under surveillance.

Where? Where were they?

He eyed the street leading to the lake. The sidewalk tables. The doorways. The parked cars. There were plenty of people enjoying a Swiss summer night, but no one paid special attention to the comings and goings at the Drei Alpenhäuser. Then he realized he was looking in the wrong place. The hunters wouldn't know if or when he was coming back to Zurich, so they wouldn't mount a stakeout from the street. An agent hanging out here for hours might attract attention from the police.

This was a long-term assignment. One bored man in a window.

Above his head were the four floors of the Opera Hotel. The corner rooms all looked down on the café entrance. He was sure that in one of those rooms a man was smoking in the darkness, binoculars on the window ledge so that he could grab them and zoom in on every face arriving at the restaurant.

Bourne didn't give the watcher a face to see. He tucked his chin down and set out across the street, not looking over his shoulder. Whoever was manning the vigil in the hotel behind him would only observe the back of his head, not enough to match to a photograph or a description. Jason shoved his hands in his pockets—a man not worried about anyone spotting him—and headed directly for the café. He waved to a stranger on the sidewalk, as if he were a local out on the town, then shoved through the heavy door of the Drei Alpenhäuser and let it swing shut behind him.

Jesus, it was all so familiar! As if no time had passed!

The sharp aroma of *raclette*. The singsong whine of the accordion as an old man went from table to table playing his Bavarian music. The candles flickering on the faces of discreet lovers tucked into their booths. And not just lovers. This was a place to meet without being seen, for deals to be made, for money to be exchanged under the table. That was why Cain had used it in the past.

"Herr Bourne!" exclaimed the maître d', returning to his podium near the front of the restaurant. He was a small man in a well-pressed suit, his hair gray, his mustache thin. "What a pleasure to have you join us again. It's been some time now."

Nothing ever changed here. The same faces. The same smiles.

What was the man's name? Jason tried to pull it out of his memory.

"Yes, thank you, Simon," Bourne told him. "I'm afraid my business hasn't taken me to Zurich for a while. I've missed it."

"Your usual table? The booth near the back?"

"Please."

Simon led him through the dimly lit café. Jason was conscious of eyes watching him from the shadows. Everyone watched everyone else here. They reached the booth, which was definitely the location Cain would have chosen, steps away from the kitchen doors, providing an easy escape in the event of trouble. The maître d' handed him a leather-bound menu and a wine list, and before the man could leave, Bourne slid a hundred-euro note across the black tablecloth. Compensation for favors in the past and future.

"I need your help, Simon," Bourne said.

"Anything, sir," the man replied, pocketing the cash.

"I'm told someone has been asking for me here."

The man's face showed surprise. "For you, Herr Bourne? I don't believe so."

"I understand she's been here several times. Blond, in her twenties."

Simon frowned. "Well, that would describe a large part of our clientele. But truly, Herr Bourne, if anyone had asked for you by name, I would remember it. In fact, I would have taken special care to find out who the person was so that I could alert you as soon as you returned. You have always been most generous."

"All right. Thank you, Simon."

"Enjoy your dinner, sir."

Bourne eased back in the booth. He tried to make sense of it. He was *known* here. This restaurant was Cain's ground zero in Zurich. According to Gabriel Wildhaber, a woman had come here looking for him, and yet the maître d' remembered no one asking about Jason Bourne. Why?

Was it a trap?

Was Simon calling in the hunters right now? This was Switzerland, and the Swiss knew how to blow with the prevailing winds. Herr Bourne was generous, but that wouldn't keep a man at a restaurant from shifting loyalties for the right price. He decided he'd made a mistake by coming here. He was too exposed. He pushed away the menu and was about to head for the café's rear door, but then he saw something that changed his mind.

That man!

He knew that man!

Through the shadows of the restaurant, Bourne spotted an obese wine steward opening a bottle of Riesling for an older Swiss businessman and his much younger companion. The steward wore a ridiculous costume, like a yodeler in the mountains, and he posted a fake smile as he extolled the virtues of the wine. But sweat covered his huge head, and his stare kept darting toward Bourne, terror in his eyes.

That man knew *him*, too.

Their relationship went way back, into the shadows that Jason didn't remember. A contact, a go-between.

When the steward had finished pouring the Riesling, he made a slow tour from table to table, checking in with the other guests, before he finally arrived at Bourne's booth. The fat man leaned forward, wiping sweat from his mustache and patting down the comb-over across his bald head.

His voice, when he spoke, was high-pitched and strained. "You! Why did you come back? Are you crazy?"

Bourne shrugged. "I'm just a man having dinner. I hear the schnitzel is excellent."

"Do not play games with me, *Cain*. I hoped I would never see you again. I am out of the business. I cannot help you!"

The man clamped his mouth shut and straightened up as one of the other guests headed for the exit. The diner, an oily young American with flaming red hair, offered a compliment on the selection of the brut rosé and pressed a tip into the steward's palm as the two shook hands. The fat man thanked him officiously and waited until the redhead was out of earshot before turning back to Bourne's table.

"Out of the business?" Jason asked. He pried open the man's thick fingers. "A two-hundred-euro tip on a fifty-euro bottle of champagne? Your advice isn't worth that much. But drugs are. Escorts are."

The steward wrestled away his hand. "I still have to make a living, don't I? I have a family, for God's sake! But finding an evening's entertainment for a lonely tourist is different from helping people like you. I want nothing to do with you!"

"What about Gabriel Wildhaber?" Bourne asked.

"Wildhaber nearly died! They tortured him! Do you think I want to end up like that?"

"What men? Who came after him?"

"I don't know! I swear I don't know!"

"I hear they were looking for *me*," Bourne said. "Have they been in here? Did they talk to you?"

"No! Why would they do that? You know how it works. They would keep the café under surveillance and wait for you to show up. Like you did! Tonight! I'm telling you, nobody talked to me!"

Bourne studied the man's nervous face and knew he was lying.

"*Somebody* talked to you," he said. "Wildhaber said a woman was asking about me at the Drei Alpenhäuser. How would he know that if you didn't tell him?"

"All right!" the man hissed, glancing around at the other tables. "All right, yes, there was a woman. She was desperate to find you. She had a photograph taken here at the café. A picture from the old, old days. But I recognized you. I told her I didn't know where you were. I hadn't seen you in years. But I said I would talk to a friend and see if he could help."

"Wildhaber."

"Yes! Wildhaber!"

"How did you find him? Where is he?"

"He's where he always is. He hasn't moved. Selnaustrasse near the Sihl. I may not be in the business anymore, but I keep tabs on people. So, yes, I talked to him. And then they came after him! I've been terrified ever since that I'm next."

"How much did the woman pay you?"

"What?"

"You sold me out, old friend. What's the price of betrayal these days?"

His eyes widened. "You must understand, I did not believe she meant you harm! She said nothing about Cain—or about Jason Bourne."

"Who is she? How do I find her?"

The fat man shook his head. "I don't have a name. I don't know where she is. All I have is a phone number. She asked me to text her if I saw you again—if you ever came in here. I swear, I know nothing else!"

Bourne frowned as he weighed the risks.

A woman trying to find him, a woman with a photograph of him from the past. It was obviously a lie, a fake. She had to be working with the killers, setting a trap to lure him from hiding. And yet the pieces of the puzzle didn't fit. This woman already knew about the Drei Alpenhäuser. She knew that he used to come here. So why torture Wildhaber for information they already had?

Something else was going on.

"Text her," Bourne said.

"What?"

"Text her right now. Tell her I'm in the restaurant but she needs to hurry."

"Yes! Yes, all right! But then we are done!"

"We're done when I say we're done," Bourne told him. "You forgot what it means to work for Cain. When someone asks, *you don't know me.*"

The man's multiple chins wriggled with moisture and fear. He grabbed a phone from his pocket, and his huge fingers stabbed at the keys. Bourne made sure he sent the correct message, and then he snatched the phone from the man and put it on the table in front of him.

The message went through, first delivered, then read moments later.

Almost immediately, a reply came back in German. *I'm on my way! Twenty minutes. Make sure he doesn't leave, please!*

"You see," the fat man said, his voice pleading. "You see, I did what you asked. She's coming. Now let me have my phone."

"You'll get it when we're done. I don't want you warning her."

"You know I would never—"

"I already know you'd give me up for the right price," Jason said. "Now get me a bottle of the Vinothek Riesling. And remember—you have a debt to pay, *mein Freund.*"

"Yes! Yes, right away!"

The fat man couldn't get away from him fast enough.

Soon after, a waitress brought the expensive wine for him and opened it and poured a large glass. Bourne took a drink of the wine, which was cold and sweet, and he kept an eye on the man's phone as the time ticked by. No other messages arrived from the woman. From where he was, he could see the entrance of the café. He slid his Sig Sauer from its holster and placed it next to him on the velvet cushion of the booth. He blew out the candle, leaving himself mostly in darkness.

The woman had said twenty minutes, but she was there in fifteen.

He was sure it was her. She looked out of breath, as if she'd been running, and she scanned the restaurant impatiently as she burst through the door. Simon offered her a table, but she ignored him. The woman was as described, late twenties, with straight blond hair that fell to the middle of her chest. Her long hair was wet; it had begun to rain outside. She was tall and thin, wearing drainpipe red jeans and a sleeveless T-shirt that hugged her body like a second skin. Her damp face was narrow, her nose long, her cheekbones high and sharp, her chin dimpled.

She was very attractive.

When she didn't see him right away, her forehead screwed up with frustration and her fists clenched. Then he stood up, and with the speed of a laser beam, her eyes found him at the back of the restaurant. She blinked, as if not believing he was real, and she rushed to his booth, every step filled with frantic energy.

"My God, it's you!" she whispered, her words tumbling together. "It's really you. I can't believe I finally found you. David! David Webb!"

3

HE UNDERSTOOD NOW WHY THE MAÎTRE D' HADN'T KNOWN THAT ANYONE was searching for him at the Drei Alpenhäuser. This woman didn't know him as Jason Bourne. She didn't know him as Cain. She knew him from an identity that he didn't even remember himself, an identity he hadn't used in ten years.

His real name. David Webb.

"You don't remember me, do you?" she asked as she slid into the booth next to him. He moved over to give her room, but his fingers closed around the Sig. Just in case.

"No, I don't. I'm sorry."

"That's okay. We only met once. It was here, right here in this café. I was in Zurich to visit my sister. Well, and to meet you, too. She'd been bragging about this fellow teacher she'd met at the college. The younger man in her life. You were as handsome as she promised." The woman reached for the bottle with trembling hands, poured herself a glass of Riesling, and drank hungrily from it. Then she smiled with relief. Her pale blue eyes glinted in the shadows like two sapphires. "Wow, I have to say, you still are."

Bourne tried to keep his face like a mask, not showing his confusion. He didn't remember any of this. Not this woman. Not her sister. *Nothing!* Some of his time as Jason Bourne—as *Cain*—had begun to creep back into his mind in fits and starts, but his life as David Webb remained almost entirely a blank slate.

"I'm Johanna Roth," the woman went on.

She reached around to the back of her jeans and pulled out a small, wrinkled photograph and smoothed it on the table.

"See? I took this picture at dinner that day. That's you and Monika."

Jason took the photograph in his hand. He focused on the man in the picture first, and it was definitely him. David Webb. He'd seen photographs going back to his childhood, so he knew himself from the past, but it was always like looking at a stranger's face. This man was younger, more boyish, more innocent, definitely not a Treadstone agent yet. Death and violence hadn't etched their scars into his features. But everything else was the same, the square jaw, the swept-back brown hair, the intense blue-gray eyes. What looked foreign and out of place in the picture was the smile he wore. He saw happiness in that smile, the kind of contentment a young man could feel when he didn't know what lay ahead.

Was it real?

Photographs could be faked. Altered. Manipulated. But he didn't think that was the case with this picture. For one thing, the background was definitely the Drei Alpenhäuser, the same booth in the same restaurant. But the décor had changed in ten years, which made the image feel authentic. The cushioning in the booth was gray now and had been red then. The painting behind him now was colorful and modern, whereas in the photograph, he sat in front of a traditional oil portrait of the Matterhorn. The details felt right, too. He could *feel* himself in that place.

Then there was the girl.

Monika.

Who *was* she? He squeezed his eyes shut and tried to remember anything about her. There was *something* hidden away in his mind, but he couldn't grasp it. His head throbbed with pain, the way it did when he forced memories to the surface rather than letting them come to him on their own.

Monika.

His brain gave him nothing, but his heart remembered her with a strange ache that was full of regret. His mouth went dry with longing. His lips felt warm, as if he'd been kissed. His arms felt heavy, as if this woman should be wrapped up in them. She was older than he'd been back then, at least in her midthirties, but age had never mattered to him. He could imagine those pale blue eyes staring back at him; he could feel the lush strands of her blond hair twisted around his fingers. Yes, he'd been in love with her. He could see it in the way he pulled her close to him in the photograph and held her like a treasure. David Webb loved this woman.

But Jason Bourne had no idea who she was.

He shook himself out of the past. The photograph had disoriented him, but he couldn't afford to lose sight of what was going on.

You're being hunted, Cain.

He focused on Johanna. She still had the wineglass in her hand, but she struggled to hold it because her body kept twitching. The frenetic energy masked something else. Fear. He took a second look at her pretty face, and he noticed the pale discoloration of bruises on her neck and arms.

She'd been beaten.

"What's going on, Johanna? Why have you been trying to find me?"

"I need your help," she replied. "My sister is in danger."

"Why do you think that?"

The woman inhaled sharply, her breasts swelling on her bony frame. "A month ago, this man showed up at my apartment. I live in Salzburg. You know, the hills are alive with the sound of music, and all that shit. I work for an IT start-up out of Berlin, but it's all remote. Anyway, this guy was about fifty years old, expensive suit, cologne, but there was something creepy about him. I don't know, it was weird, he kept taking off his glasses and cleaning them in an OCD way. I didn't like it. He said he was a lawyer, and he wanted to know where Monika was."

"Did he say why?" Bourne asked.

"He said he'd been hired to find her by a student she taught in Switzerland years ago. The kid hit it rich with some AI software, and he wanted to thank the people who'd gotten him to that point in life. Including his teachers. He wanted to give her some stock in his company. I mean, cool, right? But it sounded fishy to me."

"What did Monika teach?"

Johanna looked at him with a sudden suspicion. "What? Literature, of course. How could you not remember that?"

"Later," Jason said. "What did you tell him?"

"The truth. I have no idea where Monika is. I haven't spoken to her in ten years."

Ten years!

Bourne felt his past touching him again, like icy fingers on his neck. Ten years ago, everything had begun. Ten years ago, he'd become part of Treadstone. Like a trigger, his brain hit him with an unexpected memory, something he'd never seen in his mind before. He was in a car speeding up a mountain road. Dirt scraping under his tires, glass shattering. He felt a rush of adrenaline, his breath hammering in his chest.

You are not David Webb! You are Cain!

Just as quickly, another vision sped through his mind. He saw a woman's silky blond hair, her head trapped between his strong hands. There was a voice in his ears. He knew that voice! He knew that man!

Kill her!

"Are you all right?" Johanna asked.

"I'm fine," he replied quickly. "Go on. What else did this man say?"

"Well, he started asking why it had been so long since we talked and why we'd lost touch. Did I have any way to locate her? Did I know any of her friends? That was when I really got suspicious. So I told him to leave."

"What happened then?"

"That night I was jogging in the Volksgarten. Two men attacked me. They beat the shit out of me. They kept asking me where Monika was, and they didn't believe me when I said I didn't know. And they— they asked about you, too. Did I know where David Webb was? Did I know how to find him? I swear they would have killed me if somebody hadn't seen us and shouted that they were calling the police."

"What did you do?"

"I was in the hospital for a couple of days. When I got out, I packed a bag, and I left. I wanted to get as far away from Salzburg as I could. I took a leave from my job. I bounced around Vienna and Munich for a few days, but then I came to Zurich. This was where I last saw Monika. And it's where I met you, too. I remembered that we came to this restaurant and the people here knew you back then. Like you were a regular. So I thought I'd ask around to see if you ever came back here."

Bourne frowned as he tried to piece together the chain of events in his head, but he realized they'd run out of time. The pursuers had already caught up with him. The air in the café changed as the door to the street opened again, and he watched two men come inside. One was in his forties, with silver hair and gold-rimmed glasses. The second man was younger and smaller, with an egg-shaped bald head. Both men wore suits.

Both men were killers. He knew the look.

"The lawyer," Jason said. "And the two men in the park. Did you mention Zurich to them? Or the Drei Alpenhäuser?"

"No, I didn't tell them anything."

Jason shook his head. It didn't matter what she'd said. They'd set Johanna on the trail to find her sister, and they'd been following her since Salzburg. She had taken them right to the Drei Alpenhäuser. They might not have seen Bourne come in tonight—they might not even know what Bourne looked like—but whoever was watching from the Opera Hotel would have recognized Johanna and known why she was running back to the café.

The call had gone out. *He's here.*

He pulled her deeper into the shadows of the booth, and her eyes were puzzled as she stared back at him.

"What's going on?"

"Two men just came in," he said. "Do you recognize them?"

Johanna's gaze shifted to the door of the café. Her face blanched. "Oh, fuck! Oh my God, that's them. How did they find us?"

She began to get up in panic, but he pushed her down. "Not yet. Don't move. Stay where you are."

"What do we do?"

"When I tell you, head for the kitchen door. Don't slow down, don't stop. Keep going for the alley, and when you get outside, run. I'll meet you on the Münsterbrücke over the Limmat in one hour."

Johanna shook her head. "I don't understand. How do you know about these things?"

"Later," he said again.

Bourne watched Simon show the men to two separate tables. The smaller, younger man took a booth near the café door. He was the backup. The other man, with the gold-rimmed glasses, followed Simon through the restaurant. His eyes casually monitored the other diners, and the shadows and candlelight didn't fool him. His gaze passed across Bourne and Johanna, registering their presence without any reaction. Simon sat him at a table twenty feet away, where he had a direct line of sight on Bourne's booth.

One of the man's hands stayed out of sight behind the open wine list on the table. Jason was sure he had a gun aimed across the restaurant. Meanwhile, Bourne already had his finger curled around the trigger of his Sig, and he propped his other hand under the heavy wooden table of the booth.

"What are we waiting for?" Johanna asked, unable to drag her terrified gaze away from the man watching them.

"Hang on," Jason murmured. "As soon as I tell you, *go*. Don't hesitate, just run straight for that door and keep moving. Got it?"

"Yes, but what about you?"

"Don't worry about me. I'll meet you in one hour on the Limmat."

Bourne waited for his moment. He saw a young waiter in a red uniform emerge through the outbound kitchen door with a silver tray propped on his hand. The man headed toward the front of the restaurant on a route that would take him directly in front of Bourne's booth. The timing had to be perfect.

But the man in the gold-rimmed glasses saw what was happening, too. He shoved back his chair, the gun in his hand, his arm leveling for the shot.

The waiter would cross between Jason and the killer in *three, two—*

One!

"Go!" Jason hissed at Johanna.

She did what he wanted and bolted from the booth. In the same instant, his left hand hoisted the table into the air and sent it crashing into the waiter in front of him. The man fell; the platter flew. Bourne dove for the floor as two bullets spat into the wall above his head. He slithered forward as more bullets chased him, and a stinging pain burned across his calf. Rolling back, he aimed the Sig, but the waiter chose that moment to get to his knees, blocking his shot. The killer in the gold-rimmed glasses fired, drilling a bullet into the young waiter's head, and the innocent man crashed down onto Bourne, pinning his gun arm to the floor.

More bullets exploded, one after another, landing on the dead waiter's body.

Then a separate fusillade erupted from the front of the restaurant. The second killer fired across the café, his arms together in a tight V. Around them, diners screamed, throwing themselves under tables and scrambling for the exit. Bourne lifted his wrist and shot back, once, twice, three times, landing a shot in the man's chest with the third bullet. He fired once more, another hit, and the man fell.

But the first killer was already aiming his suppressed Glock right at Bourne. The man had the drop on him, and he wouldn't miss. Then a gruesome crack sounded, like bone breaking. Glass shattered, and blood poured over the killer's head as he pitched forward.

Except the flood of liquid streaming across the floor wasn't blood. It was wine.

The obese wine steward stood where the killer had been, the broken neck of a Burgundy bottle in his hand. The killer lay on the café floor, unconscious. The rest of the café was virtually empty now. Everyone had fled or taken refuge under their tables. But Jason could hear screaming outside and the wail of sirens already drawing closer.

Bourne scrambled to his feet and holstered his gun.

"All debts are paid," the fat man told him. "Now get the fuck out of here, Cain, and never come back."

4

BOURNE LIMPED ALONG THE COBBLESTONES OF LIMMATQUAI THROUGH the darkness. A late-evening streetcar rattled past him on its tracks. He emerged into the open square near the river, with the twin fifteenth-century towers of the Grossmünster rising over his head and the old bridge across the water immediately on his left. Sheets of rain made halos around the streetlights. He waited in the shadows, examining the archways in the buildings for threats. From where he was, he could see a lone figure in the middle of the bridge, silhouetted by the gauzy lights.

Johanna.

He'd wondered if she would really be there. Part of him had expected her to run.

Jason crossed to the railing and followed the walkway along the river. Johanna saw him coming, and she splashed forward through the puddles to greet him. When she was within reach, he spun her around and pushed her hard against the metal railing. His body leaned into her back, and his hands patted down her wet clothes.

"What the fuck?" she demanded, squirming to get away. "What are you doing?"

"Checking you for wires," Bourne said.

"You think it was *me*? You think I did this? You're crazy!"

"I don't know you," Jason told her, "and I sure as hell don't trust you."

Johanna pressed her mouth shut. Her resistance relaxed, and she spread her arms and legs to let him search her. He was thorough, and he found nothing. When he was done, Johanna turned around, her face flushed with humiliation. She put her hands on his chest and pushed him heavily, driving him a few steps back.

"Satisfied?"

"For now."

"I *didn't* know those men were coming. I swear. I don't know how they knew I was there."

"I'm pretty sure they had a spy watching the café," Bourne told her. "He saw you come in and figured you were meeting me. So he called for reinforcements."

Johanna pushed away the blond hair from her eyes. "Then I'm sorry. I don't think like that. It never occurred to me that anyone would be watching the restaurant. I'm not trying to put you in danger. I'm just worried about my sister."

Her sister.

Monika.

Jason saw the woman's face in the photograph again. For the first time, he had an actual memory of her, just a sudden flash of recollection like a short video clip. He saw Monika on the heights of a church somewhere, her sad intense gaze wrapping itself around him. She was a woman with so much depth, borne down by a weight that he wanted to lift for her. They were by the sea.

Was it France? Mont Saint-Michel?

He heard a voice in his head. His own voice.

I think we should get married.

And then he remembered her head locked between his hands, the way it would be before he broke her neck. He couldn't say to Johanna what he was thinking to himself. *You'll never find Monika. I killed her.*

"You're hurt," Johanna said with concern, noticing the blood he trailed onto the wet pavement. "Are you okay?"

"I'm fine."

"Should we go to the hospital?"

"No, I can deal with it myself."

"What happened at the café?"

"Don't worry about that. I got out. I'm here."

"But those men," Johanna said. "What about them?"

"I killed one of them. The other is still out there. They'll be search-ing the city. We can't stay in the open for much longer."

Her eyes shot open. "You *killed* him? *You* did?"

"Yes."

"My God, David, I don't—I mean, who the hell *are* you?"

He glanced through the rain at the sluggish waters of the Limmat below them. "I'm not David Webb. Not anymore. My name is Jason Bourne."

"Well, David or Jason, that doesn't explain anything. Are you some kind of cop?"

"What I am doesn't matter. The less you know about me, the safer you are. Now let's go. We need to get to a hotel."

He took her by the elbow, but she fixed her feet on the bridge. "No, wait. I have one more question."

Bourne stared at her. "All right."

"Did Monika know? I mean, did she know who you were? The things you do?"

"Back then, I was still David Webb," he replied. "At least in the beginning, that's who I was. After that, I don't know what she knew about me. I don't know what I told her. But I doubt I told her anything at all."

That was true. No matter how close he was to Monika, he would have kept her in the dark. He was Treadstone, and Treadstone kept its secrets.

Johanna shook her head. "I don't understand. How could you not know what you told her? Like in the restaurant. You didn't remember that Monika taught literature. That makes no sense."

Jason debated how much to say. He needed answers, but those answers came from a part of his life that didn't exist for him anymore. This woman knew more about those days than he did. She could guide him; she could help him. For now, he had to make her an ally. That meant telling her at least part of the truth.

"A few years ago, I was shot," he explained. "I took a bullet to the head. I survived, but the injury erased my memory. I didn't know who I was or *what* I was. Most of my past is still empty. Gone. David Webb is just a name. He's not me."

"Jesus." She came forward and put her warm hands on his cheeks. "You don't remember her, do you? You don't even remember Monika."

"No."

"My God, you were in love with her."

"Maybe I was. I don't know. I feel something when I see her picture, like an echo, but that's all."

"I'm so sorry." Johanna took away her hands and stepped back. A gust of wind on the river swirled her wet hair across her face. She looked around nervously, as if afraid that ghosts would come out of the darkness. "You don't have any way to find her, do you? You don't know where she is."

"No." He chose his words carefully. "I don't even know if she's still alive."

"But you were the one who helped her escape."

Bourne blinked with surprise. "*I* helped her escape? Are you sure?"

"Yes. You built a new identity for her. You sent her into hiding."

"How do you know that?"

"Because Monika called me," Johanna told him. "Ten years ago, she called me from Switzerland. The call came out of nowhere in the middle of the night. She said something terrible had happened. People had been killed, and she was in danger. She said she needed to start a new life, somewhere safe. She said *you* were the one helping her, and if there was some kind of emergency, I should find you. That was it. She was calling to say goodbye. I never spoke to my sister again."

BOURNE FOUND A CHEAP GUESTHOUSE FOR THEM IN HEINRICHSTRASSE.

The name and location of the hotel, in a quiet neighborhood near the St. Josef church, came to him without consciously thinking about where they could hide. The details were simply in his head when he needed them. That was how his past worked now, by instinct rather than memory. He knew the guesthouse was owned and run by a woman who didn't ask questions, and he knew she took cash to keep the names of certain guests off the register.

"I have no clothes," Johanna pointed out when they were safely inside the second-floor room. "Nothing. All my things are at my own hotel."

"Give me your key," Bourne said. "I'll go and pack up for you. I want to see if anyone's waiting for you to come back."

Johanna gave him that same confused, frightened look again. It was a look he knew well.

Who are you?

Bourne sat down on one side of the single twin bed. He patted the sagging mattress for Johanna to take the other side. She kicked off her sneakers and dragged her knees up until she could wrap her arms around her red jeans. Her face and hair were still damp, and a little shiver coursed through her body. He got up and went to the bathroom for one of the towels and brought it back for her.

"Thank you," she said.

She pushed the towel around her hair and skin and tried to dry herself. Her bare arms were muscular. She was strong, but he could still see fading bruises where she'd been beaten. Messy strands of blond hair fell across her forehead, and her face turned pink as she rubbed it. Her blue eyes had wide, round whites, giving her a vulnerable intensity. Her lips were pale, tilting naturally downward, and her teeth weren't perfectly straight. But her face was much more than the sum of its parts. It was the kind of face with interesting depths to be explored. She wasn't a one-note woman who always wore the same expression.

Abbey's face was like that, too.

He found himself staring at her features, and she noticed.

"What are you looking at?" she asked. "Are you trying to see *her* in me?"

"Partly."

But partly Jason just enjoyed looking at her.

"Well, you won't see all that much of Monika. We're only half sisters. Same father, same last name, different mothers."

Jason nodded. "You're also American. I can hear it in your voice."

"Half," Johanna replied. "Monika was all German. But her mother died when she was ten, and my father remarried a woman from Chicago. A few years after that, I came along. The marriage didn't last long, but I liked having an older sister. So I stayed close to Monika even after I moved back to the U.S. with my mother. I lived in Chicago until after college, and then I decided to move to Europe. That's how I wound up in Austria."

"How old were you when you last talked to Monika?"

"Nineteen."

"Tell me how it happened," Bourne said.

Johanna clutched her knees a little tighter. "I already told you what I know. I spent a couple weeks in Switzerland over spring break ten years ago. That's when I met you. I hung out with Monika and we had a great vacation together, and then I went home. That was that. There was nothing unusual. But over the summer, she called me, and just like that, she was gone. I never heard from her again."

"Did you correspond with her in the interim? Between your vacation and that last phone call?"

"Sure. Everything sounded normal. She didn't talk about anything being wrong."

Bourne hesitated. "Did she mention me?"

"Yes, all the time. I mean, the two of you were going to get married. You took a trip to France in June, and you came back engaged."

"Mont Saint-Michel," he murmured. "I asked her at Mont Saint-Michel."

"That's right. She told me that in one of her letters. It sounded really romantic. Do you remember it?"

He shook his head. "No, not really. I just know that's what happened. How long after that did she call to say she had to go away?"

"About a month, I think. Early July."

"And she didn't give any hints that something was wrong?"

"No."

"After her call, did you talk to anyone about it? Your father?"

"He died the previous year. I talked to my mother about it, and we reached out to the Swiss authorities to see if we could find out what was going on. But we didn't get any answers. Monika was just—gone."

"What about me? Did you try to reach me?"

"Monika told me I should only try to find you if it was an emergency. She said I'd be putting both of you in danger if I interfered. I kept hoping I'd hear from her again, but I never did."

"You're sure this was July ten years ago?" he asked. "That's when she disappeared?"

"Positive."

"And she said that people had been killed? She was in danger?"

"Yes."

Bourne got up from the bed. He went to the window and checked the street below them, which was empty. It was past midnight. He tried to make sense of the timeline in his head, but he couldn't, because he remembered none of it. The only thing he knew of that part of his life was what Nash Rollins had told him.

Ten years ago, he'd been a teacher at an elite private college in the mountains outside Zurich. David Abbott had gotten him the job. David Abbott—the man who'd raised him and mentored him when his own parents had been killed at the Pentagon that one awful day in September. It was the perfect job for a young man destined to follow his mentor into government work—a chance to observe how Europe's future leaders were being molded, to witness close-up the sociological and political forces shaping the continent.

Except that was not his destiny.

Treadstone was his destiny.

Nash Rollins had shown up in Zurich—my God, he'd met him *at the Drei Alpenhäuser*—and told David that his future lay elsewhere. That David Abbott wanted him to be a part of the new agency he'd founded. His training had begun in that city and continued for months. Physical. Mental. Emotional. He'd learned all of the rules that would guide the rest of his life, and then he'd been sent off on his own.

That was how Nash had described David Webb's Treadstone initiation to Jason Bourne.

Jason Bourne, who had no memory of his previous life.

But Nash had said nothing to him about a mission in Zurich. As far as Bourne knew, his first mission for Treadstone had been *after* he'd left the college for good. It was a routine surveillance operation in Helsinki over Christmastime that year. But now he realized that a piece of the puzzle was missing.

Something terrible happened. People were killed.

That was what Monika Roth had told her sister.

Nash had said nothing to him about violence and death that summer in Zurich. He'd said nothing about Monika. To Bourne, the woman named Monika, the woman he was going to *marry*, had never even existed.

Jason could only draw one conclusion.

Nash had lied to him about his past. There had been another mission.

And it had gone badly wrong.

5

A MUDDY TRAIL LED BESIDE THE NARROW, SURGING WATERS OF THE SIHL. A handful of windows in buildings on both sides of the river gave the only light. Jason kept his Sig in his hand. He passed under the low stone overpass of a pedestrian bridge, where the concrete footings were painted over with graffiti. He heard voices, but when he illuminated the bridge wall with his flashlight, he saw only two drug addicts shooting up, their pale faces frozen like deer in a car's headlights.

Bourne knew where he needed to go for answers. He remembered what the man in Paris had told him. *Vandal needed a cleaner for a particularly bloody scene—apparently a man you'd used yourself in the past.*

Gabriel Wildhaber. He lived here.

Beyond the bridge, a series of apartment buildings rose over the river. Their ground-floor windows, peeking out through stone foundations, were covered with bars like jail cells. A black drainpipe led down one of the walls to the grassy riverbank. Jason shimmied up the pipe, bracing his feet on the brackets, then climbed a chain-link fence and dropped onto the small patio adjoining the first apartment building. It was drab, with a few picnic tables covered with foil ashtrays and half-empty beer steins. A couple of umbrellas dripped rainwater. He crossed to the wooden door that led into the building. It was locked, but with a shove of his shoulder, he forced it inward.

He found himself in a corridor that smelled of mildew and weed. The beige carpet under his feet was damp. In the hallway, a series of doors led to river-facing apartments, and a stairwell led to the upper floors. Slowly, with the wooden stairs groaning under his feet, he climbed to the topmost floor of the building. Directly opposite the stairs, he saw the door to apartment 37.

Gabriel Wildhaber lived in that apartment. Bourne didn't remember it. He just knew it.

No sound came through the door of the flat. It was late, almost three in the morning. Silently, he tried the handle and found it open, which surprised him. He kept himself behind the adjacent wall for cover, then kicked the door inward with a tap of his boot. The hinges squealed, giving him away.

From the darkness, he heard a man's voice. "Cain. *Bitte komm herein.*"

Bourne entered the dark apartment and leveled his Sig at a sofa underneath the tall, narrow windows. A man sat there, nothing but a shadow barely distinguishable in the lights from the other side of the river. He had his hands up, his fingers spread wide. Bourne approached him, making the man squint as he shined the flashlight into his face. Wildhaber wore nothing but boxer shorts on his tall, scrawny frame, and the sofa cushions hid no weapons. Slowly, eyes on Jason, the man lowered his arms. Then he reached forward to the table in front of him and retrieved a hand-rolled joint.

"They have men out front," Wildhaber said, taking a long drag. "Did they see you?"

"I came from the river side."

"Smart."

"You were expecting me," Bourne said. "Who told you? Was it the wine steward at the Drei Alpenhäuser?"

"*Ja*, Helmut said I could probably expect a visit. But if I know that, then they know it, too. We don't have much time."

"Who are they?"

"You think I know? Cain has plenty of enemies in his past. Take your pick." He eyed Jason from behind heavy black glasses. "Ah, but you don't remember any of it, do you?"

Bourne grabbed a wooden chair and sat down in front of the man. He lowered his Sig but kept it loosely in his hand. In the dim light, he could see the injuries that Wildhaber had suffered. One leg was in a cast from the knee down. The scars of burn marks littered his chest, and his smile underneath a wispy mustache was missing a couple of teeth. Worst of all, the fingers on his left hand were bloody nubs, missing beyond the knuckles.

"I'm sorry about what they did to you."

Wildhaber shrugged. He put down the joint and shook his head back, tossing long, greasy black hair out of his face. He was in his forties, but he looked sixty, with skin hanging gray and wrinkled on his frame.

"Thank God for Vandal," he said. "I'd be dead if she hadn't showed up when she did. She warned you?"

"I got the message."

"Well, you're wasting your time with me, Cain. I don't know anything that will help you. There were three of them who worked me over, but I don't know who they are or why they want you. Only one of them did the talking. His accent sounded Bavarian, for what it's worth. Beyond that, they were too busy with their work."

"I'm not interested in them," Bourne said.

Wildhaber cocked his head. His eyes shot nervously around the apartment, drifting toward the kitchenette. "No?"

"I'm interested in you. I want to know why you're lying to me, Gabriel."

The man paled. "Lying? I wouldn't—"

Bourne raised the gun again and pointed it at the man's face, cutting him off. "They came to you because you know me. But I don't know *you*. You're a cleaner, but I don't remember ever using your . . . services. If I did, then the odds are that the job has something to do with the men who are trying to find me. You're clever, Gabriel. You've certainly made the same connection. So why are you hiding it?"

Fingers trembling, Wildhaber reached for the joint again. He closed his eyes as he inhaled, and then he stubbed it out in the ashtray. "Yeah, okay, I did a job for you. Ten years ago. It was messy. Ugly."

"What was it?"

Wildhaber hesitated, and Bourne pushed the barrel of the Sig into the man's forehead. *"What was it?"*

"Fuck, Cain, don't you get it? You're not supposed to know!"

"What are you talking about?"

"You came to me ten years ago with a job," the man said, "but it wasn't just you. Nash Rollins was with you."

Nash.

Jason wasn't surprised.

"The job," Bourne said.

Wildhaber held up his hands as Bourne's finger curled around the trigger of the Sig. "Look, look, listen to me. Ten years ago, I knew Nash. Everybody did. But you were new. Smart, fucking talented, but green.

You were on edge over what you'd done. Jumpy, pacing back and forth. You kept talking about a girl."

"What girl?"

"Do you think I asked? I don't care about shit like that. Nash told me to take care of the scene. Clean it up. So I did. End of story. You were in and out of Zurich for years after that, but I didn't deal with you again. I heard you got a new identity. Jason Bourne. Except then the word was, you got shot. You lost your memory. Crazy, right? I didn't know whether to believe it. I figured maybe it was some kind of op you were running. But then Nash showed up at my door again."

"*Nash* did. Why?"

"He confirmed what happened to you, about that bullet that cleaned your clock. You didn't remember anything about your past. Thing is, Nash wanted to keep it that way. He said if you ever showed up here asking about that job I did, I should play dumb. I should pretend I didn't know you and I never worked for you. He gave me ten thousand dollars to make sure I told you nothing."

"For God's sake, *why?* Why keep me in the dark?"

Wildhaber shook his head. "He didn't tell me, and I didn't ask. I was just as happy not to see Cain again. People who deal with you tend to get dead. So I made sure I stayed clear. That's the way it was until those boys showed up looking for you."

Bourne got up and went to the windows. He could barely see the dark ribbon of the Sihl below him. "Tell me about the job."

"Hey, Nash said—"

"I'll deal with Nash."

Wildhaber sighed. "I need more scotch for this."

The man pushed up from the sofa and dragged a crutch under

one of his shoulders. He limped to the kitchenette on the other side of the apartment, where half a bottle of Johnett Swiss Single Malt sat on the counter, with a shot glass already beside it. Wildhaber poured it to the rim and drank it down in a single swallow.

"There's a chalet in the mountains near Engelberg," Wildhaber told him. "It's located up a crazy steep road."

Jason squeezed his eyes shut. The chalet!

He felt the rush of adrenaline again, the pounding in his head. He was back on the mountain road, dirt scraping under his tires, glass shattering.

You are not David Webb! You are Cain!

He saw the woman tied to a chair. Monika.

And he saw more. He saw everything. The events at the chalet rushed back into his mind like Niagara pouring over the cliffs.

"I went down to Engelberg," Wildhaber went on. "It was a fucking slaughterhouse. Four dead bodies. One was a professor at the college. The other three were kids. Not one of them older than twenty. You—"

"I killed them."

Wildhaber reached for the scotch again. "Yeah. You remember that?"

"I remember now," David Webb said.

"I AM HERE TO SWEAR MY LIFE AND LOYALTY TO THE CAUSE," DAVID AN-*nounced.*

He placed his hands on either side of Monika's head and prepared to break the neck of the woman he loved. The chair rattled as she struggled against the bonds that held her in place, and her muffled screams filled his ears. His blood pulsed, a pounding in his skull.

Five men.

Five threats to kill.

Gavin Wright was closest, two steps away. The three boys were spread around the room, all of them with rifles pointed at him. And the leader sat in a chair by the stairs, hidden by the shadows and a cloud of cigarette smoke. David had no weapon, no gun, no knife, just his hands pressed against Monika's soft face.

But he was Cain. This was what he'd been trained for.

Turn your disadvantage into an advantage.

Treadstone.

He tightened his grip on Monika, feeling her fear at what he would do next. He didn't look down at her; he removed all expression from his face. Soldiers felt nothing. He let his gaze travel coldly from one man to the next and then finally to the man in the corner, the man he couldn't see.

Below him, where Monika's legs were tied, he braced his left foot against the rear left leg of the chair and positioned the side of his right foot against the other leg.

Noise. Noise was a distraction.

Cain shouted. His voice was like the bellow of a fierce beast. He swung Monika's head sharply between his hands, but he used his elbow to twist her shoulders, softening the blow and making it harmless. Simultaneously, he kicked out the right leg of the chair with his foot and drove both Monika and the broken chair to the ground.

For an instant, to the men watching, it looked as if he'd killed her so ferociously that the chair had collapsed.

An instant was all he needed.

"Stay down," he whispered in Monika's ear.

Then he grabbed the broken chair leg from the floor. Gavin took a step closer to examine the scene, which was what Cain expected him to do. The man loomed above him, and Cain swung the chair leg, nails protruding, into the side of Gavin's head.

The professor screamed. The man's finger was on the trigger of the rifle, and Cain shoved the barrel away and squeezed his own finger into the trigger guard, spraying wild automatic fire around the chalet. The burst struck one of the students—the math prodigy, Lukas—and nearly decapitated him with a dozen bullets through his neck.

The other two boys began firing back with roars of fury. Cain jerked Gavin in front of him, letting the professor absorb the impact of round after round, eviscerating his body. Grabbing Gavin's rifle, Cain launched the dead body into the air, then threw himself to the ground and laid down a steady rain of hate. He'd never been so calm, so focused. Bullets laced the air around him. The walls behind him erupted in stone and dust; windows exploded over his head. Cain simply fired, arcing the barrel back and forth. He took out the first threat—they were threats, not people, not teenagers—with a tight circle of fire to the chest, then the second threat with a round between his eyes, and then the third threat as the boy charged him, firing and firing, his youth and adrenaline making his aim wild. Cain let the bullets fly like shrapnel, then shot him in the knee and watched him fall. As he landed hard, Cain drew a knife from a scabbard on Gavin's body and lifted up the boy's head and opened up his throat with a single deep slash.

They were all dead.

Threats neutralized. Targets down.

Monika lay face down on the floor, vomiting into her gag. But she was alive.

Cain got to his feet and focused on the last man. The leader. The man with that strangely familiar voice that he couldn't place.

He knew that man!

But he was gone. The chair was empty.

Cain ran to the chalet window and saw the Ferrari 458 Italia already racing away down the mountain road.

BOURNE HAD CLOSED HIS EYES AS THE MEMORY STORMED OVER HIM.

Mistake.

He heard movement on the other side of the apartment. His instincts kicked in just as Gabriel Wildhaber unleashed fire from a B&T A1 that he'd yanked from a drawer in the kitchenette.

"They'll pay for your corpse!" Wildhaber shouted. "After what they did to me, I deserve something! *Le Renouveau* will pay!"

But Bourne knew—*how* did he know?—that Wildhaber was left-handed. That meant that his gun hand had been chopped to nothing by the men who tortured him. The man used his right hand to shoot, but his high, drunken aim missed repeatedly. A bullet took out one of the windows over the river. Another landed in the sofa. Another nicked the coffee table and sent up a spray of razor-sharp splinters, and Bourne felt blood on his cheek. He stayed where he was, a tree rooted to the ground as Wildhaber missed again. Then he feinted left and took a step right, raised his Sig, and fired a single round.

On the other side of the room, Wildhaber clutched at his throat. His gun dropped from his hand. The bullet severed his spine, and he fell forward, choking. Dying.

Bourne didn't wait for the end. He was already out the door. If killers were outside the building, they'd heard the shots. They'd be coming for him up the stairs.

As he made his escape, Wildhaber's last words chased him all the way back to the river.

They'll pay for your corpse.

Le Renouveau *will pay.*

6

THE ITALIAN MAN IN THE FERRAGAMO SUIT CHECKED HIS PHONE AS HE rode the escalator from the French underground station. He needed to catch up on natural gas futures before he got to the meeting, because once he was there, the guards would confiscate his phone. The precautions regarding communication devices had been established long ago by *le commandant*, and they were annoying but necessary. They couldn't take the risk of anyone recording or eavesdropping on what was said in that room.

Protocol also dictated that none of the participants arrive via personal vehicles or car services that could be tracked. Anonymity was key. That meant taking taxis or the Métro, and even taxis were discouraged. A driver might recognize and remember a face. So Franco took the subway, even though he hated it. There were no first-class compartments, the station reeked like a toilet, and the people—*mio Dio*, the people! Around him, the fat, the loud, the unwashed, and the unemployed thundered up the stairs toward the plaza, waving signs for *La Vraie* and shouting the name of Raymond Berland.

Le Roi Raymond, they called him.

King Raymond.

The European establishment was scared to death of Berland. The Italian man saw it every day, because he was part of the establishment himself, at least in the eyes of the world. Franco Antonini was only thirty-two years old and already the number four man in the continent's largest energy company. Within a few years, he would leapfrog from number four to number one as the next CEO. That destination was a certainty, regardless of what it took to eliminate his competitors. His career path had been shepherded by *Le Renouveau* since he was recruited to the cause at seventeen years old.

Franco enjoyed watching his compatriots squirm about the upcoming French election. According to the newest polls, Raymond Berland, the charismatic young leader of the True France party, was only a point or two behind the current president. This followed the president's starring role in a leaked video involving thirteen-year-old girls, which was apparently too much even for the jaded sexual mores of France. He had resigned from the race, so the elites in Brussels and the leaders of the largest French companies were scrambling to back a political newcomer, Chrétien Pau, in a last-ditch attempt to stop Berland and *La Vraie* from staging a right-wing takeover of the Élysée Palace and the Palais Bourbon.

All Franco could do was laugh.

The takeover was unstoppable.

On the escalator, a fortysomething French construction worker in a yellow reflective jacket muscled past him, chanting about *Le Roi Raymond*. Seeing Franco's expensive suit, the man hurled angry jibes about the rich and privileged. Franco ignored him and continued to study his phone. No need to feed the beast when the beast already had plenty of food. The man soon found new prey, descending on a small and pretty Muslim woman in a headscarf who rode the escalator a few steps above Franco. The construction worker shouted at her to go back to where she came from, and half a dozen other men joined in, surrounding the woman and screaming in her face. She looked down and said nothing, but that only provoked the men to make their curses more obscene.

Such fools.

At the top of the escalator, Franco smoothly stepped forward between the men, put an arm around the young woman's shoulders, and guided her under his protection into the plaza of La Défense. The gang followed at first, but there were too many other distractions, and most of them peeled away to join the latest rally for *La Vraie*. Franco walked beside the woman until she was away from her tormenters, and then he squeezed her shoulder and told her in French, *"Tu es en sécurité maintenant, ma chérie."*

You're safe now.

"Merci beaucoup," she told him. *"Vous êtes si gentil."*

He waved her away with a pleasant smile. She would probably tell her family about the nice man in the suit who helped her ward off the French Nazis. In a few more hours, as the toxin ravaged her body, she wouldn't remember him squeezing her shoulder or the prick of his ring as it penetrated her skin.

These immigrants had to learn they had no place here.

Franco paused in the huge plaza. He observed the nearby rally and shook his head at the loud idiots of *La Vraie* chanting their slogans and pretending to be tough. They were ignorant pawns to be moved where they were useful and then discarded like waste. It was the leaders of *Le Renouveau*—the men and women who had sworn their life and loyalty to the cause—who knew how to take real action.

He continued toward the hotel where the meeting would take place. The white cube of the Grande Arche dominated the plaza, like something out of a science fiction movie, a geometric counterpart to the Arc de Triomphe barely visible in the opposite direction. Some people hated the cube in La Défense, just like they hated the glass pyramid at the Louvre. Franco had no patience for those who were stuck in the past and resisted progress and change. That was the nature of the world. Sweep out the old and the corrupt, eliminate the weak and the cowardly, and let the new order take over. The higher order.

The renewal. *Le Renouveau.*

It was quarter to two in the afternoon. The meeting was to begin promptly at two. Franco bought a cone of *frites* and ate them one by one, carefully using a napkin to wipe the salt and grease from his fingers. He hummed as he watched the unrest in the square, which had been carefully orchestrated for maximum effect. Everything was proceeding according to plan. Ten minutes later, he entered the hotel and took the elevator to the private conference room on the uppermost floor. Outside the doors, two armed guards met him, checked his identification—although they knew perfectly well who he was—took his phone, his lethal opal ring, his compact Glock 43, and his SKM stiletto, and then let him enter the room to join the others. He always made sure he was the last to arrive.

The conference room was small, with twenty plush chairs set out around a glass table built in a square U. The angled windows looked down on the plaza and the modern arch. Franco made no small talk with the other members. This wasn't a place for chitchat. He took his place at the head of the table, and when they saw him, the rest of the participants took their chairs for the beginning of the meeting.

Franco's gaze went from face to face.

He knew them all well. He had known them and trained with them for years. A few had gone to college with him, and the others had attended similar schools around Europe. There were fourteen men, five women, ranging in age from twenty-eight to thirty-seven. These were the titans of the future, sons and daughters of wealth and power, up-and-coming leaders in government, the military, business, education, media, technology, and energy. Control those sectors, and you controlled the entire world. Like Franco, they had been chosen to rise to the top in their respective fields.

He tapped a pencil twice on the glass tabletop and was rewarded with instant silence.

"Buongiorno, amici," he said. *"Bonjour.* Hello. It is a pleasure to be back with all of you again. Let us dial in *le commandant."*

Franco reached for the secure phone in front of him and tapped in a number. Almost immediately, a sharp, familiar voice boomed through the room, speaking in a rugged accent that still bore traces of the man's French childhood. This was his real voice, not the voice he used in public, which he could modulate to sound like a dozen different men. His talent was to make every audience feel that he was one of them.

In this room, with these people, his words had a slashing quality that demanded obedience.

"State your oaths," the man announced over the phone.

One by one, each person in the room stood up and offered the vow they had made to *Le Renouveau* in the very beginning after their recruitment. *I am here to swear my life and loyalty to the cause.* Franco was the last to make his pledge, and then he waited for *le commandant* to continue.

"The election is in just a few weeks," the leader announced. "I hardly need to remind you of the importance of this event. This is the culmination of years of planning and patience, of eroding the status quo and feeding instability. Riots over gas prices, over pension reforms, over police shootings. The culture in France and throughout Europe is fragile, looking for change, and we are finally ready to assume power. Each of you has a vital role to play in the coming days. I assume you are ready with your reports. Franco, let's begin."

Franco nodded at the woman immediately on his right. Her name was Maryse Rouche, thirty-one years old, the granddaughter of a former German chancellor and head of European operations for one of the world's largest technology companies. Franco had recruited her to the organization himself when they began an affair in college. She was married now, with two children, but their affair continued at a torrid pace whenever they were both in Paris.

"My team and I have begun overriding elements of the search engine algorithms and replacing them with our own criteria," Maryse told the gathering, her voice bland, without any intonation. "Essentially, we'll control the news and narratives on display with stories of our own design. And of course, an evaluation of social media history using the Prescix technology will allow us to tailor posts to specific individuals and reinforce what they want to hear. Our analysis shows that this alone should increase raw approval ratings for our security objectives up to five points in the next polls."

"Naturally, the print and television media will back up this operation," added Chester Bagley, senior director of programming at Euro-News, which operated the number one network in most of the EU member states. "Our own stations will be directing content according to our specifications, but we also have people in the international affiliates of the American networks. No doubt you've observed that the uprisings are making headlines not just on the continent but around the world. Already we're enhancing the voices of those who are calling for a greater police and military presence to deal with the violence."

"That brings us to intelligence," Franco said. "Justin?"

Justin Ely nodded from the far side of the room.

He was a recent recruit to the leadership committee, having spent years as a field operative. He was also the only American in the room. Unlike the others, who had separate careers in their public lives, Justin worked only within the organization. He was the son of an American ambassador, which had led him to an elite European education in Brussels. With recommendations from senior members of *Le Renouveau*, he'd been recruited to the CIA after college. He'd spent ten years doing wet work for the agency. After his work for the Americans, he'd gone private, building relationships with contractors and mercenaries around the world. All of those contacts were now paying off.

Justin wore jeans and a leather jacket, the only person in the room not formally dressed for the meeting. He was thin to the point of being gaunt, with a bony frame that belied his strength and skills. His jet-black hair was cut short and neat. He had pale skin, reddened by sunburn, with narrow dead eyes and a thin mouth that rarely smiled. Franco liked him for his ruthlessness and cunning, although it was impossible to know what he was thinking, because nothing ever showed on his face.

"We've developed street-level chain of command with regard to the protests—" Justin began, but *le commandant* unexpectedly cut him off.

"Yes, yes, Justin, I have confidence in your strategy for the unrest. The violence is spreading as we wished. You've done well, and I acknowledge your success. Now skip ahead and tell me about your failure."

Justin glanced down the table at Franco, his jaw jutting slightly with annoyance. Franco's mouth pursed, as if to say: *Hold your tongue.*

"I assume you mean David Webb," Justin went on.

A clipped reply came from the phone. "Yes."

"All right. As you know, we recently received a tip that we believed would help us locate the assassin at the mountain chalet. The man we've been pursuing for years. The man who murdered four of our recruits."

"And almost murdered me," the voice on the phone added acidly.

"Yes, sir. He was trying to penetrate our organization back then, but fortunately, you tagged him as a mole from the beginning. His name is David Webb, but he left that identity behind not long after the incident at the chalet. That's one of the reasons he's been so difficult to find. We've now confirmed that he's an American operative known as Cain, also called Jason Bourne. Originally, he was run out of the CIA's Treadstone unit, but his relationship with them seems to be arm's length at this point."

"I'm more interested in why he's still alive," the leader snapped over the phone.

Justin took a deep breath. "He's alive because I fucked up, sir. This was my mission, my responsibility. If you want to have Franco shoot me for it, go ahead."

Franco winced. No one else in the room had the balls to talk to *le commandant* like that, not even Franco himself. But Justin didn't pull punches, and that was one of the reasons the leader had brought him into the inner circle.

After an uncomfortable silence, the phone speaker came alive again. "Continue."

"Yes, sir. We maintained surveillance on the café in Zurich, and we sent in two of my best men when we knew he was inside. But Cain spotted our men and took out one. A third party intervened and disabled my other man."

"And Webb?" the leader asked.

"He's gone underground again, unfortunately. However, I've alerted all of our cells to watch for him. He won't get far."

"I trust you're right. We can't afford any setbacks at this juncture. The last thing we need is a wild card like Cain getting in our way. We've been trying to find him and eliminate him for years, and we need to get the job done. He *saw* me in that chalet. If he makes the connection and figures out who I am, he could blow up the entire operation."

"Understood, sir. We'll find him. Now that I know he's Treadstone, I know how he thinks. I've already activated a team in Engelberg. My expectation is he'll go there next, and we'll be waiting for him."

"Except now he'll be on guard," Franco pointed out at the head of the table. "He knows we're looking for him."

"Yes, he does," Justin acknowledged, "but that may turn out to be an advantage. With Bourne on the run, I expect he'll lead us where we want him to go. To our other target. He's going to help us find the woman named Monika Roth."

7

"IF WE'RE GOING TO FIND YOUR SISTER, WE HAVE TO START HERE," JASON told Johanna. "This is where it all began ten years ago."

He drove a white Audi sedan along a narrow road that led into the mountain town of Engelberg. On his left, deep green hills rose sharply into the trees. On his right, A-frame log homes dotted the meadows, and beyond them, a saw-toothed line of rocky, impossibly beautiful mountains rose over the valley. The highest of the peaks, Mount Titlis, still wore a white cap of snow even in the summer.

Engelberg.

He'd lived here for almost a year in his twenties, and he'd taught in the classrooms of Stiftsschule Obwalden. Everything about the town was familiar to him. He could map out all of the streets in his mind; he knew the vista around each turn. He could rattle off the names of the hotels, bars, and cafés and describe them down to the last detail. And yet he also didn't know the town at all. When he tried to remember his life here, his memory descended into a fog like low clouds obscuring the mountains.

"Did you ever visit Monika here?" Bourne asked. "Do you know anything about her life in town?"

Johanna shook her head. "Only what she told me. I was living in Chicago then. I saw Monika in Zurich during my trip that spring. We traveled a little bit around the country, but she didn't take me here. She didn't even want me to meet you until I pestered her about it. Honestly, I thought that was a little strange."

"How long did she work at the college?"

"Not long. A few months, I think. She arrived midterm. That was right before the summer when she disappeared."

"How did she happen to find a job here?"

"I don't really know. I remember her talking about sending out dozens of applications. Literature majors can't exactly be choosy about jobs. I figured she found a place that was willing to hire her, so she said yes. Anyway, she must have met you pretty soon after she got here, because she started talking about you right away."

Jason said nothing. He kept an eye on the rearview mirror.

"Where did she live? At the school?"

"Yes. She said all the teachers did. There wasn't much privacy. I remember her saying the two of you had to find a hotel when you wanted to have sex. Or a mountain field if the weather was good. I thought that was kind of hot." Johanna glanced across the Audi and pinned him with her blue eyes. "It's so strange. I can't believe your mind could just ... *erase* her like that."

"The bullet erased everything," he told her. Then he studied the familiar mountains through the car windows and clarified, "Actually, that's not true. It was more like a neutron bomb that killed the people and left everything else standing. I remember places, politics, history, all of those things. But myself? The people I knew? The things we did? That's almost all gone."

"I'm sorry."

Quickly, Johanna reached across the car and caressed his leg with her fingertips and then drew her hand back.

"I've learned to live with it," Jason added, enjoying the warmth where her fingers had been. "For better or for worse, it makes everything that I experience now more intense. My senses are sharper. I have to wrestle with my emotions to keep them controlled."

"Why does that matter?" Johanna asked. "Why can't you just feel what you feel?"

He didn't answer because no one from outside his life could understand the rules. The rules were about staying alive.

Emotion kills.

Treadstone.

When the silence dragged out, Johanna turned away to watch the mountains outside the car. Her mouth puckered, as if she wanted to say something more but didn't dare cross the line. He sensed a kind of intimacy between them, a growing attraction, but he'd been burned too many times to let anything happen.

Then he saw her eyes shift to the side-view mirror on the Audi. Her body stiffened with concern.

"Jason, there's a car back there."

"I know."

"I think it's been there a while. I saw it before."

"Yes, we're being followed. A black Mercedes picked us up outside Wolfenschiessen."

Johanna swung back sharply. "Oh my God! Is it them? Have they found us?"

"I'm not sure. The driver's good. He mostly hangs back out of sight, but every now and then, he pulls close enough to make sure we haven't turned off the road. If it's the ones chasing me, they had plenty of opportunities in the last ten miles to run us off the road. But they haven't done that. That makes me think it's someone else."

"Who else could it be?"

He frowned. "I don't know."

"What do we do?"

"We set a trap for them," Bourne said. "Hold on tight."

He checked the mirror. The Mercedes had dropped back again, and he couldn't see it behind them. Immediately, he leaned his foot into the accelerator, and the Audi jumped forward with the growl of a cheetah. They were close to town, where the road was barely wider than the car. Smoothly, Jason navigated a series of tight turns and then shot down a wooded straightaway past the crowns of evergreens rising out of the valley. As they cleared the forest, the granite cliffs became a blur. His speedometer crept to eighty miles an hour.

"We're close to a hotel," Jason said. "The Waldegg."

"How do you know that?"

"I just do. When I pull off the road, go into the hotel and straight through to the restaurant on the other side. Get a table and wait for me there."

"What are you going to do?"

"Find out who's in the Mercedes."

He shot around the next curve. Ahead of him, he saw the letters of the hotel sign looming over a building that hugged the cliff on the right side of the road. He stood on the brakes, dragging the Audi to a stop and jerking off Schwandstrasse into a parking place near the hotel's porte cochere. He glanced in the mirror. The Mercedes hadn't caught up with them yet, but they only had a few seconds.

"Quickly, go into the restaurant," he told her.

Johanna climbed out of the car and hurried through the hotel's glass door. Jason shut off the engine, then got out and ran to the end of the building's flagstone wall. He took cover around the corner in a gap between the wall and a wooden balcony that hung over the cliff. Mountain peaks encircled the horizon, and the houses of Engelberg filled the green valley below him. He waited. Less than a minute later, the roar of a car engine cut through the cool air. A vehicle approached, going fast, then peeled off the road with a screech of rubber when the driver spotted the Audi at the hotel.

Bourne drew his Sig.

For a long time, two or three minutes, the Mercedes engine idled in the porte cochere. Then he heard the click of a car door opening and closing. A strange singsong tap of footsteps, slow, not fast, headed for the hotel entrance. One man. Jason took a step toward the corner of the building, but drew back as the engine of the Mercedes raced again. He pushed against the wall and watched as the car sped away from the hotel and down the hillside.

Someone had gotten out of the car.

Someone was in the hotel.

Jason hid his hands in the pockets of his leather jacket, fingers still curled around the Sig. He checked the road and made his way to the hotel door. Inside, the lobby was empty. The man from the Mercedes was already gone. Bourne continued to the back of the hotel, where a café overlooked the broad vista of the valley and mountains. A few tables were filled, but he didn't see Johanna. He checked the shadows of the doorway that led to the rest of the hotel, but she'd disappeared.

His gaze went to the outdoor patio, and he saw a man being seated at a table near the railing. The man propped a cane on the chair next to him as he sat down heavily. He was in his fifties and small, with deeply tanned skin that looked as tough and inflexible as a leather hide. His nose was long with a prominent bump, his eyebrows bushy, his hard face dotted with lines and liver spots. His wiry, greased-back gray hair struggled to cover his head.

It was a man David Webb had met at the Drei Alpenhäuser ten years ago when he learned about an organization called Treadstone. It was a man who limped with a cane because he'd been shot on the boardwalk in Quebec City.

Jason knew that because he'd been the one who shot him.

It was Nash Rollins.

"JASON," NASH SAID AS BOURNE TOOK A SEAT ACROSS THE TABLE FROM HIS Treadstone handler. "Don't you love the mountain air? It makes me feel years younger."

Bourne noted that the other tables on the patio were empty, giving them privacy. They sat on fur-draped chairs with a cool breeze billowing up from the valley. The town of Engelberg spread through the flatland below them, and green fields rose into the craggy peaks that encircled the area. He could see the towers and cables of chairlifts that brought skiers up the winter mountains.

"It's a beautiful place," Bourne agreed.

A waiter arrived at the table with a bread basket and two cups of double espresso, and Jason realized that Nash had been expecting him. Nash thanked the man in flawless German, then admired the view and sipped his coffee.

"We met here once before," Nash told him when the waiter was gone. "I suppose you don't remember that."

"Ten years ago?"

"That's right. You reached out and said there was an emergency. You needed a cleaner."

"Because I'd just killed four men," Bourne said.

Nash eyed him over his coffee mug. "Correct. Did the memory of that incident finally come back to you?"

"It did, but I had help."

"Gabriel Wildhaber?" Nash said.

Bourne nodded.

"I brought Gabriel with me from Zurich that day. He's kind of a dick, isn't he? Most cleaners are a little twisted, but I suppose you can't really blame them."

"I had to kill him last night."

Nash spread butter over a crusty slice of bread. "Yes, I heard."

"He was trying to kill me."

"Well, Gabriel was always something of a mercenary, selling himself to the highest bidder. No great loss."

Bourne leaned across the table. "Can we get down to it, Nash? How did you find me? And what's really going on?"

Nash settled back into the fur-draped chair. He wasn't a big man, and he had the gnarled look of a cypress tree battered by coastal winds. He was fifteen years older than Jason, but what he'd lost in physical stamina over the years had been replaced by his wily intelligence. Bourne never underestimated Nash. They had plenty of history together, but he also never fully trusted him. And he never told him everything.

"I was in Paris yesterday," Nash replied. "Although not to see you."

"Then why?"

Nash's voice softened to a raspy drawl. "Treadstone is keeping a close eye on the French elections. This Raymond Berland? He's the most dangerous man we've seen on the European political front in a long time. He's more extreme than Jean-Marie Le Pen ever was, and *les violences urbaines* shows that. The difference is that Berland and *La Vraie* seem to stand a real chance of winning. If this EU dark horse Chrétien Pau doesn't widen the gap soon, we may need to get involved."

"By eliminating Berland? All that will do is inflame his supporters even more."

"That's a risk, but the alternative is a Nazi takeover of the French government."

"So how does this involve me?" Bourne asked.

"Well, I don't know. Maybe it's all a coincidence of timing, but I doubt it. When Vandal reported that Gabriel was assaulted by men looking for *you*, that raised red flags. I've had our Zurich assets on alert ever since. Naturally, I got a call about an incident at the Drei Alpenhäuser and then about Gabriel's death. So I flew to Zurich this morning."

"That doesn't explain what you're doing *here*."

Nash chewed on his slice of bread. "I'm pretty good at what I do, Jason. Almost as good as you. There are only two or three Treadstone contacts you'd use in Zurich to get a car. I knew you were in a white Audi with smoked windows ten minutes after you were behind the wheel. And if you talked to Wildhaber, that meant you knew about the deaths in the chalet. I assumed your next stop would be Engelberg."

Bourne frowned. He didn't like being predictable, particularly with someone like Nash. That was the kind of basic tradecraft mistake that got agents killed. It reminded him that he'd been off his game since the death of Nova and the breakup with Abbey Laurent. He was alone. Distracted. Consumed by regret. He'd spent much of the past year in a dark place, and he wasn't sure how to climb back out.

"Why not reach out to me yourself if you were in Paris?" Bourne asked. "Vandal's message came from outside the Treadstone network."

"If the message came from me, I wasn't sure you'd listen."

"Maybe that's because you've been lying to me for years."

Nash sat in silence, not denying it. He waited for Jason to continue.

"After I was shot, after my identity was erased, you're the one who told me about my history," Bourne said. "We sat in that meeting room on 57th Street in New York, and you described every mission I'd had. Every contact. Every location. You filled in the gaps of what I'd lost. And yet somehow you forgot to mention my very first mission. Here. Four men killed in those mountains within weeks of my joining Treadstone. You left that out of the story. Why?"

Nash leaned forward, jabbing a finger at Jason. "After you were shot, you were a wreck. You were questioning everything about yourself. I didn't tell you about the mission in Engelberg because it was a *fucking disaster.* The last thing you needed at that point was a blow to your confidence. It could have pushed you over the edge. I talked to the Treadstone shrink who vetted you, and we concluded that the best thing to do was leave it out altogether. You didn't remember it, so why bring it back?"

"Well, I remember it now. What happened?"

Nash's face hardened. "I didn't come here to take a stroll down memory lane, Jason. I came here to tell you to *let it go.* Go back to Paris. Go into hiding until this blows over. We don't need you. I have other agents working this assignment, agents who won't be recognized, agents who aren't compromised."

"And yet you told me about Wildhaber," Bourne pointed out. "You had Vandal send me that message in Paris. You pulled me in, and you knew I'd come back here eventually. I'd ask you why, but we both know the answer. You wanted to use me as bait. You wanted to draw out whoever was coming after me so you could figure out who they were. Right?"

"Right," Nash admitted.

"Wildhaber mentioned *Le Renouveau.* He said *Le Renouveau* would pay for my corpse. Is it them?"

"That's my suspicion."

"Who are they? And what does this have to do with the mission ten years ago?"

Nash frowned, as if reluctant to continue. "All right, but first things first. What do you remember about David Abbott?"

"Only what you told me about him. He was my father's best friend. He raised me after my parents were killed. I lived for years at the home he kept in Paris."

"He also founded Treadstone," Nash said.

"I know."

"Abbott's goal was always to have you join the agency. Your raw skills were off the charts, and he wanted you in the field as soon as possible. Me, I thought you were still too young. You needed seasoning, and we needed more time to evaluate your strengths and weaknesses. But Abbott didn't want to wait. He had a mission that required a man like you, multilingual, educated in Europe, but with enough trauma in his past that he could be perceived as alienated. Disaffected."

"In other words, a recruitment target," Bourne said.

"Yes. That's right. You see, we'd heard rumors in Brussels. Soft in-tel we couldn't confirm. There was a far-right Nazi group forming in Europe. That's not exactly news, but this one appeared to have some sharp minds behind it, and they were pursuing a sophisticated long-term strategy. Build a grassroots network. Recruit young adults out of European colleges and indoctrinate them with extremist ideology—not for immediate action, but to lay the groundwork for a far-right takeover. Create a network of influential sleepers, elites who eventually would be in position to support their ideology in government, media, tech, the military, whatever. The Nazi danger isn't from hotheads in the street. That's just the cover. It's the shrewd minds behind the scenes who are the real threat."

"And this was *Le Renouveau?*"

"Exactly," Nash replied. "The trouble was, we knew almost noth-ing about them. We got a lead that they were planning a summit in Ibiza, and we sent in a Treadstone agent to spy on the meeting. But they're slippery. Word must have gotten out that they'd been burned, and the summit broke up early. We had hundreds of names of people on the island, but no way to tie any of them to the summit or to *Le Re-nouveau*. Our agent walked away with almost nothing. Just a possible location."

"Here," Bourne concluded.

"Yes. Our agent was in an Ibiza bar and heard someone tagging Stiftsschule Obwalden as one of the recruitment centers."

"Who was the leak?"

"An economics teacher. Man named Gavin Wright. He was one of the people you killed in the chalet. We could have taken him out after Ibiza and squeezed him, but we didn't know much about the broader organization. We wanted bigger fish. So Abbott had the idea of placing you inside the college as a teacher, with the goal of having you infiltrate *Le Renouveau* as a mole."

"Except he never told me that."

"No. He got you the job, and all he wanted at first was to have you observe. Attract no attention. Act innocent because you *were* innocent. After a few months, he asked me to go in and tell you what was really going on. To recruit you to Treadstone. To train you. And then to encourage you to become a spy inside the organization. It was a good plan, but I argued it was the wrong place to get you started. You were impulsive. Inexperienced. Abbott thought that would be an advantage. It would make you seem more genuine. If we used someone who was too smooth, they'd be suspicious. And at first, it seemed to work. You got an invitation to meet one of the higher-ups. A formal recruitment ceremony. You were in."

"But I wasn't," Bourne said. "They smelled a trap."

"Yes, and you were nearly killed, and the operation blew up in our faces. *Le Renouveau* knew we were onto them. They went underground. In the ten years since then, we've had no success breaking into the organization. All we do know is that their long-term plans seem to be reaching the first big turning point."

"You mean the election?" Bourne asked.

"Yes. There's no way the emergence of *La Vraie* right now is accidental. Guess who was 'vacationing' on Ibiza the weekend of the aborted summit? Raymond Berland. *Le Roi Raymond.*"

Bourne frowned. "The riots in Paris aren't organic. They're being carefully orchestrated."

"Yes, that's what we believe, too. Orchestrated by *Le Renouveau.*"

"If that's their agenda, why come after me now? After all these years?"

Nash eased back in his chair. His gaze drifted to the mountains.

"Partly revenge, I imagine. They've been looking for you for years. You killed four of their assets. They don't forget that. Plus—"

"Plus someone else was in the chalet," Jason said.

Nash nodded. "That's right. We don't know who, but it was definitely someone higher up in the organization. In ten years, who knows how far that person has come? He may be concerned that you can identify him."

"Except I can't."

"Which they may or may not know. Given the way your memory is returning in fits and starts, it's also possible that you *may* remember eventually. They're not going to take that chance. Either way, these people are not going to give up. You've got a target on your chest, Jason. Like I said, the best thing for you to do is go into hiding and let us deal with them. If you're out in the open, they're going to find you."

Bourne stayed quiet for a long time. "You've avoided one name, Nash. Monika Roth."

"Forget about her."

"I already have," Jason replied. "I don't remember her at all because you never told me about her. You hid her from me. Why?"

"Because she's irrelevant," Nash said.

"Not to me. Who is she?"

"An outsider. A goddamn English teacher."

"I fell in love with her," Bourne said.

"That's true. In other words, you violated our first rule from the beginning. You got involved with someone. I told you when I recruited you to Treadstone that relationships are deadly for people like us. Monika Roth had no part in any of this—but you put her in the crosshairs for *Le Renouveau*. They kidnapped her. They demanded you kill her. And as a result, you blew up the entire operation."

"What was the alternative?" Jason asked cynically. "Did you expect me to go ahead and break her neck?"

"I expected you *not* to get involved with anyone in the first place."

"Well, it's too late for that. I have to find her. If I'm a target, so is she. She was in that chalet, too. Where is she?"

Nash shook his head. "I have no idea. You sent her away. You gave her a new identity using outside resources. Even back then, you didn't trust us, Jason. By the time you came to me and told me what had happened, she was already gone."

8

THE AGENT KNOWN AS VANDAL PARKED THE BLACK MERCEDES AT THE DEAD end of a narrow lane called Haselweg. She got out of the car and picked her way through the meadow and staked out a hidden place among the evergreens. Above her on the steep green slope was the Hotel Waldegg. She could see the figures of two men seated at a table on the outdoor patio, and even at that distance, she recognized them.

Nash Rollins.

And Cain.

Vandal brought her Vortex Kaibab binoculars to her eyes, which made Cain leap into focus as if he were sitting next to her. The high-power binoculars actually belonged to him. She'd used them on their joint mission a few years earlier, when she'd served as his spotter on the assassination of a weapons trafficker in Barcelona. In the tumult following the kill, they'd been separated, and the binoculars had stayed with her.

As she spied on him, her surveillance pricked his sixth sense. Every good agent had that instinct of knowing when they were being watched.

She saw his head turn and his eyes narrow as they swept the panorama below him. She knew she was invisible, but the binoculars made her feel so close to him that she took a step backward into the trees. Which was a mistake. He might not see her, but he'd see the motion. Through the lenses, she saw Bourne's focus harden, staring straight at her location.

Had he spotted her? Did he know it was her?

I'm here, Cain.

It had been months since she'd last seen him. She'd been at the house in Maryland when he found the body of Nova. His former partner. His lover. Their relationship had been the worst-kept secret in Treadstone. She'd seen it in his face; her death had obviously wounded him deeply.

So Cain had an Achilles' heel. He was still a human being; he still felt something. Most of the other Treadstone agents became little more than robots after years of violence, but Bourne had somehow salvaged part of his soul. Maybe it was the loss of his memory. Maybe not knowing who he was had kept his humanity alive. On one level, Vandal admired him for it, even envied him. She'd turned to stone herself long ago, and there were days when she wished she could still see men as something other than sources of physical pleasure, used and discarded. Or as targets to be killed.

But she also knew that emotion was a deadly weakness. When she was young, before Treadstone, she'd been a raging river of emotion, most of it fueled by cocaine. She'd been an addict, a narcissist, an adulterer—and ultimately, a murderer.

Emotion kills.

Yes, Vandal knew that better than anyone else. Her husband had paid the price for her out-of-control life. So now she stayed clean and played by the rules. Most of the time. But there were still days when she felt like giving herself to the drug all over again.

Cain.

God, there was something magnetic about him. She'd been drawn to him in Barcelona. Treadstone agents were typically willing to release their adrenaline through sex, and it was safe because it meant nothing. They'd shared a room, and she'd seen him naked with all of his muscles and scars, a specimen more perfect because of his imperfections. His face was square and handsome, but with complexity and pain just below the surface. She'd joined him in the shower, intent on seducing him, but he'd rejected her. Not because he didn't find her attractive. Not because he didn't want her.

But she wasn't Nova.

When Cain fell, he fell hard. Vandal understood that about him. He needed someone in his life, regardless of the dangers it brought. She knew the stories; she'd heard the rumors. After Nova had come the other woman, the Canadian journalist, Abbey Laurent. Bourne had loved her, too. And lost her.

Through the binoculars, Vandal continued to stare at him. Even if he didn't know she was there, the sheer intensity of his gaze made her feel naked, the way she'd been that night in Spain. She wondered what it would be like to have those ice-blue eyes stare at her with passion and need. Not that she was ever likely to find out.

A text tone sounded on Vandal's phone. She lowered the binoculars and checked the incoming message. It was from Nash.

Time to go.

Vandal backed away from the slope. She tramped through the dense trees and made her way to the dead end where she'd parked the Mercedes. The return trip up the hillside took her less than ten minutes. When she got to the Waldegg, she did a U-turn and waited in the porte cochere. She wondered if Cain would be there with Nash and what he would say when he saw her. But the hotel door opened and Nash came outside alone.

He limped across the asphalt and slipped into the passenger seat.

"How did it go?" she asked.

"He's a stubborn son of a bitch."

"You knew that already."

"Yes, I did. Head for the train station."

"We're leaving?"

"I am. I have to head back to Paris. I want you to stay here and keep eyes on Cain."

"Understood."

Vandal put the Mercedes in gear. She navigated the turns again as they shot downhill, and then the road leveled off among the shops and cobblestones of the main street. Towering mountains dwarfed the town in every direction. She didn't say anything more until she parked across from the Engelberg train station.

"Did you tell Cain I'm here?" she asked.

"No. I don't want him to know we're babysitting him. So you'll need to be alert. If he spots you, I imagine he'll try to lose you."

Vandal smiled. "I imagine you're right."

"Keep me posted on everything he does. And particularly everyone he meets. I told him to lay low, but we both know he's not going to do that. The fact is, he's useful even when he's breaking the rules. Assuming he doesn't get himself killed in the process, he may lead us to the heart of *Le Renouveau*."

Vandal nodded. "Okay."

"One more thing. For Cain, this isn't just about the men who are trying to kill him. There's a personal factor. He's looking for a woman.

He knew her when he was in Engelberg ten years ago. Her name is Monika."

"Who is Monika?" Vandal asked.

Nash didn't answer immediately. He smoothed back his thinning gray hair, and the calculations running through his dark eyes told Vandal he was hiding things. That was Nash. He was the Treadstone master of half-truths.

"Monika Roth is the most dangerous woman in Cain's life," he told her. "No matter what happens, you have to make sure he never meets her again."

9

WHEN NASH WAS GONE, JOHANNA REAPPEARED FROM INSIDE THE HOTEL. She joined him at the outside table near the railing. He noticed that her hands were shaking. She grabbed a seeded cracker from the basket in front of her and began breaking it into pieces without eating any of it. The mountain air blew wisps of her long blond hair like string across her face and brought a flush to her pale cheeks. Once again, he found himself uncomfortably aware of his attraction to her.

"That man," she murmured. "I know you told me to stay here, but I saw him come in, and I just knew he was the one from the Mercedes. I hid down one of the hallways before he got out of the lobby. I didn't want him to see me."

"Nash has that effect on people," Jason said.

"Who is he?"

"A man I've known for a long time. He's not part of the group that's after me, but you did the right thing by staying away from him. I don't want him knowing we're together."

"Why not?"

"Because Nash made it clear that he doesn't want me to go after Monika. He's hiding something. He wants me to leave it alone, and if he finds out we're together, he'll look for a way to stop us. He knows you can help me, so his first step would be to get you out of the way."

"You don't think he'd—" Johanna began. Her face paled. "I mean, what would he do?"

"Nash can justify pretty much anything to get what he wants."

Johanna reached across the table and took hold of his hands. "Does this mean you're going to keep looking for her? Despite what this Nash wants you to do?"

Bourne didn't need to think about it. "Yes, I'm going to find her."

"Thank you," she replied, sighing with relief.

"Actually, *we're* going to find her. I need your help."

"Of course. Anything."

Jason stared over the railing at the Swiss town spread out below them. From up here, he could isolate the gray stone buildings of the Stiftsschule Obwalden and the monastery that was connected to it. The sharp geometric wings and rows of identical square windows made the facility look like a prison. It had seemed like a prison to him back then, too, the teachers in dark suits, the students in uniforms, the voices hushed in the corridors.

"Johanna, I can't tell you everything about what happened ten years ago, or why," he said. "It's not safe. But there are some things you need to know. What Monika said in that last phone call to you was true. People got killed. *I* killed them. They were going to kill me, and they were going to kill Monika, too."

"For God's sake, *why?*"

"An extremist organization was recruiting at the school. My job was to infiltrate them. I failed. I'm the one who put your sister in danger, and I'm the one who forced her to go away and adopt a new identity. The trouble is, with my memory gone, I don't know who she is or where she is."

Johanna shook her head. "Then how do we find her?"

"I had to have help in creating a legend for her. I was new, I was young. I didn't have any kind of network back then, and according to Nash, I didn't use his resources in arranging her escape. Even so, I would have needed a pro to forge identity papers for me, in order to get Monika set up somewhere else under a new name. Somebody helped me do that. Odds are, it was someone here in town. Or I would have turned to someone I knew to make a connection."

Johanna's eyes showed her frustration. "But I was never here. How can I help you?"

"You talked to Monika. She wrote to you, too, right? Letters or e-mails? You said she told you about me. Did she talk about anyone else? Mutual friends of ours. People we hung out with at the school or in town. Or did she mention things we did? The thing is, Johanna, as crazy as it sounds, you know more about that summer than I do."

"That's not saying much," she protested. "Monika was private. She didn't share a lot with me."

"Is there anything you do remember?"

She ran her fingers through her blond hair. "Well, Zurich obviously. The two of you went there a lot. And Mont Saint-Michel, where you got engaged. I heard about that."

"What about here in town?"

"I'm sorry, I can't think of anything." She nibbled on a piece of dry cracker and stared off at the mountain peaks. Then a little crinkle spread across her smooth forehead. "Well, I mean, there was one funny story. But I don't see how it could help you."

"What was it?" he asked.

"She told me that one of her favorite students had gotten into trouble. His parents had bought him a drone. This was when they were first getting popular. I guess he was flying it around the school grounds, and he accidentally—well, he said it was an accident—managed to get video of one of the male teachers doing yoga in the buff. All hell broke loose when word got out about it. It looked like he'd be expelled, but the head of security stepped in, confiscated the drone, deleted the video, and got the kid a reprieve. Monika was really relieved."

Jason frowned. "What's the connection?"

"Like I said, I don't see how it can help, but she told me *you* made it happen. You asked the security guy to go easy on the kid, and he did. Apparently the two of you were best friends back then."

BOURNE BOOKED A ROOM AT THE HOTEL WALDEGG AND TOLD JOHANNA TO wait for him. Then he drove the Audi to the east edge of town, where he parked outside the sprawling facility of the Stiftsschule Obwalden. Beyond the college's stone archway, he found a large inner courtyard that resembled the grounds of New England schools. Walkways crisscrossed the green grass, and the four-story gray walls of the school surrounded the college quad. The area was empty except for two male students, both muscular and blond, kicking a soccer ball back and forth between them.

His memory fought with itself, trying to assemble the missing pieces. He was back in a place that had been his home for nearly a year. When he looked at the school windows, he could picture the desks, blackboards, and wooden floors of the classrooms. He had visions of his own one-room apartment that looked down on the quad from the uppermost floor. The place was familiar to him, but that was all. The people were gone.

Monika was gone.

Out of the corner of his eye, he spotted a soccer ball hurtling his way. He threw up his arms and grabbed it out of the air before it collided with his head. One of the two blond students came running toward him.

"Entschuldigung!" he called to Jason in a surprisingly deep voice.

"Kein Problem," Bourne replied with a smile. *"Aber Sie brauchen mehr Übung."*

The young man, who was probably twenty years old, detected the American accent in Jason's voice and switched smoothly to English. "Yes, you are correct, sir. One can never get enough practice. I do apologize that Josef's kick got away from him. I trust you're unhurt."

"I'm fine," Jason replied, tossing the ball back to him.

"Excellent. My name is Manfred. Josef over there is my clumsy roommate."

Manfred was a solid young man, six foot three and built with the strength of one of the mountainside trees. His blond hair curled up over his head like a rising wave, and his long face made sharp angles down to the point of his cleft chin. He had pale, penetrating blue eyes and eyebrows that were much darker than his hair. He wore a white jersey and red nylon shorts, both of which emphasized his honed muscles.

"Welcome to Obwalden," Manfred went on. "Are you an alumnus, sir? Or possibly seeking employment here?"

"No, nothing like that."

Manfred smiled with only his lips, and his politeness barely hid suspicion. "Well, perhaps I can direct you to your destination."

Bourne didn't have time to respond. Manfred's companion, Josef, skidded to a stop in front of them. Josef was younger, no more than eighteen, and slight compared to his friend. He smiled nervously at Bourne but didn't join the conversation, obviously deferring to the other boy and dreading the reaction to his errant kick. Manfred turned on Josef with angry impatience, his blue eyes glinting like two knives. He juggled the soccer ball nimbly on his feet, then whipped the ball into Josef's groin so hard that the boy screamed and doubled over.

"Fehler erfordern Strafe," Manfred hissed.

Mistakes demand punishment.

"Ja, ja, es tut mir Leid," Josef choked out an apology.

"Gehen Sie weg. Jetzt!"

"Jawohl!"

Josef picked up the soccer ball where it had bounced into the grass. He cupped a hand between his legs and limped back to the middle of the field.

"Children must be taught lessons," Manfred told Bourne, calm returning to his face.

"That's quite the lesson."

Manfred shrugged. "Discipline is expected here. Now, sir, may I direct you somewhere on campus?"

"Yes, I'm looking for the head of security."

"Of course. Proceed to the building on the opposite side of the field. His office is on the third floor, northwest corner." Then the boy added, "Is there a problem? I'm happy to offer assistance."

"Oh, no, no problem," Bourne replied. "I'm in the country on vacation, and I thought I'd look up an old friend. I think he used to head the security office here, but that was years ago. He may have moved on."

"What is your friend's name?" Manfred asked.

Jason made up a name at random. "Gerhard Fauss."

The boy shook his head. "No, the head of security here is Rudolph Graz, and he has held that position for a very long time."

Rudolph Graz.

Rudy!

The name registered immediately in Bourne's mind. He saw a man twenty years older than himself, dark hair, a trimmed beard, an easy laugh. He had a vision of the two of them skiing the slopes of Mount Titlis, powder erupting in their faces.

Yes, Johanna was right. They'd been good friends.

"Well, perhaps I was mistaken about the name of the town," Jason said. "I'll check with Herr Graz and see if he's heard of Gerhard at a different school. Thanks for your help, Manfred."

"Of course, sir."

Bourne nodded at the boy and headed across the green field. He passed the other soccer player, Josef, who shot to attention as if Bourne were a superior officer. The kid looked scared out of his mind, a fish swimming in shark-infested waters. Jason gave him an encouraging smile, then continued to the next building. As he let himself inside, he glanced across the quad and noticed that Manfred was watching Bourne's every move with his arms crossed solidly over his chest.

He shut the heavy door behind him. The building was silent and appeared to be mostly deserted. The floors were made of glossy wood, giving a hollow echo to his footsteps as he marched down the corridor. He passed classrooms furnished in a severe style, no modern technology, just rows of old desks and chalkboards. One of the doors was open, and decades of dust seemed to waft from inside. He tried to remember being here, teaching here, but he couldn't. Nothing of those days was left.

However, the school itself gave him a reminder of his past.

Photographs lined the wall, group pictures of teachers in suits and dresses that went back for years. Nobody smiled. This wasn't a college for levity. He noted the dates on the pictures, and in the middle of the hallway, he found one labeled from ten years earlier. The photograph wasn't in perfect focus and included about thirty teachers. He saw men standing in the back row and used his index finger to move from face to face.

There he was.

David Webb. The young man he used to be. Before Cain. Before Treadstone. He recognized the blurry image of himself, but that man may as well have been a stranger.

He glanced at the other teachers in the picture. A handful of names came back to him with flashes of memory. He remembered debates. Faculty dinners. Arguments. He made a point of examining the women in the picture—there weren't many—but none of the faces matched the woman from the photo Johanna had shown him at the Drei Alpenhäuser.

Monika wasn't there.

Why not?

Maybe she'd simply missed the photo shoot that day. Even so, he found it strange.

Jason reached the end of the hallway and climbed to the third floor. Across from the stairs, he spotted a corner office labeled with the name Rudolph Graz. He pushed open the door and found a man napping on a threadbare sofa. The man's face was older, well into his fifties now and more gray in his beard, but it otherwise matched Jason's recollection from the ski slopes. Behind him on a small end table was a framed photograph of a pretty, plump Swiss woman with dark hair, smiling at the camera from a wheelchair.

"Hello, Rudy."

The man's eyes shot open at the unexpected voice. He blinked, as if what he was seeing had to be part of a dream. Then shock spread across his sunburnt features, and he leaped to his feet.

"*Gott im Himmel.* David! What are you doing here? Why did you come back? Are you trying to get us both killed?"

10

RUDY PUSHED BACK HIS MESSY COWLICK. HE HURRIED TO THE OFFICE WIN-
dow that looked out on the quad and inched aside the white curtain.
His body stayed concealed behind the frame. "How many people saw
you arrive?"

"Two students playing soccer. That's all."

"Two is more than enough," Rudy said. "Did you tell them you
were looking for me?"

"No, I made up a name."

"Well, that's smart, but it may not help either of us. Memories are
long around this place. You should leave. Get away from the school, and
get away from Engelberg altogether. They'll be coming for you."

"Who?"

Darkness spread like a shadow across the man's features. "There
are names we don't say out loud around here. People are always listening."

"Rudy, I know about *Le Renouveau*. Do they still exist? Are they still
recruiting here?"

"They're recruiting *everywhere*," the man replied.

Bourne joined him at the window and put a hand on his friend's shoulder. "I need your help. I'm sorry if my being here puts you at risk, but I need information."

Rudy peeled his gaze away from the window. He looked Jason up and down like a ghost and then wrapped his arms around him in a tight embrace. "Jesus, yes, of course. I'm sorry. It's good to see you, David. I've missed you. Ten years ago, I was sure I'd never see either of you again."

"Either of us?"

"You and Monika. How is she?"

Jason felt disoriented, hearing Monika's name on someone else's lips, hearing this man remember a woman whom Jason barely remembered at all. "Monika's one of the reasons I came to see you."

"All right, yes, talk to me. But I'm serious, you shouldn't be here, David. It doesn't matter how much time has passed. If you're seen, people will recognize you. And don't forget, the police would like to catch up with you, too. No one ever found the bodies in the chalet, but your name came up as a suspect in those who went missing—given that you yourself vanished soon after. As did your fiancée."

Bourne tried to stifle his reaction to the word *fiancée*. It reminded him of everything he'd lost, and he felt another wave of anger at Nash for keeping this secret from him all these years. "Rudy, tell me what you remember from back then. I need to know exactly what happened."

His friend's brow furrowed. "I don't understand. Why do you want to know that? You were there."

Bourne explained.

He gave him the shortened version of the story, and Rudy was so stunned that he made him repeat it when he was done. After that, his friend went to his desk and found a bottle of Jägermeister and poured them two shots. They sat down next to each other on the old sofa. Jason had a brief vision of being in this office in the old days, and he remembered Rudy keeping a photo of the two of them in ski gear framed above this same sofa. The photo wasn't there anymore. The only personal item in the office seemed to be the picture of his wife on the end table.

"No memory," Rudy murmured. "Unbelievable. You're saying you don't know *me*?"

"I don't. I'm sorry."

His friend sipped his drink and shook his head. "Well, I've forgotten some of those days myself, but that was all the beer we drank. We had some good long nights, David. The twenty years between us never mattered. And Monika? My God, you were supposed to marry her. I was supposed to be your best man. All these years later, I assumed the two of you were living happily somewhere under different names."

"What can you tell me about Monika?"

Rudy shrugged. "She was beautiful, of course, although it was the kind of beauty that seemed to keep people at arm's length. She was smart, well-read, which you'd expect from an English professor. She came to the college a few months after you did, and the two of you hit it off immediately. I was glad. You always struck me as a lonely soul, David. She seemed to be good for you."

"Do you remember where she came from?"

"I don't. I believe she was German, but that's all I recall. Monika didn't talk much about her past. You even mentioned yourself a couple of times that she seemed to be closed off. Like she had secrets."

Secrets. Bourne wondered what that meant.

"That last night, Rudy," he went on. "Tell me about the night at the chalet."

The man shook his head. "That's a night I wish *I* could forget."

"I obviously told you something."

Rudy exhaled loudly and settled back into the cushions of the sofa. He glanced at the photo on the end table with a grimace. "You did indeed. You told me everything. You showed up at my house after midnight. Monika was with you, but she was shell-shocked. She couldn't even speak. My wife—Lisette—she put her to bed in one of our guest rooms. That was when you told me the truth about yourself. That you were some kind of spy for the Americans. That you'd been trying to break into an extremist group that was operating on campus."

"Did you know about it?"

Rudy rubbed a hand across his beard and closed his eyes. "*Ja,* we all knew. Nobody said anything. We knew there would be . . . consequences . . . if we spoke up. Nothing has changed since then. There's still a conspiracy of silence."

"What about the chalet?" Jason asked. "What did I tell you?"

"You said you'd killed four men. Three students and a teacher. I was horrified, needless to say. But you told me the whole story—how they'd taken Monika, how they wanted you to murder her to prove your loyalty. You fought back and were able to get away. But then you said you had to escape. Leave the country altogether and start over somewhere else. Both of you."

"Did I tell you how I planned to do that?"

"You said you knew people who could take care of the scene. But you didn't trust them to help Monika. You wanted to do that yourself."

"I would have needed papers. A new ID."

Rudy nodded. "You asked if I knew anybody who could do the work fast. Someone you could trust to stay quiet."

"Did you know anyone?"

"I made some calls. That's the thing about working security. You get to know a fair number of cops and criminals. I was able to locate a twentysomething French communist who worked in a bistro on Schweizerhausstrasse. Apparently, when he wasn't dishing up schnitzel to the tourists, he was part of an underground network for refugees around Europe. That was the beginning of angry times here, you know. An anti-immigrant referendum had just passed in Switzerland."

"Is he still around?" Jason asked. "What's his name?"

"Yanis Lorchaud. Yes, he's still in town. He owns the restaurant now. All the communists become capitalists as soon as they start making money. But I'm not sure if he's still in the immigrant business."

"Did I tell you anything about Monika's new identity? Or about where I was taking her?"

"No, my friend, and I didn't ask," Rudy replied. "I didn't want to know the details. People knew we were friends. If anyone came knocking at my door, I didn't want to be able to give you away."

Something in his voice gave Bourne a chill.

"Rudy, *did* someone come knocking?"

His friend glanced at the photo on the end table. He closed his eyes tightly. "Yes, they did, David. Yes, they did. Two strangers claiming to be Interpol came to my office and asked questions about you and the missing men from the school. I told them I knew nothing. I hadn't seen you. But I made a mistake."

"What?"

"I let the name of *Le Renouveau* cross my lips. I suggested things were happening here that they should investigate."

Jason knew what was coming next.

"Two hours later, I got a call," Rudy went on. "Lisette was in the hospital. They'd beaten her and broken both of her legs. She never walked again."

MANFRED WAITED UNTIL JOSEF HAD GONE TO THE SHOWERS, LEAVING HIM alone in their college apartment. Then he went to the large digital clock hung over his desk and removed it from the wall. On the back side, he removed the plastic panel for the battery compartment and pulled out the three AA batteries inside. With his fingernail, he pried open a plastic base at the bottom of the compartment.

Inside was a small pay-as-you-go mobile phone.

He powered it up and waited for the phone to acquire a signal. When it did, he tapped in a number from memory and activated a timer to keep watch on the length of the conversation. The phone was intended for emergency use only, and even then, no call was supposed to exceed sixty seconds.

An American voice answered on the first ring. "Identify yourself."

"Wolfgabel. Location Gamma-Bravo-Alpha."

The man on the other end of the line didn't need to consult a codebook to know that the caller was Manfred Seitz of Stiftsschule Obwalden in Engelberg, Switzerland. Just as Manfred knew that the American voice on the call belonged to a man named Justin Ely, who was head of intelligence for *Le Renouveau*.

Justin was the man who'd recruited him two years earlier.

"Proceed."

"I received the communiqué about the man you are looking for," Manfred said.

"And?"

"He is here. Just as you anticipated."

There was a pause of several seconds on the phone.

"You're sure it's him?"

"Quite sure."

"How long ago did you see him?"

"Fifteen minutes. He was inquiring about our head of security. He's with him now."

"Excellent," Ely replied. "That's good work. I'll check in with our other resources in town and activate our plan. We'll need to move rapidly. I'm heading to the airport now. I'll be on-site in three hours."

11

"YANIS LORCHAUD?" BOURNE ASKED.

The Frenchman sat on a three-legged stool in a basement wine cellar underneath the main floor of his restaurant. An open bottle of Leroux Corton Grand Cru sat on a little table in front of him. He swirled a healthy pour of the wine in a fat-bottomed glass, and his nostrils flared as he waved the scent toward his nose. He closed his eyes, tilting the glass between his lips, then held the wine in his mouth for a while before letting it slide down his gullet like a raw oyster.

His lips smacked with satisfaction.

"Oui, c'est moi," he finally replied.

"My name is—" Jason began, but Lorchaud interrupted him.

"Oh, I know who you are. I remember you. Once upon a time, you were a young man called David Webb. And now, as the story goes, you are Cain."

Bourne studied the wine cellar. The arched ceiling was low, the brick stonework ancient and cracked. The damp basement smelled of mold and wood. Dusty wine racks and large casks lined the water-stained walls, flickering in the shadows cast by a droopy candle on Lorchaud's small table. He pulled a second stool from near the wall of the cellar and sat in front of Lorchaud.

"Ten years ago, I believe we did some business together," Bourne said.

"Business? I'm sorry, but I have no memory of that." Lorchaud's dark eyes brightened, and a smile flickered on his mouth. "Surely *you* know what that's like."

The man was in his thirties, but his face had a drawn yellow cast, made paler by the candlelight. His brown hair was long and greasy, which made an odd contrast to the glistening tuxedo he wore. He was tall, his knees sharply bent as he sat on the low stool. His socks had slipped down, revealing skinny bare ankles.

"Would you like some of the Corton?" Lorchaud asked, tapping an empty wineglass on a shelf over his head. The crystal made an elegant ping.

"No. Thank you."

"A shame. It's excellent. What about dinner reservations upstairs? I'm sure I can comp an old friend and get you a window table." He gave Jason a little wink. "Would that be a table for one or a table for two? Are you traveling alone?"

Bourne's eyes narrowed with suspicion. He didn't like the man's game. "I just need to ask you some questions, Yanis. Then I'll go."

"I wish I could help you, *monsieur*. But ten years? That's a long time to be asking questions. I have a different life now. I am a simple restaurateur, catering to our town's many wealthy visitors. I pour their wines. I entertain their wives. I have left my other occupations in the past."

"That's not what I hear," Bourne replied.

Lorchaud pursed his lips thoughtfully and drank more wine. "Oh? And what is it you hear?"

"I talked to one of my contacts at Interpol Paris. He's an old hand, been around for thirty years. His portfolio includes identity theft, particularly as it relates to immigration and terrorism. It's safe to say there isn't a resource in Europe for forged papers that he doesn't know about."

"And? So what?"

"I gave him your name. He said he's never heard of you."

Lorchaud shrugged and waved the wineglass in the air. "Well, there you are."

"Yes, except he *should* have heard of you, Yanis. Even if you retired from the life, he'd definitely know your name. You know what that makes me think? My friend was protecting a source."

The man's pale face got a little paler.

"After all, we both know it's easier to make money when the government isn't breathing down your neck, Yanis. No tax audits to see if your restaurant profits are being mingled with revenue from other enterprises. No warrants, no computer searches. No agents parked outside to make your clients nervous. But how to keep them away from your doorstep, hmm? A man like you might decide to play both sides of the street. Every now and then, you answer a question for a government agent. You slip a little bit of information their way. Nothing that would ever lead back to you, of course. But something useful enough that Interpol turns a blind eye to your operations."

"I have no idea what you're talking about," Lorchaud replied stiffly.

"Really? So if word were to get around on the black market that you turned over information to the authorities on the occasional client, you'd be okay with that? You don't think that would have any effect on your expected life span?"

Lorchaud's fingers tightened around the wineglass. His raspy voice took on an edge. "Exactly what is it you want, Cain?"

Bourne reached into the pocket of his leather jacket and removed a clip of bills. He peeled off five thousand Swiss francs and put the cash on the table next to Lorchaud's bottle of wine.

"Ten years ago, David Webb asked you to put together a legend. The subject was a woman named Monika Roth, an English teacher at the college here in town. You turned her into someone else. New name. New identity. I want to know *who*, and I want to know where she was resettled."

Lorchaud caressed the bills but didn't pick them up. "Ah, so it's true. The memory of the past is gone for you. How interesting. Because otherwise, I cannot see why you'd be asking me for information that you already possess yourself."

"Monika Roth," Bourne repeated.

Lorchaud scoffed. "Oh, surely you don't think I remember in my head every legend I've created. One woman so many years ago? Who knows what name I gave her? Besides, the whole point of my work is discretion. You lost your memory to a bullet, Cain. I am *paid* to have no memory."

"You don't need to remember. I'm sure you've kept records of every passport, birth certificate, and credit card that ever left this place in a refugee's pocket. I imagine sometimes your life depends on having those records." Bourne tapped the bulging pocket of his leather jacket, where he kept his Sig. "Like now. This can go one of two ways, Yanis. I can pay you, or I can shoot you. Take your pick."

Jason removed another five thousand francs from the money clip and added them to the stack. Lorchaud made the easy choice. He slapped a hand on the table, and the cash disappeared into his tuxedo pocket. The Frenchman pointed to the wall of the wine cellar behind Bourne, where the mortar around the bricks was crumbling.

"The third brick from the bottom, second from the left. Would you mind? There's a device inside."

Jason found the loose brick and nudged it free. He slid his hand deep into the crevice until his fingers curled around an oversized Samsung phone. He handed the device to Lorchaud, who tapped the power button and unlocked it with his thumbprint. Then the man entered what appeared to be a twelve-digit code to unlock a specific app. He scrolled through the records on his phone and smiled with satisfaction.

"Yes, this is her, is it not? Lovely woman. Such a distinctive face."

Lorchaud turned the phone around.

Bourne saw a photo image of a German passport, and his eyes went to the picture. His breath caught in his chest, seeing her again. She'd done her makeup before having the picture taken, and it brought out her elegant bone structure. Her lipstick was dark red, her mouth serious. Wavy blond hair swept casually over her head and fell to her shoulders. Blue eyes stared at the camera with a kind of distant reserve, keeping the photographer away. She was beautiful, refined, independent. It was definitely Monika Roth, the same woman in the picture Johanna had taken of them at the Drei Alpenhäuser, the same woman who'd cast an aura around him from the heights of Mont Saint-Michel, the same woman whose life he'd saved in a mountain chalet.

He read the passport details.

Monika had become Ella Graf, address in an apartment building in Hamburg, Germany. That was the first link in the chain of finding her again. He memorized the address, then handed the phone to Lorchaud.

"Destroy her file," Bourne said, handing the man more money.

"Get rid of any records pertaining to her right now. Forget she was ever here, and then forget I was ever here. Understand?"

Lorchaud shrugged. "Consider it done."

"Thank you, Yanis."

Bourne turned to leave the wine cellar, but the Frenchman called him back. "Cain, wait. There's something else."

"What is it?"

Lorchaud poured more Corton from the bottle. He breathed heavily and rubbed sweat from his forehead. "You've played fair with me. I'll play fair with you. There are certain other things you should know."

"Like what?"

"You've been betrayed."

Jason tensed. "What do you mean?"

"Word went out a few weeks ago that *Le Renouveau* had made the connection between Cain and events that happened here a decade ago. They certainly didn't do that on their own, not after all this time. Someone told them about you. That's why they're coming after you now. I'd suggest you watch your back."

"Do you know who it was?" Jason asked.

Lorchaud shook his head. "I have no idea. Someone on the inside, I think. Someone in intelligence. Those are the rumors."

"I appreciate it."

"There's more. This town isn't safe. They've been expecting you."

"They know I'm in Engelberg?"

"Almost certainly, yes. My connections give me access to information passed among many different groups. *Le Renouveau* anticipated that you'd come *here*. All of their agents in town have been looking for you. It stands to reason you've already been spotted." Lorchaud's face darkened in the light of the candle. "And not just you. They know you're traveling with a woman."

Bourne hissed. *"Shit."*

He ran for the old stone stairs that led out of the cellar.

When he got to the restaurant, he pushed through the tables and then out into the cool Swiss air. It was almost dark. He checked the meadow across the street that ended where the mountains rose like giants out of the valley floor. The grassland was empty. No one was waiting for him. He dug his phone out of his pocket and punched in the number for the burner phone he'd given Johanna.

She didn't answer.

Bourne swore again.

He blamed himself; he should have seen it coming. They *knew* about Johanna. They'd already taken her once. Of course they'd go after her again. Of course they would use her as leverage to get *him*.

He ran for the Audi, which he'd parked three blocks away. When he fired the engine, his tires screeched as he shot for the main road. His headlights illuminated the dark street, and the bright lights of downtown loomed ahead of him. In the crowded streets, he had to slow, creeping past shops and restaurants and dodging the tourists. The delay made him pound the wheel with impatience.

He tapped out a text to Johanna with one thumb. *Where are you?*

There was still no answer.

Beyond the town center, he pressed the accelerator down and climbed the hill toward the Waldegg. The Audi squealed to a stop in the porte cochere, and Jason ran inside and bolted up five flights of stairs. The room he'd rented was in a corner of the hotel, looking toward the mountain ranges in the east and south. But as he got there, he could see that he was too late.

The door was ajar.

Bourne drew his Sig. He held his breath, then kicked the door open the rest of the way and twisted through the frame, his gun level. Inside, he found chaos. Furniture was turned over and broken. A mirror shattered.

Worst of all, he saw a spatter of blood on the white wall.

Johanna had fought like a tiger, but she'd lost.

She was hurt, and she was gone. *Le Renouveau* had her.

12

BOURNE DROVE AWAY FROM THE HOTEL AND FOUND A PARKING LOT SOUTH of the river, near the transit station where rotating cable cars took skiers to the high slopes of Mount Titlis. At night, the idle cars dangled from the wires and swung in the mountain breeze. He got out of the Audi and paced beside a narrow stream, where rapids surged over the rocks toward the Eugenisee lake a hundred yards away.

They had Johanna. He had to get her back. *But how?*

Think! Make a plan!

He didn't believe *Le Renouveau* would kill her, not right away. She wasn't the one they wanted. They wanted *him*. But they'd left no message in the hotel, no threats, no place to meet. They wanted him off balance. They wanted him to make a mistake. Let him panic the more time passed, the way he'd panicked ten years ago.

But that wasn't going to happen. A young man named David Webb had made mistakes, but not Cain. Cain was death.

He went to the water's edge, letting the noisy flow of the river over the rocks clear his mind like white noise. Across from him, giant boulders piled high on the bank made a flood barrier that kept snowmelt from the heart of the town. Not far away, a wooden footbridge led over the stream, and he saw lights burning in a few apartment buildings. When his eyes examined the shadows, he saw no one, and yet he was sure he wasn't alone.

They're watching me.

Then his phone rang, interrupting his thoughts.

He didn't recognize the number, and he wondered if this was the call. The outreach from the enemy. *We have the woman. She dies if you don't give yourself up.*

Instead, the voice belonged to a friend. It was Rudy Graz.

"David! I'm so glad I reached you. Where are you? Are you still in town?"

"Yes, I'm at the river. What's going on?"

"I'm not sure. I can't reach Lisette."

Jason inhaled sharply. He didn't like coincidences. First Johanna, now Lisette.

"When did you last talk to her?"

"Right after I saw you. She was fine, but I told her to be careful and let me know if she spotted anything unusual. Now she's not answering her phone. That's not like her. I'm worried."

"Are you still at the school?"

"Yes, but I'm leaving now. We have a farmhouse north of town."

"Give me the address. I'll meet you there. When you get to the house, *don't* go inside."

"Don't go inside?" Rudy protested. "This is my wife! If something's wrong, I need to be with her."

"I understand, but you don't know who may be waiting for you. I'll be right behind you. Stay outside, Rudy."

Bourne hung up. He turned toward the Audi, then stopped. Across the river, car high beams passed like searchlights along the opposite bank. For just an instant, the light revealed a figure hidden among the trees, with what looked like binoculars aimed at *him*. Bourne reversed course. He sprinted for the footbridge and pounded to the opposite shore. It only took him seconds, but by the time he reached the trees, whoever it was had already melted away.

He heard running footsteps in the distance.

But he'd been right. Someone was watching him.

The words of Yanis Lorchaud echoed in his head. *You've been betrayed.*

Jason crossed back over the river and ran to the Audi. He headed west, passing the Eugenisee and following the river northward. Quickly, he left the town of Engelberg behind and found himself in the high hill country. The road climbed like a terrace cut into the mountainside, and his headlights were the only lights in an otherwise pitch-black night. He drove fast as the highway climbed, then braked when the road descended sharply in horseshoe curves toward the next valley.

The turnoff to Rudy's house was a gravel lane joining the road at a tight angle. He had to do a U-turn to reach it. Then he followed the trail downward through dense trees on both sides. He turned off his lights, letting the grind of rocks under his tires tell him he was still on the road. Where the trees ended, a meadow opened up under the starlight. A handful of lights glowed in a farmhouse a hundred yards away.

He saw a car outside the house, its driver's door open, its headlights on.

Rudy had beaten him here. He'd gone inside.

Bourne swung the Audi into the soft grass and parked. He got out, his Sig in his hand. Around him, evergreens lined the field like a wall.

As his eyes adjusted to the night, he made out ruts in the grass, and the tracks led from the road to a black SUV hidden next to the trees. It was nearly invisible. Rudy wouldn't have seen it as he sped toward his house.

He wouldn't have known he was walking into a trap.

Rudy, why didn't you wait for me?

Jason ran through the damp grass. As he neared the house, he stopped, hearing the hum and crackle of power lines suspended over his head. A car engine rumbled. Rudy had left his car running as he bolted for the house to check on his wife. The front door was open, with lights shining from inside.

He approached the house, which was two stories, built into a shallow slope so the second floor exited into fields out back. A large patio came off the front porch, with a firepit to warm the winter nights below the mountains. Near the corner of the house, he saw a lean-to stocked with chopped wood. Jason avoided the open front door. Instead, he climbed the grassy slope to approach the house from the rear. He found glass doors that led into a master bedroom suite, and when he tried them, the doors slid open, unlocked. It was dark inside, and he switched on a penlight to examine the room.

His light revealed heavy Swiss décor, like a cottage out of a fairy tale. An elaborate pattern of red and gold diamonds adorned the wallpaper. A cherrywood four-poster bed occupied one wall, along with carved end tables and a huge five-drawer dresser. He saw an overstuffed leather recliner facing a flat-screen television, and next to the recliner was a C-table with a bottle of vodka, an ice bucket, and a halffull tumbler. The ice in the glass had long since melted.

As he neared the other side of the C-table, he spotted the metal frame of a wheelchair.

Bourne froze.

When he stepped closer, the tiny beam of his light shined down into the face of Lisette Graz, her body and head slumped sideways, her hair falling toward the floor like a waterfall, a bullet hole in the middle of her forehead.

He swore under his breath.

Rudy's car was outside, but Rudy wasn't in the bedroom with his wife. Jason knew what that meant.

He headed for the upstairs hallway. The lights weren't on, but a glow from the foyer carried up the stairs. With his back to the wall, he sidestepped along the corridor and looked over the railing to the ground floor below him. His breath caught.

At the base of the steps, spread-eagled on his back, was Rudy. His friend.

Dead like his wife.

A flurry of shots had caught him in the chest, followed by a final kill shot to his temple. His mouth was open, eyes wide with surprise at the ambush. The blood still dripped down his face like a slow red creek. It couldn't have happened more than a few minutes earlier. Bourne had seen no one in the field, and the black SUV was still hidden in the trees. So the killer or killers were inside the house. They hadn't left.

Why were they still here?

Then Bourne knew. They were waiting for him.

He assumed at least two men downstairs. Did they know he was already in the house? Not likely. His footsteps had been silent.

From where he was, he studied the foyer, which was lit by a hanging chandelier. He had a partial view of the living room on his left and what looked like an office or library on his right. The lights in both of those rooms were off. The front door opened inward toward the office, so he guessed that the killers were hiding there, out of sight, as they waited for their target to clear the door.

He had to draw them out of the house.

Bourne backtracked to the master bedroom. He slipped through the doorway, past the body of Lisette Graz, and grabbed the bottle of Xellent vodka from the C-table. In the walk-in closet, he ripped a sleeve from one of Rudy's shirts. Then he let himself back outside into the darkness. He made his way down the slope and approached a set of large windows that opened into the office. Nudging his face only an inch or two past the frame, he looked inside, but if anyone was waiting there, they were hidden where the foyer lights didn't reach.

Ducking under the window, he continued to the front of the house. At the lean-to, he searched a metal shelf above the stacks of firewood and found an old can of lighter fluid. He uncorked the vodka bottle, poured some of it off, then replaced the missing liquid with kerosene from the can. With what was left, he doused the shirtsleeve and stuffed it into the neck of the bottle.

He crept around the corner toward the porch steps and the open front door. With a cigarette lighter from his pocket, he ignited the doused sleeve into a burning torch, then lofted the Molotov cocktail through the doorway. It landed on the tile floor, glass shattering. In the next instant, an explosion of flame erupted inside, reaching almost to the ceiling. Smoke, heat, and a sweet-sour gasoline smell billowed into the night air. Panicked gunshots cracked behind the walls, followed by the shouts of an angry voice.

"Nach oben! Nach oben!"

Upstairs. They were heading upstairs.

Bourne retraced his steps and sprinted to the top of the slope. He kept his gun aimed at the doors that led out of the bedroom into the fields. A few seconds later, the doors flew open with a bang, and a boy bolted outside, semiautomatic rifle slung around his neck. Jason recognized him. It was the teenager with the bad soccer kick from the college quad, the kid who'd taken a ball to the groin in retaliation.

Josef.

Bourne's finger curled around the trigger, but he held his fire. He let the boy run. Josef was the sacrificial lamb. The real assault came next. Jason ducked behind the corner just as the older student from the quad, Manfred, charged through the door, sweeping fire from his rifle around the field. Jason let him get off several shots in a semicircle, then spun back and laid down a rain of pinpoint bullets from his Sig. He caught Manfred facing the wrong way and cut him down with four shots in the middle of his back.

As the boy collapsed, Bourne walked over and ended him the way they'd ended Rudy, with a coup de grâce to the temple.

He holstered his Sig and took Manfred's rifle into his hands. It was a Slovenian gun, a Tinck Perun X-16. When he swung it toward the meadow behind the house, he saw Josef in the grass, absolutely motionless, arms in the air and panicked terror on his face. He'd dumped his rifle on the ground at his feet.

"Nicht schiessen!" the boy pleaded.

Bourne walked up to Josef, the X-16 pointed at the teenager's chest. His heart was cold. He shoved the hot barrel into the bottom of Josef's chin and forced his head upward to look at the stars.

"Who killed them?" Jason asked.

"Was meinen Sie?"

"Who killed Rudy and Lisette? Was it you?"

"Nein, nein, es war Manfred! Ich schwöre!"

Bourne squatted and closed his hand around the Perun on the ground at Josef's feet. The barrel was cold. It hadn't been fired. He stood up again, gun still pointed at the boy.

"Bitte, mein Gott, schiesse nicht!" Josef cried.

"I won't shoot you. Not if you do exactly what I say."

"Ja, ja, alles was Sie willst!"

"Where is Johanna? Do you know where they took her?"

"Ja, sure, yes, I know," Josef replied, switching to accented English. "Manfred told me. She is in the chalet where you killed our men years ago. The same place! If we find you, we are to bring you there!"

"How many are waiting?"

"I don't know. I swear I don't know! Manfred didn't say. But there is an important man there."

"Why is he important? Who is he?"

"He is a leader. One of the top men of *Le Renouveau*. Manfred called him Justin. He's American like you. He came here to lead the operation. First they kill the woman, and then they kill you."

Bourne gestured with the barrel of the X-16 toward the black SUV that was parked in the trees.

"Drive," he told Josef. "Take me there."

13

DÉJÀ VU.

Bourne had traveled this road ten years earlier. It led up into the mountains, and the boy, Josef, squinted to follow the twists and turns at the end of his headlights. A granite cliff loomed over their heads on one side, and a steep drop-off fell into air on the other. Jason could smell the kid's sweat and see his hands slipping on the steering wheel. The SUV crawled, barely going twenty miles an hour.

Josef's stare drifted to the mirror. He'd done that several times.

"Focus on the road," Bourne snapped.

"*Ja*, of course, but I think—"

"What?"

"I think someone is following us!"

Jason twisted around in the passenger seat. He looked down into the blackness of the mountain road. At first, he saw nothing, but then a flash of headlights came and went somewhere in the curves below them. Josef was right. Coming up the mountain road, another car was in pursuit.

"Did Manfred have any other backup at Rudy's?" Bourne asked.

"I don't think so. It was just us. Justin told us to stay at the house of Herr Graz in case you showed up. But he believed you would go to the chalet. He assumed you'd guess that was where they had taken the woman."

Bourne frowned.

"Faster," he told Josef.

"*Mein Gott*, on this road? Do you want to die?"

"*Faster.*"

The boy accelerated, making the tires scrape. Josef's arms and legs quivered with fear, and Bourne had to grab the wheel to make sure he didn't drive them off the cliff. He was glad when they finally emerged onto the high plain, where rolling hills spread out under the night sky. The mountains made silhouettes on the horizon. The chalet wasn't far. He could see it in his mind from a decade ago.

His first mission.

His first failure.

"What now?" Josef asked.

"Let me out before we get to the chalet. They'll have guards waiting. Drive right up and tell them it's done. Go in and tell Justin that I'm dead. You killed me."

"He'll never believe me!"

Bourne shrugged. "Then tell him Manfred killed me, but I was able to kill Manfred with return fire. Say you came up here to inform Justin in person, but you need help to get the bodies away. He needs to send men there."

"I—I don't know if I can," Josef protested.

"If he doesn't believe you, he'll shoot you on the spot."

"Oh, fuck!"

Jason spotted lights ahead of them, appearing and disappearing with the swells of the road. They were almost there. He looked behind them, and whatever vehicle was chasing them hadn't reached the summit of the mountain yet. Bourne put a hand on the wheel, and Josef slowed the SUV to a crawl. He dug inside the inner pocket of his jacket and handed the teenager a miniature receiver.

"Put this in your ear. I'll be able to hear you."

Josef did as instructed.

"Okay, let me out," Bourne said.

The vehicle stopped, and he climbed out and pointed his Sig across the seat. "Remember what I said. Make the story good. If Justin doesn't believe you, you're dead. I'll hear everything you say. If you tell them I'm outside, I'll be the one to kill you, and you won't like what I do to you."

"No! Not a word, I swear!"

"Good. Now go."

The SUV sped away over the hill that led to the chalet. With the vehicle gone, the night turned black, and he could barely see his hand in front of his face. He backed away into the field and stretched out in the wet grass. Soon after, in the mountain silence, he heard the approach of a car engine. Two headlights came around the curve and then were extinguished, making the vehicle virtually disappear. The car passed him and stopped halfway up the low slope. The engine shut down.

He crept forward, approaching the Mercedes sedan from behind. As the door opened, he dragged out the driver and threw her to the ground. He held her there with a knee to her chest and the barrel of his Sig pushed into her throat.

His flashlight blinded her. The woman opened her eyes, squinting and blinking into the bright light.

"Cain," she said, gagging as she tried to speak. "Nice way to say hello."

"Vandal."

"Are you going to let me up?"

Jason didn't move the Sig. "That depends. Who are you working for?"

"Come on," she hissed. "I'm on your side. I'm Treadstone. You know that."

"Do I?"

"Fuck, Cain, I'm the one who sent you the warning in Paris!"

He kept the gun pressed hard against her neck. "Someone gave me up. Someone working in intelligence. *Le Renouveau* made the connection between me and David Webb. How did they do that?"

"I don't have a clue. It wasn't me."

"Then what are you doing here?"

"What do you think? Nash told me to follow you."

Jason stared into Vandal's dark, fiery eyes. His light shined on the lavender streaks shooting through her black hair. The last time he'd seen her had been in the woods in suburban Maryland, and she'd done something Treadstone agents didn't do. She'd hugged him and let him cry about Nova's death in her arms.

He holstered his Sig and let her go.

"Did Nash tell you about Monika?" Bourne asked.

"Only that I should keep you away from her."

He shook his head with no surprise. "What about Johanna? I came to Engelberg with a woman. She's the one who was hunting for me at the Drei Alpenhäuser. Does Nash know about her?"

"No, I only picked you up after your meeting with Nash, and you were alone," Vandal said. "Who's Johanna?"

"She's Monika's sister. *Le Renouveau* have her in the chalet."

The Treadstone agent got to her feet and brushed mud from her clothes. "Well, I've got gear in the trunk. Let's get her the fuck out of there."

JUSTIN ELY SAT IN A CHAIR IN FRONT OF JOHANNA AND CASUALLY CROSSED his legs. A Marlboro dripped from his mouth, and he removed it and blew smoke toward the vaulted ceiling of the chalet. He nodded at one of his men to remove the woman's gag. There were ten agents of *Le Renouveau* with him, seven inside, three monitoring the exterior on timed shifts. He'd read up on the incident with David Webb ten years earlier. This time he was taking no chances on being outmaneuvered by the agent known as Cain.

"Johanna Roth," he announced to the woman, who was tied to a chair by her wrists and ankles, with the chair pushed against the wall. "American sister to Monika Roth. You could save all of us a lot of time if you told us where she is."

"I wouldn't tell you if I knew," she spat back at him, "and I don't."

"No? You don't? I have a lot of trouble believing that. Two sisters. Sisters stick together. I'm sure you and Monika found a way to stay in contact somehow, even if you don't know her actual location. Phone number? Email? Social media account? Give me any of those, and we'll track her down."

Johanna worked her jaw to loosen the stiffness. "Fuck you."

"What about Cain? Or *David Webb,* as you know him. Does he know where Monika is?"

"Fuck you," she repeated.

Justin sighed. "We know Cain arranged Monika's new identity ten years ago. But from what I've learned about him, he doesn't actually *remember* doing so. So now he's trying to cover old ground and figure out where he hid her away. I expect he told you how he plans to do that. Has he given you names? Locations? And yes, yes, I know, fuck me. The thing is, you're only alive as long as you're useful to me, Ms. Roth. I want Cain, and I want your sister. I don't give a shit about *you*. That might work to your advantage if you helped me."

She clamped her mouth shut, saying nothing.

Justin blew smoke in the woman's face, making her cough. His fingers stroked along her cheekbones and played with her blond hair. He popped open two buttons on the shirt she was wearing and put his palm on the swell of her breast.

"Your heart is going fast," he murmured. "Are you scared of me?"

"What do you think? Of course I am."

"I'm sorry about that. I wish circumstances were different. You know, you're a very pretty girl. Has Cain told you that? Have you fucked him yet? Or is he still pining for that mystery woman from his youth?"

Flame erupted in her eyes, making him smile. That was fine. He loved the ones who hated him.

Justin heard a disturbance at the chalet door. He spun, his Glock already in his hand, and saw one of his men muscling a teenager into the house. He snapped his fingers for the man to bring the pimply-faced child closer. The boy stood in front of him, knees knocking, Adam's apple bobbing as he swallowed down bile. He brushed brown hair out of his face and came to attention.

"Ich bin hier, um der Sache mein Leben—" he began.

"Yes, yes, I know how it goes," Justin interrupted. "Who are you?"

"Josef. I am from Stiftsschule Obwalden."

"Right. You were with Manfred. Where is he?"

Josef's nervous face grew more nervous. "Manfred is dead."

"How?"

"The one you wanted. David Webb. Cain. He killed him at the house of Rudolph Graz."

"And not you?" Justin asked. "How is it that you're still alive? Where's Cain?"

"Cain is dead, too."

Behind him, he heard a gasp and a low moan from the woman tied to the chair.

Justin frowned with suspicion. "What are you saying, Josef? *You* killed Cain?"

"No, Manfred did that. There was an exchange of gunfire. Both of them were killed. I came here immediately to inform you. But the scene is unchanged and must be attended to. The dead bodies are there, not just them, but the two others you ordered us to kill. Herr Graz and his wife."

Justin walked a slow circle around the teenager. He saw no injuries, but the boy's face was smeared with dirt, and he smelled of gasoline. "Where are your weapons, Josef?"

"I—I lost them, sir."

"You lost them? How?"

"Cain started a fire. There was an explosion. In the chaos, I left my weapons behind."

"And then you drove here? By yourself?"

"Yes."

Justin nodded at the man who'd brought Josef into the chalet. His name was Beau, a local agent he'd used in Geneva. "Is the boy's SUV outside?"

Beau nodded.

"Search it thoroughly. Then report back."

"Yes, sir."

As the man left, Justin studied the unimpressive teenager in front of him. Something about his story didn't add up. He knew Manfred, who was one of his own recruits. A rock. A superb fighter, a perfect physical specimen. He found it hard to imagine this boy Josef surviving an encounter with Cain when Manfred did not.

"Take off your clothes," Justin snapped.

"What?"

"Your clothes. Now."

Josef hesitated only for a moment, then began to strip. He removed his shirt and undershirt, then stepped out of his shoes and pulled down his pants and underwear to his ankles. His body was scrawny, his limp dick shrinking up to nothing. Justin confirmed that the boy wasn't wearing a wire, and he saw no injuries to suggest he'd been beaten or influenced in other ways.

So perhaps even the strangest stories could be true.

Justin grabbed a radio from his belt. "Beau, give me a report. The boy's vehicle, do you see anything of concern?"

He waited. There was no response.

"Beau?"

Justin instantly shot a severe look at Josef. He watched the teenager, who had a damp sheen of sweat on his sunken chest. The boy's eyes began to blink at a rapid pace. Justin clicked the button on the radio again and continued to transmit to the other two guards outside. "Pieter? Drobac? Report immediately."

The guards didn't answer.

"Report," he repeated, but he no longer expected a response.

Calmly, Justin raised the Glock and fired a single shot into Josef's head.

The boy collapsed forward, dead. In the chair by the chalet wall, Johanna reacted to the killing with fevered screams. Justin turned and fired again, burying a bullet in the wall less than an inch from her face. He drew a finger across his throat, and her screams cut off into silence.

Below him, next to Josef's head, he spotted a small radio transmitter that had slipped from the boy's ear. He crushed it under his boot with a curse.

"Cain is out there," he announced to his men. "Go get him."

14

BOURNE STOOD OVER THE BODY OF THE GUARD KNOWN AS BEAU, WHO BLED
out at his feet, his throat cut open by a slash from a Thompson SOCP
knife. The second guard—it was either Pieter or Drobac—twitched
ten feet away, his neck broken, his last breaths gasping into the Swiss
night air. He didn't know where the third guard was, but the man hadn't
responded to Justin's query, so Bourne assumed that Vandal had removed the threat while she was checking the perimeter of the chalet.

"Vandal, what's your position?" he murmured into his radio.

She didn't answer. Instead, out of the darkness, Vandal appeared at
his side like a phantom, the lean curves of her body glowing white like
a sculpted angel. They both wore helmet-mounted Nightfox goggles,
which she carried as part of her Treadstone equipment. Each of them
now also carried Perun rifles from the *Le Renouveau* guards in addition
to their pistols and Thompson knives.

"They know we're here," Bourne said.

"Okay. I'll shut off the lights."

Vandal retreated around the corner of the chalet toward the

electrical box. Bourne crept toward the front door but stayed low and wide, expecting a volley of fire. He wasn't disappointed. Like a thunderstorm, rifles erupted, peppering the door from inside and spraying bullets around the exterior. One of the windshields in the three SUVs parked outside shattered. Jason crouched below the chalet windows, letting the men exhaust their onslaught. The deafening noise stopped as quickly as it had started, and silence followed. The smell of smoke leached through the destroyed door.

He waited for the power to go out so he could pick the assailants off one by one as they emerged in the darkness, big white targets for his rifle. But the next trap sprang before Vandal could cut the electricity.

From two sides, near the chalet roofline, floodlights burst to dazzling life, blinding him and forcing him to rip off his night vision goggles. In the same instant, the door crashed open, and footsteps pounded outside. He heard a deadly hail of fire and felt a round thud directly into his Kevlar vest like a jackhammer, knocking out his breath. He fired back round after round, high, low, wide, desperate to pin the killers down as he staggered to find cover without being able to see.

The power finally went dead. Overhead, the floodlights shut off, restoring the blackness of the night. Immediately, Bourne moved, knowing the men would fire at his last position. He shunted sideways, barely escaping the next siege of bullets as he rammed into the wall of the chalet. Then an arm around his throat jerked him off the ground and dragged him around the corner of the house.

Vandal.

She dropped to her knees, pivoted around the corner, and laid down fire one slow round at a time, bullet in the head, bullet in the head, bullet in the head. Three men had come outside, and three men, glowing white in the darkness, went down.

"Here," she murmured, handing him his Nightfox goggles.

Bourne felt his breath slowly come back to his lungs. He repositioned the goggles on his head and blinked until his eyes recovered and the night world came alive again. "Thanks for the rescue."

"No problem. How many more?"

"I don't know," he replied. "Let's find out."

Bourne sank to the ground and slithered around the corner, leading with the rifle. The chalet door was now open, but he saw no movement from inside. When he was below the edge of the front windows, he stood up long enough to see shadowy ghosts changing positions throughout the chalet. One of them must have spotted him, a darker silhouette against the night, because a new burst of fire showered him with glass as the window blew apart. He jerked back and retreated around the corner.

"Four, maybe five more," he said.

"Well, fuck, that seems like overkill," Vandal replied. "What does that make, ten men for little old you?"

"I'm glad I have you with me."

"So what's next?" she asked.

Bourne took the Perun and aimed around the corner. With a handful of shots, he took out the front tires on each of the SUVs, hearing the rubber explode with a hiss and watching the vehicles lurch to the ground.

"Justin won't be getting out that way," he said. "I'm going in."

"I'm right behind you."

He checked the front of the chalet and confirmed that the area was empty, except for the bodies of the guards, which lay on the ground white and motionless through the lenses of his goggles. The other killers were inside. He approached the shattered front door, which hung open, clinging to one set of hinges. He held up his hand to stop Vandal behind him, then crouched and rolled past the doorframe to the other side. The darkness covered him, but not enough. At least two men waited beyond the threshold, and orange flashes of gunfire erupted and barely missed him.

Through the radio in his ear, he heard Vandal's whispered voice. "I'll fire through the window. That should pin them down and let you get inside."

Bourne gave her a thumbs-up. He watched her back up until she was below the front window frame, which was littered with broken fragments around the edges like shark teeth. She lifted her hand to signal him, and in the glow of his night vision, he saw her swing up the barrel of the Perun and begin to fire, her aim high. Simultaneously, Bourne pushed off his knees and ran through the door, unleashing bullets toward two white silhouettes crouching twenty feet behind the frame. One fell, at least four bullets in his torso. The other threw himself to the floor but came up firing, and Bourne heard the spit of rounds chasing him into what looked like a formal dining room. He leaped, hitting the floor hard and sliding around the wall.

"I'll draw their fire," he hissed to Vandal. *"Go."*

He sent several shots into the next room to buy them time, then uncoiled his body and half jumped, half crawled to the opposite wall. The killer near the door squeezed off half a dozen rounds, and one came so close that it shattered Bourne's Nightfox goggles and ripped the helmet off his head. Now he was blind again.

But more fire exploded from the chalet door as Vandal roared inside, taking down the man in front of her and sliding to the floor like a runner stealing a base as two more men from the huge great space opened up with their weapons.

"Two to go," Vandal told him.

"What about Johanna?"

"I don't see her."

"Do they have night vision?"

"I don't think so. If they did, I'd be dead. I'm out here on the floor, exposed. They're targeting our barrels when we fire."

"Okay, be my eyes."

Bourne dropped to the varnished floor. He kept the rifle off the ground, finger around the trigger, and slid forward, propped on one elbow and pushing with his knees. As he neared the open door, the night sky gave the faintest brightness to the room, and he stopped. He knew Vandal was close, and he could barely make out the shape of her body among the two dead killers slumped on the floor.

He pressed ahead, trying to picture the layout of the chalet from ten years ago. Flashes of memory came and went in his mind. As he cleared the foyer, he felt hardwood turn to plush carpet, and he remembered two steps leading down into a great space below a vaulted ceiling. Yes! He could see it now. Two walls boasted mountain views through high narrow windows, a wall on his right and another directly ahead of him. The third wall to his left featured a huge flagstone fireplace and rough-hewn beams.

Two men were here. Somewhere.

And Johanna. *Where was Johanna?*

"Anything?" he murmured to Vandal. "Do you see them?"

"No. They're hiding under cover."

"Time for a diversion," Jason said.

He knew she could see him, even if he couldn't see anything himself. Silently, he shifted his weight from his left elbow to his right elbow, keeping his finger on the Perun's trigger. Then he slid his left hand back to a tight rear pocket and fished a penlight out of his black pants. He cocked his arm, then hoisted the flashlight through the darkness to the opposite side of the room.

It landed against the wall with a bang.

Gunfire followed.

He aimed toward the flash of one of the barrels. The clatter of broken glass mixed with the thunder of the rifle as he took out windows on the south wall. Then he made a tight roll to his left, barely escaping the barrage of the second man returning fire at the flashes of Bourne's gun. Behind him, he heard Vandal shoot from the foyer, and a body nearby made a heavy thud as it fell.

Bourne lay on the carpet, breathing hard.

"Both down," Vandal murmured.

"Any others?"

"I don't see anyone else."

Jason allowed himself to call out. *"Johanna!"*

He got no answer. The chalet was silent.

"I'll get the lights back on," Vandal said.

He heard the thump of her footsteps, and he stood up but had no way to move in the darkness. He listened, hearing only a whistle as cold wind blew past broken glass. Less than a minute later, he squinted as the lights came to life inside the chalet. When he could see, he noted the bodies on the floor, blood pooling beneath them. Among the bodies was the Nazi teenager, Josef, naked, the back of his skull nothing but a gaping hole of bone and brain.

Johanna was gone.

He saw cut lengths of rope near a chair on the floor.

Justin had taken her.

Bourne's eyes spotted wrought-iron stairs that wound like a snake to the second floor of the chalet. A memory sent shock waves of pain through his head. Jason saw an image of a man in shadow, the silver frames of his glasses glinting in the light, cigarette smoke clouding in front of his face. He was there, and then he was not there, escaping up the stairs.

That was what Justin had done.

He'd escaped, and he had Johanna.

Bourne flew up the steps two at a time, feeling the metal staircase quiver under his feet. He found himself in a dark hallway confronted by double doors. Sconce lights on two walls lit up a billiard room furnished with a professional pool table and the stuffed bodies of deer, ibex, and bears. On the far side of the room, a peaked wall made of glass let in a fierce mountain breeze through open sliding doors. He bolted across the room. The doors led to a large deck, where wooden steps descended to the green fields behind the chalet. The black night made it virtually impossible to see, and he closed his eyes to listen.

Somewhere, not far away, he heard footsteps in the damp field.

He took a chance and called again. *"Johanna!"*

This time she screamed for him. The scream cut off immediately, choked by someone's hand, but *she was there!*

Jason charged down the steps and shot across the field. He heard Johanna again, gasping out his name with a cry before she was shut down.

"David!"

His arms and legs pumped, and he closed the distance quickly. The two of them were right in front of him, a man dragging a woman, the woman stumbling and trying to slow him down. Bourne measured his steps and threw himself forward, colliding into the man's back and taking him hard to the soft grass.

With a cry, Johanna broke free and staggered away.

Below him, the man—he knew it was Justin—bucked like a bull and threw Bourne off. Justin slashed with his arm, and Jason felt the sting of a knife cutting through the tough hull of his vest. The fibers slowed the blade, but it cut him anyway, hacking across his skin. Jason grabbed the man's wrist, turned it, and broke it. Justin screamed as the bone snapped. The man's other fist slammed Bourne's face, jerking his head back and dizzying him. He felt Justin's movement rather than saw it, and he knew the man was reaching for a gun. Barely a second later, an explosion went off near his ear and heat seared his skin. Bourne used one boot to push off the grass and hurl himself forward, landing heavily against Justin and shoving him backward. Following the man's arm, he located the gun and slammed Justin's hand down until his grip loosened. Jason pried away the pistol and tossed it into the darkness.

His hands found Justin's neck. He locked his fingers around arteries and cartilage in a vise grip, thumbs pushing into the man's windpipe and cutting off his air. Justin struggled below him, jerking against Bourne to get free, landing furious blows with his damaged hands. A knee punched Jason's groin. A thumb gouged at his eye. But Bourne held on, squeezing harder, until the movements underneath him finally grew faint and then the man's entire body sank back, motionless and lifeless.

Justin was dead.

Bourne's grip was so tight that he found it hard to disengage his fingers from the man's neck. Finally, he peeled them back one at a time and rolled away. The grass was wet under his body, the stars shining in the mountain sky far above him. He tried to stand up, buckled, then stood up again.

Arms flew around him.

"Oh my God, Jason, are you okay?"

Johanna clung to him tightly, her head on his chest. Her perfume gave a floral hint to the sweet mountain air. She held on, sobbing, and then her wet face lifted and she kissed him, pressing her lips hard against his mouth.

"You saved me," she murmured between kisses. "Jesus, you saved me."

He found himself lifting her off the ground and kissing her back. The pain and the tiredness and the blood suddenly didn't exist at all. Johanna was in his arms. His hands sifted through her blond hair, and his lips found her mouth and cheeks and nose and neck and ears. He didn't want to let go. Neither did she.

They wouldn't have let go at all if Bourne hadn't become aware of a strange, muffled music filling the night. He forced himself to detach his arms from Johanna, and he listened to the music and realized it was coming from the dead body at his feet.

Justin had a phone, and it was ringing.

15

NO NAME AND NO NUMBER CAME IN WITH THE CALL. BOURNE DUG THE phone out of the dead man's pocket, then silenced Johanna with a finger over her lips. He tapped the button to take the call, then put a hand over his mouth and used a breathless, muffled tone to answer with the phone at his ear.

"Yeah?"

There was a long silence on the other end. Jason heard nothing in the background, no clues as to where the caller was located. The only noise was in the field around him as mountain air whipped into a frenzy and made a whistle through the trees.

Finally, a voice responded, low and calm, barely louder than a whisper. "Is it done? Do you have David Webb?"

In the pause that followed, the voice went on.

"Or is he dead?"

Jason squeezed his eyes shut.

He *knew* that voice. He *remembered* it. Was it from his past? Or was it from the present? Maybe it was both. His mind raced back to that night in the chalet ten years earlier and to the man in the silver glasses orchestrating the action from a chair in the corner of the room. He *knew* him. This was the man on the phone, and he was still in control, still stage-managing the scene like a director.

Who was he?

Bourne tried to pair a face in shadow with the voice in his mind, but forcing his brain to remember brought stabs of pain behind his eyes. He only knew one thing. When he thought of that voice, he thought of Monika. It wasn't just about the chalet. This was something else. Somehow the two of them were linked in his memory.

How? *Why?*

"Justin?" said the voice, now with faint suspicion.

Bourne said again, "Yeah." Then he added, "Webb's dead."

The empty silence stretched out, but he checked the phone and saw that the call hadn't dropped. When the man finally spoke again, Jason heard a dark smile in the voice, and he knew he hadn't fooled him at all.

"Well, well, well. *Cain.*"

Jason shrugged. "That's right."

"And Justin?"

"Dead. I killed him."

"I assumed as much. That's impressive. He had a similar background to yours and similar skills. Well, I warned Justin not to underestimate you, even with greater numbers. He was talented, but sometimes too arrogant."

"He shot a confused teenager in the head," Jason snapped.

"And didn't you do the same ten years ago? Three of my men were your own students at the college. You're not so different from us."

Jason didn't take the bait. "So it *was* you back then. In the chalet."

"Yes, it was. You're right. We have history, you and I. I've been trying to hunt you down for a long time."

"You got away from me ten years ago. Don't count on it happening again."

"Brave talk. I respect that. I respect *you*. Actually, I suggested to Justin if we took you alive, maybe we could persuade you to join our organization. You might find that our values aren't so misaligned as you would think."

"Or maybe I wouldn't."

"Oh, surely you don't condone the chaos in the West. The U.S., France, Germany, Britain, all of them weak-kneed democracies letting their own cultures be erased by outsiders. Inviting their enemies in by the millions. Don't you think China is laughing at us? Our goal is to stop the decline. We intend to restore the values that built Western civilization in the first place."

"I've heard speeches like that before," Jason replied. "Thank you, next."

"That's a shame. Because we *will* win in the end. It's inevitable. Our philosophy cannot be stopped. I'd rather have you on our side because you're a formidable adversary. But you should know that we are formidable in our own right."

"I don't doubt it."

"You were able to defeat Justin, but don't think you're safe with him gone. There are many more of us to follow. We *will* meet again, Cain, and I don't think it's likely to end well for you." He added with what sounded like a wicked grin, "Or for Monika."

"I'm the one you want, not her," Bourne snapped. "It's been ten years. She's no threat to you now. Monika had nothing to do with any of this."

His forehead creased with puzzlement as he heard the man chuckling softly on the phone.

"Oh, David. Do you mind if I call you David? After all, that's still who you really are. All these years, David, and you've learned nothing. I know what happened to your memory, but trust me, it wouldn't help you to remember everything about your past. You see, even back then, you had no idea who Monika Roth really was."

VANDAL USED HER TRAUMA KIT TO STITCH UP BOURNE'S CHEST.

They stood outside in the darkness, with Jason holding a flashlight to illuminate the deep wound caused by Justin's knife. Her movements were quick and skilled. When she was done, her fingers lingered for a while on his chest, tracing his other scars. Then she seemed to realize what she was doing and pulled her hand away.

Close to them, Johanna sat in the back seat of the Mercedes. She was visible through the open window. Dirt smeared her face and hair, and dried blood made a ribbon from her temple onto her cheek. Jason hadn't wanted her to go back inside the chalet, which was strewn with bodies, so he'd carried her here from the mountain fields, with her arms around his neck. Her eyes had the shell-shocked emptiness that came in the wake of violence.

"You like her," Vandal said, noting his fixed stare on the woman in the car.

Bourne shrugged. "It's nothing."

She wiped a red smudge from his face. "Her lipstick tells a different story."

"Stress, adrenaline, sex. It all gets mixed up. You know that."

Her eyes were dark in the glow of the light. "I do know that."

Briefly, Jason had a flashback of their mission in Barcelona. He thought about the night before the assassination and how Vandal had come up behind him in the shower and molded her naked body against his. He remembered her hands reaching around to caress him, teasing out his arousal with sharp fingernails. The memory, hot and vivid, began to work its magic on him again.

But for now, Vandal was all business.

"I checked the bodies. They're clean. There's nothing to give us any leads on *Le Renouveau.*"

"What about Justin?" he asked.

"Facial recognition came back with a hit in our own records. His name was Justin Ely. He spent a decade working for the CIA in Eastern Europe."

"That must be what the man on the phone meant," Bourne said. "He said we had similar backgrounds. But if *Le Renouveau* methods haven't changed, the odds are that Justin was a mole from the beginning. They probably recruited him in college. That's what makes this whole operation so insidious. Most of the assets in the group won't have any red flags in their background that we can use to ferret them out."

"Well, I can use my sources and see what else I can find about Justin. We might find clues to other recruits."

"Okay, good."

"And you? What do you do next?"

Bourne hesitated. "I have a lead on Monika."

Vandal glanced at Johanna in the Mercedes. "You're still a target, Cain. *Le Renouveau* is still after you. If you can get a lead on Monika, so can they. Tracking her down might put all three of you at risk. Why not go underground for a while? Find a beach somewhere. Take the girl with you, and the two of you can swim and drink and fuck for a few days. You know she wants it. I'm pretty sure you do, too."

He heard a twinge of jealousy in her voice. Or maybe that was his own ego telling him what he wanted to believe.

"Monika's her sister," Bourne replied. "Johanna's not going to give up looking for her, even if I back out. And the fact is, I want to know who Monika is. I'm beginning to wonder if she's connected to this in ways I didn't understand."

"How so? You think she's part of *Le Renouveau?*"

"I don't know. I can't believe that, but at this point, anything's possible."

"Maybe that's how they got onto you in the beginning," Vandal suggested. "I mean, someone gave you up."

Bourne didn't answer, but he had been wondering the same thing.

He thought about the warning from Yanis Lorchaud. *You've been betrayed.*

"Regardless, I need to find her," he said. "Whatever her role is in all of this, *Le Renouveau* are looking for Monika, too. She's not safe."

A frown creased Vandal's face. "Just to be clear, Nash wants you to stand down. My job is to make sure you do."

"Nash isn't telling us everything he knows. He never does."

"I still have my orders."

Bourne retrieved his shirt, which was slung over Vandal's shoulder. He shrugged it onto his chest, buttoned it, and left it untucked. He glanced toward the nearest hill that led to the chalet, but there were no lights inside the house. They'd switched off the power again, letting the interior grow cold with the overnight temperatures. Then they'd dragged the bodies from outside back into the chalet.

"You can try to stop me if you want," he told her.

"Or?"

"Or you can help me."

Vandal glanced up at the dark sky. Her face began to glisten with dampness as cold mist fell from the clouds. "I have to stay here and wait for the cleaners."

"Okay."

"Go ahead and take the Mercedes. I'll catch a ride back to town when the job's done. That will be hours from now. Plenty of time for you to get away."

"Thank you."

"Are you going to tell me where you're going?" Vandal asked.

He knew what the question meant. Did he trust her? Would he tell her the next step in his plan? Cain had been betrayed by Treadstone too many times to trust anyone, but he also knew that Vandal couldn't help him if he wasn't willing to share intelligence with her. Either she was an enemy or she was an ally.

Or she was both.

"We're going to Germany," Jason told her, fighting his own instincts. "That's where I sent Monika ten years ago. I set her up in an apartment in Hamburg."

"Do you think she'll be there?"

"I don't know."

"Well, if you need me, say the word."

"I will."

Vandal slid her phone out of her back pocket and dialed. The man on the other end answered immediately, and Jason recognized Nash's raspy voice. As Vandal talked to him, her eyes never left Bourne.

"It's me," she said. "Sorry for the delay. Yeah, I'm still alive, but I'm on a fucking mountaintop in the rain, and I've got a bunch of dead bodies in a chalet. Send a crew. We need to clean this up and keep it quiet."

Bourne heard Nash say one word. His own name.

"Cain?" she replied. "Yeah, Cain's alive, too. But the bastard lost me. I don't know where he is or where he's heading next. I only know that you were right. He's going after this woman, Monika. He's going to find her sooner or later. You'll never stop him."

16

THE NORTH SEA LICKED AT THE CAUSEWAY AS THE TIDE BROUGHT THE WA-
ter closer.

The woman didn't want to be trapped on the mainland for the
night. It had never happened to her before, but there had been times
when her tires splashed through a couple of inches of water as she sped
back to the island. One time, using her binoculars from the coast, she'd
seen a man escape from his BMW and climb to the emergency refuge
shack, while his vehicle floated away with the rising tide.

It was a gray day, slate clouds filling the sky and spitting out rain.
Wet sand stretched across the lowlands, interrupted by isolated lakes
and rivers left behind the last time the sea had retreated. Damp moss
and green algae lined the narrow road on both sides. She checked her
mirror, the way she always did, but she had the causeway to herself in
both directions. Usually, there were a couple of other drivers racing the
tide, but not today. No one else was heading home to Holy Island, and
those who were still there were trapped for at least seven hours until
the road reemerged.

As she neared the island, sand gave way to grassy marshes. Low hills rose in front of her, dotted by sturdy evergreens windblown by the fierce sea gales. Finally, a road sign welcomed her to Lindisfarne. She was home again. This time she'd been away for nine weeks. Sometimes it was only a few days; sometimes it was months. But eventually, she always returned to her cottage off the Northumberland coast, as she had for ten years.

When she was clear of the incoming tide, she pulled onto the shoulder near a grassy sand dune. She turned off the engine and opened the window, and the late-day chill spread through her Volkswagen. She took her binoculars from the glove box and zoomed in on the causeway, confirming that no cars had followed behind her. That was the reason she always kept an eye on the tidal schedule and waited until the last minute to return to the island. She liked to know who was making the crossing with her.

But today she watched the road flood, and she was alone.

The woman fired up the Volkswagen again and returned to the lonely road, which continued through empty land for two more miles. The rain increased, forcing her to turn on her windshield wipers. She soon reached the town, which consisted of little more than a few blocks of old stone buildings and white cottages clinging to the island's south- ern shore. Tourists came to visit the ruined priory and the sixteenth- century castle built on a pillar of land to guard the approach from the sea. A few of the visitors stayed overnight, but most left before the tide rose, leaving the town to its two hundred or so permanent dwellers.

The rain kept the streets mostly deserted. She passed a couple of hardy souls walking their dogs, and they tipped their wool caps at her to welcome her home. Everyone knew everyone else on the island. Her neighbors knew her as Sarah Tedford, forty-five years old, training supervisor for a company called Peterman Resources Ltd. No one knew what the company did, and no one asked. They only knew that Sarah's job took her away for long stretches at a time, and when she came back, she mostly stayed at her cottage, drinking tea on a garden patio that overlooked the sea.

That was okay. Recluses were a staple of island life.

She didn't park near her house. She never did. Instead, she found a grassy area near the old priory and left her car there. She went inside a whitewashed two-story pub and inn called the Crown & Anchor. It was late, and she didn't feel like cooking, and nothing in her refrigerator would still be good after all these weeks away. The barman behind the brick bar was a strapping twentysomething kid named Nicholas, and he began pulling a half-pint of hard cider as soon as he saw her. That was her drink whenever she came here. She asked for an order of fish and chips, and then she took her cider to a table near the coal fireplace to dry off.

Nicholas had hit on her a couple of times when the pub was empty, as it was now. She was flattered by the interest from a kid who was young enough to be her son, but she'd never done anything about it. She knew she was attractive. Men had told her that often enough, but she'd made a point of never letting anyone get close to her. Not in a long time. Her wheat-blond hair was wavy, sweeping over her head and falling to her shoulders. She had pale blue eyes, focused and sad. Her bone structure was sharply defined, and she could dazzle when she needed to, but she made a point of removing her makeup before she came home. Otherwise, she looked too royal for the hardscrabble island life. However, she always kept her lipstick perfect. She was vain about her deep red lips, maybe because her mouth turned naturally downward in a frown, and she didn't often smile.

"You back for a while then, Sarah?" Nicholas called from the bar. "We've missed you around here."

"Oh, I don't know yet," she replied. "I never know from day to day. But thank you. I've missed you, too."

Her English still bore a trace of her German accent from her childhood. People on the island talked about that. Where was Sarah from? How had she come from Germany to England? She'd told them that her father had emigrated from Berlin when she was a child, and after she'd grown up, she stayed in her adoptive home country. That wasn't true, but if anyone took the time to look, they'd find immigration records to back up her story. To the outside world, she was Sarah Tedford.

Her fingers parted the damp strands of her hair with long, slow movements of her fingers. She noticed Nicholas watching her, and she knew the gesture was seductive, although she had no erotic intentions. Or did she? Why had she told Nicholas she missed him? That was a lie. She never gave him a thought, in or out of the pub. But she hadn't made love to anyone in a while, and she missed the physical release of having someone in her bed. It would be easy to take Nicholas home. But he was a boy, and boys could be complicated. She'd learned that ten years ago. Boys had a way of falling hard, and that was a problem for her. So she stopped twisting her hair and took out her phone, deliberately ignoring Nicholas. He continued to shoot smiles her way, but she pretended not to notice.

Ten minutes later, he brought her food, tied neatly in a plastic bag to take away. She thanked him, gave him a generous tip to make up for leading him on, and went back out into the rain. She left her Volkswagen where it was. Her cottage was only a minute's walk away. She followed the stone border of the graveyard past the priory ruins and the ghostly, skeletal statue of Saint Aidan lifting a torch to the sky. In the other direction, on the far side of the island harbor, the fierce old castle jutted out of the flat land. She passed the church and continued to the seafront, where a flower-lined wall surrounded her property. The wall wouldn't have been hard to climb, but she'd installed sensors at regular intervals, and notifications went to her phone if anyone came inside. She unlatched the wooden gate and let herself into the garden.

Her stone cottage was small, two stories plus an attic, with a blue painted door. When she was gone, she paid an old man in the village to mow her lawn and tend to her landscaping so everything looked manicured when she returned. She liked to keep a precise, ordered life. According to her security system, Mr. Aubrey had last been here to maintain the place two days ago, and no one had tripped the motion detectors since then.

And yet something was wrong.

Right in front of her blue door, in the shelter of the overhang, she saw a plastic-wrapped bouquet of red roses and baby's breath. The flowers looked fresh; they couldn't have been here long. She dug out her phone and checked the video database, but somehow the person delivering the flowers had done so without triggering her devices and cameras. She didn't like that. For the moment, she ignored the bouquet and took a walk around the exterior of her property. Nothing looked out of place. The windows were still closed on both levels, and the rear door was deadbolted from the inside. She did a complete circle of the yard, past the back gate and steps that led down to the beach, and she saw no evidence that anyone had been here.

But when she returned to the front door, there were the flowers.

She squatted in front of the arrangement. A square white card was tucked inside the plastic. Carefully peeling the wrapping back, she removed the envelope and saw a word written in script on the outside.

Shadow

Her breath caught in her chest.

She ripped open the envelope and took out the card inside. The message contained a single sentence neatly written in the same script, but she didn't even need to read it to know what it would say. She'd been dreading this message for years.

Ten years.

Ever since she met David Webb.

The note said: *He's coming.*

PART TWO

17

THE MORNING TRAIN TOOK JASON AND JOHANNA FROM ENGELBERG TO THE river town of Basel. He opted for a slow route via Bern, requiring two changes and three hours of travel time. At each station, he made sure they weren't being followed. When they got to Basel, they wandered the city on foot for the rest of the day. He led them on a random route through the storybook streets of the medieval Old Town and on the path by the Rhine, with the twin spires of the Münster rising above the rest of the village.

His goal for the detour was to confirm that he'd evaded surveillance from both Nash Rollins and *Le Renouveau*. But he couldn't deny that he enjoyed the brief respite from violence, walking hand in hand with Johanna.

That evening, they returned to the Basel Bahnhof and he booked them on an overnight train. Near midnight, they changed at Frankfurt for the multi-hour trip to Hamburg, and he got them a private first-class couchette. As they headed north out of the city, the train car window looked out on the German countryside, which gave the compartment its only light when they passed through the small towns. Otherwise, the carriage was dark, and the rattle of the train provided a hypnotic clatter. They didn't talk, but they also didn't sleep. Bourne stretched out on his back on one side of the compartment and Johanna stayed on the other, but soon he heard her slip out of her bed. She moved in beside him, their bodies squeezed next to each other in the cramped space.

"Do you mind?" she murmured. "I want to be with you."

In fact, he did mind. He knew he should tell her to go, to stay away from him, to keep distance between them like a solid wall. Johanna was Kryptonite, and letting himself get close to her was dangerous for both of them.

But he heard himself whisper, "No, I don't mind."

She faced him in bed. She was so close that her breath blew softly on his cheek. In the darkness, he could barely see her, but every few seconds, light would flash across the window, and he would catch a glimpse of her blue eyes staring at him and of her pale lips parted just inches away.

Her arm went around his waist. Her hips molded against his.

"Tell me something," she said softly.

"What?"

"Do you still love Monika?"

"Love her? How can I? I don't even remember her."

"Do you feel like you owe her some kind of loyalty? I mean, because of the past."

"No."

"And yet I can feel you hesitating with me," Johanna said. "Pulling away. You won't let me get close to you."

"That's true."

"Why? Do you think you'd upset her by sleeping with me?"

"No. Whatever happened between us was a long time ago."

"Then what is it? Because I'm not shy. I never have been. I nearly died last night, and that only confirmed for me how much I want you. I won't apologize for that, not to you, not to her. I mean, I think I fell in love with you a little bit ten years ago when we first met in Zurich. I couldn't have you then because you belonged to my sister. But there's nothing standing between us now." She added after a pause, "Is there?"

Jason watched her face appear and disappear with another glimmer of light.

He could have told her that his life was complicated and impossible.

He could have told her that he was still in love with Abbey Laurent.

He could have told her that he hadn't gotten over finding the bullet-riddled body of his previous lover, Nova, months earlier.

He could have told her that every woman who'd come into his life had paid a terrible price for knowing him. Including Monika.

But he didn't.

He pulled her against him. She came to him quickly and hungrily, her tongue exploring his mouth, a purr of desire rumbling in her throat. Her hands slipped under his shirt to massage his back. He undid her nylon belt, shimmied her pants down to her thighs, and found the warmth and wetness between her legs. His fingertips caressed her and slipped inside. She pushed hard into his hand, wanting more, but the tight couchette was too cramped for their impatience. They scrambled out of bed and stripped off the rest of their clothes in the darkness. Naked, they embraced, and she fell back with him onto the cot, her legs spread wide. He sank easily inside her, bringing a soft cry, and her thighs wrapped around his back as tightly as a vise.

The first time, wet and wild and urgent, took no time at all. The second time, minutes later, was slower, their invisible movements gentle and unhurried. He got to know every inch of her body with his fingers and lips, and she did the same to him. When he finally entered her again, face-to-face, their coupling built like a fire, a long fuse burning to an explosion that left them clinging fiercely to each other and moaning with release.

Sated, they fell back against the pillow, still tangled together. The clatter of the train shook around them. For a while, all they could do was breathe and recover. Their bodies had grown slippery with sweat, and her blond hair stuck to his neck and shoulders as if pasted there. He heard her giggle in the darkness.

"Jesus," Johanna said. "I needed that."

"Me too."

"I want to do that with you a lot. Okay? A lot. For a long time."

"Okay."

But Jason knew that was an easy promise to make and even easier to break. Tomorrow might change everything. Johanna seemed to realize that, too, because she grew silent and didn't say anything more. She simply held on to him and idly stroked his skin. Eventually, her chest fell into a steady, swelling rhythm against him as she slept.

Bourne slept, too. Not for long, just enough to refresh his mind. When he opened his eyes again, he eased out of the bed, leaving Johanna where she was. He dressed quickly and let himself out of the couchette into the rattling train corridor. When he found the dining car, he bought espresso and croissants. Back in the compartment, he found the lights on and Johanna sitting up, still naked. She looked relaxed and comfortable, her blond hair tangled, her breasts on display below her skinny shoulders.

"Oh, good job," she said, seeing the food. "I'm starved."

They ate breakfast together and made small talk. The coffee was bitter, the pastries dry, but he didn't care. He talked about living in Paris, and she talked about living in Salzburg. They avoided the subject of death on the mountain. When they were done, she helped him out of his clothes and they made love again.

Finally, as morning neared and the sky began to lighten, they sat on the floor of the compartment with their backs against one of the beds.

"We'll be in Hamburg in a few minutes," he said.

Johanna nodded. "Yeah. I'm anxious to be there, but I don't really want this night to end. Does that make any sense?"

"I get it. I know how you feel." He kissed her and went on in a darker voice. "Listen, it would be better if you don't come with me to the apartment building. I can drop you near the river, and you can hang out there for a while. If I find Monika, I'll bring her to you."

"Why don't you want me with you?" Johanna asked.

"Because if I was able to find out where she is and who she is, it's possible *Le Renouveau* did, too. They may have figured out that I went to Yanis Lorchaud, and they may have gotten him to talk. If so, they could have people waiting for us at the apartment."

"I don't care. I'd rather stay with you, David." Johanna shook her head. "Sorry. I keep doing that. *Jason*."

"Johanna, I'm not going to put you at risk—"

"I know, but I'm already at risk, and I feel safer when we're together," she broke in. "Every time we're separated, I wonder if I'll see you again. And whoever these people are, I don't want to be left alone to face them by myself."

He hesitated, but he found himself unwilling to say no. "Yes, all right. But stay close and do exactly what I say."

"Of course." She glanced out the train window. The countryside had given way to office buildings and apartment towers as they neared the city. "Ella Graf. That was the name you gave her? That's who we're looking for?"

"Yes."

"Strange. You were David Webb. She was Monika Roth. Now both of you have new identities. And then there's me. I'm the same person I always was."

"Listen to me, Johanna. It's been ten years since you saw your sister. A lot may have happened to her in that amount of time. You have to be prepared for that."

"I know. A lot already has happened. I wonder what she'll say to me. To you, too. I mean, I wonder what she'll say about *us*. Suddenly, I'm nervous to tell her that we're involved. I thought I wouldn't care, but I do."

"Don't worry about that now."

Johanna touched his face, and her fingers were warm. "What are you not telling me?"

"What do you mean?"

"There's something else about my sister, something you're not saying."

He chose his words carefully. "There may be things about her that you never knew."

"Like what?"

"Someone high up in *Le Renouveau* said I didn't know who she really was."

"What does that mean?"

"I don't know. It could simply be a game he's playing with me. A misdirection. Sowing mistrust."

"But you don't think so," Johanna said.

"I don't know what to think. How well did you actually know Monika?"

She frowned. "I thought pretty well, but I was just a teenager. She was much older than me. We were in separate countries most of the time, her in Germany, me in the U.S. Looking back, I guess I didn't really know her well at all. I only knew what she told me about herself."

"Did anything she told you ever strike you as odd? Or out of character?"

"Not that I remember. Or that I would have even noticed as a kid. She was a teacher. It seemed to me she mostly liked to read books. She talked a lot about what she was reading. That was it."

"Where did she go to school?"

"I don't even know. Somewhere in Germany or Switzerland, I guess. Like I said, she was a lot older. Jesus, you don't think she's one of *them*, do you?"

"I hope not." Bourne looked out the window as the train started to slow. He heard the noises of people in the corridor getting ready to disembark. "But that's why you'd be better off letting me do this alone."

Johanna shook her head firmly. "No. I started this. I found you so that I could find *her*. I want to be there when you do."

"Okay," Jason agreed. "We'll do this together. But you may not find what you're looking for. Whenever we find Monika, she may not be the person you remember. She may be a stranger."

18

THEY AVOIDED THE EARLY-MORNING TAXI LINE OUTSIDE THE HAMBURG train station. Instead, Jason led Johanna across Kirchenallee and hailed a cab in a plaza around the corner. When the driver asked for their destination, he told the young woman simply to drive and he'd provide the directions. He also asked her to adjust her side mirror so that he could see the traffic behind them. She gave him a curious look, but when he passed one hundred euro across the front seat, she complied.

For the next hour, he led them across the bridges over the Hamburg canals. It was Sunday morning, and they had most of the downtown streets to themselves. He *knew* he'd been here before. He didn't remember many of the details, but he remembered the city itself. Hamburg was a place of business and brawn, a German version of Chicago with big shoulders. At least once, he was sure he'd come here by ship out of the North Sea. He could picture the industrial ports on the south side of the river and see himself navigating a nighttime maze of shipping containers stacked five high. He had his Sig in his hand.

But the when and the why of being here was gone.

His sense of direction came only from instinct, but his instincts were sound. When they headed toward the Elbe on Sandtorkai, he could picture the scalloped glass tower of the symphony hall in his head before they reached it on the street. When they passed the rough red stone of St. Catharine's Church, he knew there was a Chinese restaurant in the next block, and he could taste their Hunan beef on his tongue.

Hovering over all of it was a ghost. Monika.

Had he been here with *her*?

When he was sure they weren't being followed, he directed the cabbie to a residential neighborhood near Fischers Park, a few blocks north of the river. He and Johanna got out on a cobblestoned alley, and the taxi drove away. On their right, apartment buildings lined the street, most no more than three or four stories tall. Cars crowded the curb beneath leafy ash trees, and dozens of bicycles were chained to a railing beside a neatly trimmed hedge outside the apartments. The railing was mounted on a low stone wall, covered over with graffiti and spray paint. Across the street, dense foliage marked the fringe of the park.

"Is Monika's place near here?" Johanna asked, looking at the deserted avenue.

"In the next block. Bernadottestrasse."

"So why aren't we there?"

"I want to check out the area first," he said.

She took his hand as they crossed the street. They walked to the next intersection, where there was a stoplight but no Sunday traffic. He noted the handful of people around them. An old woman made her way toward the park, walking her schnauzer on a leash. Two twentysomething men jogged eastward in the opposite direction. On the far corner, a man stood next to his bicycle with a dark cigarette hanging from his mouth. Bourne studied him closely, but concluded that he wasn't a threat.

The entire neighborhood looked secure.

And yet. He had a bad feeling anyway.

"Is everything okay?" Johanna asked, reading his face.

"Something's off."

"What is it? Do you see something?"

"No."

"Then I don't understand," Johanna said.

"This feels too easy. I don't like it when things come too easy."

"Did this man Lorchaud lie about the location?"

Jason shook his head. "No, I saw the actual papers. The identification data on Monika was legit. But I'm starting to wonder if Lorchaud only gave it to me because he knew I wouldn't find anything."

Johanna squeezed his hand tighter. "Which building is hers?"

"The last building across from the park," he said, analyzing the location with a quick glance. Most of the buildings on the street were elegant *Altbau*, old buildings, freshly painted in bright white and built with arches over the windows and gabled dormers on the roofline. The last building was newer, but boxy and unattractive. It was five stories high, built of tan brick, with balconies stretching across each level. The apartment number for Ella Graf put it on the building's top floor.

"What do we do?" Johanna asked.

"We go inside."

They stayed adjacent to the park as they headed down the street. He noted the cars around them, but the vehicles were empty. So were the balconies and windows in the nearby apartments. Somehow he expected to spot surveillance, but he saw nothing. When they were across from Monika's building, he checked the balconies of the two upper-floor apartments, but both were empty, the drapes pulled shut.

Even so, the foreboding that tightened his gut got worse.

Your body senses danger faster than your brain.

Treadstone.

Bourne put his hands in the pockets of his leather jacket, his fingers curled around the Sig. Together, he and Johanna crossed to the glass building door. It was smoked, and he couldn't see inside. Each apartment had a buzzer and a metal mailbox beside the door. The boxes had handwritten names, and he noted the name GRAF written in block letters next to the mailbox for an apartment on the top floor.

"Is that Monika's handwriting?" he asked.

Johanna shook her head. "I can't tell. I don't think so, but I could be wrong."

He examined the label more closely. It didn't look as faded and dirty as the others, as if it had been recently added.

Or was he being paranoid?

Jason studied the other names on the building roster. One label for the lone ground-floor apartment said: BAUER—MANAGERIN. He pushed the buzzer, and a few seconds later, a woman's voice answered. *"Ja, ja, wer ist da?"*

"Polizei," Bourne said.

"Polizei? Gibt es ein Problem?"

"Wir müssen mit Ihnen sprechen."

"Ja, natürlich, bitte kommen Sie herein."

The glass entrance door clicked open with a buzz and let them inside. The manager already had her own apartment door open, and she met them at the stairs. She was a small woman and younger than Jason expected, about thirty, with a trim runner's physique. She had short brown hair, red glasses, and a face full of earrings and piercings. She wore a black Lycra top and bottom, with a gold chain belt dangling around her waist. She introduced herself as Greta Bauer.

Bourne used a badge that identified him as Jean-Pierre Larousse of Interpol, and he gave his German a hint of a French accent. "Ms. Bauer, my associate and I are looking for a woman named Ella Graf. Our records show this apartment building as her last known address. Are you familiar with Ms. Graf?"

"Ella? Sure, of course. She lives on the top floor. She's been here for years—longer than me, anyway."

"Can you tell us what she looks like?"

The manager shrugged. "Pretty, wavy blond hair, very elegant appearance. I imagine she's around forty, or midforties, hard to tell. She's very nice, very friendly, never a problem or complaint. I can't imagine she's done anything wrong."

"Do you know if she's home?"

"I don't. I'm sorry."

"Have you seen her recently?"

"Yesterday morning was the last time. She was coming in as I was going out."

Next to him, Bourne felt Johanna tense, and he knew why. It was beginning to feel real to both of them. Monika was here.

"Thank you for your help," Bourne told her. "Please go back into your apartment now and stay there until I give you the all clear."

The young woman blanched and quickly retreated behind the door of her flat.

Bourne climbed the stairs slowly, with Johanna a couple of steps behind him. On the top floor, they found doors leading to two apartments, one on either side of the stairwell. The metal number on the door on his right matched the number on the mailbox for Ella Graf.

He told Johanna to stay a few steps back, then slid his Sig from his jacket pocket.

"Jesus, is that necessary?" she whispered.

"I hope not."

But his instincts hadn't stopped broadcasting a warning.

He put an ear to the door and listened. There were no sounds from inside the apartment. Cautiously, he did the same to the door of the opposite flat, and it was silent, too. Staying to the side of the frame, he rapped sharply on Ella Graf's door. There was no answer and no sound of movement from the other side.

He knocked again and this time called, "Fräulein Graf?"

Nothing.

"She could be out," Johanna said.

"Maybe, but it's pretty early to be out on a Sunday."

He didn't mention his fears of what they might find inside.

Bourne slid two stiff wires from the lining of his jacket and set to work on the lock. He worked fast. Less than a minute later, the lock clicked and he nudged the door open with his foot. He moved inside, arms extended with both hands on his Sig. Turning his shoulders swiftly, he confirmed that the living room was clear.

"Stay here while I check the rest of the place," he told Johanna.

She came into the foyer behind him, but didn't go farther. The apartment wasn't large, two bedrooms, both of which had access to an outside balcony, plus a small kitchen and a single bathroom. He checked the whole unit in a few seconds and confirmed that the rooms were empty. No one was here, but there were women's clothes in the main bedroom closet and dishes in the dishwasher.

Someone lived here.

Was it Ella Graf, the woman who'd once been Monika Roth?

And if so, where was she?

Bourne returned from the bedroom. Johanna remained in the foyer, studying the apartment with a frown on her face. She smelled the air, as if she could pick up her sister's scent. Her stare went to every piece of cheap Ikea furniture, then to the walls, which were decorated with framed prints of the old masters. A crinkle of doubt furrowed her forehead, and she shook her head.

"This place doesn't feel like her," she murmured.

"How so?"

"The furniture's wrong, and so's the artwork. None of this is Monika. I don't know, maybe that's the point. You adopt a new life, you become a new person."

"There's nothing personal here," Bourne said. "I would have told her to keep it that way. But after ten years, people usually slip. Their new identity creeps into the place. You can't help it."

"So what does that mean?"

He didn't answer right away. He went to the patio door and stepped onto the balcony. The wicker furniture looked worn and heavily used. Five stories below him, the street was still mostly empty. He could see into the park, where a few teenagers played basketball. It was a normal Sunday morning, but it didn't feel normal.

"Excuse me, hello, is everything okay?" a woman called from the apartment doorway. "Did you find what you were looking for?"

Bourne spun around, pointing the Sig with his right arm. The manager, Greta Bauer, shot her hands in the air and gave him a nervous smile. She glanced back and forth between Jason and Johanna.

"It's just me," she said brightly.

He took several steps back into the room, and he didn't lower the gun. "Fräulein Bauer. I told you to wait in your apartment."

"Yes, but I looked outside, and I didn't see Ella's car on the street. Usually that means she's gone. I thought you might want to know that."

"Thank you. You can go back downstairs now."

"Oh, yes, all right. Okay."

But she didn't move. Her smile seemed frozen, her stare transfixed by the gun. She tugged at the piercing in the middle of her lower lip like a kind of tic. "Ella drives a Mini Cooper, by the way. She typically parks in the same place every day."

"Thank you."

"I'm trying to remember if I saw it when I got back yesterday, but I'm not sure."

"I said you can go, Ms. Bauer."

"Yes, of course. Sorry. I didn't mean to interrupt you."

The woman pushed her red glasses nervously up her nose. She turned and disappeared through the apartment door. Bourne waited a couple of seconds before letting his gun arm drop, aiming the barrel at the floor. He regretted it as soon as he did. With the speed of a snake, Greta Bauer shot back into the room. Bourne jerked his Sig up, but he was too late. The woman wrapped an arm around Johanna's waist and jammed the blade of an eight-inch knife against her throat. Her smile had vanished. Her dark eyes behind her red glasses turned to stone.

Jason's finger curled around the trigger, but the woman pushed hard on the blade, drawing blood from Johanna's neck.

"Put down the gun, Cain. If you don't, I'll cut her throat open right now."

"Then you'll die, too."

"Machts nichts," she said with a shrug. *"Ich bin hier, um der Sache mein Leben und meine Treue zu versprechen."*

He remembered the oath of *Le Renouveau*. He'd seen what its members would do for the cause, and he didn't doubt for a moment that this woman would kill Johanna, even if it meant sacrificing her own life.

Bourne bent down and put his gun on the hardwood floor of the apartment.

19

"KICK THE GUN TO ME," THE WOMAN SNAPPED.

Bourne used the toe of his boot to slide the Sig across the floor, and it came to a stop halfway between them. Meanwhile, Johanna struggled in the woman's arms, her eyes wide, her lips trembling. The blood at her throat looked cherry red against her pale white skin as it dripped down to her chest.

"Now the rest. I'm sure you have other weapons."

He did. He had a dagger sheathed at his belt and a Glock in a holster on his ankle. The woman cupped her hand, waving with her fingers for him to disarm himself and push the weapons toward her. Slowly, Bourne knelt, raising the cuff of his pants and disengaging the Glock, which he pushed away on the floor. He did the same with the knife.

She nodded at the armory at her feet. "That's a good boy. Thank you. Wow, the intel on you was dead-on, Cain. Your weakness is always the woman. It's like having a tell in the poker game. Justin was right. It's too bad he made the mistake of using brute force to take you out rather than something a little more subtle."

"Where's the real Greta Bauer?" Jason asked.

"Downstairs in her apartment. She's still breathing for now. I thought we might need her, but as it turned out, you swallowed my act."

"And Monika?"

The woman shook her head. "No fucking clue where she is. Some lesbian engineer has lived here for the last four years. I asked if I could borrow her apartment for a couple of days until you showed up, and she said no. Weird, huh? So I strangled her with my belt. I put her body across the hall with the married couple from the other flat. The husband heard me doing the engineer and knocked on the door to see what was going on. Dumbass. I cut his throat and then drowned his wife in the bathtub."

"Jesus!" Johanna gasped.

She struggled to get away, but stopped as the knife cut her again.

"Oh, don't worry, honey. I'll come up with something even nicer for you. And I'll make sure your boyfriend here watches me do it." She yanked hard on Johanna's blond hair, pulling her head back to expose more of her throat, and she grinned at Bourne. "Or you could make it easy and tell me where Monika is."

"I have no idea."

"That's too bad. Justin told me about your memory issues, but I wasn't sure whether to believe him. But even if you don't know where she is, I'm sure you've got a way to contact her. Agents like you always leave a back door."

"Not this time," Bourne said. "There's no back door. Not with her."

"No? Sorry, Cain, but I don't believe you. I think you're lying. But that's okay. When you see what I do to your girlfriend here, you'll have plenty of incentive to tell me what I want to know."

The woman bit down hard on Johanna's ear, making her cry out and drawing a new trickle of blood. With her tongue, the woman licked the blood away like it was fine wine. "This one feels like a screamer. She'll be fun to play with."

Jason watched a flush of panic cross Johanna's face. Their eyes met, and he knew she was about to do something foolish. He tried to send her a message—*Don't! Don't do it!*—but he didn't have time to stop her, only to help her. In the next instant, Johanna flinched. She reached over to the arm locked around her waist and snapped the woman's index finger with a sickening crack. Caught by surprise, the woman howled in pain.

Bourne had barely a second before the woman dragged the blade across Johanna's neck. He shot forward. His fingers closed around the woman's forearm and jerked the knife away. Suddenly free, Johanna leaped to the floor, leaving Jason and their assailant intertwined. As Bourne twisted the woman around, she spun with him and piled her shoulder into his chest. They both toppled backward, and she landed on top of him. The knife clattered out of her grasp, but she rolled free, crawling toward the blade a few feet away. He took her foot and hung on, then delivered a heavy boot to the middle of her face.

Cartilage smashed, and her nose erupted in blood.

"Fuck!" she screamed, wriggling out of his grasp. "Fuck you, you son of a bitch!"

She scooped up the knife and came for him. With a sweeping arc, she swung it toward Bourne's thigh. He pushed away just as the point of the knife shot downward. It missed him by an inch and shuddered into the wooden floor, where it stuck hard. He kept rolling. He scrambled to his feet, but the woman was waiting for him and jabbed a kick deep into his stomach that sent him reeling backward. As he gasped for breath, she kicked again, her body a blur of motion. His knees buckled.

A second later, her foot shot straight upward like a chorus line Rockette, connecting with the bottom of his chin and snapping his neck back with an impact that felt as if his teeth had rattled into his brain.

He staggered away, colliding hard with the glass door of the balcony.

"Never send a man to do a woman's job, Cain," she hissed. "Justin should have known that."

She reached under her black Lycra top to a holster, and her injured hand reemerged with a Beretta 92. The barrel pointed at his chest from ten feet away. She held the gun awkwardly, her middle finger grasping for the trigger because her index finger was broken and useless. Even so, she was so close that she couldn't miss. Bourne stared into the black hole of the barrel, expecting a spit of flame.

Then a flurry of gunfire erupted from a new direction.

Johanna stood on the other side of the room, Bourne's Sig cradled between her hands. She fired wildly, a shot in the wall, a shot in the ceiling, two shots in the floor, two shots piercing the glass of the patio door. She didn't come close to hitting her target, but the assault forced the woman to duck, and Bourne took two dizzy steps and kicked the Beretta out of her hand.

The woman came off her knees with a growl and launched her body at him, her head like a battering ram. The collision took them both full speed into the cracked patio door, which shattered outward under their combined weight. Amid a field of glass, they landed in each other's arms against the balcony railing, five stories above the street. The woman, her face a mass of blood, snapped her teeth at him. Her fingernails came like claws for his eyes, but he slammed her chest hard with the heel of his hand, breaking a rib in a sick pop and forcing her backward. With insane energy, she shook off the blow and drove at him again. This time he tagged her chin with a sideways blow from his fist, and once more she fell back, just out of reach.

Standing by the shattered patio door, she paused, catching her breath. He saw her eyes flick past him to the open air beyond the railing, and he guessed her next move. Kill them both, or die trying. She charged toward him again, and she was all speed, no chance to stop. He barely managed to throw himself out of her way just as she hit the railing hard. Her momentum catapulted her over the edge, and her body made a somersault, flipping twice as she crashed to the street below. He looked down in time to see her land on the pavement headfirst with a cracking force that drove her skull deep into her neck.

He was still holding on to the railing when Johanna rushed up beside him from inside the apartment. She peered at the street and then reared back and slapped a hand over her mouth when she saw the body.

"Holy shit," she said. *"Holy shit!"*

"Yeah, she's done." Bourne steered Johanna from the railing and took her face in his hands. "Are you okay?"

"I'm fine, but what about you? Look at you! Jesus!"

"Don't worry about me. We need to get out of here."

He put an arm around her waist to help her, then realized that he was the one who needed help. His weight felt as if it were pushing him to the ground. Johanna let him lean on her, and the two of them limped across the apartment toward the door. He retrieved his weapons and managed to stand on his own when they made it to the stairwell. He used the wall as leverage, leaving streaks of blood on the paint as they headed downstairs.

At the ground floor, he saw the crushed body of the agent from *Le*

Renouveau where it had landed outside the building door. Three people already stood over her, filming the scene with their phones. More people were running toward the building from both directions.

"Not that way," he told Johanna.

He tried the door to Greta Bauer's apartment. It was unlocked. He led Johanna inside and closed the door behind them. Hopefully, there was a door or window that would let them slip out the rear of the building. He headed down a hallway toward the back of the apartment, but Johanna tugged on his arm.

"Jason, wait. What's that noise?"

He listened.

Somewhere in the apartment, he heard a muffled cry, and he followed the noise into the master bedroom. Someone was inside the closet, beating against the door and struggling to call for help. When he pulled the door open, he found an older woman hog-tied on the closet floor, a gag taped securely over her mouth.

Greta Bauer. The real Greta Bauer.

Bourne used his knife to free her, and he and Johanna helped her to the bed. Sweat bathed her limbs, and she choked as she tried to suck air through her nose. He eyed the bedroom window, where he could see more than a dozen people outside gathering around the dead body. Time was short.

"You're Mrs. Bauer?" Bourne asked quickly. "The building manager?"

Tears and streaks of makeup streamed down her face as she nodded. She was in her sixties, heavyset, with thinning blond hair. A lilac housedress fell to her knees. He carefully cut away the strips of tape that were wound around her head and removed the gag from her mouth.

"You're safe now," he told her. "The woman who did this to you is dead. The police will be here any minute. They'll get you to a hospital and make sure you're okay."

Greta Bauer cleared her throat and spoke raggedly. "Oh my God! That woman—she was going to kill me!"

"I understand. I know how terrifying this experience was. But I need you to answer a few questions for me. Time is critical. This woman may have associates in the city that we need to track down."

"Who are you?" she asked, her eyes dazed. "What is this all about?"

"My name is Larousse. I'm with Interpol. We've been after this woman and the group she's part of for a long time. These people are ruthless and dangerous, as you saw. Can you tell me what she wanted? What did she say to you?"

"Well, it was crazy! Madness! She asked me about some woman who booked an apartment here ten years ago. Ten years!"

"Ella Graf," Johanna murmured.

Greta touched the raw skin on her face and winced. "Yes! Yes, that's right. That was the name."

"Did you know Ella Graf?" Jason asked. "Were you the manager here ten years ago?"

"I was, but I didn't recall anyone named Graf living here. But she made me check my records, and of course, I remembered it then because it was so strange."

Bourne heard a wail of sirens drawing closer outside the building. Johanna glanced over their shoulders toward the apartment door.

"Why strange?" he asked. "What was strange about Ella Graf?"

"Well, it wasn't her really, but what happened. It was all in the file. I kept notes about it because I didn't know what to do."

The sirens were nearly at the building.

"Go on," he said, impatience creeping into his voice. "Quickly."

"Well, I got a booking for the top-floor apartment ten years ago. It came in long distance, a full year paid in advance under the name Ella Graf. This woman showed up a few days later to move in. No furniture with her, just a small suitcase. She was pretty. There was something very distinctive about her. Honestly, she didn't look like the kind of woman who would be living in a place like this. She seemed higher class, you know? Anyway, she introduced herself as Ella Graf, and I remember she had a man with her."

Mrs. Bauer stopped.

Her stare went quizzically to Bourne's face, and he knew from her expression that *he* was the man who'd shown up at this place. He'd taken Monika Roth to this apartment building to begin her new life. But the building manager squinted at him, then shook her head, as if it were too long ago to make the connection.

"The man took her upstairs to the apartment," she went on. "Then he left later that evening."

"What about Ella Graf?" Johanna asked.

"Well, that was what was so strange," Mrs. Bauer replied. "The next day, she left, too. She took her suitcase with her, and she disappeared. She never moved into the apartment, and she never contacted me to tell me what to do. The apartment sat empty for an entire year, all paid for, but with no one in it. I never saw her again."

20

FIREWORKS EXPLODED OVER THE ARC DE TRIOMPHE IN STARBURSTS OF blue, white, and red, matching the colors of the French flag. The same colors rippled from floodlights flashing across the monument, making it seem as if it were waving in the breeze. Thousands of people filled the traffic circle, squeezed shoulder to shoulder and blocking traffic. Their voices made a rhythmic chant, the same two phrases over and over.

The first phrase was *La Vraie.*

The second was *Le Roi Raymond.*

It was another burning summer night in Paris. The crowd had been waiting for hours, from dusk into darkness, for the arrival of Raymond Berland. Sweaty faces glowed in the reflections. The early comers had staked out places below the platform where Berland would speak. A high stage had been constructed to face the wide, elegant stretch of the Champs-Élysées that led like an arrow of yellow light toward the Place de la Concorde. Chairs lined the stage in rows, divided by a center aisle that led to a podium and microphone illuminated by a searchlight. Mayors, police officers, assembly members, and other supporters of *La Vraie* from around the country filled the chairs and shouted with the crowd. For those not lucky enough to be close to the action, huge video screens had been set up at intervals around the arch to broadcast the speech.

Berland was late.

He'd been expected at ten o'clock, and now it was almost midnight. But impatience only fed the crowd's excitement as the arrival of *Le Roi Raymond* drew near. A bubble of voices rose among those closest to the arch, and the rumor tore in an undercurrent through the crowd. People had spotted the armored car.

Il est là.

He's here.

An attractive dark-haired woman in the front row of chairs stood up. That was enough to trigger an enormous cheer around the Arc de Triomphe, loud enough to be heard like thunder blocks away. The woman—Jeannette LaTour, the mayor of the town of Nice—took a position at the podium and waited as the chants began again. *La Vraie! Le Roi Raymond!* Ten minutes passed before she even tried to speak, and then she opened with a single sentence that set the crowd on fire all over again.

"Êtes-vous prêt à reconquérir la vraie France?"

Are you ready to take back the real France?

The people shouted their approval, and their cheers quickly turned into another call for *Le Roi Raymond.* They knew what they wanted, and Mayor LaTour didn't make them wait any longer. She took her prepared remarks, held up the sheet of paper so the cameras could see it, and ripped the page into pieces that she scattered into the air. With her fists raised over her head, she leaned toward the microphone and announced, *"Le prochain président de la vraie France . . . Raymond Berland!"*

A man appeared at the back of the platform, captured by the light.

Around the circle, the video screens showed him in close-up, drawing a sustained primal scream from his followers. He was a small man, lean and not physically imposing. He wore a white suit, perfectly fitted, and a red tie. His sandy-blond hair was greased back on his head in tight waves. He had a square jaw with a jutting knob of a chin and blue eyes that found the camera as if it were a window into the minds of his supporters. He didn't smile. He didn't wave. He marched toward the podium with an angry passion, ignoring the people on the stage who stretched out their hands to him. The boom of the crowd grew into a deafening thunder, but Berland made a slashing motion with his hand. Thousands of people fell silent at once, leaving the plaza as still as a church.

He didn't shout. He started low, his voice smooth, like a preacher. His charisma held them in his palm.

"More than eighty years ago," Berland began, "invaders paraded past this monument and took possession of our homeland."

No one said a word.

It seemed as if everyone gathered around the arch was holding their breath.

"Nazis. Killers. They murdered our grandparents. They defiled our great land."

Berland stared out at the crowd for a long moment, letting his words sink in. The silence dragged on.

"And what did the heroes of the real France do in those years?" he finally continued. "They fought back. They resisted. Thousands and thousands of men, women, and even children put their lives on the line. They wrested our country from its occupiers. These were ordinary citizens. Ordinary heroes. People like *you*. People who were committed to their belief that the real France would rise again."

A roar began, but again Berland cut it off with a simple wave of his hand. His voice continued to rise, its cadence hypnotic.

"But now what do we see around us today? We see new invaders. New occupiers. Aliens to our values. They are taking over our cities, rotting us from within, telling us we must live by their rules, telling us we must tolerate their beliefs. Our women must walk in fear of them. Our people must hold their tongues so as not to offend them. Is that the real France? I ask every one of you, *is that the real France?*"

This time the crowd erupted with a single word.

Non!

"No, it is not," Berland went on. "That is not the France I love, that you love, that you wish to leave to your children. That is a France I don't even recognize. And yet we must acknowledge the bitter truth. We have done this to ourselves. We have allowed the elitists in the Élysée Palace and the Palais Bourbon to bow down meekly in front of our enemies. The *government* has allowed this to happen. The *government* has told us that *we* are the ones who must be stopped because we dare to believe in the real France."

Boos and hisses muttered from the crowd.

"That's right. They call *us* Nazis. They call *us* extremists. They call *us* racists. They say we must accept a new France. They say we must change with the times. But you know what must change? The *government* must change. It is time to put *us* in charge of the government. Those who led the Vichy regime were cowards and enemies of the real France, and the same is true today."

Berland gripped the podium with both hands.

"You can feel their fear, can't you? You see it in the Assembly, in the media, in the interference in our affairs from the EU and the United States. They are all terrified that the *people* will finally take charge. They all claim to be scared of *me*, but the truth is, my friends, they are scared of *you*. Well, soon you will show them—"

Suddenly, Berland stopped.

His face darkened. Only a second or two passed, but the ominous silence felt as if long minutes were going by. Confusion rippled like a deadly virus through the crowd, and people began to murmur questions back and forth.

What's going on? What's happening?

Calmly, Berland extended one arm, his finger pointed below the stage. All the cameras followed him, showing a chaos of hundreds of faces. And then, shrill and terrified, a solitary voice rose from the crowd. A woman screamed from below Berland, shouting one unmistakable word at the top of her lungs.

"Pistolet!"

Gun.

Before the echo of her warning even died away, cracks spat into the silence. A barrage of metal pings ricocheted off the stage and podium. Berland didn't move. Bullets filled the air around him, but he remained where he was, a statue staring down at his attacker and showing no fear. Everywhere else, anarchy spread. The crowd moved like a living thing, animals lurching into a stampede. Behind him, VIPs sprang to their feet, some running for the stairs, some charging forward to pull him off the stage.

The mayor of Nice got to Berland first. LaTour yanked at his arm, but *Le Roi Raymond* shook her off and raised his arms to settle the crowd.

"You see?" he bellowed into the microphone as gunfire continued to burst around him. "You see the desperation of our enemies? You see the lengths they will go to stop us? Do not let them frighten you! Stay where you are! Take hold of the attackers! Show them what French heroes do! Resist!"

Mayor LaTour grabbed his arm again, and the microphone broadcast her panicked voice begging him to go. *"Raymond, mon Dieu, nous devons partir. Maintenant!"*

She pushed forward, coming between Berland and the podium.

In the same moment, a bullet found her, and her head exploded.

Limp and lifeless, the mayor's body crashed down into the crowd as blood sprayed in a crimson shower across Raymond Berland.

THE OVERNIGHT EVENTS PLAYED ON A VIDEO SCREEN AS CHRÉTIEN PAU waited to go live on the early-morning news show on BFM-TV. For the hundredth time, he watched the death of the pretty young mayor from Nice and saw her body collapse into the waiting arms of the crowd. The crack of bullets filled the air for several more seconds until the assailant, a Turkish immigrant named Rafez, who'd arrived in France only six months earlier, disappeared under the gang of men who surged on top of him and wrested away the gun.

Rafez would not be arrested. He would not be brought to trial for murder.

He was already dead.

The crowd had beat him to death right there in the shadow of the Arc de Triomphe. Now half a dozen members of *La Vraie*, caught on video as they pummeled the shooter until his body looked like *confiture de fraise*, were wanted by the police. Half the country was calling them heroes and demanding they go free.

That was the beginning of the night, but not the end.

On the screen, Pau watched the next video footage as hundreds of outraged rioters flooded down the Champs-Élysées, breaking the windows of upscale restaurants and shops, setting cars on fire, assaulting tourists, and drawing a violent police response that left three more people dead and dozens hospitalized. Tonight, the rumors said, *La Vraie* would take its campaign of terror and revenge beyond Paris to the cities of Nice, Lyon, Toulouse, and Marseilles. They would shut down the Métro. They would block highways all over the country.

Bedlam.

"Monsieur Pau?"

He looked away from the screen.

His interviewer, a thirtysomething woman named Camille with messy dark hair and round tortoiseshell glasses, checked the clock on the studio wall and told him, *"Quatre-vingt-dix secondes, Monsieur Pau."*

Ninety seconds.

"Oui, d'accord," he replied absently.

The woman primped her hair as they prepared to go on the air. She was pretty, but not as pretty as the American journalists, who all seemed to be hired for their resemblance to Scarlett Johansson. Pau smoothed the sleeves of his dark suit, drank from the bottle of water in front of him, and rubbed his index finger against his middle finger, feeling the absence of a cigarette. He took eye drops from the pocket of his suit coat and moistened his contact lenses. The monitor highlighted his bright blue eyes.

Behind him, the video screen froze on an image of the angry face of Raymond Berland covered in blood. What a symbol it was of the choice the voters had. Berland was the candidate of chaos and violence, and Pau was the candidate of order. In the end, people always voted for order. They would not tolerate death on the streets. It had to be stopped.

Pau was much taller than Berland, nearly six foot three, and athletically graceful. A stylist cut his short brown hair every week to keep it at the same length. He had a chiseled, handsome face, marred only by a scar on his forehead he'd received during army counterterrorism operations in Mali. The two men were both young, in their midforties, but Berland liked to emphasize his lower-class upbringing on the docks of Le Havre and contrast it with Pau's rarefied childhood as the son of a French oil executive and a senior attorney in the European Court of Human Rights.

A vote for Pau, Berland liked to say, was a vote for the system, and Pau didn't disagree. He was the system to its core.

The camera lights went on. The host, Camille, opened the show.

"*Les violences urbaines continuent,*" she told her viewers soberly. "Shocking events overnight have rattled the presidential race yet again and put Raymond Berland, the right-wing leader of the *La Vraie* party, not only in the middle of an assassination attempt but also in the middle of a new and more deadly round of urban riots. Meanwhile, the current government's challenger to Berland is a political newcomer, Chrétien Pau. Monsieur Pau, who was thrust into the spotlight after the incumbent president resigned from the race following exposure of sexual misconduct, has not held elective office before. However, he has been a government policy adviser for the past ten years, and he is a member of a family with deep roots in European business and government. His selection to stand in this election, ahead of other more experienced candidates, was described as a 'house cleaning' for a mainstream party that has been too often rocked by corruption in recent years. Monsieur Pau joins us in the studio this morning. Welcome, sir."

"Thank you, Camille," Pau replied.

"Let me ask you first to respond to the overnight violence, which is the worst we have seen in an already dangerous summer."

"It is," Pau agreed, "and it is unacceptable. It is unacceptable that anyone should attempt to murder Raymond Berland. I find that horrifying. Agree with him or disagree with him, this is France, and we settle our arguments with votes, not with bullets. My heart goes out to the family of Madame LaTour of Nice, who lost her life in the attack. This is an unspeakable tragedy. We cannot and *will not* tolerate any violent act that is designed to censor our democracy. However, it is no less unacceptable that the supporters of Monsieur Berland should defy our laws and bring death and unrest to our cities, as they have been doing for weeks. Monsieur Berland should condemn this behavior without reservation, but instead, he has celebrated it. He has stated that there will be no peace absent a victory for *La Vraie*. That is the talk of a dictator, not a president."

"Monsieur Pau, your campaign literature calls you the right man for the right times. The right experience, the right family, the right values."

"I believe that with all my heart, yes."

"And yet the polls are close. Some people are suggesting this could be the year that the far right finally triumphs with the voters, after many failed attempts. Monsieur Berland has said that the only way he can lose is if the election is rigged. He has not promised to abide by the outcome."

Pau shrugged and pointed at the screen, which replayed the fires along the Champs-Élysées and finally focused on a dead body in the street, surrounded by blood and broken glass. "Polls mean nothing. Events are everything. Look at the streets of Paris! Look at the violence! The people of France will never vote for this. Never! There is only one issue now for families in this country who wish their children to grow up in a safe environment. Restore peace. Restore order. End the violence. That is my mission. I promise you, I will do whatever is necessary to make it happen. I have seen the worst of the current party and the worst of those who wish to take over, and I owe nothing to either side. So yes, I am the right man for the times. The supporters of Monsieur Berland say they want to restore *La Vraie France*. To them I say, I agree with you. We share the same goal. But if that is the country you want, you are backing the wrong candidate."

21

BOURNE AWAKENED WITH SUN SHINING THROUGH HIS APARTMENT WINDOW.

It took a moment for his mind to catch up to his surroundings. He lay naked on a twin bed, and Johanna lay naked beside him, her bare arm thrown across his chest and her long blond hair covering her face. An old ceiling fan rattled over his head, making more noise than air. He blinked, his brain shaking off a fog that lingered from the morphine shot the doctor had given him the previous night.

With *Le Renouveau* and the local police both hunting for him, he'd booked third-class train tickets out of Hamburg. They'd arrived in Paris hours later in the middle of the evening. From the Gare du Nord station, he'd taken Johanna to his backup apartment above an alley in the artsy, seedy Pigalle neighborhood, home to the Moulin Rouge and ground zero for most of the city's sins. It was easy to stay anonymous in this area because everyone else who lived here wanted to fly below the radar, too. There were also plenty of street people he could pay to be his eyes and ears.

He'd dealt with the worst of his injuries on the train, but by the time they got to the flat, he knew he needed something stronger. A thousand euro later, a discreet doctor named Richet made a midnight visit and gave him an injection that dulled the ache. The pain came back now as he woke up and the drugs wore off. His jaw felt stiff, and the blows he'd taken to his chest ached in his ribs. He was slow to get up. When he finally pushed himself out of bed, he limped to the window and nudged aside the curtain. In the street below, it was morning in Pigalle. The sex shops, strip clubs, and massage parlors were closed, their metal shutters pulled down and locked. A couple of drunks slept off the night on the sidewalks. But when he opened the window, he smelled coffee and sugar. The patisserie on the corner was open.

"A flat in the red-light district," Johanna said, coming up behind him and peering at Pigalle over his shoulder. "Nice. Do you take all your girls here?"

"Just you."

"Well, how special do I feel. And a massage parlor right across the street, that's convenient. What's their specialty? Swedish? Shiatsu?"

"I think it's more like one hand or two," Jason said.

"*Very* nice."

He touched the bandages on her neck. "How are you? How do you feel?"

"I'm okay. You're the one I was worried about. By the time we got here, you looked as white as a ghost."

"I'm fine."

"Well, you still don't look good. Come back to bed and rest."

He let her take his hand and pull him across the apartment. In bed, he turned on the flat-screen television to the morning news and then lay back against the pillow, his brain spinning. Around him, the small apartment was sparsely furnished, little more than the bed, a table with two chairs, an armoire with one broken leg, and a desk by the window. The walls were empty, and he kept only some basic clothes and necessities in the armoire and bathroom. He'd rented the flat two years earlier, but since then it had sat locked and unused in case he needed a place when he was on the run.

"Jesus," Johanna commented, pointing at the television screen. "Looks like we missed all the fun last night."

Bourne turned up the volume. He saw a replay of the night's events, including the attempted murder of Raymond Berland near the Arc de Triomphe. Seeing that, he couldn't help but think of Nash Rollins, and he wondered whether the assassination plot had somehow been spearheaded by Treadstone. Then the video shifted to the destruction along Paris's most famous avenue. At sunrise, the Champs-Élysées was unnaturally deserted, closed by the police in both directions.

"Sometimes I think the world is coming apart at the seams," Johanna said.

"Sometimes I think you're right."

She took the remote control from him and switched off the television. She propped herself on her side, and her fingertips played across his bare skin. They were very close to each other in the small bed. She leaned into him and kissed him softly, her breasts grazing his chest. He responded automatically and tried to reach for her, but she pushed him away with a toss of her hair.

"Whoa there, lover, no exertion like that for you this morning. Not in the shape you're in. You need to save your strength. But play your cards right, and maybe later I'll pretend I work at that massage parlor."

She patted his cheek with a grin, but the teasing smile quickly vanished from her lips. Her expression turned serious as she brushed back the blond hair from her face.

"You know, we didn't talk on the train, but I've got a lot of questions. What do you think happened to Monika? I don't understand. You set her up in the apartment in Hamburg, but then she left the next day? Why?"

"She was scared," Bourne concluded. "She didn't trust me. I can't blame her for that. She let me take her to Hamburg, but as soon as I was gone, she ran. Obviously, she built a new identity for herself somewhere else. And that's the problem. I have no idea where. Not the city, not the country. She may not even be in Europe."

"But why wouldn't she trust you? She was going to marry you."

"Yes, and then I almost got her killed."

Johanna shook her head. "I hate to think of her alone like that. On her own, no parents, no me, no you. I can't imagine where she went or what she did. Assuming she's even still alive. I guess we don't know that for sure, do we?"

"No, we don't," Jason said, "but *Le Renouveau* is still looking for her. That's a good sign. If they'd already found her, it would be all over. So we have to assume she's still alive and still in hiding."

Johanna sank back next to him onto the bed, and her fingers laced with his. "Okay, but how are we going to find her? Hamburg was our only lead."

His breath exhaled in a heavy sigh, which rippled through his chest with a stab of pain. "Honestly? I don't know. I was thinking about that all night. Monika had to have had help creating her new identity. She didn't do it herself. But any of the big cities would have people like Yanis Lorchaud who could produce false documents for her. For all I know, I *gave* her other names myself in case she needed to run. But finding out who she used would be impossible after all this time."

"What about photo recognition? Can't we run some kind of search with her picture? If she got a passport, then she must be in a system somewhere, right? Or maybe she got a teaching license in another country."

"I think it's unlikely she went back to teaching," Jason said. "That would be the first place people would look for her. I can reach out to an IT contact of mine and see if he can find her photo online. It's worked before. But ten years is a long time to match up faces on such a large scale."

They were silent for a while, both of them frustrated.

Then Johanna said, "What's a back door?"

"I'm sorry?"

"That woman from *Le Renouveau* talked about you having a back door to contact Monika. What is that?"

"She was wrong. I don't have one for her."

"Yes, but how does it work? I mean, in the tech biz, a back door is a fast way inside a password-protected system. What is it in your world?"

"It's a safe protocol for establishing contact," Bourne explained. "Low-tech. No phones, no computers. Those things can always be hacked and tracked. It goes back to the Cold War days of dead drops and double agents. You have to set it up in advance, but once you do, you've got a secure way of getting and receiving messages."

"Have you ever used something like that yourself?"

Jason pushed himself up to a sitting position. "Sure. I've used boutique hotels and third parties for extra security. I'll leave a message at the desk for the person I want to reach. Different name, fake identity. Then I'll drop a signal in some crowded part of the city that indicates a message is waiting. Whoever I'm communicating with typically uses someone else—like a lawyer on retainer—to keep an eye out for the signal. If they see it, the lawyer goes to the hotel to collect the message and then passes it on to the person I want to reach."

He thought about Abbey Laurent.

He'd set up a bank account for Abbey to hire a lawyer in Paris to walk past the Bastille Métro station every day—either to leave a signal if she needed to reach Bourne, or to pick up a message if Bourne needed to reach Abbey. He didn't know who the lawyer was. He didn't even know if Abbey had kept the protocol in place, or if she'd decided it was better to leave herself with no way of keeping in touch with him.

But he knew Abbey. He was sure a lawyer still walked by that station every day. And every day there was no message at the hotel off Rue Saint-Antoine.

Abbey!

God, he missed her.

"Jason?" Johanna asked quietly.

He shook himself. "Yeah. What?"

"You were a thousand miles away for a second."

"Sorry."

She rubbed his arm with a fingernail. "I know that look. That look's about a woman. What's her name?"

Jason chuckled softly to himself. Johanna was smart. "Abbey."

"Are you in love with her?"

Abbey was gone from his life, so there was no point in denying it.

"Yes," he said.

"Is she in love with you?"

"She was once. Now, I don't know. We went our separate ways."

"Because loving you is dangerous," Johanna concluded.

"Right."

"Is that your way of saying I should leave you, too?"

Bourne turned and stroked her soft face. "Yes. I won't lie. The safest thing for you is to get far away from me. Just like your sister did. She was smart. Running away was the right call."

"Well, for now, I'll take my chances with you, Jason Bourne."

He didn't reply.

"This Abbey of yours," she continued. "Did you establish a back door with her? A way to stay in touch?"

"I did, but I've never used it."

"Well, wouldn't you have established the same thing with Monika? I can't believe you wouldn't have given her a way to get in touch with you in an emergency."

"Even if I did, that won't help us."

"What do you mean? Why?"

"Because I don't remember," Bourne said, his voice harsh with anger at himself. "Did I set up a back door with Monika? Probably. But I have no memory of the details. I don't know what the protocol was. Which hotel did I use? Was it in Paris or somewhere else? What's the signal? Where do I leave it? Even in the *very* unlikely event that Monika would still have someone looking for a message, I have no way to leave it for her."

Johanna shifted behind him in bed. She swung her legs on either side of his hips and kneaded the muscles in his neck with her strong fingers. Her body leaned against him. "What about hypnosis?"

"I've tried that. No luck."

"Would you have told anyone else about it? Or written down how it worked?"

"No. The whole point of a back door is that nobody else knows the details. Just me and the contact. Don't you see? I'm out of ideas. I don't know how to find your sister. You might as well go back to your own life, Johanna, because the longer you stay with me, the greater the chances that you get killed."

She was quiet for a while, and so was he, with nothing but the noisy ceiling fan over their heads. Then she murmured something in his ear with a tentativeness that made it sound like a question.

"The hotel in Zurich," she said. "The one near the church. You took me there after we escaped from the Drei Alpenhäuser."

"Yes, what about it?"

"How did you pick that hotel? Did you remember it?"

He shook his head. "No, I just knew it was there. I knew where to go. That's the way my mind works now."

"Right. That's what you said. It was the same way in Hamburg, wasn't it? Places, people, resources, they're in your head when you need them. So you haven't lost everything. Somewhere in there, you *do* remember details."

"That's true, but I can't call them up on demand."

"Sure. I understand that. But you talked about this woman in your life. Abbey. You said you set up a back door in Paris in order to be able to contact her. I don't know, is it possible that—"

Johanna stopped.

She didn't say anything more because she didn't need to. Bourne's mind took over her thoughts, and he knew where she was going. If the details for a back door with Monika were hidden somewhere in his head, had they shown up again when he needed them? Just like the hotel in Zurich. Or the hotel in Engelberg. Or the layout of the streets in Hamburg. Instinct, not memory.

Was it *possible*?

He'd set up a back door with Abbey.

Had he used the same one he'd used with Monika?

He remembered explaining the protocol to Abbey and how easily the details had flowed off his tongue. The Bastille station. The little hotel in Rue Saint-Antoine. The bank account to pay the lawyer. He didn't need to think about them; he didn't need to decide where they would leave messages or how the signal would be exchanged. No hesitation. No thought. The whole plan simply came to him.

Now he knew why.

Because he'd used it before.

22

THE BRASSERIE ON BOULEVARD DE STRASBOURG FACED THE STONE ARCH-
ways at the entrance to the Gare de l'Est station. Passengers came and
went through the wrought-iron gates, and Jason could hear the screech
of train wheels. He sat next to Johanna at an outside table, with two
chilled glasses of Sancerre in front of them. Taxis and buses belched
exhaust on the crowded street, and waves of stifling heat rippled off the
pavement.

He checked his watch. It was ten minutes past six in the evening.
The train had arrived seven minutes ago, right on time. He expected
to see Vandal outside the gates in the next sixty seconds, and he wasn't
disappointed. She blew through the crowd at a fast walk moments later.
Her black-and-purple hair was tied in a ponytail that hung through the
gap at the back of a white baseball cap. She wore a loose-fitting sleeveless black shirt that showed off her strong arms, along with tight blue
jeans and burgundy boots. Sunglasses covered her eyes, but her head
swiveled just enough that Bourne knew she saw them. She made no

acknowledgment, and she continued away from them without crossing the street.

"Where is she going?" Johanna murmured.

"She'll clear the area ahead. I'll make sure no one's on her trail. In half an hour, we'll rendezvous in our next location."

"This world of yours," Johanna said.

Jason didn't reply, but he remembered Abbey saying the same thing to him the previous year.

He spent ten more minutes watching the people and vehicles outside Gare de l'Est, until he was sure that Vandal hadn't been followed, either by Treadstone or anyone else. Then he took Johanna by the hand, and they strolled southward at an easy pace like Paris lovers. His eyes remained alert, but he saw no evidence of a trap being set for them. At the next narrow street, Rue Saint-Laurent, he turned left and led them three more blocks to the flower gardens of Jardin Villemin.

Vandal was waiting on a bench near a cluster of red French poppies within sight of the Canal Saint-Martin.

"Give us a minute alone," Bourne said to Johanna. "Stay where I can see you, okay?"

"Sure." Johanna took a few steps onto the green grass, then stopped. "Not that it matters or anything, but I'm curious. Did you and she ever—?"

"No. Never."

Johanna shot a look at Vandal, whose face wore no expression, and then she looked back to Jason. "Yeah, okay."

She settled on the grass and began doing yoga.

Bourne continued along the path and took a seat on the bench next to Vandal. The Treadstone agent kept her sunglasses on and stared straight ahead. She'd bought a cone of takeaway *frites*, which she ate one at a time.

"Cain," she said.

"Thanks for coming. Are you clear?"

"Yes. For now, I'm off the Treadstone grid."

"What did you tell Nash?"

"I said I needed to take a couple of days after the shootout in Switzerland."

"He believed that?"

"Probably not. But I said I'd help you, so here I am. Just know that I'm walking a fine line on this one."

"I do know that."

"What happened in Hamburg?" she asked.

"It was a dead end."

Her head turned, and he could feel her eyes studying him. "From the looks of you, I take it the dead end included a welcoming party."

"Yes. *Le Renouveau* was there."

"Do you think they got Monika?"

"No. She left Hamburg ten years ago. She didn't keep the flat or the identity I'd set up for her."

Vandal glanced at Johanna on the grass. "And you're still with the girl, huh?"

"For the moment."

"Well, at least you took my advice. The two of you are having sex, right?" Vandal's mouth showed a ghost of a smile. "A woman knows, Cain."

Bourne ignored that. "Whenever we find Monika, I might need Johanna to get close to her. After what happened in Switzerland ten years ago, Monika's not likely to welcome me with open arms. But she'll talk to her sister."

"Do you have any idea where Monika is now?"

"No."

"Then why am I here?" Vandal asked. "What's your plan B?"

He explained his suspicion that he'd set up a back-door protocol with Monika that matched what he'd created for Abbey Laurent.

"Of course, it may be one more dead end," Bourne admitted. "I may have used a different setup in a different city, or Monika may have cut it off as soon as it started. But for now, that's all I've got."

"What's my role?"

"I need help with surveillance. Even if the protocol is still in place, I can't leave an actual message because I don't know what name to use with her. Plus, getting a message from me might drive her further underground. If she finds out I'm looking for her, she might run again."

"In other words, you want to grab the middleman," Vandal concluded.

"Right. If we identify him, he can lead us to her."

"And then what? What happens when you actually find Monika?"

"I get answers," Bourne said.

Vandal tossed a French fry to a bird on the grass. "Answers are overrated."

"Not to me."

She shook her head. "I don't get it, Cain. Why is this so important to you? Why can't you let it go? It was ten years ago. You're not David Webb anymore. You're not the man you were then. Neither is Monika, whoever she is. What do you think you're going to find out that will make any difference now?"

Vandal was right.

Nothing from the past would change who he was. But that didn't matter.

"Those who can't remember the past are doomed to repeat it," Bourne said. "I can't remember my past at all. I only know what I've been told by people like Nash. Or the handful of broken pieces my mind chooses to let me see. I need to fill in the gaps. I need to get past the lies. Otherwise, I'll never know what land mines are waiting for me."

"Fair enough. I guess if I were in your shoes, I'd do the same thing." Vandal stood up from the bench. "When do we start?"

"There's a church called the Temple du Marais on Rue Saint-Antoine. It's just up the street from the hotel I use for messages. Meet me there at nine in the morning. We'll set up radios and cameras."

"I'll be there," she said.

She turned toward the canal, but Bourne stopped her.

"Hey, Vandal?"

"Yeah?"

"There's a quid pro quo whenever you need it. I owe you. But we don't know each other that well, and yet here you are ignoring orders from Nash to put your ass on the line for me. Why? Why are you helping me?"

She looked down at him from behind her sunglasses. When she didn't answer immediately, he wondered if she'd simply walk away and leave him to wonder.

"I don't know, Cain," she said finally. "Maybe I like you. Or maybe I feel bad about what happened to you and Nova. Or maybe one of these days I'd like to wake up and look in the mirror and not hate the person that Treadstone made me."

THE COLD RAIN POURED DOWN OVER THE LONELY COUNTRY ROAD THAT LED inland from the Northumberland coast. On both sides, farm fields rolled over the hills, turning a shadowy color of emerald under the charcoal sky. Tall grass twisted in the wind. The woman who went by the name Sarah Tedford could barely see through the sheeting rain on the windshield of her Volkswagen, but she knew every turn of this road like an old friend. She was only a few miles from the intersection with the A1, close enough to ping on the nearest cell tower regardless of the storm.

She steered her car into the long grass. From inside her glove box, she retrieved a white USB charging cable and a pay-as-you-go mobile phone still in its original plastic packaging. She always kept a burner phone in the attic of her Holy Island house. With a knife from her jacket, she cut open the plastic and inserted the prepaid SIM card into the Alcatel phone. Then she connected the USB cable and waited as the phone screen awakened.

The phone took a few minutes to find the nearest cell signal. When it did, she dialed a number from memory, let it ring a few times, then hung up. She didn't expect anyone to answer. She waited two minutes, repeated the process, and hung up again. Two minutes later, she dialed once more, and this time a male voice answered.

"Shadow," he said.

"It's been a long time," she replied.

"Yes, it has." She heard a dark cast to his voice. "I thought we agreed that it was safer not to use direct communications. This call probably isn't a good idea. You're leaving a trail that someone might follow."

She knew he was right, but leaving a trail was part of her plan. She listened to the rain hammering the Volkswagen and studied the grim English sky. The clouds overhead moved so quickly that they looked alive.

"I got your flowers," she said. "They were lovely."

"I trust you took my message to heart."

She glanced at the backpack on the seat next to her, which she always kept packed and ready to go. "I did, but maybe not in the way you intended."

"What does that mean?"

"It means I decided to reach out to him. Make contact."

The man on the phone took a long time to answer, and all she heard was the tumult of the storm, whipping across the countryside toward the sea.

"That's a bad idea," he told her finally. "It's better to lay low. Do nothing. He has no way to find you."

"You don't believe that, and neither do I. It's only a matter of time. He's too good. I can't hide from him anymore, and I'm done running. If it's going to happen, it needs to happen on my terms."

"And what do you plan to tell him?"

"The truth. Or at least the version of the truth he needs to hear. Monika Roth doesn't want him back in her life. He and I were over a long time ago. I'm going to tell him to stay away and leave me alone."

"Do you think he'll listen?"

She closed her eyes briefly. "No. I don't."

"So what, then?"

"If he won't be dissuaded, then I may need to tell him the rest of the story," she said. "He's probably already guessed some of it. He's smart. He must know I'm not the person he thought I was."

The man's rumble of displeasure carried across the miles between them. "You told me once it would be catastrophic for him to learn what really happened."

"I know, and it may be."

"This isn't a game. Do you remember Storm? When she found out the truth about you, she blew up your car. Then she committed suicide."

"Oh, I remember. Believe me."

"Then why go down the same road with David Webb?"

She sighed. "I didn't want this. You know that. After he lost his memory, I was hoping we could keep him in the dark forever. I wouldn't even *exist* for him. That was best for all of us. But now that he knows about me—or he thinks he does—he'll never stop until he gets the truth. In the end, that could be useful."

"I still think you should reconsider. This isn't only about David. You're putting yourself at risk by reaching out to him. Remember, *Le Renouveau* wants you dead. They're looking for both of you. This isn't the time to come out of hiding."

She hesitated. "Are you sure about *Le Renouveau*? I don't understand what they would want with me. Not after all this time."

"You were in that chalet."

"I know, but why come after me? I couldn't see or hear a thing. They made sure of that. There's no one I can identify."

"Maybe they don't realize that. Anyway, it's confirmed. You're a target."

Her brow furrowed. "I don't know. Something about this feels wrong."

"What do you mean?"

"I mean, there's something else going on. We're missing a piece of the puzzle. Why is this all happening *now*? I don't like it."

"All the more reason to stay out of sight," he said.

"I understand how you feel, but it's too late for that. I have a plane booked across the Channel tonight."

"How do you plan to make contact?"

She steered back onto the country road and accelerated through the rain toward the A1. "You forget who I am. I know exactly what David will do next and how he plans to find me. Believe me, I know his mind better than he knows it himself."

23

"I'M COMING UP BEAUMARCHAIS," BOURNE MURMURED INTO THE MICRO-
phone. "I'll leave the signal at the Métro stop. Once I do that, I'll head
to the hotel and wait. Are the cameras working?"

Vandal replied from her position at a café across the street from the
Temple du Marais. "Roger that. I can see everyone coming and going
from the hotel, and we've got video coverage on both ends of the street."

"Got it."

Jason walked slowly toward the Place de la Bastille through a version of Paris he barely recognized. Most of the shops were closed, ca-
sualties of the latest unrest. The windows of the BNP Paribas bank were
boarded up with plywood. He passed an abandoned taxi that had been
turned upside down and set on fire, with a charred smell of smoke and
rubber poisoning the air. At the corner, near the Colonne de Juillet,
police in riot gear patrolled the plaza with automatic weapons.

It was as if *La Vraie* had already won the war. Paris was a ghost
town.

He reached the café where he'd been sitting just a few days earlier, when the message from Vandal had sent him back to Zurich and the Drei Alpenhäuser. It seemed like a lifetime ago. That was when his world had turned upside down, like that burned taxi.

You're being hunted, Cain.

The café was open despite the violence. They'd swept up the broken glass and hired a bored, overweight security guard to stand watch near the door. Someone had hung a handwritten sign on the shot-up window that read *Baise les politiciens. Boire du vin.*

Fuck the politicians. Drink wine.

One of the waitresses at the café recognized him and waved. He nodded back at her. He could have sat outside and ordered his *steak au poivre* the way he always did when he was looking for a message from Abbey. A message that never came.

But not today.

He approached the large sign for the Métro station that was mounted in front of the escalators. The sign included a map of the Paris rail network and the name of the station—BASTILLE—in white letters. He stood in front of it, his hands in his pockets, as if studying the route for his next trip. Then he slid an orange piece of chalk from his pocket and drew a small hashtag symbol on the sign.

It was done.

If the protocol was in place, someone would pass the Métro sign and take note of the hashtag and know that a message was waiting at a hotel a few blocks away.

If.

Bourne continued past the station. He turned right at the next street, which was Rue Saint-Antoine. The farther he walked from the Place de la Bastille, the more the city came back to life, crowded with people, cars, bicycles, and motorbikes. He made two sudden stops at store windows, and he crossed the street in front of a taxi that blared his horn at him, to confirm that no one was on his tail. The dirty gold stone and gray dome of the Temple du Marais loomed ahead of him. He passed a café at the corner and noted Vandal at one of the outside tables, a copy of the French edition of *Marie Claire* in her hands. She had a latte and an almond pastry in front of her, along with a phone in a bejeweled purple case. Her hair was loose and long. She wore a black jacket over a white shell, with jeans and high-heeled boots. Oversized rose-colored sunglasses covered her eyes.

They didn't acknowledge each other.

Bourne turned the corner. Rue Castex was quiet, which made his footsteps on the pavement sound loud. He crossed the street and walked beside the old stone wall of the Marais church. Pausing, he lit a cigarette, which gave him time to examine the doorways and windows of the buildings down the block. He saw nothing, and yet his instincts came to life, warning him of a trap.

You're being watched.

How could that be? He didn't see how anyone could know about this back door. It was his protocol. He'd picked the location; he'd set up the plan. There should have been only two other people who knew the details: Abbey Laurent and Monika Roth. Even the intermediaries who made the drops, whoever they were, had no way of connecting Cain to the messages that were being left.

Had Abbey told someone? No. Never.

Had Monika?

Jason frowned at the possibility. He wondered again: Who *was* Monika?

"Is there a problem?" Vandal murmured through his earpiece. She could see him frozen outside the church, smoke drifting from his cigarette.

"Who have you seen on the street today?" he asked.

"About a dozen people over the past hour. No one went into the hotel. A few people came out, but no one raised red flags for me."

"Okay."

Bourne had faith in Vandal's observation skills, but he'd learned long ago to listen to his paranoia. Someone on this street, behind one of the windows, had him under surveillance. If they hadn't passed Vandal coming or going, that meant they had already been in place, waiting for him to arrive.

And yet *no one* could have known he would come here.

No one except Abbey and Monika.

He crushed the cigarette under his shoe without smoking it and continued down the street. If he was being watched, the goal wasn't to kill him, because anyone above him had an easy sniper's shot as he neared the hotel. He narrowed his eyes, alert for movement or the swish of a curtain, but if there was a watcher, he or she betrayed nothing.

Ahead of him was the Temple Hotel, a narrow white building five stories tall. He was sure he'd been here before. When setting up a back door, he always scouted the location. Size was important—too big, and a message might get lost or forgotten; too small, and a strange request might raise suspicions. He would have stayed overnight to become familiar with the flow of guests and traffic. He would have tipped the staff to be sure that enough money greasing someone's palm would make sure that a message could be left for a stranger and not get thrown away.

Yes, he'd been here before—but he didn't remember it.

Would they remember *him*?

Bourne opened the glass door of the hotel and walked inside. The lobby was small, decorated with flowers, the walls adorned with sconce lights and hanging tapestries. There was no counter, just a wooden table with a registration book to welcome guests. A balding, fortysomething man staffed the table, wearing a short-sleeve white dress shirt that had grayed with age, and a paisley tie. He sized up Bourne with the uncanny French ability to recognize Americans, and he greeted him in English. But his face showed no recognition that they'd met before.

"Hello, *monsieur*. Welcome to the Temple Hotel. How may I assist you?"

Jason added a little Texas twang to his voice and adopted one of his usual covers. "The name is Briggs. Charlie Briggs. I was hoping you'd have a room available."

"Do you have a reservation?"

"No, no reservation. Just one bed is all I need."

"I see. Yes, we do have a room available, but . . ."

His voice trailed off. The man took note of Bourne's lack of luggage, and his mouth formed a little frown. Jason could see him anticipating the prospect of this crude American coming back with a prostitute in tow.

Jason allowed a little embarrassment on his face. "The truth is, I'm hoping I don't actually have to spend the night. I mean, I'll pay in advance, no problem about that. But this is my honeymoon trip, and my wife and I had a big fight this morning, and she told me in no uncertain terms to get my keister out of our hotel and not come back until I was ready to apologize."

"Keister?" the man asked.

Bourne grinned and slapped his backside. "I guess you'd call it the derriere over here."

"Ah. *Oui*, I understand."

"I figure an expensive dinner, nice bottle of wine, and we'll be good to go, but if not, I'd like to make sure I have a place to sleep tonight. So anyway, one room, see voo play. How much will that be?"

The hotel clerk quoted him a price. Bourne dug in his pocket for a wrinkled stash of euro, and as he pulled out his hand, the bills fluttered to the floor. He squatted down with a curse and began gathering them up, and as he stood up again, he affixed a miniature receiver the size of a postage stamp to the underside of the registration table. Then he counted out the bills and added a couple hundred euro to what he gave the man.

"There's a little extra in there for ya."

"Merci beaucoup."

Jason smiled. Yes, this was the perfect place for a back door.

"Say, mind if I ask you a question?" he went on. "On the QT, as it were. Antree nouz."

"Of course, sir. How can I help?"

"I noticed a very lovely woman at a restaurant up the street yesterday. In fact, I spent a little too much time noticing her, if you catch my drift. That was part of what caused the fight with my wife. This woman, well, she was a looker, but in an upscale way, refined, upper-crust, know what I mean? Long, wavy blond hair, sad blue eyes, deep red lips. About forty-five or so, I guess. I heard her talking, and she sounded German, not French."

He described Monika as the photograph from the Drei Alpenhäuser had showed her and hoped she still might look a little like that.

"I'm pretty sure I saw her come into this hotel," Bourne went on. "Does she ring any bells with you? Do you know who she is?"

"I'm afraid not," the clerk replied stiffly. "There's no one staying here who matches that description."

"Ah well, too bad. Heck, probably just as well that I not find her, right? I don't need any more trouble at home."

The man handed Bourne a room key, and he headed for the hotel stairs. There was no elevator. He climbed to the second floor and let himself inside a small room with an arched ceiling and painted timbers lining the walls. In addition to a single bed, there was a writing desk and a chair, which he pulled to the casement window. He opened the window to see the street below him, and then he synched the app on his phone to listen to the microphone in the lobby of the hotel. From inside his jacket, he took out a small but powerful pair of binoculars, which he used to study the windows in the buildings across the street.

If anyone was surveilling him from there, they were well hidden.

"I'm in position," he murmured to Vandal. "Are you picking up the lobby sound?"

"Loud and clear. Was that Monika you were describing?"

"Yeah. It was a shot in the dark."

"Did he recognize her?"

"Maybe. If he did, she paid him not to remember her."

"So now what?"

"Now we wait," Bourne said.

THE WAIT LASTED THE REST OF THE DAY.

For several hours, he listened to the dialogue of people checking in and out of the hotel, but none of the conversations raised suspicions with him. At one o'clock, the clerk went to lunch. A young woman took over the registration desk and spent most of the time on the phone discussing her sex life with a level of explicit detail that made Vandal groan through the microphone in Bourne's ear.

But as the afternoon wore on, no one took the bait. No one came into the hotel to ask about messages.

Until six o'clock.

At six o'clock, Vandal reported a young woman in a tailored business suit and sky-high heels entering the hotel. She went to the desk—the original clerk was back on duty—and told the man that she understood a message was waiting for a woman named Marella Vaughn.

In the room overhead, Bourne felt the breath escape from his chest. He should have expected this, but it still came as a shock.

Marella Vaughn. Yes, of course.

The woman downstairs was here to collect a message from Jason—but not for Monika. Marella Vaughn was the false name Abbey had chosen, the name under which he would reach out to her in an emergency. Abbey was still following the protocol. Every day, she sent someone past the Bastille station to look for a sign that a message was waiting at this hotel. And now, for the first time, the sign had been there—but there was no message.

Jason wondered if the woman would contact Abbey and let her know. Of course she would. Any lawyer would report a deviation in the norm to her client.

The signal was there, but there was no message.

What would she think?

"Cain?" Vandal asked, interrupting his thoughts. "Is this it? Is this the courier?"

"No. This is something else."

From the window, Jason watched the woman in the business suit exit the hotel and head toward the far end of Rue Castex. A part of him wanted to break cover and catch up with her. Give her a message. Tell her to tell Abbey that Jason says—

What?

What could he say?

There was nothing in the world he could say that wouldn't turn Abbey's life upside down, and he wasn't going to do that.

"Hang on," Vandal said in his ear.

"What is it?"

"We've got another visitor. Opposite direction. I like the look of him."

Bourne checked the street. He saw the man that Vandal meant, and he agreed with her instincts. This wasn't a tourist; this was a man on a mission. He was in his fifties, medium height, stocky build, with a receding hairline and gray beard. His face had the sunken lines of alcohol and age, but he wore a gray suit that was tailored and expensive. He looked successful but not smooth, not corporate. If he was a lawyer, Bourne suspected that he represented a rougher kind of client.

"He's going in," Vandal said.

Jason heard the noise of the hotel's front door. He thought about going downstairs to the lobby to see this man and watch how he behaved. But he couldn't do that. Whoever the man was, he might be prepped to look for someone matching Cain's description.

He listened to the clerk greeting him.

"Bonjour, monsieur. Puis-je vous aider?"

"Do you have a message for Patricia Tuile?" the man asked. "I'm supposed to pick up a note that was left for her here."

"Tuile?" Vandal asked Jason through the radio. "Is that the code name for Monika?"

"It has to be her," he replied. "This is our guy."

Ten years later—and the protocol was still in place. Monika was still waiting for him to make contact.

"Non, je regrette, pas de message," the clerk replied.

There was a long pause on the microphone downstairs.

"Rien?" the man asked, his voice turning harsh and suspicious. Nothing?

"Non, monsieur."

"Es-tu sûr?"

"Oui, il n'y a pas de message. Et je ne connais pas cette femme Patricia Tuile. Elle n'est pas une cliente de l'hôtel."

The clerk was certain. No message. No Patricia Tuile staying at the hotel.

Another long pause followed, and Bourne knew what the man was thinking. This made no sense. The hashtag had been placed on the sign at the Bastille station. The note should have been there! Something was wrong!

He'd leave the hotel and report the situation to his client.

There is a problem. We're being played!

But that was exactly what Bourne wanted. Once the man had made contact, he and Vandal would track him back to Monika.

"Get ready to follow him," Jason said into the radio.

"On it."

But then Bourne heard the man's voice through the microphone again. The courier sounded strangely calm for someone who'd just had a decade-old messaging protocol turned on its head.

"Ah, well, apparently the message hasn't been dropped off yet. I will try again tomorrow. In the meantime, I'd like to leave a note with you from Ms. Tuile. Would five hundred euro make sure this gets to the man who comes to collect it?"

"Certainement," the clerk replied. "And who will pick it up?"

"His name is David Webb."

24

HIS NAME IS DAVID WEBB.

For a moment, Bourne froze with disbelief. His head pounded, the roaring of pain back between his ears. A message for him? Here and now?

Impossible!

There was no way the note could be from Monika. And yet she was the only one who knew about the back door. It had to be from her. She was reaching out to him after all these years, in the one location where she could expect to find him. Now! At the very moment when he was looking for her!

The timing couldn't be a coincidence.

Somehow she *knew* he was searching for her.

He shook himself out of his thoughts and focused on the mission. Through the microphone, he heard the clatter of the hotel door opening and closing. Downstairs, the courier was leaving.

"He's on the move," Vandal reported.

"Follow him," Jason said. "See where he goes, and find out who he is. Keep me posted. I'll rendezvous with you as soon as I can."

Bourne went to the window and watched the man leaving the hotel. On the street below him, the lawyer headed south, alone, and disappeared around the corner on Boulevard Henri IV, turning toward the Seine a few blocks away. Soon after, Vandal appeared, walking quickly to catch up with the man. She shot a glance over her shoulder at the hotel and nodded silently at Bourne when she spotted him in the window.

He took the stairs to the lobby. The balding clerk in the paisley tie recognized him.

"Ah, Monsieur Briggs. Have you been outside to enjoy the city?"

"I'm afraid not."

Bourne dropped the room key on the registration table. He also dropped the Texas accent, and his voice hardened. "Here you go. Keep the money, but I won't need the room tonight."

The clerk blinked, trying to match the different voice to the man he'd met earlier. He stuttered with surprise. "I see. Well, I hope this means you have reconciled with your wife, and you won't be sleeping in an empty bed."

"I have no wife," Bourne replied, "and you have a message for me."

The man stared at him. "A message? I'm sorry, there is no message for you, Mr. Briggs."

"It's Webb. My name is David Webb."

The man's hand went to the drawer in the registration table, where he'd obviously deposited the envelope from the courier. But he didn't open it. "I don't understand. Your passport did not have that name."

Bourne put five hundred euro on the table, matching what the lawyer had given the man. "You're having a lucrative day, *monsieur.* Don't do anything that would turn this into a bad day for you."

"You are putting me in a difficult situation, Mr. Briggs," the clerk complained. "I accepted this message for a specific person. I'm not sure how I would explain giving it to someone else. Are you with the authorities? Do you have some official identification? Otherwise, I would need to have the permission of the man who gave me the note in order to deliver it to you. He said he would return tomorrow. Perhaps you can come back and talk about this with him yourself."

Bourne reached into his pocket and slid his Sig out just far enough for the man to see the butt of the gun.

"The message," he repeated.

The clerk swallowed hard. "*Oui!* Yes, yes, of course! I will get it for you!"

The man yanked open the drawer of the table and spilled out a collection of cigarettes, breath mints, and paper clips as he pulled the envelope from the back. He shoved it across the table as if it couldn't be out of his hand fast enough. Bourne took the envelope and dropped another large euro note in front of the man.

"A *very* lucrative day for you, *mon ami.* Now you will forget any of this ever happened. Understood?"

"It is forgotten! I swear! But what if the other man returns? What should I say?"

"He won't return. Don't worry about that. However, *I* might come back. I may have other messages to leave with you in the future. I'll be generous if I can count on your discretion. If I can't—"

"Oh, you can rely on me, *monsieur.* Always!"

Bourne shoved the envelope in his pocket and left the hotel. He walked to the busy intersection ahead of him and turned toward the river, but he stopped in the doorway of the first apartment building he reached. He examined the envelope, which had the name *David Webb* written in a masculine hand on the outside—probably the lawyer's handwriting. Jason ripped open the flap and unfolded the paper inside.

The note was written in a different hand. A woman's.

Did he *know* that writing? Had he seen it before?

He closed his eyes, trying to peer through the shadows in his brain to an echo from ten years earlier, but his mind gave him nothing but darkness. If he knew that handwriting, he'd forgotten it long ago.

He read the note.

David,

I know you're looking for me. If you value my life, if you value what we once meant to each other, you must stop. Don't try to find me. Time buries us all like a rising tide. Let the past stay buried.

Monika

BOURNE MET UP WITH VANDAL ON ÎLE SAINT-LOUIS IN THE MIDDLE OF THE Seine. She licked a Berthillon ice cream cone as she waited for him on Pont de la Tournelle on the island's south side. Barge traffic slouched under the bridge, and a dank smell rose from the river. He leaned on the bridge's stone wall beside her, and automatically he reviewed the people around him to check for surveillance. A twentysomething girl who looked like a fashion model carried a bag from Printemps. A blonde in a calf-length white trench coat, her back to him, smoked a cigarette and stared upriver toward the Eiffel Tower peeking above the trees. A man in a leather jacket sat astride his motorbike outside a wine bar.

He felt that same sensation in his gut that he'd felt outside the hotel. He wasn't alone. He was being watched. But who was it?

"What did you find out about the courier?" Bourne asked Vandal.

"He's got an office in the middle of the block," she replied. "Rue des Deux Ponts. His name is Christophe Chouat. Criminal defense lawyer. I looked him up, and if you read between the lines, his client list sounds like a who's who of organized crime. Interesting choice for a go-between. But he's definitely the kind of guy who wouldn't ask questions about a back-door arrangement."

"Is there anyone else in the office?"

"A secretary. Young redhead. I don't think he hired her for her typing skills. They looked pretty friendly." Vandal licked her tongue around the scoop of pistachio ice cream. "So, are you going to tell me about the note?"

Jason handed it over without a word and Vandal's eyes flicked over the page. Her full lips puckered with suspicion.

"Do you think it's real?" she asked. "Or is someone playing games with you?"

"It's hard to tell. I sent Johanna a picture of the note to see if she recognized the handwriting. I haven't heard back from her yet. If it's fake, then Chouat is part of a trap to pull me in, and we need to spring it back on him. But even if it's real, we need to get to him. It means he's in contact with Monika. Not just in the past, but recently. That's how we find her."

"If the note is real, it also means Monika wants you to stay away from her," Vandal pointed out.

"I know."

"But you don't intend to do that."

"No, I don't."

He felt a buzz on the phone in his pocket. When he pulled it out, he saw that Johanna had replied to his message.

Jesus! Yes, I think that's really her! I'm virtually sure that's Monika's hand-writing. What does that mean?

He texted a short reply. *No info on Monika yet. Do you recall her mentioning a lawyer named Christophe Chouat?*

I don't think so.

What about Patricia Tuile?

Sorry, Jason. No.

Okay. Stay where you are. I'll be in touch soon.

A few seconds later, Johanna added a final note. *Will do. I miss you.*

He read the text thread to Vandal, leaving out the personal part of the exchange.

"Well, the note could still be fake despite the handwriting," she said with a frown. "Anyone with a sample from Monika could match it using AI or a good forger."

"Either way, we need to put the squeeze on Chouat," Bourne said.

"Well, here's our chance. He's on the move."

Bourne glanced toward Rue des Deux Ponts. Four doors down, he spotted Christophe Chouat emerging from the building with a curly-haired woman beside him, probably no more than twenty-one or twenty-two years old. In her stilettos, the attractive young secretary was taller than the lawyer by a couple of inches. Chouat checked the street in both directions, then headed toward the north side of the island. The girl kept a possessive arm locked tightly around the man's elbow.

"Let's go," Jason said.

They dodged traffic across the cobblestones, where the water-stained stone buildings rose on both sides of the one-way street. He'd only taken a few steps when he felt that same sixth sense of eyes on his back. In one seamless move, he turned around and scanned the bridge for unexpected motion.

He found it.

There!

Earlier, he'd spotted a blond woman in a trench coat admiring the view of the Eiffel Tower. Now, when he made his sudden turn, she twisted away with unusual speed. All he caught was a vanishing glimpse of her profile, not enough to see her features. The woman put her head down and shoved her hands in her coat pockets as she marched across the bridge toward the Latin Quarter.

"Stay with Chouat," he told Vandal.

"What's going on?"

"We're being watched. I'll be back."

Bourne reversed course.

He crossed the intersection diagonally and took the bridge over the water. To his right, he saw the fire-damaged façade of Notre-Dame encased in a web of scaffolding. One of the Bateaux Mouches riverboats cruised the Seine below him. He maneuvered among dozens of tourists, trying to keep the blond woman in view as she kept up a fast pace away from the island in her high heels. The low sun over the buildings ahead of him dazzled his eyes, making him squint. The woman's blond head came and went, bobbing among the crowd. He saw her, didn't see her, and then saw her again. But as he took long strides, the distance between them shrank second by second.

Then she disappeared.

As she reached the city side of the bridge, she squeezed through an American tour group, and he lost her.

Where did she go?

Bourne slowed, trying to locate the woman amid the crush of people and vehicles. His mind broke the scene into its components, isolating the clues. The bicycles wheeling across the intersection. The tour bus stopped at a red light. The lineup of people at a takeaway crêpe stand. The dense trees lining the sidewalk. He watched for anything that might give away the woman's location, a swish of blond hair between the cars, a white reflection of her trench coat in the shop windows.

Her *coat*!

When he rounded the corner of the bridge, there it was. It lay in a pile near the stone wall. She'd shrugged it off and walked away. And yet she couldn't be far. He'd only been steps behind her.

Bourne shut out the other noises of the city. He heard it. Close by, footsteps hurried away, high heels tapping like Morse code on stone. He glanced toward the stairs that led down to the riverbank of the Seine. A woman in a red blouse and white skirt rushed along the water's edge, the towers of Notre-Dame framed beyond her. She wore a floppy beige rain hat that covered her hair, but the gait was the same. It was her.

He charged down the stairs. She heard him coming and, kicking off her heels, she ran without looking back. Bourne ran, too. He was faster—in just a few seconds, he'd be on her—but whoever she was, the woman was smart.

She veered away from the river. A group of three French teenage boys smoked cigarettes near the wall below the street, and she intercepted them and pointed behind her. She pointed *at Bourne*. As soon as she did, the young men came off the wall and formed a barricade to block his path. Two dug in their pockets and came out with knives; the third had a gun. Bourne had no choice; he skidded to a stop on the loose gravel.

The boys marched toward him in a semicircle that blocked his advance. Meanwhile, behind them, the woman kept running, making her escape.

"Pourquoi cours-tu après cette femme?" the largest of the teenagers called to Jason in a guttural voice, rotating the blade of his knife in the air. *"Tu veux nous essayer, connard?"*

Bourne held up his hands. He backed away from them.

There was no point in a fight. It wouldn't take long to dispatch the three boys, but he'd already lost the chase. The woman had reached the next bridge. She sprinted up the steps to the streets of Paris, and she was gone.

25

NIGHT FELL AN HOUR LATER. THE LIGHTS OF THE CITY CAME ALIVE.

When it was fully dark, Bourne hailed a cab near the Sorbonne and then used his Sig and two thousand euro to convince the scared driver to let him take the taxi for the night. He told the man where to pick up his vehicle in the morning and said another five thousand euro would be waiting in the glove box.

From there, he returned to the near-empty streets of Île Saint-Louis, where Vandal was waiting for him. He found her sitting in the doorway of a closed pharmacy, with a view on an elegant corner bistro called L'Îlot Vache. She handed him a pair of binoculars, and he focused on the brightly lit interior of the restaurant. He could see Christophe Chouat at a small round table, flirting with his young redheaded secretary over glasses of white wine.

"Any activity?" Bourne asked.

"Only under the table. Chouat's been feeling up Little Miss Muffet between bites of escargot. What is it about French girls and daddy complexes?"

Bourne smiled. "Any phone calls or texts?"

"Plenty. His phone has been practically glued to his hand."

"So Monika probably knows I got her message."

"Probably," Vandal agreed. "What about the woman on the bridge? What was that about? Could that have been her?"

"Maybe. I never saw her face. As soon as she realized I was onto her, she bolted."

"*Le Renouveau?*"

"I don't see how they could have found us that quickly."

Vandal frowned. "What the fuck's going on? Are we running the show here, Cain, or are we dancing to somebody else's tune?"

"It could be both. All we can do for now is stay with the plan."

"All right, what's next?"

"It's time to shake things up for our lawyer friend," Bourne said. "We need to get Chouat off balance."

"He works for the mob. He'll be tough to rattle."

"Not necessarily. Sooner or later in that biz, you know they're going to come for you. Did you track down his phone number?"

"Yeah. I gave it a wrong number call earlier just to be sure. It's him."

Bourne retrieved his burner phone. He keyed in the number that Vandal gave him, and then he tapped out a text to Christophe Chouat.

You're being watched.

He pushed to send the message and used the binoculars to focus on the lawyer inside L'Îlot Vache. The man heard the buzz of his phone and retrieved it from the restaurant table. His mouth puckered with concern as he read the message. He grabbed his glass and gulped wine and took a casual look around the half-full bistro.

Then Chouat keyed in a reply. *Who is this?*

Bourne ignored the question and sent another message. *Don't tell the girl anything.*

He watched the lawyer check his phone as the next message arrived. When he did, the man's bloodshot eyes focused on the young girl with the big lips and overdone blush. She smiled and made a kiss at him, but when she reached for his hand, he pulled it away from her.

Why not? the lawyer texted.

Why do you think, Christophe? Do you think she fucks you for free? She's a spy, you fool.

Vandal glanced at the exchange on Bourne's phone. "Aw. Someone's not getting laid tonight."

"We need the girl out of there," Jason said. "She's a complication."

Bourne focused on Chouat again. As the man read the latest message, the wrinkles on his forehead deepened, and the bags under his eyes seemed to get heavier in the shadows. Sweat glistened on his face in the flickering candlelight. The lawyer studied the girl darkly, as if replaying their entire relationship in his head. She blinked in confusion at the new, hostile expression on his face. She leaned forward, putting her hand on his knee, but he peeled away her fingers.

The lawyer tapped out a new message. *Who the hell are you?*

Your friends sent me, Bourne replied.

What friends?

Oh, for God's sake, Chouat. Do you think we're not always watching you?

He could see the man breathing harder now. The lawyer's shirt collar seemed to choke him, and he wrestled it with his fingers. His eyes shifted to the door of the restaurant and then to the windows, as if expecting gunmen to storm inside or a bomb to go off in a hail of flying glass.

Bullets. Bombs. A knife in the alley. When you were a mob lawyer, you never knew how the end would come.

I've been loyal! You know that!

Bourne took a chance. *Then why have you made new alliances?*

New alliances? My God, what are you talking about?

Jason texted: *Le Renouveau.*

He watched the man's fingers fly on his phone. *That is mad! Insane! Me in bed with those maniacs? Never!*

You're doing their bidding.

I am not. I swear I am not! Why do you think that?

The hotel on Rue Castex.

Again Chouat studied the bistro in fear, trying to identify whoever was watching him. His secretary put a palm softly on his face—*"Mon cher, quel est le problème?"*—and Bourne watched him slap her wrist down to the table and hiss at her to be quiet. His fingers assaulted the keyboard of the phone.

The hotel? That is nothing! What about it?

The hotel is a drop for Le Renouveau. You are delivering messages for them.

Impossible! You are wrong!

Who is your client? Who sent you there?

I don't know her. I don't know her name. We have never met! I get a monthly retainer through a Swiss account. I check for a signal that tells me to go to the hotel, but until today, there has never been a signal. This was the first time!

And David Webb? Jason texted.

I delivered the message to him. That is all!

Chouat, don't you know who Webb is? He is an assassin!

In the bistro, the lawyer paled as he read the latest message. The word wrapped itself around his mind. Assassin.

Jesus! I had no idea!

Where did the message come from?

It was waiting at my office this morning. I don't know who delivered it, and I don't know what it contained. I did not read it!

Bourne delivered another twist. *We intercepted the message at the hotel. The note was instructions for a hit. A target. An account number for the funds. Le Renouveau is hiring Webb to kill for them.*

I swear I did not know! What do I do?

Jason texted: *First get rid of the girl.*

In the bistro, Chouat snapped at his secretary and jerked a finger at the door. The girl pointed at her half-eaten dinner and began to complain, but the lawyer took his wineglass and poured it over her salmon tartare. That was enough. She slapped a hand across his face and stomped out of the restaurant.

Half a block away, Bourne watched the girl march down Rue des Deux Ponts in a spitting rage. Chouat had lost a secretary and a lover.

She's gone! What now? What do you want from me?

You need to run, Chouat. Do you think Webb will let you live? You're the link that connects the killer to his employers. The first thing he will do is get rid of you. He has already been following you! He was there tonight!

Oh my God!

Don't go home. Don't go to your office. He will have both places under surveillance.

My home? But my wife!

Give her an excuse, Chouat. You're good at that. You weren't planning to be home tonight anyway, were you? You must leave now.

Where? Where do I go?

Take a cab. Don't take your car. It's almost certainly wired with explosives. Go to the Hotel Mercure near Charles de Gaulle. Await further instructions.

Yes! Yes, okay!

Bourne put away his phone.

"Time for phase two," he told Vandal, handing her the binoculars. "Chouat and I are going to take a little ride."

"What do you want me to do?"

"Go back to his office and search it. See if you can find any client or bank records for Patricia Tuile. He claims not to know anything about who Monika is, but he could be covering for her. I'll meet up with you later tonight."

"I hope you know what you're doing, Cain."

Bourne didn't answer. He returned to the stolen taxi, started the engine, and turned on the call light. He kept an eye on the door to L'Îlot Vache, inching the cab down the empty street and waiting for Chouat to appear. As he waited, he thought about other scared, nervous men he'd dealt with in his life. Antoine d'Amacourt—the Paris banker who'd been part of the money trail after he lost his memory. Carson Gattor—the New York lawyer who'd helped Bourne and Abbey make the connection to the Medusa group after he'd been framed for a congresswoman's murder.

Pressured little men in over their heads.

In the lights outside the bistro, he saw the door fly open. Christophe Chouat hurried onto the sidewalk. The lawyer saw the light on Bourne's cab and flagged him down.

"WHERE TO, *MONSIEUR*?" BOURNE ASKED AS THE LAWYER PILED INTO THE back of the cab and slammed the door shut.

"Hotel Mercure. It's near de Gaulle."

"Ah, fuck no, that's out of my way," Bourne told him, feigning reluctance in a guttural Marseilles accent. "I'm supposed to be off duty soon. Find another cab."

"No! No, I'll pay you whatever you want. Forget the meter. I'll give you cash."

"Cash?"

"Yes. Plus a tip. Twice the usual fare."

"What the hell, okay."

Bourne drove.

He kept an eye on his passenger in the rearview mirror as Chouat slumped low in the seat and kept twisting around to stare through the rear window. The man flinched whenever he saw headlights. Bourne navigated off the island and crossed to the north side of the Seine, and when he reached the wide, tree-lined river road, he headed southeast. A mile later, signs ahead indicated the lane for the Périphérique, the highway that skirted the city, but Bourne took an exit before they got there. He swung the cab into the Parc de Bercy.

Chouat noticed the detour. "Hey, where are you going? This isn't the way."

"Accident," Bourne told him. "An hour's delay. We'll pick up the highway near Vincennes."

He sped through the deserted park, crossing under a series of pedestrian overpasses. On the other side of the park, a few blocks away, the road dipped into a tunnel below a maze of train tracks leading in and out of Gare de Lyon. Flickering overhead lights lit up the lanes like strobes. Halfway through the tunnel, Bourne suddenly twisted the wheel hard, driving up onto the adjacent sidewalk and pulling the cab next to the stone wall that supported the steel girders for the tracks. Before Chouat could react, Jason was out the driver's door and in the back seat with the lawyer.

Chouat saw the Sig in Bourne's hand. He grabbed for the passenger door on his right, but the door only opened a couple of inches before colliding with the stone wall. The lawyer's eyes went wild with fear.

"Oh, fuck, who are you? Were you the one texting me? I did what you wanted!"

Bourne pointed the gun between the man's eyes. "Once upon a time, my name was David Webb."

"Webb? Jesus! You're Webb? I swear, I know nothing! I didn't read the note!"

"Shut up, Chouat."

He waited as a train boomed like thunder on the tracks over their heads, making the taxi shake. The lawyer clapped his hands over his ears at the noise and tears leaked from his bloodshot eyes.

"Please," he murmured. "Please, I delivered the note. That's all! I don't know anything else!"

"Where did the note come from?" Bourne asked.

"I have no idea! It was waiting at my office this morning. Someone pushed it through the mail slot."

"How did you know what to do with it?"

"There were instructions," Chouat went on quickly. "It said I should follow the protocol for the Patricia Tuile account."

"On the phone, you said you didn't know the client's name."

"The phone? My God, that *was* you? How did—"

"Patricia Tuile," Jason snapped. "Tell me about the protocol."

"Mademoiselle Tuile is the name on the account, but for God's sake, I'm sure it is an alias! I do not know her real name! I do not even know whether it is really a woman. The protocol has been in place for years. Every day, I am to go past the sign for the Bastille station. If there is a hashtag on the sign in orange chalk, then I should stop at the hotel on Rue Castex, and there will be a message waiting under the name Patricia Tuile. Sometimes I go past the sign myself, and sometimes I send my secretary. But there has never been a signal to indicate a message. All these years, never!"

"Until today," Bourne said.

"Yes! Yes! But it was strange. If my client wishes to *leave* a note, I am supposed to make the hashtag on the Métro sign myself. Then I take the note to the hotel for the recipient to collect. I planned to do that today, but when I passed the sign at Bastille, I saw that the hashtag was already there. Someone else had left the signal. That meant a note was supposed to be waiting for Patricia Tuile, but when I went to the hotel, there was nothing. So instead, I left the note—the note for you! If there was something wrong with the contents, it was not me. I only followed the protocol!"

The flashing lights in the tunnel sent Chouat's face in and out of shadow.

"What if there had been a message for Patricia Tuile?" Bourne asked. "What do you do with it?"

"I make contact and await instructions on how to deliver it."

"How do you make contact?"

"I have a phone number. Several times over the years, the number has changed. A new number is left at my office. That is all I know."

"You call the number?"

"No, I send a text. I do not know who is on the other end!"

"What's the number?"

The lawyer squirmed. "I don't remember it. I'm terrible with numbers. I keep it written down at my office."

Bourne shoved the barrel of the Sig into Chouat's forehead. "I tolerate one lie. The second lie, and I pull the trigger."

"Yes! Yes, all right! A new number arrived today along with the note of instructions. Plus—I don't know what it means—plus a bottle of mead."

"Mead?" Bourne asked, puzzled. "The drink?"

"Yes. No explanation—just a bottle of Lindisfarne Mead."

"Does that usually happen?"

"No, never before. I put the new number in my phone, and then I destroyed the card."

A new number.

Multiple new numbers over the years.

Had it started with Monika? Was it *still* Monika? Or had the protocol been intercepted? When spies broke a code, they usually kept it going to see who answered. That was smart tradecraft.

"Did you text her today?" Bourne asked. "Does she know what happened at the hotel?"

He nodded frantically. "Yes, of course. She is a client. When I got to my office, I used the number, and I texted her about the hashtag. I said there was no note waiting, but I had left the note for David Webb as instructed."

"Did she reply?"

He shook his head. "I got nothing back."

Jason dug into the man's suit coat pocket and slid out his iPhone. "Get me the number."

Chouat fumbled with the phone, using Face ID to unlock it. His fingers shook as he scrolled through the keys. "Here. Here it is! I put it under a different name. Not Tuile."

Jason memorized the phone number. Then he called up the lawyer's messaging app and confirmed the man's story. Hours earlier, Chouat had sent an update to that number explaining what had happened at the hotel in Rue Castex. Whoever received the message had sent nothing back in reply.

Bourne noted the twelve digits and the UK country code: 44.

Was Monika hiding in England? How long had she been there?

But now he had a way to reach her. He had twelve digits to send her a message. Twelve digits to go back into a past he didn't remember.

If it really was Monika on the other end of that number.

Bourne got out of the cab and flung Chouat's phone into the traffic lane. A few seconds later, a van speeding through the tunnel hit the phone and smashed it into fragments of metal and glass.

"Get out of here," he told the lawyer, leaning back through the open door. "If you hear anything more from Patricia Tuile, tell her David Webb needs to talk to her. It's urgent. She's in danger."

26

VANDAL WALKED TO THE END OF RUE DES DEUX PONTS IN THE DARKNESS.
She crossed the quai to the river and leaned against the stone wall over
the Seine. With a vape pen, she inhaled and blew steam into the air. It
was late and quiet on the island, and there was almost no traffic, just a
handful of shadows on the sidewalks. She spotted a couple kissing in a
doorway, hands all over each other. A man walked a terrier. Two children passed on bicycles. There was no one who smelled like a threat.
And yet this whole mission felt wrong.

She'd said to Cain: *Are we running the show here, or are we dancing to
someone else's tune?* More and more, she felt like a puppet, at the mercy of
an invisible hand pulling the strings.

She thought about calling Nash. Give him an update. Confess her
sins. She could tell him about Bourne and Monika and the search that
seemed to be nearing a climax. But then what? If Cain found out what
she'd done, he'd disappear and continue his hunt for Monika alone, and
Nash would have no idea where he was. By keeping the secret, Vandal

could stay close to Bourne. But sooner or later, she would have to pick sides.

She was Treadstone. There was only one side.

Vandal pocketed her vape pen and pushed off the wall. The street ahead of her was empty. She crossed the cobblestones into Rue des Deux Ponts and passed a closed brasserie on her left. Four doors down, she stopped outside an old building with a blue door. Bars secured the windows. She slid a leather pouch from her pocket and selected two slim metal tools that she used to disengage the lock. When she pushed on it, the heavy door swung inward, leading to a dusty hallway that had a sweet smell of garlic. She closed the outer door behind her and found another door halfway down the wall on her right.

An etched metal sign above the door knocker read CHOUAT.

When she nudged her weight against the door, it inched open. A burnt smell drifted from the shut-up space, and she immediately backed away and retrieved her Glock from the holster at the small of her back. She heard no movement from the other side of the door. No lights lit up the darkness of the interior. The office was empty.

But a gun had been fired there, and it smelled recent.

Vandal shoved the door open with her boot. She had her Glock aimed and ready. When she came inside, the smell of the discharged weapon grew sharper in her nose. Her hand searched the nearest wall for a light switch. She clicked it on and found herself in a small, windowless anteroom decorated with dark, heavy wallpaper. There was a sofa and armchair, a small desk, and then another door leading to a second room that faced the street.

That door was partially open, blocked by a body whose bare legs jutted through the doorway.

"Shit."

Vandal approached the inner office, not lowering her Glock. At her feet, a woman lay on her back, brown eyes huge and wide as she stared at the ceiling, her curly red hair soaking into the pool of blood behind her head. Her mouth hung open in surprise. A single bullet had burrowed between her eyes, killing her instantly.

It was Chouat's pretty young secretary. She'd left the bistro barely half an hour ago, and she'd come back to the office to find herself face-to-face with an assassin. A block away, in the silence of the night, Vandal was sure she would have heard the shot. So she assumed the killer had used a suppressor.

This was a pro, not a burglar surprised in the act of ransacking the office.

Had the assassin been waiting for Chouat?

Vandal stepped over the body and swung the pistol around the space, but the office was empty. Three tall windows looked out on Rue des Deux Ponts, the blinds closed and dark. The light behind her threw her tall shadow across the hardwood floor.

The office had been searched thoroughly, the kind of search she'd intended to do herself. But she was too late. She saw a charging cord on Chouat's desk that had once been connected to a laptop, but the laptop was gone. The lawyer had a metal file cabinet in the corner, and dozens of file folders had been yanked out of the drawers and strewn around the floor.

She checked to see if anything had been left behind. The killer couldn't have expected Chouat's secretary to return so quickly and wouldn't have wanted to linger in the office after the shooting. She examined the lawyer's desk. He had mail in his inbox, and she quickly went through the envelopes, looking for names she recognized. She did the same with the file folders on the desk, but the killer had obviously been through them, too, and left them in a disorganized pile. There was also a bottle of Lindisfarne Mead on the desk, open, with an empty glass next to it. She checked for a note or card and found nothing.

Vandal checked the desk drawers, looking for thumb drives or other electronic records, but if Chouat had kept any, they were gone now. Then she turned her attention to the sea of client files on the floor. It would take her more time than she had to go through them all, but she knew the name Chouat had used at the hotel on Rue Castex.

Patricia Tuile.

She hunted through the folders on her hands and knees and found a stack that had obviously come from the drawer labeled P–Z. In a couple of minutes, she located what she was looking for—a folder identified with a printed label for P. TUILE.

The folder was empty.

"Shit," she said again.

Then she sprang to her feet.

In the anteroom, she heard a low click, just loud enough to disturb the silence. She led with her Glock back into the outer office and saw that something was different. She'd left the door to the hallway wide open.

Now it was fully closed.

Her mind made the leap: *The assassin was still here!*

He hadn't had time to make his escape before Vandal arrived, so instead of returning to the street, he'd gone up the stairs and waited to get out of the building.

Vandal charged to the hallway door, but as she turned the knob, the door suddenly crashed open from the other side, slamming into her face and knocking her backward off her feet. Her body flew. She hit the ground hard, dizzy, and she was vaguely aware of the pound of foot-steps outside.

As her mind cleared, she got to her feet and staggered into the hall-way. The outer door to Rue des Deux Ponts was ajar. She steadied herself on the wall, then limped out to the street and pointed her gun both ways. On the bridge, she saw a shadow passing in and out of the glow of the streetlights. The killer wore black, but at that distance, she couldn't even be sure whether it was a man or a woman. Vandal took a few steps to give chase, then stopped. She had no hope of catching who-ever it was. All she could do was watch the killer disappear toward the maze of streets beyond the bridge.

Someone was willing to kill to keep them from finding Monika.

Or was it Monika herself?

CHRÉTIEN PAU ASKED THE DRIVER TO DROP HIM ON A QUIET STRETCH OF Rue de Grenelle near the Swiss embassy. He got out of the passenger side of the inconspicuous black Volvo, then leaned through the window.

"Meet me back here in one hour."

"*Oui, d'accord.*"

Pau waited on the street until the Volvo disappeared.

He checked in both directions, but no one was around. It was late, and this area of the city was free of the violent protests by *La Vraie*. He tugged a beret low on his head to cover his brown hair and squinted through his sunglasses in the dark. Despite the heat, he'd slung a white scarf that he could swish over the lower part of his face if necessary. He wore a dark sport coat over a collarless red shirt, plus jeans and old sneakers, not the attire anyone would have expected from a candidate for the presidency of France.

He walked to the corner. The Eiffel Tower gleamed in gold against the dark horizon. Crossing the intersection, he continued in the shelter of the trees until he reached the oxidized-green cannons of the Musée de l'Armée, pointing their barrels toward the esplanade and the river. The shining dome and steeple of Les Invalides, where Napoleon was buried, peeked over the roof.

As he neared the gates that led into the museum grounds, he saw a fiftysomething man seated on the stone wall, a cane nestled between his knees and his chin on top of the cane. The man was small, but built like a sturdy fire hydrant. His wiry gray hair had tufts that didn't fall into place, and his skin had the leathery look of a comfortable old shoe. His clothes were loose. He whistled loudly, and Pau recognized a snippet from Camille Saint-Saëns's *Carnival of the Animals*.

That was the signal; all was well.

The older man's eyes were dreamy as he stared down the long avenue toward the Grand Palais, but that was a ruse. Pau was sure that Nash Rollins could have described the face of every pedestrian and rattled off the license plate of every car that had passed him in the last half an hour.

"This meeting is ill-advised, Nash," Pau commented, sitting down on the wall a few feet away from him.

"It couldn't be helped," Nash replied in his typical raspy drawl. "But I thought a midnight rendezvous would be more discreet for you."

"Well, you're right, I don't need to be seen talking to an American spy in the middle of the campaign. If anyone from *La Vraie* spotted us? Berland would build a guillotine for me in the Place de la Bastille."

"*Le Roi Raymond,*" Nash murmured. "That's what I wanted to talk to you about."

"I assumed so."

"You've been very helpful to us over the years, Chrétien. Your information about policy discussions at the EU has been extremely valuable. Treadstone and the American government are grateful."

"You're welcome, but I'd rather we keep that fact to ourselves."

"Yes, of course. Needless to say, we want our relationship to continue after the election. We were among those lobbying behind the scenes for you to be the replacement when your current president decided to bow out. So I'm here to offer our help in making sure the election goes your way."

"You can help by doing nothing," Pau said.

Nash pursed his lips. "I understand, but that may not be possible."

"Meaning what?"

"Meaning we can't let Raymond Berland win. An extremist right-winger as president of France? Unthinkable."

"I share your goal in that regard," Pau replied.

"Maybe I misspoke. We *will not* let Berland win. We will do whatever it takes to make sure that doesn't happen."

Pau stripped off his sunglasses and eyed Nash in the darkness. "What are you suggesting? Voter fraud? Hacking our machines? Or something worse? France is not one of your play toys in the Americas or the Middle East, Nash. You can't use the CIA to meddle in our elections."

"You think we're alone in doing that?" Nash replied. "You think the Russians aren't trying to put a thumb on the scale in favor of Berland? Probably the Chinese, too."

"I think social media manipulation is very different from what *you* have in mind. Do you think I'm naïve? I've known you too long, Nash, and I know the kind of people and tactics you use. In fact, I suppose I should ask you directly. Was Treadstone behind the assassination attempt on Berland?"

Nash shook his head. "No. That wasn't us. In fact, we have reason to suspect Berland orchestrated the shooting himself. To make himself a martyr and to drive more anti-immigrant sentiment."

"I suspected the same thing," Pau admitted.

"We also believe that *Le Renouveau* is stage-managing the urban riots around the country. Revving up the outrage, turning the protests violent. All in support of Berland."

Pau exhaled with a loud huff. "*Le Renouveau* again. You and your conspiracy theories."

"This is not a conspiracy."

"No? I remember a Treadstone briefing in Brussels after their so-called leadership summit in Ibiza more than a decade ago. Your spies came away with nothing. I'm not saying *Le Renouveau* doesn't exist, but I think you're greatly exaggerating its influence."

"Berland was in Ibiza that weekend," Nash pointed out.

"And so what? Berland and *La Vraie* are the culmination of some kind of yearslong plot to take over France?"

"Maybe so."

Pau stood up from the stone wall and replaced his sunglasses on his face. "I appreciate the intelligence you provide, Nash. I always do. But keep Treadstone's dirty little fingers out of the election. France has flirted with Jean-Marie Le Pen and Marine Le Pen and now *Le Roi Raymond*, and always the Americans and the media pitch a fit, believing this time the Nazis will win. Hitler is on the march. Well, the right wing always comes up short with the voters, and they will again."

The American spy's face was stone. "We're prepared to make sure they do."

"Then let me be clear," Pau told him. "If you interfere, I will expose American involvement in the election, and you'll lose France as an ally for the next generation. I imagine that would be the end of NATO, too. Think about that, won't you? Good night, Nash."

27

BOURNE ABANDONED THE TAXI AT THE SIDE STREET HE'D CHOSEN NEAR LES Halles and then walked a few blocks to the plaza in front of the Hôtel de Ville. It was after midnight, but hundreds of lights gave the palace-like city hall a yellow glow. So did the bonfires in the plaza, dozens of empty oil drums filled with wood and set ablaze by supporters of *La Vraie*. Their angry chants bellowed into the night, calling for a new revolution and repeating the name of *Le Roi Raymond*. Most carried French flags, along with posters bearing the photograph of Raymond Berland, his fist raised in a power salute.

Jason found an empty bench and slid his phone from his pocket.

First he reviewed the message from Vandal. Chouat's secretary had been murdered, the lawyer's office ransacked. If there had been evidence about Monika left behind, it was gone. That meant his last chance to reach her was the phone number Chouat had given him.

Twelve digits, one UK number.

All he needed to do was send a message.

We need to meet, he typed. *It's David.*

Then he erased the message without sending it. First he needed to talk to Johanna. She was supposed to be here with him, and she was late. He opened the messaging app again, and he sent a message to the burner phone he'd given her. *Are you okay?*

"I'm fine," said a voice behind him.

Johanna slid onto the bench, with the lights of the Hôtel de Ville glowing behind her. Her face was flushed from the heat of the fires, but she kissed him and stayed close, their thighs pressed together. They'd only been apart for a day, but he felt her absence, and he was glad to be back in the aura of her perfume.

"Sorry," she said. "The Métro is a fucking disaster with all the rioters and police. What's going on?"

He gave her an update on what had happened during the evening, and he ended with the UK phone number.

Johanna shivered despite the heat in the plaza. "Jesus. Do you think that's really Monika's number? After all this time? We finally have a way to reach her?"

"We have a way to reach someone. It may be her, it may not."

"Did you text the number?"

"No. I wanted you with me before I did."

Her forehead wrinkled with confusion, but then she understood. "You mean, to help you figure out whether it's really her?"

"Exactly."

"Do you think she'll answer?"

"If it's a trap, if it's *not* her, she'll answer and try to lure us in," Bourne said. "And if it *is* her? She may answer, or she may simply run. But right now, this is as close as we've come to finding her."

He tapped in the same message he'd already deleted once before.

We need to meet. It's David.

This time he sent it and watched as the text was delivered.

"Now we wait," he told Johanna. "We'll need to be patient. If we hear anything back at all, it might not be until tomorrow."

But he was wrong.

Not even a minute after he sent the message, the phone buzzed with a reply.

David, it's me.

Johanna expelled her breath loudly. "Oh my God!"

"Hang on," he murmured. "We don't know who's talking to us."

Where are you? he wrote back.

A few seconds later, another text arrived. *Paris.*

"She's here!" Johanna exclaimed.

"Someone's here. It may be her, it may not."

I got your note at the hotel, he typed.

Then you know I don't want you to find me. Leave me alone, David. Go back to your life. Let me go back to mine.

We're both in danger, he wrote.

You put me in danger once before.

Yes, I did. I'm sorry.

I'm safer without you, David.

I know why you feel that way, but this is different. We need to talk. In person.

A long pause followed. Then a new text arrived. *That's a bad idea.*

And yet you're here. You came to Paris. Why?

Because I know you. You wouldn't give up, you wouldn't stop searching unless you heard from me. So I came here to send you a message. But now I'm telling you to go.

"We need some way to confirm it's really her," Bourne said. "I need to ask her something only she would know."

Johanna bit her lip in thought. "She's got a tattoo of a rose on her ass."

"No, it can't be anything physical," Bourne said. "If someone has Monika—or even if they *had* her and killed her—they can identify anything we ask about her body. They'll have taken pictures of her, too, in case we ask for a photo. That won't tell us anything."

"But if they have her, won't they just force her to answer our questions?"

"If she's being held against her will, then I hope she's smart enough to lie."

"Well, what about where you asked her to marry you? Mont Saint-Michel. That's not the kind of thing someone else is likely to know."

Jason didn't want to ask that question or go down that road, but he did anyway. He wrote: *Years ago, we got engaged.*

Yes, we did.

Where did I ask you?

He held his breath, waiting for the reply. It seemed to take longer than he expected, but that may have been his own anxiety.

Finally, she wrote back.

Mont Saint-Michel. Another text arrived a couple of seconds later: *It really is me, David.*

"Oh my God!" Johanna said.

He read the words again: *It really is me.*

But was it?

Could someone else know the answer to that question? Could he have told someone about Monika and Mont Saint-Michel *himself* sometime in the past? Because he remembered none of it.

"Give me another question," he said quickly to Johanna. "Something personal, something even *I* wouldn't know about. Just you and her."

Johanna cupped her palms over her face. "I don't know—there's so much—wait, wait, our father had a favorite movie. He used to watch it all the time. It was a Hitchcock film. The Cary Grant one. *North by Northwest.*"

What's your father's favorite movie? Bourne texted.

This time there was another long pause from the other phone.

How do you know about that, David?

You told me.

Another pause.

No. I didn't.

What was it? I need to know it's you.

Again she took a long time to answer, so long he wondered if she was going to stop responding at all.

Then the message came through.

North by Northwest.

Next to him, Johanna exhaled loudly.

It was her. It was Monika.

Jason felt the roaring he always felt in his head as memories fought to come back and bumped hard into a wall of nothingness. His brain grasped to remember this woman. He'd loved her. He'd wanted to spend his whole life with her. But then his life had changed overnight. He became Treadstone. He became *Cain.* From that moment forward, there was no turning back.

The man who'd once been David Webb disappeared into the mist.

He needed so many answers. This woman had been there at the crossroads of his whole life, and he didn't know her at all. The only thing he had was an old photograph of her from the Drei Alpenhäuser. He ignored Johanna, who was clutching tightly to his shoulder, and his fingers tapped urgently on the keys.

Why did you run, Monika? I took you to Hamburg, but you left and didn't tell me where you were going.

He watched the screen and saw that she was typing a reply.

After what happened, do you really need to ask? Can you blame me? I thought I was going to die in that chalet. I was terrified, David. Not just of them. Of you. You weren't the man I thought I knew.

I never meant for you to be involved in that.

Does that change anything? They terrorized me. So did you. I thought you were going to kill me.

I would never do that. I can't believe you would think that.

The man I loved would never do that, but you weren't that man anymore.

Yes, I know.

And later, when we were free, you said I had to leave my whole life behind. Leave you behind.

It was necessary. It was the only way to keep you safe.

Well, I did what you wanted. I left you behind. I left everything behind. I ran. I didn't trust you anymore.

And yet you kept the back door going. All this time. The signal. The hotel. Why?

She didn't answer right away. He thought she might have quit the conversation entirely, but the phone told him she was still crafting a reply.

I couldn't shut you out entirely. Not after what we'd meant to each other.

Jason frowned as he read the answer. Johanna picked up on his emotions.

"What is it?" she asked. "What's wrong?"

"She's lying."

"I don't understand."

"She's saying what she thinks I want to hear, but it feels false. Like her answers have been rehearsed."

"Is it not her? But she knows things only Monika would know."

"It may be her, it may be your sister, but you have to remember what I told you. Monika may not have been the person either of us thought she was. She was keeping secrets back then. She still is."

"What are you going to do?"

"I have to meet her," Bourne said.

He tapped out another text.

I need to see you. Now. Tonight. Name a place and time.

"Will she do it?" Johanna asked.

"I think she will," he replied. "I've peeled back every layer of her identity, and that's the only one left. Whatever's going on between us, it will only be resolved face-to-face."

He didn't have to wait long to be proved right. His phone buzzed.

La Villette. The dome. One hour.

28

ELABORATE STREET PAINTINGS ADORNED THE FOUNDATIONS OF THE
bridge that led across the canal near the park called La Villette, in the
far northeast part of Paris. Aztec ghost masks. Wild multicolored gi-
raffes. A graffiti-style *Mona Lisa* with a blue face and yellow headscarf.
Between the bridge columns, near the dark green water, Bourne saw a
homeless man under a Mexican blanket.

Or was the man really a scout guarding the entrance to the park?

Jason drew his Sig and watched the man's eyes blink open as he stood
over him. The stranger, the gun, elicited no reaction, and the drugged
eyes fell shut again.

The man was no threat.

Bourne stayed at the water's edge. He headed east through the
glow of streetlights on Quai de la Marne. Low apartment buildings
butted up to the canal, and houseboats were tied up at the pier. Ahead
of him, more graffiti covered the girders of an old railway bridge. He
walked with his hands in the pockets of his jacket. The area around him
was quiet but not deserted. An Asian prostitute strolled in the opposite

direction, clutching a black purse. A bulky teenager smoked near the bridge; he had a knife dangling on his belt, but the kid took the measure of Bourne and let him pass. In a nearby doorway, he heard the masculine grunts of two men having sex.

"Do you see anything?" he murmured into his radio.

"Nothing yet," Vandal replied.

"What about Monika?"

"No sign of her, either."

Bourne checked his watch. The rendezvous was scheduled in fifteen minutes. He closed in on La Villette from two blocks to the west, and Vandal approached from the east, making a pincer as they zeroed in on the mirrored dome known as La Géode. He was prepared for a heavy reception, but so far, he saw no one other than the usual Paris night creatures.

He crossed into the huge park itself, which was a maze of museums, concert venues, and children's rides tucked among trails and trees. An elevated walkway called the Galerie de l'Ourcq bordered the canal, and he climbed the steps, listening to the scrape of his footfalls on the metal. There were no other sounds around him. A few lights glowed on the opposite shore, but the park was mostly dark. Over the railing, he spotted shadows moving near a carousel, but none had the look of killers.

"I'm crossing the canal," he told Vandal. "I'm five minutes from the sphere."

A footbridge led over the water. Bourne crossed quickly, feeling exposed if anyone was watching him through night vision goggles. On the far shore, he took steps back down to the quai that led along the canal. He passed a children's park, where a multicolored dragon towered over his head, its tongue forming a giant slide. Beyond the slide, he veered from the canal sidewalk to a path that led through a small cluster of trees, where it was almost impossible to see anything around him.

Again he stopped to listen, but he heard no voices, no radios, no ambush waiting.

He thought about texting Monika. *I'm here. Where are you?*

But he kept his phone in his pocket.

Bourne took out his gun and leveled it as he moved forward. The path through the trees wasn't long. Where the trail ended, he saw a wide expanse of green grass dotted with LED lights like a field of candles. The canal was on his right, the metal beams of the science and industry museum on his left.

"Are we still clear?" he murmured to Vandal.

"So far."

He left the trees and moved into the center of the lawn. The grass was wet under his feet. An arc of concrete, like a huge wing, bent across the grass. He walked beside it, and something huge and bright, as unreal as a silver planet, crept into view. The mirrored dome of La Géode towered in front of him, its luminous panels reflecting the sky and the shadows of the park. He could see himself in the gleaming metal, a lone figure standing near the concrete arc in the middle of the grass.

Then he wasn't alone anymore.

"Someone's coming," Bourne told Vandal.

Footsteps made a distinct noise not far away, the tap of heels on stone. He swung his gun, aiming for the sound. Immediately adjacent to the sphere, a silhouette rose into view on the steps that led from the lower level of the museum. At first, he couldn't see who it was, male or female. The figure was in darkness, but when it cleared the stairs, he knew it was a woman. She took the walkway beside La Géode and stopped in front of the huge dome, its shimmering reflective panels making her thin shape look absurdly tall and large.

Was it her?

Bourne took a few steps forward, leaving twenty yards between him and the woman. He still had his gun level, pointed at her, and she must have spotted it, because she spread her arms wide, her fingers apart. Without saying a word, she sent a message: *I'm not a threat.* But he didn't believe that. Not yet. She was too far away, too lost in darkness, for him to identify her.

Slowly, Bourne closed the distance between them.

His gaze locked on her as he tried to pick out the details of her features. With each step toward her, she became real, not a ghost, not a phantom from the mists of his memory. She was very tall, nearly his own height, but pencil thin. She wore a black coat, long, draping to her ankles. Her hair, wavy and blond, cascaded to her shoulders. Her skin glowed white where the lights by the canal shined from the mirrored dome. And her mouth. Her mouth was the smallest flash of deep cherry red against that white face.

She wore no smile. But that was typical, he remembered now. She almost never smiled; her lips always turned downward. She still bore the weight of some sadness that never went away. Just as she had in the past. Ten years ago.

He *knew* her.

Jesus, *yes*, he knew this woman!

This was the woman in the photograph Johanna had given him. The woman from his past, so beautifully distant and lonely. His feelings came back, complicated and strong. As a young man, he'd wanted to erase the sadness of this woman. Save her. Rescue her.

From what?

He didn't know. He'd *never* known.

But it was her. It was really her.

Monika.

And with that, memories tumbled out of the shadows. A kaleido-scope of images rushed madly through his brain, hot and fast like an explosion. Monika in his Swiss apartment, reading Goethe to him in German and Baudelaire to him in French, her accents perfect. Monika asking endless questions about his parents, his childhood, his dreams, his desires, his fears, and then ducking every question he asked about her own past. Monika, naked under him in bed, impossible to reach even when they made love, unhappy even when her climax rippled through her body.

His fiancée.

I think we should get married.

He could hear it; that was his voice on the parapets of Mont Saint-Michel.

Yes, all right, came her strangely casual, careless reply. As if even then she had no intention of going through with it.

He remembered more and more details, like a dam giving way and flooding his mind. But these weren't memories he wanted back. He could have left them in the mist. These were *terrible* memories.

Monika, tender and loving one moment, cold and cruel the next, like a split personality.

Monika, introducing him to a friend outside the Drei Alpenhäuser.

An old friend from Paris.

But this man was more than a friend. David Webb had known it at once, had seen it in both of their eyes. This man was her lover. He could still feel rage twisting his stomach, raw jealousy at the thought that the woman he loved, the woman he was going to marry, was sleeping with another man.

Who was he?

You must remember! It's *urgent*!

Somehow he knew it was vital that he see who that man was. But the face of his rival, his enemy, refused to emerge from the shadows, and searching for it only brought pain behind his eyes.

One more memory stormed back to him. An empty apartment. *Her* apartment. It had been that same day! That awful day of death and blood at the chalet! He'd gone to Monika's apartment, and it had been empty, stripped of everything, her life, her possessions. She hadn't just run away *after* the violence in the chalet, after he'd given her a new identity in Hamburg. She'd run *before*. She'd already been running away from him when *Le Renouveau* kidnapped her.

Monika.

There she was. She stood in front of him, only ten yards away. He knew her, and yet he didn't know her at all. His face darkened with everything he remembered, and he was close enough to see cold recognition cross her beautiful features. She could read his mind. That had always been her special talent. Her superpower. She knew the veil had been lifted from his eyes.

Bourne called to her, his voice as bitter as smoke.

"Who are you?"

VANDAL HEARD SOMETHING. OR SAW SOMETHING. OR SMELLED SOME-thing. Her instincts reacted to the sensation before her brain did. That was how Treadstone trained their agents—to listen to the things that weren't there.

She slowed as she walked through a concrete plaza beside the ground floor of the museum. Its huge wall of glass glowed with lights. A handful of trees rose from planters in the stone, dead leaves scattering across the plaza in the wind. Ahead of her, the giant dome rose several stories tall, as high as the building next to it. She heard a voice near the sphere, echoed in her radio. Cain's voice.

The woman, Monika, was with him.

But something else was going on. Vandal felt it, just as she had on Île Saint-Louis.

"Cain, I don't like this," she murmured, but she got no response.

She swung her gun in a circle, watching everything around her and absorbing the silence. The museum. The bright dome. The stone benches. The black superstructure of an old French submarine on display, the *Argonaute*. No one was here. If there was a threat, it was in the park above her.

Where Cain and Monika were.

On her left, Vandal saw a series of slanted concrete walls, where fountains typically ran during the day. The fountains were turned off now, and the sharply angled walls led up to a fence at the upper level of the park. She went to the low railing beside the fountain, climbed it, and jumped to the base of the wall. With her fingers and boots clutching for seams, she made her way up the slimy, slippery surface to the top, then climbed the six-foot chain-link fence and dropped to the ground.

She found herself on the edge of another plaza. Close by, she saw the black hull of the old submarine, with the top of the mirrored sphere glowing behind it. Ahead of her was a cluster of trees built into a berm near the open grass.

She sensed danger very close. Someone was here. Her gaze went to the trees, picking out each individual tree trunk in the shadows.

There!

A dark figure floated from one tree to the next like a spirit. Someone was stalking Bourne and Monika.

Vandal sprinted across the plaza. She knew the slap of her boots on stone gave her away, but she couldn't help that. Hearing her coming, the person in the trees vanished, as if melting into the ground. Vandal reached the berm and skidded to a halt. Her gun was level, her eyes and ears pricked up for clues.

"Cain, we've got an intruder."

Still no answer.

She moved into the trees, and her boots sank into the soft earth with each step. The stranger couldn't be far from her. A few feet away, no more. *But where?* Her eyes scanned each tree trunk for the telltale silhouette of someone hiding behind it. She studied the up-and-down ground of the berm, like a black shroud in the darkness. If someone was stretched out across the dirt, she couldn't see them.

Another step.

She heard something behind her, but when she spun, she saw nothing. She stood like a statue, alert for any disturbance, any clue as to where the person had gone. But her foe was good. A professional, like she was. Dead silent, giving nothing away.

A rustle of wind made its way through the trees. Was that what she'd heard?

Where are you?

Alarm bells exploded in her mind, red flares of warning. Somehow she knew—*she knew*—that whoever had kicked that door into her face on Île Saint-Louis was here with her now. Inches away. Waiting. Watching.

A gun in hand, a suppressor threaded onto the barrel.

She took another step. Her finger slid over the trigger of her Glock. She couldn't see; the world inside the trees was black on black. But all she needed was the barest sound, a breath, a finger, a knee, a foot moving in the dirt. Pinpoint the noise and fire.

I'm Vandal. I'm fast, you fucker. Try me.

Then the noise came. Not behind her. It came from in front of her, a crackling like a footstep near one of the trees. Vandal swung her arms, aimed the gun, but she realized at once that she'd been fooled by the oldest trick of all. There was no one! Nothing! Someone had tossed a rock toward the grass.

The noise was a ruse, a split-second distraction to break her concentration.

The stranger was *behind* her, leaping off the ground and separating like a ghost from the darkness.

Vandal corrected, lurching away, twisting around. Yes, she was fast, but not fast enough. She had a vision of a horrible caricature, of a Guy Fawkes mask grinning at her as something hard and metal whipped through the air. A length of pipe crashed into the side of her skull. The night turned to day inside her head with a blinding explosion of pain and light, and she wasn't even aware of crumpling to the ground.

29

"WHO ARE YOU?" BOURNE CALLED.

Monika said nothing, her face devoid of expression. That face remained one of the most beautiful he'd ever seen, but it had a hardness to it. Get close to her, and she threw up a wall. It was strange. He remembered being in love with her once, but he felt nothing for her now. Her sister, Johanna, far younger and less polished, pretty but not beautiful, was the more attractive to him of the two.

Bourne had no interest in rekindling an affair with Monika. What he wanted from her was answers.

What really happened in Switzerland ten years ago?

Who was the man—her lover—at the Drei Alpenhäuser?

Why had she run away from David Webb?

He heard Vandal's warning through the radio. *I don't like this.*

Bourne didn't reply; he didn't want Monika to realize he wasn't alone. His head twisted slightly, seeing no one in the shadows. If *Le Renouveau* had a team of assassins here, he was sure they would have spotted it by now. But he trusted Vandal's instincts, and it occurred to him that the danger might not actually be from *Le Renouveau*. It might be from the woman in front of him. *She* could have brought backup with her, the same way he had with Vandal.

"You're in danger, Monika," he called to her. "The group that came after me ten years ago in Switzerland is after me again. And they're after you, too. They're trying to find you. If they do, they'll kill you."

She spoke for the first time.

That voice! Words dripped smoothly from her lips like melting ice.

"I can take care of myself, David."

He didn't doubt that was true. There was a depth of resourcefulness to this woman that he hadn't perceived ten years ago. Maybe because, back then, she'd been hiding it from him. Hiding who she was.

"I know that," he replied.

"Then what do you want? Why have you gone to so much trouble to find me? I told you to stay away."

He debated what to say to her. With his memories broken or gone, he wouldn't know a lie from the truth, no matter what she told him. Not that she would know that about him. He could have been honest—*I have no past; it was erased; it was taken from me*—but he felt wary of showing weakness in front of her. Somehow he knew this woman could be a tiger, alert for wounded prey.

"Ten years ago, that summer changed my whole life," Bourne said. "*You* changed my life."

"Did I? No, I don't think so, David."

She said it like he was a rare breed of moth pinned to a card and she was studying him through a magnifying glass.

"What do you mean?"

"I mean, men like you never change."

"I was young. I had no idea who I was."

"Well, *I* knew who you were. David Webb the orphan. David Webb the brilliant, talented loner. Except you were never really a loner, were you? That was a lie. You needed someone in your life, and there I was. I filled your bed. I filled the empty spaces. That's all I was to you."

He felt slapped by her harsh judgment, but she wasn't wrong.

Had he ever really loved her? Or had it been something else? He'd been *obsessed* with her—in thrall to her. She hadn't even existed for him in ten years, and yet seeing her now, she still had a hold over him that was different from any other woman he'd ever met. He was fooling himself to say he felt nothing. Something about her still pulled him in. She could still control him and wrap him around her finger.

He didn't like it.

He was struggling with what to say next, when she called to him again.

"You still haven't told me what you want, David. Why am I here? Because if you can't tell me that, then let me go."

He heard his old name on her lips. *David.*

With her, he was David Webb again, caught at a crossroads in his life, trapped between two worlds. Bourne had to remind himself that David Webb was dead. He didn't exist anymore.

David Webb was *Cain.*

"What I want is for you to stop hiding from me," he shot back at her. "Answer my question. *Who are you?*"

This time, he could see a crack of doubt and guilt opening up on Monika's face.

"You know who I am," she replied.

"What?"

"You know who I am," she repeated, spitting out each word slowly.

No! he wanted to scream at her. *No, I don't know! That's why I'm here!*

Or was he wrong?

Did Jason Bourne know something about Monika that David Webb had never understood? Suddenly, he began to feel as if all the pieces had already been laid in front of him, but he hadn't assembled the puzzle. He was so close to the truth, and yet the answer stayed just out of his grasp.

But it didn't matter. Not now.

In the next moment, Vandal's voice came through the radio.

We've got an intruder.

Bourne swiveled toward the trees on his right. Vandal was on the east; the threat came from the east. His eyes hunted the darkness. He saw nothing, but he heard a sharp crack through the radio, the sound of an assault, and then the crash of someone falling. He hissed out Vandal's name now, but he got no reply.

He knew what came next. He threw himself to the wet grass.

Seconds later, the barrage of bullets began. Sparks of fire blinked from the woods. Bourne shouted for Monika to get down, but she seemed frozen in front of the mirrored sphere, almost in disbelief at what was happening. A bullet sent up concrete dust from the sidewalk. Another bullet hit the wall behind her and ricocheted. Another pinged off one of the metal panels over her head.

"Get down!" he screamed again.

He drew his Sig and fired toward the shadows where the gunfire had erupted.

When Monika didn't move, Bourne got to his feet and ran. He pounded across the grass, closing the distance between them. She watched him come with a bizarrely curious expression on her face, as if the bullets were blanks, unable to hurt her. But they weren't blanks. Another succession of low spits hissed through the air. More bullets burned through earth, metal, and stone. He watched in horror as a round hit Monika squarely in the chest, drawing a cry of pain from her mouth. The impact made her lose her balance, and her legs skidded out from under her. She fell backward, her head bumping into the grass.

Jason was on her in an instant. He covered her with his body and sheltered her from more fire. When he lifted her head, she looked dazed, but she stared up with that same distant coolness.

"I'm fine," she said.

"You're not fine, you've been shot."

"I'm fine," she repeated. "Really."

Bourne wrenched aside the flaps of her long coat. He saw a bullet hole torn through her blouse right where her heart should be. A perfect shot. Blood should have been pouring out of the wound, pouring away her life, but no blood soaked through the fabric. She was right; she wasn't hurt. He ripped her blouse open and saw the slug mashed against a black Kevlar vest that had absorbed the energy of the shot.

She was *wearing a vest?*

"Go get them," Monika murmured. "Quickly, get them, don't worry about me. Find out who they are, that's important. I'm okay. *Get them.*"

Bourne slid off her body and aimed his gun toward the trees. For now, the assault had stopped. He scrambled to his feet and ran, expecting bullets to track him, but he made it to cover without drawing fire. Breathing hard, he stopped and listened. The killer couldn't have escaped, not yet. He heard no running footsteps escaping from the park. Someone was still here, still close to him.

He picked the thickest of the young trees near him and hid there, crouching low. From the other side of the canal, he heard shouts. Voices. People had heard the shots. Soon there would be sirens closing in on the park.

Where was the killer?

Bourne sidestepped between trees. His movement caught the assassin's eye, and the suppressed gun fired again, bullets going high but forcing Bourne to the ground. His gun level, he eyed the shadows. He fired and rolled, fired and rolled, then waited for the killer to shoot again.

But no bullets came. Bourne had no target.

He heard movement above him and swung his gun upward.

It was Vandal. Ribbons of blood poured down her face. She had her gun in her hand, but loosely, as if she could barely carry it. Shots erupted again, so close that the bark of the tree exploded across Vandal's face. Bourne grabbed her by the belt and dragged her out of the line of fire. She collapsed, then swore as the pain caught up with her.

Not far away, Bourne heard someone running. He separated himself from Vandal and scrambled to his feet. He ran a few steps toward the plaza, then stopped. His gun was ready, but he couldn't see enough to get a clear shot. He heard the killer bolting over the berm and pounding toward the east end of the park.

Out of reach.

Bourne returned to Vandal and helped her to her feet. "How do you feel?"

"Like a cracked fucking egg. Sorry. I was trying to help you, but I didn't realize how weak I was."

"Sit down and stay here. I have to check on Monika."

Vandal didn't protest. She grabbed the nearest tree and slid to the soft ground, then held her head in her hands.

Bourne ran out of the trees into the middle of the open grass, and his gaze shot to the mirrored dome of La Géode. The walkway in front of the sphere was empty now. Monika was gone. He holstered his gun and sprinted to the area where she'd been lying on the ground, but nothing was there. He turned in a circle, trying to find her. He ran to the edge of the sphere and peered down at the lower level near the museum. Then to the trees where he'd come from the canal. Then to the shelter beneath the *Argonaute* submarine.

But Monika hadn't taken cover. She wasn't hiding and waiting for him to come back. She'd disappeared.

Jason took his phone from his back pocket. He found the message thread where he'd written to her from the bench at the Hôtel de Ville, and he tapped out a new message. *Monika, where are you?*

He sent it.

A second or two later, he heard a text tone close by. He used a penlight to hunt in the grass in front of the walkway, and he saw Monika's burner phone lying on the ground.

She'd abandoned it. She'd left behind his one way of reaching out to her.

He'd lost her again.

30

BOURNE KEPT AN ARM AROUND VANDAL'S WAIST AS THEY ESCAPED FROM
the park. When they reached the outside streets, she felt strong enough
to walk on her own, but he knew she was badly hurt. They'd left a stolen Kia a few blocks away, on a street that bordered a huge railway yard.
When they reached the car, he let her stretch out in the back seat, her
head against the window. He used a medical kit from the trunk to clean
her up, but the slightest touch of a gauze pad on the side of her head
made her wince. He tested her focus by moving a finger in front of her
eyes. He didn't like what he saw.

"I've got a doctor I use in the city," he said. "His name's Richet. I'll
take you over there."

"Fuck that," Vandal replied wearily.

"You may have a concussion."

"I'm fine."

"How's your memory?" he asked.

"How's yours?"

Bourne couldn't help but smile. "Did you see anything in the trees?"

"I saw a Guy Fawkes mask about a second before my lights went out. Shit, those things are creepy."

"Those masks are all over the *La Vraie* riots," Bourne said. "And someone in a Guy Fawkes mask killed the messenger you sent me near the Bastille."

"Does that mean it was *Le Renouveau*?" Vandal asked.

"I think somebody wants us to believe it was *Le Renouveau*. But it doesn't feel like their style."

"So who was it?"

Bourne frowned. "Lone assassin. Stealthy. Highly skilled. Enough smarts to get the drop on a pro like you. Deliberately wearing a disguise to make us think somebody else was behind the hit. Who does that sound like?"

Vandal's eyes narrowed as she understood what he was saying. "You think it was one of us? Someone from *Treadstone*?"

"That depends."

"On what?"

"On whether you told Nash about the meeting tonight," Bourne said.

She stuttered, which was as good as a confession. "Look, Cain—"

"Somebody knew where the meeting was going to go down," he snapped, cutting her off. "Monika picked the spot. That was only two hours ago. And yet a killer—a *pro*—was already waiting for us."

"My situation is complicated," Vandal told him.

"Yes, I get it. I know you've got divided loyalties. But you said Nash would do just about anything to keep me away from Monika, right?

Now we've got a lone killer wiping out the connections at Chouat's office and targeting Monika. The whole thing smells like a Treadstone operation."

"Why would Nash go that far?" Vandal asked. "I mean, *killing* her?"

"This is Nash. The ends always justify the means. It all depends on what secrets he's trying to protect."

Vandal's head sank back against the car window, making her grimace. "Fuck. I'm sorry."

Bourne said nothing.

She closed her eyes and kept talking. He could hear the exhaustion in her voice.

"I don't know how you do it, Cain. Seriously, I don't know how you stay sane. The things they do to us. Jesus. They look for lost souls, you know? That's their whole game plan. Like Nova. Everything she went through as a kid? Her parents getting killed on that boat? Treadstone only wants the damaged ones. The ones they can manipulate. The ones with nothing to live for."

He shifted into the other seat in the back of the Kia and let Vandal drape her legs across his. He made sure no one was watching them from the street. "Does that include you?"

"What, damaged? God, yes. Of course. Like I said, it's complicated. I never told you about it?"

"No."

She looked away, avoiding his eyes. Nervously, she stroked her fingers through her black-and-purple hair. He could see remnants of blood on her face, and her mocha skin looked dirty and drawn. Her muscles twitched, her whole body tense.

"Eight years ago, I murdered my husband," Vandal said.

Jason waited in silence for a while. Then he asked, "Did he deserve it?"

Her lips made a scowl. "Like, did he beat the fuck out of me? Or shove his dick into half my friends? No. It wasn't like that. People always assume it's the guy, but I was the bad one. I was a cocaine addict, in addition to being a cheating bitch. Lloyd stuck by me a lot longer than I deserved. Big mistake on his part. Finally, he gave me an ultimatum to quit, but I was high as a kite. I told him I'd see him dead before I quit. I backed that up with four shots from a Glock."

Bourne closed his eyes. "Shit."

"This was in Los Angeles. Even with the lefty loonies in charge out there, it's hard to get off if you do that. I pled guilty, got twenty years."

"But here you are."

"Yeah. Here I am. Guess I've got a guardian angel, huh?"

"A guardian angel named Nash," Bourne said.

She nodded. "I got clean behind bars. I went back to what I used to be really good at in high school."

"Which was?"

"Gymnastics." She bent her arm to show her muscles. "I'm really good. So good apparently somebody noticed my physical skills and thought I might be useful to them. Three years into my sentence, I got a new cellmate. Short-timer, check fraud. Not the kind of person who would normally get put in with a murderer, but I didn't think about that. She and I hit it off. She was smart, got me to open up, talk about things I never talked about with anybody else. Then again, what else is there to do in there, huh? I told her my life story, and she sussed out everything that was in my head."

"She was a shadow," Bourne concluded.

"Right. Not like I knew what that was at that point, but yeah, Treadstone sent her in to check me out. See if I was good raw material. Figure out all my strengths and weaknesses, whether I was mentally up to the job. Not long after that, she got sprung from my cell. A week later, I got called to a room to meet with a tough little son of a bitch. Said his name was Nash Rollins. He offered me a choice. Sit and rot in prison for half my life, or sign my soul away to an organization called Treadstone. That was an easy call. At least it was back then. I don't know, if I could go back in time, I might tell him to shove it and take my chances with the parole board."

"So you're loyal to Nash because you made a deal?" he asked.

"I'm loyal because if I fuck up, he sends me back."

"Ah."

"I guess the bottom line is, you can't trust me."

"I don't trust anyone," Bourne told her. "But I still need your help."

"Why? We've lost her, right? Monika's gone underground again."

"Maybe. Or maybe not." Jason dug Monika's burner phone out of his pocket. "She left this in the grass. She knew I'd find it. At first, I thought that meant she was cutting me off, but now I'm not so sure. I mean, if she wanted to make sure we had no way to track her, the smart play would have been to toss the phone in the canal, not leave it behind where we could trace the pings and see where she's been."

"Or she dropped the phone when she got hit," Vandal suggested, "and she didn't take the time to find it when she was hauling ass out of here. She probably knows there's nothing on it that could compromise her location."

"It's still a risk. Fingerprints. DNA. Would you leave a burner behind like that?"

Vandal shrugged. "This woman nearly died the last time she was with you ten years ago. Now you're together for like five minutes and somebody sends an assassin to take her out. If I'm in her shoes, you're the last person I'd ever want to see again. So if she's leaving you any clues, I'd have to ask *why*."

"Well, first let's find out if she did," Bourne said. "I've got a contact at MI5. Actually, he was Nova's contact. But he should be able to run the data on Monika's phone."

He retrieved his own phone and found the contact information he wanted. He dialed, and a stuffy British voice answered before the phone had a chance to ring twice.

"Who is this, and how did you get this number?" Anthony Audley asked sharply.

"Hello, Tony."

There was a long pause on the line. Then Audley said in a frosty tone, "Cain?"

"That's right."

He wondered if the man would hang up on him. They'd never met, but he knew that Anthony Audley had had an on-again, off-again affair with Nova. He'd also heard rumors in the intelligence community that Audley blamed Bourne for Nova's death.

"It's been a long time," the Brit went on finally. "Since the fracas at the WTO."

"I remember."

"I wish I could say I miss our little chats, but that would be a lie. Are you in the UK? I'd appreciate a warning about your arrival in future, so I can alert my team about the inevitable violent and suspicious deaths."

"I'm not in the UK," Bourne replied, ignoring the jab, "but I'm looking for someone who may have a home base there. She was using a burner phone with a 44 country code."

"And you want me to run the pings and see where she's been?" Audley guessed.

"Yes."

The British agent hesitated. "You do realize I'm under no obligation to help you. You're not even officially part of Treadstone anymore, are you? The word is, you're at arm's length from your old colleagues."

"True."

"So who is this woman? Is she a British citizen?"

"I don't know. She's German-born. If she's in the UK now, she's living under a false identity even if she's naturalized."

"Why do you want to find her? To kill her?"

"No."

"And yet the women around you have a way of winding up dead, Cain," Audley said acidly.

"In fact, I'm trying to keep her alive."

"Is this a Treadstone operation?"

"No, it's personal," Jason said. "She's part of my past."

"The past you don't remember."

"Yes."

Audley was silent again. "One question."

"Okay."

"It's about Nova," he said. "Were you with her when she died?"

"I wasn't, but we were working on an operation together. So if you want to blame me, Tony—"

"I don't," Audley replied. "Truly, I don't. I knew who Nova was. Whatever the operation was, she knew the risks. And she had plenty of opportunities to live a safe life with me. She chose you instead. I have no problem with that. But I do want to know if she suffered in the end."

"I don't think so. She was shot. And she killed the woman who shot her before she died."

"Good for her." Audley sighed. "All right, give me the phone number."

Bourne rattled off the digits.

"I'll call you back," the man told him.

Jason ended the call. In the back seat, Vandal shook her head. "It's funny."

"What is?"

"All of us in the business pretending that we're robots. We don't feel a thing. We don't care. We fuck each other, but hey, it's just sex. What a crock of shit. That guy loved Nova, didn't he?"

"Yes, he did," Jason agreed.

"Did you love her, too? That was the whisper back then."

"I did at one point," he admitted. "Or I thought I did. We were making plans for the future. That was stupid for people like us."

"Then came Abbey Laurent," Vandal went on. "The writer. You loved her, too, right? And now you're fucking Johanna and pretending you don't care about her, which is so obviously a lie."

Bourne's jaw hardened. "What's your point, Vandal?"

"No point. I like you, Cain. When you put four bullets in your husband, it kind of sours you on men, you know? But you I like. I think if we fucked, I could fall for you. And there's probably a good sixty or seventy percent chance that I wouldn't end up shooting off your balls with my Glock."

"Sixty or seventy, huh?" Jason asked.

"Maybe as high as seventy-five."

His phone rang, and Vandal gave him a grin.

"Tony," Bourne said, taking the call. "What did you find out?"

"That phone has only been active for one day," Audley replied. "It signed on for the first time yesterday evening."

"Where?"

"In the middle of nowhere. It pinged off an A1 cell tower south of Berwick-upon-Tweed, near the coast in Northumberland."

"What's near there?"

"There's a causeway to Holy Island, one of those roads that's only accessible at low tide. Not much except a lot of sheep out there, plus the old Lindisfarne Castle. Pretty spot, but cold as hell when that North Sea wind blows. A couple of hundred hearty souls live in the village, but that's about it."

"Thank you, Tony."

Bourne hung up the phone. "A tidal causeway. Remember the message she sent me? 'Time buries us all like a rising tide.' I thought she meant Mont Saint-Michel, but now I wonder if this was about Lindisfarne."

"When I searched Chouat's office, there was a bottle of Lindisfarne Mead on his desk," Vandal added.

Jason nodded. "Chouat said it came with the note for David Webb. Sounds like Monika's leaving me a trail of breadcrumbs."

31

DAWN WAS STILL AN HOUR AWAY WHEN BOURNE ARRIVED BACK AT THE apartment in Pigalle. He found Johanna sitting up in bed, the white sheet nestled around her. Half a bottle of white wine sat on the nightstand; she'd been drinking. He said nothing at first, and neither did she, but they both knew what they wanted. He took off his clothes, showered, then climbed into bed with her and pulled her body against his. Their kisses grew from soft to hungry, and they made urgent love in the darkness.

He tried to keep Vandal's words out of his mind.

Now you're fucking Johanna and pretending you don't care about her, which is so obviously a lie.

When they were done, she poured Chardonnay for them. They drank it, although the wine was warm. The apartment was warm, too, and he got up and opened the window, letting in the wet-dog morning smell of Paris. He got back into bed and lay on his back next to her, their hands intertwined.

Finally, Johanna broke the silence and asked what she really wanted to know.

"Was it her?"

Jason didn't answer right away. He pictured Monika in his head, standing before La Géode, the woman from his past come to life again. Her elegant features. Her burgundy-red lips. A woman who kept a cool distance from him, who kept herself hidden behind a wall of puzzles and mysteries. And here he was in bed with her younger sister, who wanted no distance from him at all.

"Yes," he said. "It was her."

Johanna's hand flew to her mouth. "You saw her? You talked to her?"

"Briefly. But it was Monika. No question about it."

"Where is she? Can I see her now, too?"

"She disappeared from the park. Someone tried to kill her."

"Oh my God! Fuck! Was it the assholes from *Le Renouveau*? How did they find you so quickly?"

"No, I don't think it was them. They may not be the only people going after Monika. I think—I think it could be my people, too. I have connections to an organization in the American government. They have resources they use in these situations."

"Resources," Johanna said, frowning. "You mean people like you. Killers."

"Yes."

"But why would they want to kill Monika?"

"To cover up something from my past," Bourne said. "I don't know what. Not yet."

Johanna kissed him and caressed his face with her fingertips. "It must have been strange for you seeing her again."

"It was. It was also a trigger, sort of like watching your life pass before your eyes. I remembered things."

She heard the darkness in his voice. "Things? Like what?"

"None of it was organized. It was just a rush of jumbled memories. But my relationship with Monika was more complex than I realized. *She* was more complex. I don't know what to think about her now. She told me I already *know* who she is, or who she was. But I haven't been able to put the pieces together into anything that makes sense."

"Tell me," Johanna said. "Maybe I can help."

He stared at the ceiling and let the images wash over him again. Thinking about Monika brought it all back.

"That day when everything went to hell, when I went to the chalet, when I found that *Le Renouveau* had kidnapped her ... I'd forgotten something. Her apartment was empty. She was gone. She'd already left me."

"*What?* That can't be right."

"Did she say anything to you? Did she talk about being unhappy with our relationship?"

Johanna looked shocked. "No. Not a word. As far as I knew, you were the love of her life."

"I don't think so. Something had gone wrong between us. Maybe it was wrong from the beginning."

"Well, if that's true, then she was lying to both of us," Johanna said. "But I don't get it, Jason. Afterward, when she was running, she told me I could find you if I ever needed to reach her. She kept the back door going, too. Why would she do that if you weren't important to her?"

"I'm not sure. I'm still missing something." Bourne shook his head and added, "But she isn't hiding from me anymore. She's not running away. She wants me to chase her."

"What do you mean?"

"She left clues behind about her location, which she knew I'd find. They all point to a place called Holy Island on the British coast. It's remote, rugged, sparsely populated. I think that's where her home base is. Where she's been hiding. Do you know if that place had any special significance for her?"

"Holy Island?"

"It's also called Lindisfarne. There's an old castle there and a ruined priory."

Johanna closed her eyes. "I'm not sure. There's something, but it was long before I was born. Before my father remarried. I remember Monika telling me about a trip she took when she was a girl. It was the last trip she took while her mother was still alive. I don't know where it was, but she talked about a castle on a hill by the sea."

Bourne nodded. *A castle on a hill by the sea.*

"That's where we're going," he told her.

"We? I'm coming with you?"

"If you're willing. But I don't know what kind of reception to expect when we get there. *Le Renouveau* may already be waiting for us."

He thought: *Or Treadstone.*

"I'm not worried about that," Johanna said. "You'll keep me safe. If Monika's on that island, I want to see her again. I don't care if she's not the person I thought she was. She's still my sister."

"Okay, let's get dressed. We'll meet Vandal at Gare du Nord and take the Eurostar to London."

He got out of bed and went to the window. Johanna came up behind him and wrapped her arms around his waist. They stared out the window at the shadows of Pigalle, which were lightening with the dawn.

"You don't have to tell me this if you don't want to," Johanna murmured, her head leaning into his shoulder. "I mean, it's probably not fair of me to ask, but I sort of want to know what to expect. Am I going to lose you to her?"

"What?"

"Well, it's not like you owe me anything, and I'm not looking for promises. But when you're together with her again, are you going to want her and not me? What if Monika wants you back? What will you do?"

He turned around. Their bodies pressed tightly together as if they were made that way. He took her face in his hands. "Actually, I was just thinking about how much I like *you*. I haven't been involved like this with anyone since Abbey. And I told you, whatever I had with Monika isn't what I thought it was."

"You can't be sure about that," Johanna said.

"I'm not sure of anything in my past." Jason stroked along the soft line of her jaw. "There's one other thing I haven't mentioned. This is very important. Back then, did Monika talk about anyone else?"

"Anyone else? Like who?"

"Another man she was involved with."

Johanna's blue eyes widened with surprise. "Monika? No, of course not. She told me about you, and that was that. I mean, the two of you were engaged. Why would you think she was seeing someone else?"

"A memory came back to me in the park. I remembered Monika introducing me to someone at the Drei Alpenhäuser. It was just a casual thing at the door of the café. But I knew. I could see it in both of their faces. The two of them were lovers."

"This man," Johanna said. "Who was he? What did he look like?"

"I can't see him in my head. All I remember is—"

Jason stopped. In the warm morning air, his skin went cold.

"What is it?" Johanna asked.

"I remember his voice," Bourne said. "I remember, because I heard it again a few days later. Back then, I couldn't place who it was or where I'd heard it. Now I know. It was *him*. His voice. He was the man in the chalet."

VANDAL KNEW CAIN WAS RIGHT. SHE SHOULD HAVE SEEN A DOCTOR.

Her head throbbed with pain, making her dizzy whenever she turned too quickly. The swelling above her temple felt like an alien pushing its way out of her skull. Her vision kept blurring, and the brightness of the morning sun made her squint. For all she knew, she was bleeding into her brain.

She sat on the ground near Gare du Nord, and across the street was a hospital. She could have gone in there to be checked out. Do an MRI, a CT scan. But she knew what would happen then. A doctor would pull her out of the game, and she needed to be there at the end. On the island.

With Cain. With Monika.

Vandal checked her watch. She knew what she had to do. *Make the call.* Cain and Johanna would be arriving soon, and once they were together on the Eurostar, the risk of making contact would be far higher. Cain already didn't trust her. He'd be keeping a close eye on her as soon as they were together.

And if she said nothing?

What would happen then?

She squeezed her eyes shut against the bright light and the hammering inside her head. Then she forced herself to open them again.

Focus on the *mission*! She was the advance scout, the one who had to surveil the people at the train station and make sure it was safe to make the channel crossing by Eurostar.

Were the police monitoring the station, matching photos? Was a team from *Le Renouveau* watching the trains, expecting Cain might try to leave the country that way?

Was Treadstone?

But so far their escape route looked clear.

Vandal closed her eyes again. She covered her ears to quiet the persistent ringing, but that didn't work. A wave of nausea rose in her throat, and for a moment, she thought she'd have to get on her hands and knees and vomit. Then the wave passed. She was okay.

No. She wasn't okay.

As she sat on the ground, she found herself thinking about Lloyd. Her husband. She could still picture the scene in her head, four sadistic bullets in the man she loved, his agonized screams before she gave him the mercy shot between his eyes. And the *look* in those eyes. Pleading, disbelief—and, despite everything, love. He'd still loved her at the end even as she killed him.

My God!

What had she done?

She told herself that she wasn't the same woman she'd been back then. She was different. The drugs were gone. Her anger was gone. But none of that mattered. She still had to live with the memory.

Unlike Cain.

She couldn't believe she'd told Cain the truth about herself. She'd exposed her real identity to him, made herself vulnerable. He could have found her with a simple Google search. Every rule in Treadstone said not to let any of that happen.

Never give away who you really are.

Treadstone.

"You aren't that woman anymore," Vandal murmured aloud to herself.

She wasn't Sylene Jasper of East Los Angeles, addict and murderer. She wasn't staring at two decades of her life behind bars. Nash Rollins had taken her from that life and given her a fresh start. All she had to give up in return was everything—*her whole fucking identity!*—but she'd decided that there was nothing from her past that she wanted to keep with her. Sylene Jasper was dead.

Now she was *Vandal.*

That meant walking a moral tightrope every single day. All Treadstone agents did that, balancing the evil with the necessary. Right now she felt like she was on a wire strung between two high buildings and the wind was blowing hard.

Vandal stared at her phone. She punched in the digits.

"It's me," she said when she heard the voice on the other end. "Cain's found her. She's on an island off the northeast British coast. Lindisfarne. That's where he's going next. You better move fast."

32

FERMÉE.

The closed sign outside the entrance to Sainte-Chapelle explained why the Boulevard du Palais was empty today, rather than crowded with a long line of tourists waiting to gawk at the amazing stained glass. Franco Antonini checked the street anyway from behind his sunglasses, alert for anyone who might have followed him. It paid to be cautious. Even among the elite of *Le Renouveau*, moles were always a risk. He couldn't afford to be seen—or worse, to have this meeting recorded.

Not when they were so close to their objective.

He noted the town car parked in the taxi lane at the curb. It was unmarked, and the windows were smoked so that no one could see inside. Franco knew the driver; he'd selected him personally. When it came to the security and anonymity of *le commandant*, he took no chances. The driver would have made sure that the street was clear before letting his passenger disembark for the short walk to the chapel. The only people outside would be police, six of them, all armed with automatic weapons. They, too, had been individually selected for this assignment.

Their allies in the police and the military would be vital in everything that came next.

Franco approached the soot-stained entrance. The tallest of the police officers, rifle in hand, Kevlar vest over his blue uniform, nodded at Franco and gave the smallest of nods to the man at the gate.

The gate opened for him and Franco strolled inside. Alone, he crossed the interior courtyard to the front of the Gothic chapel, where dual archways pointed up to the massive rose window. Another police officer waited at the entrance and waved him through. He took the stairs to the upper chapel and emerged into the otherworldly glow of window after window of multicolored stained glass rising over his head. Sculptures of saints and angels looked down at him as he marched along the aisle. His leather dress shoes echoed on the marble all the way to the vaulted ceiling.

One man waited for him in the center of the chapel, caught in streaming rays of sunlight. He was tall and slim, in a perfectly fitted navy blue suit. His arms were folded as he admired the gold and glass.

"The majesty of what our ancestors built, hmm?" *le commandant* murmured. "We owe them a debt, Franco. And an obligation."

"Yes, sir."

"This is one of my favorite places in Paris."

"Mine, too, sir. But the tourists—"

"Oh, yes. Horrible people. No appreciation of sacredness and beauty. It's like going to Arpège and having them serve chicken nuggets. That's why I arrange for private reflection a couple of times a year."

"A very good idea, sir."

"Well, give me a report. I don't want either of us to remain here longer than necessary. Outsiders could see us."

Franco nodded. "The foreign media are in an uproar at the very possibility that *La Vraie* could win the election. The polls show a close race, but of course, the polls are irrelevant, other than for their public relations value. Our people are in place in key areas to manipulate the paper ballots. The recent expansion of voting machines in the denser urban areas will allow our IT experts to massage the results as necessary. We will win."

"Winning is only phase one," *le commandant* pointed out. "The results must also be challenged. Questioned. Disbelieved. That is how we sow the seeds of division."

"Yes, sir. The final tally will be well within the margin of error, even if our actual victory is sizable. Our media teams have begun seeding stories about the risks of fraud in both the primary round of voting and the inevitable recounts. We'll be arranging a sufficient number of minor irregularities to feed the conspiracy theorists. We have 'witnesses' ready to talk about improper ballot handling, voter suppression, invalid identifications, and so on. Computer experts will question the integrity of the voting software. From there, we'll be ready to make sure protests spill into violence, just as we've been doing throughout the campaign. What we've seen in the cities up to now will be mere prologue. The real revolution is coming. The country will explode."

Le commandant stayed silent for a moment, continuing to admire details in the stained glass. His arms remained folded over his chest. "And so our crackdown will be justified," he went on finally. "A national emergency that necessitates authoritarian rule. Order must be restored. The violence stopped."

"As we've planned for years," Franco agreed. "Naturally, our people in business, nonprofit, and the media will be ready to voice their support for the emergency measures. Already you can see widespread calls among the population for greater police action to quell the riots. Many are demanding a military response. Their voices will only grow louder with the next wave of violence."

"Meanwhile, the EU will mumble their displeasure and let us do what we want. The fat bureaucrats fear chaos above all else."

"And the Americans?" Franco asked.

Le commandant chuckled. "The Americans will play right into our hands as they always do. Divided and impotent. Half of them will call us Nazis, and half will call us the defenders of democracy. That will make it easy to isolate them."

"And after France, the movement spreads across Europe," Franco said.

"Yes, one by one. My God, Franco, we are so close. Can you feel it? All these years of planning, and we are so very close. France is the first domino. From there, the others will begin to fall. Germany next, and the rest will tumble easily after that. Either the Americans will eventually follow suit, or they'll be bystanders in the new order."

Franco watched *le commandant* clench his fists with enthusiasm.

"I also have news about David Webb," Franco added.

"Excellent. Tell me."

"Obviously, we were disappointed in Justin's failure in Switzerland and then the collapse of our trap in Hamburg. We've been trying to recapture Webb's trail since then without success, but fortunately, our source just checked in with new information. Webb—or Cain, as he is known now—is on his way to a location in the UK. Holy Island, also known as Lindisfarne. We believe this is where the woman, Monika, is located, so we'll be able to deal with both of them together."

"An assault team is ready?"

"Yes, sir. I've already organized a team that we'll dispatch to the island. Mercenaries. Untraceable."

Le commandant tapped a finger thoughtfully against his chin. "I want to be there."

"Sir?"

"At the end. When you have them. I want to be there. Arrange a helicopter. Obviously, we'll need a cover story for me, too. I don't expect any questions, but just in case, we'll want to be able to prove I was somewhere else."

"With respect, sir, I think that's very unwise," Franco replied, choosing his words carefully. "There's too much risk of exposure. Perhaps I could arrange to have them relocated once they've been isolated. You can deal with them here."

"And risk them escaping again along the way? No, no. When they are secure, I'll go in and out. An hour, no more. No one will see me."

"If that's what you want, I can arrange it, of course. But I strongly advise against—"

"Enough, Franco!" With a swipe of his hand, *le commandant* cut him off. "I am not a coward hiding in the shadows. I want to be there to witness the executions. You know that Webb and I have history. There are moments when you need to be face-to-face with your enemies to celebrate your victory."

Franco hesitated. He was on delicate ground now that he had his orders. But certain things had to be said, even with *le commandant*. He knew this man well, and he knew this situation was personal for him. In ten years, this was the only area where Franco had ever found his judgment to be compromised.

"I must ask, sir, is this really about Webb?" he went on quietly. "Is he the one you want to witness our triumph? Or is it about *her?*"

"I NEED TO GO," MONIKA TOLD HIM, GLANCING AT THE CLOCK ON THE HOTEL
nightstand. "I'm supposed to meet David at the Drei Alpenhäuser in half an hour."

She began to climb out of bed, but he took her hand and pulled her naked body beneath him again. "First we fuck one more time. I'll be quick. I want you to see your fiancé freshly fucked."

Her beautiful face screwed up with anger. "Shut up. Don't talk like that."

"Why not? You said yourself that you don't intend to give me up. Nothing changes if you get married. So why should you care what we do?"

"It's complicated."

He scoffed. "If you were French, you would realize it's not complicated at all. We don't let marriage get in the way of sex. Come, have more wine. Then I get between your legs and you come again."

Monika pulled brusquely away from him. She got out of bed and went to the armoire, where her clothes were neatly hung. "You misunderstand our relationship."

"Do I?"

"We're useful to each other. It's business. That's all."

"Really? That's all? And yet we have sex whenever we're together. Is that part of the business? What does that make you, my darling?"

Her eyes shot daggers at him, but he liked seeing her angry, because her face rarely showed any emotion at all. More often, she was like a sculpture in the Musée d'Orsay, immovable and inscrutable. Truly beautiful women were rarely good in bed. They acted as if you should thank them when they spread their legs. But that was fine. He had others to satisfy his baser desires. With Monika, the victory was in having her surrender to him even when she hated doing so.

He watched her from the bed as she got dressed. What a show she put on! First her makeup, so careful, so perfect, the faintest blush on her cheeks. And those lips! My God, the deep red of that mouth, like a gorgeous vampire. Then her lush blond hair, brushed and smoothed until it was a golden waterfall; the flimsy silk of her bra and panties; the dress clinging to her milky skin; the straps of her high heels tied with those elegant fingers. It was like watching Aphrodite come to life.

She began to fit her jewelry to her ears, wrists, and neck. Paste, but high-class paste. Everything about Monika was high-class. He'd known that since he first met her in Brussels three years earlier—two people staring at each other across a conference table, in a stuffy room filled with stuffy people. He couldn't remember whether he had seduced her or she had seduced him, or whether they had both assumed they were manipulating the other. But it didn't matter. As she'd said, they were useful to each other.

Oh yes. Monika was very, very useful. In so many ways. More than she ever knew. Like the time he'd checked her phone while she was in the shower and found her travel plans for Ibiza two days later.

A catastrophe for Le Renouveau *narrowly avoided.*

"So tell me more about this mysterious David," he said.

Her head turned slightly from where she was considering herself in the mirror. "Why do you care?"

"Because as long as I've known you, you've been a free spirit, and yet here you are engaged after mere weeks together. How oddly impulsive of you."

"My personal life isn't your concern," *she snapped.*

"I'm not prying, darling. I'm merely curious. What is he like? What kind of man is he?"

"Do you want the truth?"

"From you? Always."

She pierced him with her blue eyes. Her Gothic mouth seemed to smile without any movement of her lips. "David could kill you with his bare hands."

For just a moment, he blanched with surprise. "Seriously?"

"Seriously."

"Well, how very interesting. Is that what drew you to him? His physical prowess? Does he bring out the animal in you in a way I can't, darling?"

"I'm drawn to him because he's the best man I've ever met," Monika replied, but he noted that her typical sadness had returned to her face.

He got out of bed and began to get dressed himself, retrieving his suit from the floor where he'd shed it as they went from the hotel room door to the bed. "That's quite a compliment coming from you, given your acute observations of human nature. Obviously, I must meet this man."

"No. Definitely not."

"Oh, not to join you for dinner. Don't worry. I'm a friend of yours from Paris, that's all. You introduce me, and I leave."

"That is not going to happen."

"I'm not asking, my darling. I'm saying I will meet him. Either you introduce me to him, or we go back to bed and fuck again, which is likely to muss up all that lovely makeup. Take your pick."

Monika stared back with barely disguised contempt. "A friend from Paris. A minor acquaintance. Thirty seconds at the restaurant, and then you leave."

"Merci beaucoup, my love."

He finished putting on his suit. It didn't take long. Men were so much faster at such things than women. He was already putting on his raincoat when he heard a text arrive at his phone, which he'd been expecting. He checked it and found a message from one of his recruits in Engelberg, an economics teacher named Gavin Wright.

Do you have any information on David Webb?

With a smile at Monika across the room, he tapped out a reply.

Oh, yes. Mr. Webb is most definitely a spy.

Then he turned off his phone. "Shall we?"

They left the hotel room, and he insisted on her taking his arm. They took the elevator to the lobby and exited into the summer streets of Zurich, where a light mist was falling. The Drei Alpenhäuser was four blocks away, and Monika stayed archly silent next to him as they made their way to the restaurant, him covering her with an umbrella. He wondered if her tension was fear of what he would say, or of what he would do—or fear of her young man realizing the truth about their relationship.

Because, of course, he would. Men always did. Those were things you couldn't hide.

He recognized David Webb from a block away. Gavin had already sent photos and a full bio of the teacher who was trying to make his way inside Le Renouveau. *Webb was standing outside the Drei Alpenhäuser, waiting for Monika. His gaze picked out the two of them on the street immediately. And yes, he knew. Webb's eyes took his measure and sussed him out as a rival with barely a second glance.*

He also saw a brutal hardness in Webb to go along with his obvious intelligence. He was definitely a threat. Monika was right. Given the opportunity, this young man could kill him in an instant.

They crossed the street.

Monika greeted Webb with such naked discomfort that she may as well have been wearing a scarlet A in the swell of her lovely breasts. She knew her fiancé knew. All three of them knew, and none of them said a word.

"This is an old friend of mine from Paris," Monika said awkwardly. "He's in Zurich for the day. We bumped into each other."

Webb extended a hand to him. His handshake was absolutely crushing. My God, the strength the man had!

"I'm David Webb."

"A pleasure, David," he replied. "My name is Chrétien. Chrétien Pau."

PART THREE

PART THREE

33

AS NIGHT BEGAN TO FALL, THE ISLAND OF LINDISFARNE TOOK SHAPE
through Bourne's binoculars. The landmass was small, barely two
square miles located not even two miles off the Northumberland coast.
He could see the causeway stretching across damp sand, with the rising
tide already encroaching on the lonely road from the North Sea. A
charcoal sky hung low and menacing over their heads, blowing mist on
the Land Rover he'd parked in the tall grass. He could see a few cars
racing to reach the mainland before the water submerged the causeway
and isolated the island for the next seven hours.

"Should we be heading over there?" Johanna asked with concern
as a wave slithered across the road like a lookout and then withdrew.

"Soon," Jason replied. He checked his watch and saw that they were
five minutes past the safe crossing time. "If anyone's coming for us,
they'll head over when they think no one is coming behind them. So I
want to see who crosses at the last minute."

"By playing chicken with the tide?"

"Yeah. Pretty much. But we'll be fine."

He felt a cold wind on his face, mixed with rain. The stiff sea breeze whistled in his ears. Johanna stood next to him, her arms wrapped tightly around her chest. Her face glistened with dampness, and her long hair clung to her neck. Her blue eyes had a faraway look as she stared at the low hills of the island.

"Do you really think Monika's over there?" she murmured.

"I do."

"Does she know we're coming?"

"I think so."

In the trees behind them, a branch snapped like the crack of a gun. Bourne swung that way, Sig in hand, but he relaxed when he saw Vandal making her way back to the Land Rover. He was surprised that she'd made any noise on her approach, and he noticed that she took a wrong step in the dirt, then recovered.

"Anything?" he asked.

"One car parked near a farm road a quarter mile away."

"Who is it?"

"It's a young couple. They're watching the sheep in the field, but mostly they're making out. I don't know whether they're planning to cross, but if they are, it'll be soon. I don't see any other traffic heading our way."

"What's your take on the lovebirds?"

"They look harmless," Vandal said.

Bourne pricked up his ears as a vehicle approached on the mainland road. A small red Ford Fiesta crept between the marshlands, its engine putt-putting like a mouse on a squeaky treadmill. He aimed the binoculars toward the car in time to spot a dark-haired woman in the passenger's seat, her hands clenched around the dashboard. She didn't look more than twenty years old.

"That's them," Vandal said.

Jason couldn't see the driver from this angle, but he agreed with Vandal that the woman didn't look like a threat.

"All right, time to go."

The three of them clambered into the Land Rover. Johanna took the back, Vandal rode shotgun, and Jason sat on the right-hand driver's side. The vehicle bumped out of the trees and back onto the narrow road, and he turned toward Lindisfarne. Daylight was fading fast and the rain intensified, falling in sheets from the dark clouds. He drove past tidal pools and bright green moss that inched up to the edge of the causeway. The wide swath of brown sand beyond the road had already disappeared as black water slouched in from both sides.

Not far offshore, he reached a turnaround where a sign warned them to turn back if the tide had reached the pavement, which it had. Ahead of them, the incoming sea no longer receded from the road with each wave. He accelerated into the water, kicking up a cloud of white spray. Ripples from the tires spread out with a roar behind them. From above, rain poured across the windshield.

It didn't take him long to catch up to the young couple in the Ford Fiesta. The smaller car inched through the water, taking the dead center of the two lanes and making it impossible for him to pass. Bourne came within a car's length of their bumper, but he had nowhere to go. They reached the middle of the causeway, where a weather-beaten refuge tower rose on stilts above the tide. The low bridge near the tower hadn't taken on water yet, but only a few feet ahead of them, the sea had already begun to claim the rest of the road between the bridge and the island.

Momentarily on dry land, the Fiesta stopped.

"Aw, Jesus, guys, come on," Vandal murmured.

Jason tapped the horn gently, trying to nudge them forward, because they only had a few minutes before the water would be deep enough to float the two vehicles off the road. But the Fiesta remained where it was, its engine idling, its brake lights on. Suddenly, the passenger door jerked open. The young woman got out onto the bridge, screaming at her companion behind the wheel.

"You fucking idiot, look what you've done! I told you not to cross, I told you! Now we're trapped! This is my mom's car, Donny, shit! I am so screwed!"

Bourne got out, too. He stood behind the driver's door and called to the woman. "You should be fine if you leave now and go slowly. It's not too deep yet. But don't wait. Another five minutes, and we've all got trouble."

The young woman stared back at him with wild eyes. She pointed to the far side of the bridge, where bare pavement descended into the dark sea. The rain soaked her clothes and the wind tossed her dark hair into a tornado.

"Fine? Does that look fine? Does that look fine to you? Are you crazy?"

She kept screaming at Bourne, and her keening voice distracted him as the driver's door of the Fiesta swung open. He lost a split second of concentration.

He'd forgotten the rule.

Looks can be deceiving.

Treadstone.

The woman's companion emerged from behind the wheel. The speed of his movement suddenly alerted Jason's mind to imminent danger, and before he even spotted the semiautomatic rifle in the man's hands, he shouted a warning.

"Get down, get down, get down!"

The driver began firing. In the same instant, the young woman dug under her T-shirt and came out with a Glock, and she opened fire as well. Bourne threw himself off the bridge into the shallow water, then splashed backward to put the frame of the Land Rover between his body and the killers. The windshield of the SUV exploded like popcorn as bullets raked the interior. The passenger doors flew open, and Vandal and Johanna dived for the water on the opposite side of the bridge. The pillars of the refuge tower gave them cover, but the woman with the pistol shifted her aim to the water, while the driver advanced toward the Land Rover, firing his HK416 as he came.

Bourne dug his Sig from the holster in the small of his back. Around him, bullets punctured the water like a hailstorm. He scrambled out of the rising tide and ducked behind the SUV. The Land Rover rocked with the wind, and more glass flew as the driver fired through the vehicle, sending shrapnel over Bourne's head.

Behind the refuge tower, he heard Vandal shooting back. The young woman, whoever she was, was no match for the Treadstone agent. With a handful of shots, Vandal took her down, and the explosions from the Glock ceased. But the other shooter re-aimed his rifle toward the tower, and Vandal and Johanna both splashed away in the water with bullets chasing them. Bourne rose up and fired through the broken rear window of the Land Rover, one shot, two, three, four. The fourth bullet found its mark in the shooter's temple, and the man keeled sideways into the water. The rifle spilled from his hands to the pavement of the bridge.

Bourne ran to the tower and extended his hand to help Johanna out of the water. He did the same with Vandal, but as Vandal reached the pavement, one of her legs buckled, and she slipped heavily against the tower's wooden frame. Her eyes went blank for a moment, then refocused. Jason grabbed her and held her up, and he slapped his hand gently against her cheeks.

"Are you okay? Are you hit?"

She blinked, then shook her head. "No, I'm fine, just a little dizzy. Come on, let's go."

He helped her stretch out across the back seat and took his place behind the wheel. Johanna was already in the passenger seat. He tapped the accelerator of the Land Rover, bringing the SUV up against the rear bumper of the Fiesta. The motor made a grinding noise as he forced the smaller car out of the way. Slowly, the Fiesta jerked forward, and Bourne kept pushing until the other car tipped from the side of the bridge and rolled into the waves, which swarmed over its tires.

Beyond the bridge, there was nothing but unbroken sea stretching ahead of him. The shore of Holy Island still looked distant, a smudge of land against the horizon, which was black from the storm and the growing darkness. The road dipped down, and the SUV churned forward, sinking into the water. He drove slowly, hearing waves slap against the doors, alert to the moment when the tires might lose their grip on the road and leave the SUV floating and spinning toward the North Sea.

His windshield was gone except for a few jagged glass teeth. The rain and gales pounded his face. He tried to wipe his eyes, but even when he could see, his headlights blurred under the rising water. He kept driving, foot by foot, inch by inch. Thirty seconds passed. Then a minute. Then another minute. Slowly, the hills of Lindisfarne grew larger and closer. He felt the Land Rover buck as if it would lift off the ground, but then it landed solidly on the pavement again. Squinting, blinking, he spotted green scrub rising above the waterline. The tide seemed to suck the vehicle down, desperate to hold it in its grasp, but with a squeal, the tires broke free and the SUV swerved out of the sea and onto the rain-soaked road.

They were on the island.

Bourne drove another half a mile, until they were well into the rolling meadows. Then he let the Land Rover drift to a stop. The ice-cold rain pounded on the roof like thunder, whipping through the SUV and stinging their skin. He tried to orient himself, but they were in the middle of nowhere, with no light to penetrate the night. All they could do was keep driving until they reached the town.

"Those two," Johanna said. "The ones in the Fiesta. Who were they?"

"A welcoming party," Bourne replied. "The killers are already here."

NASH ROLLINS SPENT THE EVENING NURSING A SMITH'S ALE AT A PICNIC bench outside the Crown & Anchor pub. He sat under a patio umbrella while the downpour turned the streets of the town into black rivers. As darkness fell, he'd had the village to himself for the first hour. The tourists were gone, and the locals were tucked inside their homes out of the cold and rain. But now he had company. A few minutes earlier, he'd heard the throb of helicopters getting closer. He'd seen their lights in the sky and followed their track as they descended to land in the empty green fields behind the village.

Now an assault team had begun to spread one by one through the deserted streets. He counted at least a dozen men, dressed to blend in, no heavy weaponry in view, but no doubt with plenty of firepower under their nylon jackets. They didn't know where to go—they didn't know where *she* was yet—but it was a small town. It wouldn't take them long to zero in on their target. The woman the villagers knew as Sarah Tedford was the woman formerly known as Monika Roth.

It was time to move.

From where he was, Nash could see the beachfront street a block away and the pretty little house by the sea with the stone fence and the garden. Her refuge. Her getaway. He pushed himself up from the bench, not bothering with an umbrella. He let the rain soak his swept-back gray hair and drip in streaks under the collar of his long coat like icy fingernails. With one hand, he kept a tight hold on his cane. His other hand stayed secure inside his pocket.

He limped down the alley behind the Lindisfarne Priory. He stayed close to the green hedge, not trying to hide. He whistled and sang off-key—"Raindrops Keep Fallin' on My Head"—the way an old man who's had a little too much might do. Ahead of him, at the corner, he saw one of *them*. From the helicopters. It was a man in his twenties, six feet tall, wool cap over his head, wearing a brown waxed jacket, jeans, and Wellingtons. The man's hands were loose, but Nash assumed one of his guns was in a jacket pocket, and he could see the bulge at the man's ankle where he kept his backup pistol.

The man saw Nash coming. He wasn't worried about an old man in the rain. Instead, he saluted Nash with a finger at his cap and said, "Good evening, sir."

"Good evening to you," Nash replied, adopting a British accent and noting that the man's husky voice was Eastern European. The killers were hired help. Contract mercenaries.

"What brings you to the island?" Nash asked. "Or did you get caught by the tide?"

"I'm looking for a friend who lives in town," the man replied. "Maybe you know her. Blond hair, forties, very attractive."

"What's your friend's name?"

The man hesitated, which gave away the game.

"Monika," he replied finally.

Nash shook his head. "Sorry, there's no Monika on the island. Believe me, I know everyone. Lived here for years."

"Then I must have it wrong. Is there anyone else who matches that description? Maybe under a different name."

Nash chuckled. "You don't know your friend's name?"

"She's more like a friend of a friend. We've never met."

"Ah, I see. Well, I'm afraid there are no attractive blondes around here to keep an old man awake. If only there were, this place might be a little less bleak when the tide comes in. Sorry, I hope you find her."

He continued past the man with a friendly shake of his cane. Then he turned around, drawing his Ruger SR22 with its Silent-SR suppressor. Without a word, he calmly fired a single shot into the man's forehead. The gun made a muffled crack that the noise of the wind covered. The hired help, who didn't even have time to look surprised, went down like a heavy sack of flour.

Nash glanced around the empty street to make sure that he was alone and that no one else from the assault team came running. He took the man's collar and dragged his body behind an overgrown bush of Russian sage outside a nearby cottage. A trail of blood followed, but the rain quickly washed it away into the dirt and rocks of the alley.

He returned his gun to his pocket. He popped his Union Jack umbrella and crossed the street to the stone wall that ringed the beachfront house. A row of daffodils grew along the base of the wall. On his left, he could see headlands rising above the North Sea, the walls of St. Mary's Church, and the ruins of the old priory, which was surrounded by the graves of a medieval cemetery. Down the path that curled around the church, he saw the bobbing beam of a flashlight. They didn't have much time. More men were coming.

A wooden gate led through the stone wall. He let himself inside and closed the gate behind him, and when he turned toward the garden, he found himself staring into the black barrel of a Glock. A beautiful blond woman, her face elegant even in the driving rain, held the gun at the end of her outstretched arms. She stared darkly at him, but the suspicion fled as she recognized his face under the umbrella.

"Nash," she said. "Jesus. I almost killed you."

She lowered the gun, and he leaned forward and kissed her like a daughter.

"Hello, Shadow. Sorry for the late visit, but we need to get you out of here right now."

34

BOURNE DROVE THE LAND ROVER INTO THE CENTER OF THE LINDISFARNE village and parked it near a café that was closed for the night. The buildings around them were small and old, mostly constructed of rough stone to withstand the extreme North Sea climate. Other than a few lights in the handful of inns and cottages, the island was dark. The rain showed no sign of stopping, but the noise covered their footsteps.

The three of them were alone, but not for long. At a corner half a block away, he spotted the flash of someone struggling to light a cigarette in the downpour. Bourne signaled Vandal and Johanna to stay back, then watched as the man, who was dressed in black, spoke into a radio on his wrist. A few seconds later, he marched away down the middle of the narrow lane, his boots splashing through puddles.

"We've got company," Jason murmured.

"Our friends in the Fiesta must have radioed ahead when they spotted us coming up behind them," Vandal said.

Bourne nodded. "So they know we're here. The question is, who finds Monika first."

He paused at an intersection and glanced toward the far end of the street.

"Let's split up," he told Vandal. "We'll cover more ground that way."

Then he took the measure of the other agent with a frown of concern. "If you're okay to be on your own."

"I'm fine," Vandal snapped. "Don't worry about me."

She pushed past him through the intersection, crossing under the gauzy halo of a streetlight. Jason took Johanna's hand, and they turned left down a village street lined by stone walls overrun with ivy. He looked for anyone outside—a teenager on a bicycle, a tough islander walking his dog in the rain—but for now, the population of the town was just them and the unseen killers from *Le Renouveau*.

And, somewhere, Monika.

They passed the island post office, then a small church. Neither building had any lights on inside. At the end of the block, a crumbling wall led into farm fields that stretched toward the sea and the horizon. Where the clouds met the land in the middle of the emptiness, he could see a lone hill with sheer cliffs rising above the rest of the island. A few squares of light outlined the fortress walls of Lindisfarne Castle.

He listened carefully, hearing nothing but the rain.

Where are they?

Bourne took Johanna down a cross street that ran beside the meadow. He kept his Sig in his hand. The road ended at Marygate, which followed the island's half-moon harbor toward the castle. The opposite direction led back into town. He braced his gun hand when he saw a dark figure emerge from an alley near them, but he let the Sig go loose when he realized that it was Vandal.

She joined them in the middle of the one-lane road.

"Nothing so far," she said.

They walked three abreast, filling the street shoulder to shoulder like gunfighters in an old Western. The storm lashed their faces, and their wet clothes became a second skin. Block by block, they explored the town, but he found no one who could give them a clue about Monika's identity.

Then, as they reached a small plaza near the town's priory, a guttural noise erupted outside the whitewashed wall of an old pub. The slap of fists landed heavily on skin, followed by a heavy grunt.

Bourne squinted through the rain. In a small stretch of green grass, two men in black held a third man against the fat trunk of an oak tree. Jason whispered to Johanna to wait in the shadows, and then he and Vandal closed on the scene, their movements covered by the roar of the wind. When they were within twenty feet, he could hear one of the men demanding answers from the man held against the tree.

Answers about Monika.

"You know who the fuck she is! Don't lie! Where the hell is she?"

Another heavy blow followed the questions, then another loud grunt of pain. But the young man at the tree spat blood and said nothing. He was a Brit, and he wasn't about to give up his neighbor.

Bourne aimed his Sig, then lowered it again. The wild gusts off the sea made it impossible to keep his arm steady. The three men were clustered so closely together that he couldn't shoot without the risk of hitting the man in the middle. He gave a hand signal to Vandal. They separated, both crouching low, both silent and invisible. Step by step, they approached the killers, Bourne coming up directly behind the man asking the questions, Vandal behind his partner.

Neither one saw them.

They inched closer. Ten feet away. Then five feet. As Bourne drew within striking distance, he slid his Thompson dagger from the scabbard on his calf. Vandal did the same. He raised three fingers toward her, signaling a countdown for a simultaneous assault.

Two fingers.

One.

Now!

Bourne sprang off his knees, fast and deadly. His right arm sliced the knife around the man's neck, his blade severing the carotid artery and showering them both with blood. He threw the man to the ground, holding his twitching body in place with his knee, the killer's face staring up with shock and terror.

Next to him, Vandal did the same, but the assault went wrong.

Her boot skidded on mud as she jumped, and the man heard her coming. As she swung her blade, he deflected the blow. Her knife slashed across his forearm, but his finger squeezed the trigger of his pistol, unleashing muffled spits in the air before Vandal was able to grab his wrist. The two of them struggled hand to hand, like arm wrestlers. From the ground near them, Bourne saw that Vandal was weak and easily outmatched by the man's strength. When the man got one hand free, he drove a fist into Vandal's throat, making her stagger backward, choking. He brought his gun around, not even six feet away, and fired point-blank. Blood and rain made his fingers slip, and he missed her head by a fraction of an inch.

But he wouldn't miss twice.

Bourne threw himself at the man and took him hard to the ground, burying his dagger to the hilt under the man's arm as they fell. The man clung to the gun with his other hand, letting off another wild round, but Vandal was back on him a moment later. She crushed his wrist with her boot, then kicked the gun away. She kicked him again as Bourne held him, a steel toe to the skull that made his eyes roll back into his head and fall shut. He'd be out for a long time.

Vandal helped Jason to his feet.

"Don't say it," she murmured. "Don't fucking say a word."

He didn't have to. They both knew. She'd nearly gotten herself killed. She wasn't operating at one hundred percent; she was barely at fifty percent and getting worse. For now, she was more liability than asset.

Bourne checked the other killer—he was dead now from the knife across his throat—then turned his attention to the man at the tree. The young man had slid to the wet ground, his face swollen and bruised, his mouth bloody. He was solidly built, but he'd taken a beating and was going to be hurting for a while.

"Who are you?" Jason asked.

"Nick Landy," the man replied, awkwardly spitting out a loose tooth. "I work at the pub. I came out for a smoke after I cleaned up the place for the night, and these guys grabbed me. Jesus Christ, that one's dead, isn't he?"

Bourne didn't answer. He took the picture of Monika from his pocket and illuminated it with a penlight. "Were they asking you about this woman?"

Landy studied the photo. He took a moment to recognize the younger face, then nodded. "Yeah. They called her Monika, but that's Sarah. Sarah Tedford. She's lived on the island for years."

"Did you tell them who she is? Or where she lives?"

"Fuck no. We protect our own around here."

"Good," Bourne said. "Then talk to me. Tell me where I can find her. It's urgent."

Landy looked back and forth from Bourne to Vandal. "Who are you guys? What is this about?"

"I can't tell you that, Nick. I'm sorry. But these men want to kill her. There are others like them on the island, and even if you kept quiet about her, somebody else will break. They'll figure out where she is soon enough."

Landy assessed Bourne's face, which was streaked with the dead man's blood. Then he raised an arm and pointed down the block. "She's right down there. A minute away. The seaside cottage at the end of the street."

"Thank you, Nick."

Bourne grabbed Vandal's shoulder, and they retreated from the plaza. They rejoined Johanna, and the three of them followed the alley behind the priory. The rain hadn't stopped; the wind off the sea roared in their faces. Jason saw the outline of a small cottage ahead of them, with lights burning inside the windows. Monika's cottage. He felt Johanna tense, and he knew she was thinking the same thing.

This was the end of the road. The end of the hunt.

But when they got to the road that ran beside the coast, Bourne saw that the gate leading into the garden ahead of them was open. Beyond it, the door to Monika's house was open, too, the rain pouring inside.

"Oh my God," Johanna murmured. "Oh my God, they already found her."

He checked in both directions and saw no one nearby. To their left, a wall led along the church grounds and past it to the priory ruins and the island's old cemetery. To their right, he saw more headland cottages, mostly dark. He stepped through the wooden gate into the garden, which looked out on the sea. Smoke from a fireplace charred the air. There were footsteps in the mud, already blurred by rain. He noted security cameras glowing with dots of red light along the old eaves of the cottage.

But he didn't see what he was afraid he would see—Monika's dead body in the grass.

The three of them headed for the open front door. He crossed the threshold, moving left with his Sig, and Vandal followed, moving right. A few steps led him down into a living room paneled in dark wood, with lights dimmed and a fire still burning hot in the fireplace. He noted a mug of tea on a coffee table and a leatherbound copy of *Tess of the d'Urbervilles* beside it. When he checked the mug, he found the porcelain still warm to the touch.

Monika had left only minutes earlier, and she'd done so in a hurry.

Johanna joined him from the foyer. She looked around the room with a kind of shocked disbelief. "This is her. This one feels like her place."

"How so?" he asked.

"Remote. Lonely. That's Monika."

Jason noted the cottage's furnishings, which were antique and beautifully crafted, but not made for comfort. The house had a clean, elegant look, but it also had a sterile feel to it, like a museum display rather than a home. Johanna was right; that fit with what he remembered of Monika. Beyond the living room, he found a small library. Books and compact discs filled one wall, and he didn't see an author or composer from the twentieth century. Ocean paintings adorned the brickwork on the other walls—original oils, all expensive—but he didn't see anything personal in the room. No photographs of people. No souvenirs. No computers or devices. No clutter, no papers, no mail on the rolltop desk.

Nothing that would give an outsider any idea who this woman was. She was not Sarah Tedford and not Monika Roth.

But he doubted that many outsiders ever saw this place. The owner of this cottage lived alone in her own world, an island on an island on an island.

Vandal joined them. "The rest of the cottage is empty. No one's here. But there's something you need to see."

Bourne frowned. He and Johanna followed Vandal to the stairs directly opposite the front door. The steep, tight staircase led up into a small master bedroom, where a bay window looked out over the garden and the sea. Here, like the rest of the house, he saw nothing identifiable or personal. There was makeup and perfume on a mirrored desk, but that was all. When he checked the bathroom, he saw a couple of prescription medicines on the shelf—simvastatin for cholesterol, olmesartan for blood pressure—but the name and barcodes on the bottles had been scraped off.

"In here," Vandal said.

She pointed to the walk-in closet, which was barely six feet deep and neatly organized with women's clothes. Bourne noticed a pull-down ladder leading up to a small square hole in the ceiling, which gave access to the sharp gables of the attic. He glanced upward into the darkness.

"I checked it out," Vandal said. "I thought maybe she was hiding up there."

The expression on her face made him curious. He took hold of the ladder and climbed, and behind him, Johanna did the same. When he got to the attic, he helped her through the small opening. The space was unfinished and cold, the floor irregular with wooden beams and protruding nails. He found a light switch on an overhead timber, and he turned it on. A single bulb dangling over their heads gave off a dim glow.

But that was enough to see what was around them.

"Fuck," Johanna murmured.

The attic was filled with guns. Semiautomatic rifles from American, European, and Russian manufacturers. A Steyr sniper's rifle. At least thirty pistols, including Sigs, Glocks, Rugers, and HK models, along with ammunition and multiple suppressors. Explosives. Daggers. Ninja hand claws. Fighting sticks. Garrotes. Lockpick sets. It was an arsenal to rival anything Bourne kept himself.

Based on the open spaces he saw among the rows of weapons, at least one rifle and accompanying ammunition were missing. Monika was armed.

He crossed to an oversized jewelry box on a wooden table. When he opened it up, he found a trove of diamonds—plus thousands of dollars in cash in multiple currencies and at least ten passports from different countries, American, British, German, Swedish, Icelandic, and others. Every passport had a different name and the same photo.

Monika's photo.

Bourne knew this scene. He knew what it meant.

He'd asked Monika in Paris: *Who are you?*

She'd told him: *You know who I am.*

And she was right. He looked around the attic, and he knew exactly who she was, who she'd always been, now and ten years ago. He realized with a cold wave of bitterness that everything he'd been told about his past was a lie. A cover-up. But this was more than simple deception; this was worse. David Webb had lived a lie even before he became Cain, even before Nash recruited him. He'd been played, manipulated, twisted, every movement skillfully controlled like a marionette.

Controlled by one woman.

You know who I am.

Yes, he knew now. Monika was Treadstone.

35

JASON HAD NO TIME TO PROCESS THE IMPLICATIONS OF WHAT HE'D FOUND.
Through the drafty walls of the attic, he heard cracks of gunfire outside
the cottage. *Le Renouveau* was on the hunt. He grabbed an Astra StG4
rifle from Monika's arsenal, then jumped down the ladder to the floor
of the bedroom closet. Reaching up, he let Johanna slide into his arms.

"Stay in the house," he told her. "I have to go."

"What? No! I'm coming with you."

"Not now. Not into a firefight." He turned to Vandal, who was waiting in the bedroom doorway. "You stay here, too. They may make a
move on the cottage if they don't realize Monika is already gone. Take
cover up in the attic if you need to, and blast anyone who comes up the
stairs."

Vandal stared at him coldly. "What do you think you're doing,
Cain? You can't take them on alone."

"Do I have a choice? Look at you. You can barely stand up, Vandal.
Your vision keeps blurring, and you've got a headache like a spike
through your skull. Right? You're no help to me that way."

She said nothing, which told him everything.

"Stay here," he repeated. But as he left, he suddenly reached out and grabbed her by the neck with one hand. His voice was harsh, like the burnt ash of a thousand lies. "Tell me one thing first. Did you know?"

"Know what?"

"Don't play games with me. Did you know Monika is *Treadstone*?"

She shook her head. "I didn't. I didn't, Cain, I swear. I guessed it when I saw what she has upstairs, but that was the first time I even suspected. Nash didn't tell me. He kept me in the dark as much as you."

"Does Nash know I'm here?" Jason asked.

He tightened his grip on her neck.

"Did you *tell him* I was coming to the island?" he asked again.

Vandal struggled to take a breath. "Yes."

"Fuck!"

Bourne wrapped his other hand around Vandal's throat and pushed in his thumbs against her windpipe. The other agent didn't fight back; she just squirmed and choked in his grip. But Johanna screamed and jumped across the closet at him, prying at his hands and trying to dislodge him.

"Jason, no! Don't! Let her go!"

He felt the wave of anger drain from his body, and he backed down. He dropped his hands from Vandal's neck, and she jerked away from him, massaging her throat and coughing as she tried to speak. "I'm sorry, Cain. I had no choice. I told you my situation. You know why I had to tell him. Nash swore he had *nothing* to do with the assault in Paris. It wasn't him. And now that you know Monika is Treadstone, does it make any sense? Nash wouldn't go after one of our own."

"Nash is capable of anything."

"Maybe, but not this," Vandal insisted. "He *didn't* do it."

Downstairs, outside, Bourne heard more gunfire. He couldn't wait any longer.

"Keep Johanna safe," he told her.

He slung the StG4 into firing position and hurried down the cottage's old stairs. He ignored the front door and ran the opposite way, locating a back door that led from the kitchen. Outside, he found a gate through the seawall at the rear of the garden, which took him to a trail running along the shallow cliff. Below him, angry waves crashed against the shore, and the bay was laced with whitecaps. The rain had finally stopped as dark clouds raced across the sky, but the wind nearly blew him off his feet.

Another shot cracked nearby. He could barely hear it as the gusts whistled.

Bourne crept to the end of the wall that bordered Monika's house. There, he found an empty field, its long grass swirling. Ahead of him, against the night sky, he saw the dark silhouette of the Church of St. Mary. A flashlight beam swept across tall panels of stained glass; someone was in the churchyard. He inched forward, the rifle propped in the crook of his arm. At the end of the field, he climbed a low wall onto a path that led behind the church and into the cemetery. The high walls of St. Mary's rose above his head, and he could hear the humming vibration of the bell in the steeple. Around him, moss-covered old headstones leaned toward the ground. He stayed low, switching his position from grave to grave. A muzzle flashed not far away, but whoever was there wasn't firing at him. The bullet whipped the other way, toward the ruins of the medieval priory.

Someone moved. A man had been crouched behind one of the headstones, and now he stood up. His outline revealed a tall, lean man, a suppressed pistol in his hands. He was no more than thirty feet away. The man put his wrist near his mouth and whispered into a radio. His gun arm shifted, and Bourne heard a new magazine being snapped into the pistol. He narrowed the gap between them, timing his footsteps in the wet grass with the thunder of waves on the beach. He slipped the strap of the rifle over his neck and leaned the weapon against the nearest headstone.

He found his knife in its scabbard, still wet with blood, and he tensed, ready to spring.

Then, out of nowhere, the man fell. His body shivered, and he pitched face-first into the grass. Bourne scrambled forward and turned the man over by the shoulder. He found a single bullet hole neatly placed in the man's forehead, a perfect kill shot.

Someone in the churchyard was on Bourne's side.

Monika?

She was good with a gun. She was Treadstone.

He checked the body and found an earpiece for receiving instructions. Bourne took it and placed it in his own ear. For now, he heard nothing but empty static. He retrieved his rifle, then kept moving forward, using the headstones for protection. On his left was the arched doorway leading into the church, and ahead of him was the crumbling red façade of the old priory ruins. He kept looking for the shooter, but he saw no one.

Overhead, the clouds separated. The darkness lightened under a sliver of moon. He could see the land more clearly now, but that meant he was no longer an invisible target in the cemetery. As if to punctuate the threat, a shot careened off the stone near his head. He ducked down, barely escaping a barrage from the ruins. Muffled bursts from a suppressed pistol kicked up mud and mortar, but after half a dozen shots, the gun went silent.

Not far away, he heard a gasp of pain, and then a voice rose above the wind. *"Fuck you, don't—"*

The voice cut off with the spit of another round. His unseen ally had made another kill.

Bourne dared to call out. "Monika?"

No one answered.

He checked the grounds but still saw no sign of his supposed partner. With his rifle at the ready, he continued his slow march toward the ruins. He reached the main tower, its façade worn by weather and time. A body lay outside the wrought-iron gates, this one with two bullet wounds, one in the chest, one in the neck. Another enemy down.

How many are there?

He slipped through the gate into what had once been the interior of the priory. Eroded fragments of archways and walls rose around him. In the distance, under the moonlight, he saw the dark expanse of the sea, a few boats in the island harbor, and the castle standing watch on the summit of the hill. A movement in the shadows drew his attention. He swung his rifle that way, his finger on the trigger. A man appeared near one of the priory's stone columns, and Bourne saw that the man had one hand—his gun hand—high in the air. The other hand supported his weight on a cane.

Bourne recognized him immediately, just as the other man had recognized him. It was Nash Rollins.

He didn't lower the rifle. Instead, he crossed the grass to Nash, finger still on the trigger and ready to fire. His Treadstone handler had blood on his face and hands. He looked old and tired leaning on his cane, his clothes wet, his gray hair limp on his head. But with Nash, looks were deceiving. Even one-handed, the man still had a sharp-shooter's aim, which he'd already demonstrated by making two kills in the darkness with a silenced Ruger.

"Where is she?" Bourne asked him. "Where's Monika?"

Nash didn't pretend not to know the score. "I sent her to the castle. One of the National Trust directors has family ties to MI5. He gave her a key to the property in case she needed a place to hide."

"You lied to me in Switzerland. You called her an *outsider.* But she's not."

Nash shrugged. "I also told you to let it go and stop looking for her. You didn't. And now you know things you were better off never knowing."

"She's Treadstone. She always was."

"Of course."

"What was her mission in Engelberg?" Bourne asked.

Nash said nothing.

"Was she after *Le Renouveau?*" Jason went on. "And if she was, why didn't you have us work together?"

"That wasn't her mission," Nash replied curtly.

"Then *why* was she there? It can't be a coincidence that she and I were in the same place at the same time."

"That's for Shadow to tell you, not me."

"Shadow?"

"Her code name."

Bourne raised the StG4 rifle and pointed it into Nash's face. Not that he would fire. They both knew that. But *Jesus,* there were moments when he wanted to pull the trigger and end the games once and for all.

"You're her handler, Nash. You *know* why Shadow was there. *Tell me.*"

"I'm not her handler. I never was. You have it backward, Cain."

"What are you saying?"

"*I* report to Shadow. Or rather, I report to people who report to Shadow. She's far above my pay grade."

"*What?* You're lying again."

"I'm not. Shadow was David Abbott's golden girl. Right from the beginning. Abbott loved *you*, Jason, of course he did. You had crazy skills, but we all knew you were meant to be in the field. You'd never make it as part of the deep state bureaucracy. You can't make compromises. You can't handle the shades of gray. But Shadow was born for that life. In fact, with Levi Shaw out of the way, I expect her to take over."

"Take over? Take over what?"

"She'll be the next head of Treadstone."

Bourne heard those words and tried to absorb them. He tried to make sense of all of it. Monika Roth.

The next head of Treadstone.

David Abbott's golden girl.

The roaring of memory whipped through his mind like the ocean wind. He had so many visions of that woman from his past.

Monika in his arms as he asked her to marry him. Monika breaking his heart with her lover at the Drei Alpenhäuser. Monika, hot and cold, real and false. And now Monika, a Treadstone agent at her refuge off the British coast, hiding from assassins at a medieval castle.

Monika. *Shadow.*

Not just Treadstone. The *head* of Treadstone. The master manipulator. The heir to David Abbott's empire.

Bourne shoved the butt of the rifle into Nash's neck, forcing the older man to take a stumbling step backward in surprise and lean into his cane. His voice rose into a threat. "Why was she in Switzerland? Goddamn it, Nash, tell me. *What was her mission?*"

Nash's eyes looked like hard black pearls in the darkness.

"*You* were her mission."

Jason felt his mind spinning. He found himself caught in a vortex of lies, a *lifetime* of lies, a centrifuge where the forces of gravity got heavier and heavier, pressing in on his skull. He blinked, a stabbing jolt of pain behind his eyes. He tried to breathe and could barely drag air into his lungs. The words echoed in his mind.

You were her mission.

All of the lies took shape in the man standing in front of him. He wanted to hurt him. Kill him. Bourne took a step toward Nash, and that single step saved his life. A bullet scorched past his head, so close that the heat burned him. Jason went to the ground, pulling Nash with him, but the old man came down too slowly. The next shot tunneled into the lean flesh of Nash's side. He heard Nash swear in pain, and blood oozed through the man's shirt and between his taut fingers.

More bullets blasted the ruined walls around them.

Three men.

Bourne spotted three men closing on them through the ruins of the priory. The barrage was ceaseless. He had nowhere to hide, and all he could do was stare into the fire and bring up the barrel of the Astra rifle. He was nothing but hard, furious death. He brought down the shooters one at a time, round after round with each pull of the trigger. They outnumbered him, but he had the advantage of a tsunami of adrenaline coursing through his veins. Six shots later, he took out the first man. Eight shots after that, the second fell. The third, watching his odds disintegrate, gave up the fight and ran for the church, but Bourne's fire trailed him step by step and brought him down with a shot to the leg and then ten more shots that pummeled the fallen body.

Long after he knew the man was dead, he kept firing, his anger pouring out of him with the cracks of the rifle.

You were her mission.

Nash finally took hold of his arm and stopped him.

"Jason. *Enough.*"

Bourne lay back heavily against the stone column. He breathed hard, his nostrils flaring. He closed his eyes. The rifle in his arms felt hot to the touch. He didn't want to move, but he had to move anyway. There was no time to stay in place. The shots of the Astra were loud; more men would be coming to get them.

He pushed himself to his feet, his legs unsteady. Nash lay propped against the ruins, blood everywhere.

"Get to the castle," Nash told him in a weak voice. "You've got to save Shadow."

"What about you?"

"Fuck me, Cain, you don't like me anyway. And I'm not going to die. One shot can't kill a son of a bitch like me. *Go.*"

36

THE BLACK HELICOPTER SAT IN THE EMPTY PARKING LOT OF AN INDUS-
trial plant north of Newcastle. The pilot stayed inside, waiting for the
order to fly, along with more men and more guns. The factory owner—
a member of the House of Lords and also of *Le Renouveau* ever since his
recruitment at Cambridge—had made sure the overnight security
guards at the facility would be deaf, dumb, and blind.

Chrétien Pau paced impatiently near the trees at the back of the
lot, waiting for the signal from the island. When it came, the helicopter
was less than half an hour from Lindisfarne.

Only minutes from his final encounter with David Webb.

And with Shadow.

Pau shook his head. Shadow. *Monika.*

He hadn't seen her since that last night at the chalet ten years earlier. Of course, she had no idea that *he'd* been there, that it was her on-
again, off-again French lover and spy who'd orchestrated her abduction.
That he'd been ready to kill them both when Webb exposed himself as
a traitor trying to burrow into their network. That during all the

months she had been manipulating him as a source for the Americans, he'd been stealing her intelligence on *Le Renouveau*.

After that night—after that fucking magician David Webb had saved her life and *murdered* all of his men—Shadow disappeared. He'd wondered at first if she'd resigned from Treadstone, if she was hiding in some remote corner of the world, living an ordinary life. But it was hard to imagine anything ordinary about her. She could make a man do anything. She was the best spy he'd ever met. The best *liar*.

Except for himself.

As she would discover tonight. God, for that moment when he saw her face again!

Pau kicked at one of the puddles in the parking lot. He stared at the crescent moon. The rain had stopped, and he grew nervous when the signal didn't come.

Tell me he is there! Tell me you have found them both!

But the radio was silent.

Instead, in his pocket, he felt the buzz of his KryptAll phone. The device was secure, no listeners from Interpol and the NSA eavesdropping on his calls. Only one man ever called him on that phone.

"*Le Roi Raymond,*" Pau answered with a smile.

"*Bonsoir, Chrétien,*" Berland said, all business. "Give me the update. What's going on? I expected a call from you before now."

Pau knew that Berland rarely indulged in humor. He was a serious man for serious times. "As did I. I'm still waiting to confirm that Webb and Monika are both on the island. It should be any minute now."

"Where are you?" Berland asked.

"A few minutes away by helicopter. I'll be in and out in an hour or so, and our work will be done."

There was silence on the line.

"I'm wary of the risks of this operation," Berland finally went on. "I don't like *your* involvement in it."

Pau shrugged. "The risks are low, Raymond. I have a ready alibi. At this moment, I'm at dinner with my parents in an estate outside Bordeaux. We'll post about it online. There will be pictures and witnesses. No one knows I took a private jet to Newcastle. And the Americans and British will be anxious to cover up what happens on the island. They won't ask questions, and even if they do, no one will be left behind to give them any answers."

"Still," Berland murmured unhappily. "We're very close to the election. This is the most delicate part of our yearslong dance. We need all of the pieces to fall into place."

"Which is *why* Webb and Shadow must be killed," Pau replied. "We can't leave them alive. If Webb remembers me—if he tells *her* about me—then I'm finished. Treadstone will end me. Plus, my exposure would be a body blow to *Le Renouveau*. It would set us back by years. The risk is too great."

"I agree that the two of them must be removed. But it doesn't explain why *you* need to be there to see it done. That is personal, Chrétien. It's self-indulgence we can't afford."

Pau didn't try to deny it. "Yes, I understand, and I know you're right. If you tell me to stop, Raymond, I'll stop. You know that. I'm *le commandant* to our men, but ultimately, *Le Renouveau* is your organization. Your vision. Whatever your orders are, I will follow them. But a true general also cannot be afraid of the front lines. I was there at the chalet ten years ago. I should be there at the end."

Berland was silent for a while. "This mission is obviously important to you. Very well. See it done."

"Thank you, my friend."

Pau breathed a sigh of relief. If Berland had told him to stand down, he would have done so, but he was glad to have permission to proceed.

Raymond and Chrétien. What a duo they made!

Their relationship went back many years, to when both of them were in their early twenties. As a young dockworker in Le Havre, Berland had led a wildcat strike that turned violent and led to a blockade at the port. Pau, then an up-and-coming staffer in the French State Secretariat for the Sea, had been sent to gather intelligence on the man behind the unrest. He'd expected a foulmouthed manual laborer of little refinement, but instead, Raymond Berland turned out to be a political philosopher who could quote Edmund Burke from memory and lay out all the details of his grand plan for the future of France and Europe.

His intellectual side was balanced by cold, brilliant political calculation.

"We will never defeat the system, Chrétien," Berland told him. *"The system will never give up its power. So we must* become *the system. We must take it over from the inside, recruit the best and brightest to our side and watch them assume positions of control. Then and only then will we see the renewal of France as a superpower, true to its heritage and roots. And from there, our message will spread across the continent."*

Renewal.

Le Renouveau.

Pau had signed on with the man that weekend, and he'd never looked back. He became Berland's greatest friend and ally. Berland was the master architect, and Pau was his secret weapon—the political engineer who would bring all of his plans to life.

"I wish we could see each other before the election," Pau said. "I miss our chats."

"I do, as well," Berland replied, "but you know it's impossible. You must be completely independent of me for now. That's the only way this works. Any hint of our alliance would bring everything tumbling down. Imagine if you hadn't found out that the Americans were spying on our meeting in Ibiza—if you and I had been seen there together! It would have eviscerated our plans before they even started. Instead, here we are, with you finally on the verge of bringing our vision to reality."

Pau found himself stirred, the way his friend's words always stirred him. "I only wish you could be the public face of the movement, Raymond. This is *your* victory. You deserve to win, not be on the sidelines."

"I am the sacrificial lamb, Chrétien," Berland reminded him. "That's how it must be. We've known it from the beginning. No one will ever tolerate me and my party taking that kind of power, no matter what the polls say. The voters disappoint us time and time again, because the establishment keeps them under their thumb like scared little sheep. But they will support *you*. You can accomplish what I never could."

"I have always appreciated your faith in me," Pau told him.

"And you have always earned it."

Pau heard the ping of an incoming text. He checked his other phone and finally saw the message he'd been waiting for.

Webb is on the island. So is Monika.

"Raymond, I must go," Pau told his mentor. "It's time to fly. Soon we will tie up the last loose ends from the past, and we can move forward. I'll be in touch when it's done."

"Good hunting, my friend," Berland said. "But I'm also curious.

Who is your source? Can this person be trusted? Their information about Webb and the woman has proven reliable to date, but now you are putting your own future on the line. *Our* future."

"I don't know who the source is," Pau admitted. "I only know *what* they are. And that is what makes me trust this person. They have nothing to gain and everything to lose. We have a mole in Treadstone."

37

"LE COMMANDANT *IS COMING.*"

Bourne heard those words through the stolen radio in his ear.

He sprinted down the beach road. Ahead of him, Lindisfarne Castle loomed at the end of the spit of land, rising like a lone rook on an empty chessboard. Craggy stones marked the slope, overgrown with emerald grass. As he ran past the curving harbor, waves crashed in from the sea and cast up cold spray across the path.

He listened, but the radio went silent again.

Le commandant. The commander.

Jason knew what that meant. The trap was closing around him. His nemesis at *Le Renouveau* wanted to be there to see it spring shut.

His nemesis. The man whose voice echoed in his memory. The man who'd slipped away from him in Switzerland ten years ago. The man who'd taunted him on the phone outside the chalet.

Even back then, you had no idea who Monika Roth really was.

Monika's lover.

He was coming to the island.

Bourne heard the whiny throb of an engine. He saw the lights of a helicopter approaching at high speed across the dark sea. He stopped, watching it come. The helicopter's powerful engine fought the night wind, which made the sailboats and trawlers in the harbor strain against their anchor lines.

In the darkness, Jason was invisible, one man on the empty path, but then a search beam split the night and swept across the beach, its cone of light dazzling Bourne's eyes. He was pinned in the middle of it, like a prisoner caught in his escape. He heard the pops of rifle fire banging off the dirt and grass around him. As the helicopter hovered above him like a black spider, he dove off the road, taking cover behind a crumbling stone wall. The earpiece of the radio dislodged as he jumped, but he had no time to hunt for it. He was on his own.

He slung the Astra rifle into his grip, then rose up and fired back, shooting at the machine hanging motionless in the sky. Most of his rounds ricocheted harmlessly off the chopper's metal floor, but one bullet thudded through the open side door. A lucky shot. With a shout, a man in black tumbled forward out of the helicopter and dropped a hundred yards to the rocky beach. His body hit with a sickening thud.

The helicopter veered upward and away from the rifle fire. It soared northward across the island, looking for a safe place to land. But they knew he was here now. They knew where he was going. He only had minutes.

Get to the castle. You've got to save Shadow.

Bourne leaped over the wall and ran. He wasn't far away. The castle perched atop the rocky summit, its stone walls high and sheer.

As he got closer, the cobblestoned path sloped upward. He bent around a curve that followed the base of the castle wall, where a windswept wooden railing clung to the edge of the narrow walkway. As he ran higher, the ground got smaller, and the sea stretched across the distance toward the shadowy coast of the mainland. He reached a set of stone steps that led inside the walls. Taking them two at a time, he emerged onto the lower battery, where the fierce wind grew fiercer, roaring across the heights.

In front of him, a heavy wooden door gave entrance to the castle itself. The door was open. Behind the double rows of mullioned windows, the lights had gone off.

He leveled his rifle and went inside.

Cold air blew through the fort. The interior was clammy and claustrophobic, a relic of old centuries. He moved slowly in the gloom. Beyond the entrance hall, he had to bend down to walk through a corridor with a low ceiling. He passed a set of steps leading to the fort's upper battery and then emerged into a nautical-themed room, where a few flickering candles lit the darkness. The walls and arched ceiling were all made of rough stone. A worn patterned rug was spread over the floor, and a dead fireplace whistled with wind on the far side of the room. A model of a large wooden ship dangled over his head. The square windows cut into the walls showed nothing but black glass.

A woman stood by the fireplace, aiming a matching StG4 rifle at him.

It was Monika.

"Hello, David."

He pointed his own rifle back at her, and he didn't lower it. He crossed the room until they were directly in front of each other, barrels nearly touching.

"I'm not David Webb anymore," Jason replied. "But you know that better than anyone, don't you? After all, you're the one who turned me into Cain. Not Monika Roth. *Shadow*. That's an ironic code name for you, isn't it? Because that's what you were. That was your mission. You were my shadow. My profiler. You were the one who did my psychological evaluation for Treadstone."

"So you finally know. I'm glad. You saw Nash? He told you?"

"Yes."

"Is he okay?"

"No. They shot him. He's badly hurt. But he wanted me to come here to save you."

She shook her head. A tactician. A strategist. David Abbott's golden girl. "How did *Le Renouveau* find us so quickly? That doesn't make sense."

"Obviously, someone told them I was coming. I wondered if it was you."

"Me? My God, of course not. We have a leak somewhere. You should have stayed away, David. Now we're both at risk."

"Except *you* wanted me to come here. You left breadcrumbs for me to find."

She sighed and let the rifle sag in her arms, its barrel pointed at the floor. "Yes, you're right, I did. Nash didn't approve. He thought we should keep you in the dark. But once you found out about me, I knew that was impossible. You needed the truth, and you wouldn't stop until you heard it directly from me."

"The truth," Jason said cynically. "What's that?"

She shrugged, as if all the lies meant nothing. "Switzerland was a mission, David. For me, for you. That's all. By now, you should understand that. We do what we're told."

"This was more than a mission."

Monika crossed the room. She checked the dark windows, seeing nothing, then went to the doorway and glanced down the corridor toward the castle entrance. "What's the situation outside?"

"*Le Renouveau* is on their way," Bourne said.

"How much time do we have?"

"Five or ten minutes. Not more."

"I called for backup from the Brits. If we can hold them off for an hour, we'll have support. How many are there?"

"We eliminated several in the village, but another helicopter just arrived. I'm sure it includes reinforcements. As well as *le commandant*."

Monika looked at him in the candlelight, her face confused. "Who?"

"The leader, the one who's running the show. He's here to deal with us in person. Your old friend from Paris. Your *lover*."

"My lover? David, what are you talking about?"

Jason's voice was sharp. He wanted the news to hurt. "The man at the chalet who tried to kill us is the same man I met with you at the Drei Alpenhäuser. I'm sure you remember that night. He's the one who's hunting us now."

"*Impossible.* You're wrong."

"I'm not wrong. You were sleeping with a senior agent from *Le Renouveau*, Monika. You got played back then. He was twisting you around his finger."

"You have no idea what you're saying. You have no idea who he *is*."

"There are things I remember now," Bourne said, "and I *remember* that voice. Believe me, it's him."

He saw genuine shock—something close to primal fear—spread across her face.

"If you're right, the stakes just went way up. This is about more than us staying alive. We need to kill him, David. We can't let him leave the island."

"Right now, I'd say he has the advantage."

Monika looked lost in mental calculations. She pushed past him through the shadows toward the heavy castle door, and he followed her. She went out onto the lower battery, all the way to the edge of the wall that looked down on the beach below them. The wind made tangles of her blond hair, and the moon turned her face stark white. But the path toward the castle was dark. There were no lights in the fields.

Le Renouveau hadn't made its move yet.

She turned around. Seeing her in the moonlight, he realized again how beautiful she was. It was impossible to look away from her face. But being this close to her, he knew that she was also cold. Unreachable. From this side of his life, he found it hard to imagine that he'd once been in love with her.

"I know you hate me," she told him calmly, with that Treadstone ability to read his mind. "I don't blame you after what I did to you. Guilty as charged. But what's the rule, David? What's the one you always forget?"

"Emotion kills," Bourne replied.

"Exactly."

"You said I needed to hear the truth," he said. "We don't have much time. Tell me the truth."

Monika brushed the hair from her face. "Okay. Where do you want me to start?"

"Start at the beginning. You and Treadstone."

"All right. That means starting with David Abbott. I got to know him at Georgetown. He was an amazing man; you know that. Brilliant. We hit it off. My specialty was political psychology. Know your enemy. Read them from across the negotiating table. Understand who's lying, who's bluffing, who's vulnerable. Abbott thought my skills would be useful, so when he created Treadstone, he brought me on board. Partly,

I was supposed to assess missions and enemies—give us a psychological edge in dealing with our adversaries. But it was more than that. You're right, my code name Shadow reflected what I did. I led the program to analyze our recruits. Shadow them. Measure their abilities. I designed the processes by which we test our agents, train them, mold them, push them to their emotional limits. It's not just about physical skills, you know that. We had to know who would be able to handle the pressure and who would break."

"You mean, who you could manipulate," Bourne said. "Who you could control."

She made no excuses. "Yes. Absolutely. Do you expect me to apologize for that? Treadstone was asking its agents to operate under extreme conditions in a gray zone of morality. Some can't handle it. We had successes, and we had failures, even among the very best. Last year I dealt with an agent named Storm. Probably the best natural-born agent I've worked with since you. I like to deal with the special recruits myself. Everything seemed fine no matter what I threw at her, but I had a bad feeling, like I was missing a weakness. So I pushed seriously hard, and this time, she fell apart. She tried to kill me, and then she killed herself. The pressure destroyed her."

"*You* destroyed her. And you feel no responsibility for that?"

"Better we found out early. She could have compromised a mission."

"Jesus," Bourne said, shaking his head.

"Obviously, I pushed hard with you, too, David. In a different way. Abbott was convinced that you would be a superior operative in the field. Your intellect, your physicality, they were both off the charts. But you were like a son to him. He loved you—so much that it blinded him to your weaknesses. I reminded him that you were young and you were damaged. What would happen when you faced the kind of existential stress we knew was coming? We had to know how you would react, how you would deal with emotional or sexual attachments that might conflict with the mission. So Abbott asked me to assess you directly. Myself, in the field, not just on paper. It was the deepest study I ever did, in person, over several months. I needed to know everything about you."

"And me falling in love with you? Was that part of the plan?"

Monika stared back at him. Jesus, the ice in that face!

"Yes, it was. Abbott and I talked about it. I went there to seduce you. Physically. Romantically. We needed to know if you could walk away from me and put Treadstone first when the situation demanded it."

"Abbott knew?" David asked.

"You said you wanted the truth. Of course he knew. The whole operation was his idea."

Bourne wanted to feel angry. He wanted to explode with rage. David Abbott, the closest thing he'd ever had to a father, the man who'd loved him and educated him and taken him at his side all around the world, had been the one to betray him. Abbott had been the source of the lies. But he couldn't feel anything now. He was numb.

"The plan was always for you to walk away," Jason concluded.

"Naturally."

"I remember going to your apartment in Engelberg, and you were gone. It was empty. That was before *Le Renouveau* took you. You were simply going to leave, and I'd never know what happened to you. Right? Then after everything that happened at the chalet, you let me set you up with a new identity, take you to Hamburg, and then you vanished again. Back to Treadstone."

"Do you want me to say I'm sorry, David? Will that make it better? Well, I won't do that. I had a job to do. Like you. I've followed your record with Treadstone ever since. It's impressive, just as Abbott knew it would be. But I know the things you've done over the years. I hope you're not suggesting that what *you* do is any more morally acceptable than what I do. That's the life we lead."

Jason felt the weight of the rifle in his hands. As with Nash, he thought about putting the barrel to her chest and pulling the trigger. He examined her face for some kind of emotion, some kind of guilt or regret. But he saw none.

"After I lost my memory, Nash lied," Bourne said. "He never told me about you."

"That was at my request. Since you'd already forgotten me, I figured it was better that you never learn about our relationship."

"In other words, you didn't want me to find out that I'd been betrayed from the beginning. By Abbott. By Nash. By you."

"Yes."

He shook his head in disgust. "Was any of it real? Did you feel anything for me at all?"

"No. I didn't. I told you, it was a job."

"You're that good an actress?"

"I am. I've trained myself for missions like that. I don't feel anything for anyone. *Emotion kills*, David. But for what it's worth, you've surprised me over the years. After the mission, I wrote in my report for Abbott that you would most likely crash and burn. You'd get involved with women. You'd fall in love. And I was right. Marie St. Jacques. Nova. Abbey Laurent. I get the reports, I see you making the same mistake over and over. But somehow you've made it a strength, not a weakness. You're still what Abbott thought you would be. The best agent Treadstone ever produced."

"I'm not Treadstone," Bourne reminded her. "I told Nash that two years ago. I'm out."

"Don't be naïve, David," Monika snapped. "That's not how it works. You're never *out*. Not until the day you die."

She glanced over the castle wall again at the island below them. The wind howled. The sea roared against the beach. On the harbor path and across the green fields, they saw lights moving their way.

"But maybe that day is today," she said. "They're coming for us. It's time to fight."

38

FROM A BACKPACK INSIDE THE CASTLE, MONIKA RETRIEVED NIGHT VISION goggles for both of them. They reloaded their rifles and took up positions at the far end of the lower battery, behind the castle's stone wall. When Bourne put on his goggles and assessed the glowing white lights of the invaders, he counted a dozen men, six running across the fields, six on the path along the harbor.

Twelve to two. Bad odds.

Was *le commandant* among them? Or was he waiting for the bloodshed to be over before he made his appearance?

Bourne took one end of the wall; Monika took the other. He leaned over the edge as far as he could, balanced his weight on his elbows, and tried to keep his aim steady in the shifting gales. The Astra rifle wasn't a sniper's tool for picking off men one by one. It was a blunt instrument. All he could do was fire as many bullets as fast as possible and hope some of them found their marks.

"Not yet," Monika murmured. "Let them get a little closer."

Below them, the two groups began to converge, the killers in the field meeting up with their colleagues storming the path. Soon the angle of fire over the wall would be too steep to target them. Bourne trained his barrel through the darkness, and he'd already begun to ease the trigger back when he heard Monika whisper, *"Now."*

They both fired.

Again. And again. And again.

They unleashed one bullet after another, but at that distance, in the crosswind, nearly all of their shots went astray. For a while, the wind covered the noise of the assault, and the men below them didn't seem to notice that they were under attack. Then one man fell. Bourne didn't know if it was his shot or Monika's that struck him, but a man clutched his throat and slumped to the path. Almost immediately, a second shot found its mark and took another man down.

Now the killers knew.

They separated as they charged up the path, widening the field of fire. Two stayed behind and swung up their own guns to aim for the shooters above them, but they had no hope of hitting their targets. Bourne kept raining down bullets from the heights of the castle, and so did Monika. In the group moving up the castle walkway, he saw another man fall. Then another. That made a total of four hits.

Now the odds were eight to two. But the men would be on them in moments, firing as they came up the castle steps. They had to fall back and retrench.

Bourne and Monika retreated inside the stone fortress. He shut and latched the heavy door behind them, but the door wouldn't hold the killers back for long. They swapped out thirty-round magazines in their Astras, then Monika blew out the candles in the ship room, leaving the interior of the castle blacker than night. Wearing their night vision goggles, they staked out a location in the corridor opposite the entrance hall, near the worn stone steps that led to the upper battery. They stretched out on the cold floor, their bodies squeezed next to each other, their rifles aimed toward the door.

Thunder boomed outside, but not from the sky. The killers aimed their guns around the door's iron hinges, blasting wood dust and splinters through the entrance hall and turning the stone walls into a shooting gallery of ricochets. Bourne and Monika covered their heads as bullets flew. When the wood gave way, the killers used the weight of their shoulders and forced the heavy door inward. They entered firing, but they were blind, and their shots went wild, and at least one bounced back and struck the first of the men, eliciting a scream.

From the floor, Bourne and Monika trained their rifles on the invaders. They could see two men through their goggles, and they took them both down. The others hung back, then aimed return fire through the darkness, zeroing in on the two of them with enough accuracy that they had to slither backward away from the entrance hall. Their faces were scratched and bloody from the flying debris.

There was nowhere to go but up.

They pounded up the stone steps, then stripped open the door and burst outside into the cold night air. They threw aside their goggles. The upper battery was long and narrow, making a dogleg to the right around the small living chamber of the fort. Up here, they had no escape. The only way out was back down into the faces of the killers or over the castle wall one hundred feet to the rocks.

Bourne checked his watch. Not enough time had passed. The two of them would be dead long before backup arrived. And he was low on ammunition in his magazine. He glanced at Monika, and her face told the same story.

This was the end.

They split up. Monika veered to a triangular notch jutting from the castle wall that blocked her from the interior stairs. Bourne took position along the wet stone floor where the battery turned to the right. From where he was, he could see her and she could see him. They trained their barrels at the doorway and waited.

The noise of footsteps thumped above the wind. *Le Renouveau* had learned its lesson; the six remaining men didn't rush outside and offer themselves up as targets. Instead, the assault team sprayed bullets around the upper battery from cover, forcing Bourne and Monika back behind the walls. Two killers shot from the stairs and rolled toward an angled wall on the other side of Monika's position. Bourne reacted in time to fire several shots, but the bullets nicked harmlessly off the battery floor.

He raised a hand toward Monika, signaling her to hold her fire. For now, he was the only one shooting, and that meant the killers didn't know where she was. If he could lure them out, they'd run into her crossfire. She nodded her understanding and got herself ready, aiming her rifle toward the castle's upper chamber and waiting. Bourne fired a couple of shots, then jerked back as the two men hiding on the upper battery sent a barrage his way. When they'd forced him back behind the corner, more men flew through the doorway, boots heavy on stone.

They headed for the far end of the battery, where Bourne was. They didn't see Monika, and her rifle fire cut them down like prisoners before a firing squad. Two men went down, but a third reacted quickly enough to shift his momentum sideways and roll back behind the cover wall, where the others were hiding.

Bourne held up four fingers to Monika. Four to two. Their odds were improving.

But the last man in the stairwell took a chance and opened fire toward Monika. She hesitated before pulling back, and in that split-second delay, a bullet struck the barrel of her rifle, mangling it. Furious, Monika threw the rifle down and yanked her Glock from its holster. But in a face-to-face match of pistol versus rifle, she had no chance, and they both knew it.

A silent siege ensued atop the castle. The charred smell of the fire-fight lingered in the air despite the wind. A chilled sea gale gusted across Bourne's body, making the sweat on his skin turn cold. He felt the weight of the Astra in his hands and concluded he only had three or four bullets left in the magazine. Not nearly enough. Across the plaza, he saw Monika's face turn toward the clouds, scanning for American or British helicopters. But no rescue was coming from the sky.

Le Renouveau broke the stalemate by sacrificing another of its men like a pawn on the chessboard. The last man, the one hiding on the stairs, threw himself forward, running toward the notch in the wall where Monika had taken cover. He fired as he ran, and Bourne had no choice. He spun around the corner and exhausted his last few shots, hitting the man but not taking him down. His barrel clicked as he yanked on the trigger; the rifle was empty. The killer ran into Monika's fire, screaming as one of her bullets hit his leg, but he stayed on his feet long enough to knock the pistol out of her hand with a swing of his rifle.

When he fell, the others came.

Monika leaped for the Glock, but she stopped when the barrel of a rifle pushed into her forehead. Bourne had his Sig in its holster under his jacket, but he had no chance if he drew it now. They'd cut him down before he could get off a shot. Two of the men aimed their barrels at him, but they stayed ten feet away on the battery, and they held their fire. He didn't expect them to shoot. Not yet.

These men were the hired help, and one man was missing.

Le commandant.

The killer with his rifle trained on Monika gestured with the barrel to get her to move. She got to her feet, and Bourne could see her eyes shifting from man to man and taking the measure of the situation. For now, they had no viable strategy to escape alive. She allowed herself to be pushed across the battery toward Bourne. As the three men with rifles inched closer, Bourne and Monika moved backward, until they were both pinned against the castle wall, with nothing but the long drop behind them.

The men took positions in a semicircle, four feet apart. They didn't close the gap; they stayed out of range if Bourne or Monika made a sudden charge. Smart. They might get one, they might even get two, but not three.

Then they heard footsteps.

Someone else had arrived at the summit of the castle.

Bourne saw a man emerge from the stairs. He was very tall and good-looking, his short brown hair whipped by the wind, his handsome face chiseled and a lone scar on his forehead marring the smoothness of his skin. He had no gun in his hands. The commander needed no weapons. He wore a long black coat that draped to his knees, a black turtleneck and slacks, and buckled French cowboy boots that were wet and dirty with island mud.

Le commandant.

Bourne knew him.

This was the man who'd been sleeping with Monika, the man who bragged about it with his smile. This was the man who'd directed the trap at the chalet. And now—Bourne recognized the man's face from the newspapers and television, and he understood why Monika said this man had to die.

Chrétien Pau was the man who was supposed to save France from the extremist grip of Raymond Berland and *La Vraie*.

Chrétien Pau was also a senior commander of *Le Renouveau*.

The man's sharp gaze shifted between their faces, noting the blood and dirt and their tired eyes. His own face was flushed with victory.

"Ah, Monika, my love," Pau said in a voice Bourne recognized, a voice that was honey-smooth and cruel at the same time. "There you are at long last. How long has it been? Ten years? I was so afraid you were dead. But spies never really die, do they? They simply become ghosts."

Monika stared back with a frozen hatred, her lips pushed together into a hard, cherry-red line. She said nothing.

"No valentines for your old lover?" Pau asked. "Are you not surprised to see me? I suppose *Cain* finally figured it out and told you about me. That's why I needed to make sure we took care of both of you. It's been a long game of cat and mouse, but here we are. Does it get under that pretty skin of yours to know what I did to you? You were so proud of how you manipulated me back then. Gathering information from me on EU defense and policy. Watching your American spy climb the ranks in the French government and do your bidding. You had no idea you were playing into our hands. Setting the stage for the rise of *Le Renouveau*. Congratulations, my love. Raymond and I truly couldn't have gotten this far without your help."

Monika tossed her windswept blond hair. She finally spoke. "Fuck you, Chrétien."

He laughed. "Marvelous. Oh, that's marvelous. Truly, I'm honored.

I do believe that's the most emotion I've ever seen from you, in or out of bed."

Pau turned his attention to Bourne.

He came up closer, parting cautiously between two of his men, but keeping a safe distance with a careful respect for Bourne's fighting skills. "*Cain*. Face-to-face once more. I told you we'd meet again soon. I also told you that you had no idea who Monika Roth really was. You should have listened to me. But I assume you know the truth about her now. She betrayed you more than I ever did. In fact, I'm curious, David. If you'd realized who she was back at the chalet—if you'd understood that your lover was a liar and a fraud—would you have killed her when I told you to? Would you have sacrificed her for the mission? That's what Treadstone agents do, after all. The mission always comes first."

Bourne didn't answer. He stared back at the man, his mind furiously calculating Pau's next moves and evaluating whether they had any way to strike back. But their options were few. Monika was unarmed. Three men with rifles stood guard around them, and he had nothing but a Sig hidden inside his jacket with a full magazine and one in the chamber. A few quick shots would change the dynamic, but by the time he drew the gun, he'd be dead.

"Ah well, it doesn't really matter," Pau said. "As it happens, I'm giving you another chance to make up for the past."

Jason's eyes narrowed. "What does that mean?"

"It's simple," Pau replied. "Ten years ago you were a young spy, and you failed to follow my orders. Now I'm back to make sure you do. That's how this ends, David. That's why I'm here. You can never run from your destiny. Eventually, it always catches up with you. You see, it's time to prove yourself to *Le Renouveau* once and for all. I want you to kill Monika."

39

VANDAL AND JOHANNA SAT IN THE COLD DARKNESS AMID THE HEAVY equipment of Monika's arsenal mounted on the walls. Every light in the house was off, and the attic itself was pitch-black, without any windows. The rain had stopped, but wind shrieked through the centuries-old frame, making the house groan like a wounded animal.

"What is that noise?" Johanna asked, breaking the long silence between them. "It sounds like fireworks."

"Gunfire," Vandal replied. "It's coming from the other end of the island. The castle."

"Oh my God. We need to do something. We need to help Jason. Jesus, we can't just sit here and let him die!"

Vandal said nothing.

She felt her own frustration deepen because Johanna was right. Vandal wanted to *be* there, in the middle of it, gun in hand. It killed her to know a firefight was going on—that Cain was in jeopardy—while she sat here on the sidelines. But when she stood up, she had to grasp for one of the angled roof beams in the attic to keep herself from falling. Far away, the gunfire continued in booms of thunder.

"I'm no help to anyone like this," Vandal murmured. "I'm fucking useless."

"Then let *me* go," Johanna said.

"And get you killed? No way. Cain said to keep you safe."

"What the fuck does it matter if I'm safe? He's out there. He needs help."

Vandal grabbed a flashlight from her pocket and pointed it in the woman's face. Johanna's long blond hair was soaking wet, her ivory skin shiny and damp. Her blue eyes stared up at her with frantic intensity. Vandal was sure that if she said yes, Johanna really would grab a gun and run for the castle.

"Seriously," Johanna went on. "Let me go."

"Not a chance. You don't know what you're doing, and you'll make it worse. Look, Cain's a survivor. He's better off alone. If you're out there, he'll protect you instead of himself. No, I'm sorry, you're not going anywhere, and neither am I. We both need to stay here. We wait."

Slowly, Vandal slid back down to the floor. By habit, she pulled the Glock from her holster and checked it and rechecked it and then shoved it back in the leather case. Despite everything she'd said, she was tempted to ignore Cain's instructions, ignore her concussion, and make a run for the castle. She could draw fire. She could give them a distraction. Something. Anything.

Her mind told her again: *Cain's better off alone.*

But what if he needed help?

Johanna spoke out of the darkness. Her voice had a calm bitterness. "You don't like me, do you?"

"Whether I like you or not makes no difference," Vandal replied.

"You say that, but I see something else in your face whenever you look at me."

"There's nothing in my face."

"Is it Jason? Is that the problem?"

"I told you, there's no problem."

Johanna was quiet for a few seconds. "You know, I didn't ask to fall in love with him, if that's what bothers you. But it is what it is. I think he's falling for me, too. Is that why you don't like me? Are you jealous?"

"No. I'm not."

"I don't believe you."

"Well, believe it. I don't care what's going on between you and Cain. I feel absolutely nothing about that."

"Why, because emotion kills? According to Jason, that's the rule."

"Yes, it does."

"Jason told me the two of you never had sex," Johanna murmured. "Is that true?"

"It's true."

"Did you ever want to?"

Vandal didn't bother lying. "Once, for one night, but it didn't happen. He was right, and I was wrong. End of story."

"I know it can't last between us," Johanna said, "but for right now, he and I—"

She stopped midsentence.

Her body twisted in the darkness, and she was only inches away, her breath fast and hot on Vandal's face. She clutched Vandal's arm, her nails pinching, and her voice sank into an urgent hiss. *"Jesus."*

"What? What is it?"

"Don't you hear that? Someone's in the house."

Vandal closed her eyes and listened. At first, she thought Johanna was wrong—how could this amateur have heard an intruder before Vandal did?—but then she felt the frame of the cottage shift below them. A door had opened somewhere, letting in the roaring wind. Vibration crackled like electricity through the old timbers.

Footsteps.

In an instant, her Glock was back in her hand.

"Stay here," Vandal whispered.

"Fuck no."

"Johanna—"

"I'm coming with you unless you shoot me."

Vandal sighed. Using her flashlight, she made her way to the hinged door in the attic floor. The door opened silently; Monika obviously kept it lubricated. She let the ladder drop to the bedroom closet, and she slid down the rails, with Johanna following closely behind her. The house was dark. She scoped their route out of the bedroom, but when they reached the old cottage stairs, she switched off her flashlight and held Johanna back. They both listened to the whistle of the wind.

The vibration in the house had stopped.

"Nothing," Vandal murmured.

"He's gone?"

"Maybe. Or maybe he's waiting for us."

Vandal took the stairs slowly. As she neared the ground floor, the wind got louder. She smelled the chill of fresh air and felt it raising goose bumps on her skin. The front door was open. The outside gales pushed the door back and forth soundlessly like a seesaw. The house felt deserted now, but was it? She stayed where she was, playing a waiting game to see whether the intruder would move first.

Johanna reached the lowest step right behind her. Vandal swiveled and put her lips to the younger woman's ear. "I'm going to check the garden. Don't move. Even if you hear something, *don't move.* I'll be back in two minutes."

Vandal went outside, leaving the door to swing with the breeze behind her. The cold air helped with her dizziness. Her eyes adjusted to the darkness, and she could make out the shapes of the trees and the horizontal line of the stone wall. Around her, branches and leaves rustled together as if shouting out a warning. She moved into the wet grass, far enough that she could see the wooden gate leading to the street. Like the front door, it was open. She knew they had closed it when they arrived.

Someone had come inside.

Slowly, she circled the house. The pound of the waves increased as she got to the back garden that looked toward the sea. When she crossed to the rear gate and checked the cliff's edge, she saw no one in the moonlight in either direction. The area looked empty. And yet her Glock itched in her hand. That was instinct. Something was wrong. Her mind tried to separate the wind from the other noises around her, but her brain kept sending crazy signals.

What was that?

Was that a gunshot?

Or was she hearing things that weren't there?

When she checked her watch, she saw that almost ten minutes had passed while she left Johanna alone. Too long. She needed to get back to the house. She continued around the garden until she reached the open door, but when she went inside, she saw in the gloomy shadows that the area in front of the stairs was empty now.

Johanna wasn't there.

Shit!

Had she gone upstairs again? Had she heard something and taken refuge in the attic? Or had she run outside?

Vandal risked a low call. *"Johanna?"*

Then once more, urgently. *"Johanna, are you there? Where are you?"*

No answer.

Shit shit shit!

Vandal risked turning on her penlight, and she aimed it at the floor. Her heart sank when she spotted a dark red reflection shining back at her. From the doorway, she saw a trail of blood.

A lot of blood.

She followed the glow of her flashlight, but her brain did somersaults that made her stagger. She slumped sideways and banged her head. Propping herself up with one arm against the wall, she descended a couple of steps to the sunken living room with its brick fireplace. It smelled of old ash, and the wind howled down the chimney like a banshee. Vandal swung her light around the room, and then she stopped in horror with her flashlight beam aimed at the middle of an antique rug.

The bloodstains led there drop by drop.

To a body.

THE TOP OF THE CASTLE FELT LIKE THE ROOF OF THE WORLD. THE NIGHT sky stretched endlessly in every direction, and the island spread out below them, barren and dark. In the tumult of the wind, Bourne could barely stand up straight. He noted the positions of the killers, ten or twelve feet away, rifles ready with fingers on the triggers, each of them separated from the other by about six feet. Chrétien Pau stood in the middle, slightly in front of the rest, no gun. The wind blew his long coat back like a cape, and his face had the grin of a devil.

Four men.

Four men against eighteen rounds in his SIG P365-XMACRO. Plenty of firepower if he could reach it. But he couldn't. As soon as he tried to draw, they'd shoot him.

Monika stood next to him, close enough that he could feel her shoulder brushing against his. The words from Pau—*I want you to kill her*—elicited no reaction. She didn't tense or flinch; he felt no fear from her. Fear was an emotion, and Monika had deadened herself to emotion years ago.

She was Treadstone.

He imagined her mind whirling with possibilities, the way his was, searching for a way out. The only no-win scenario Bourne believed in was death, and until you were dead, there was always a chance to turn the game around.

"You have ten seconds, David," Pau continued. "Make your choice."

Bourne made sure his face showed nothing. Poker players never did. "And if I refuse?"

The man from *Le Renouveau* shrugged. "I'm not really giving you a choice. You know that. You both die either way. But there are many ways to die. If you kill her yourself, it will be fast and painless for her. If not, if I'm forced to let my men deal with her, then it will be agonizing and slow. I'll make you watch her suffer an excruciating death before you face the same punishment yourself. But it doesn't have to be that way. You see, David, for me the satisfaction is in making you do it. Having you *submit* to me at long last. That's worth giving up the pleasure of Monika screaming for my mercy. But it's a fine line, and my patience is limited. *Kill her.*"

"Monika means nothing to me," Bourne replied. "This isn't ten years ago. Maybe I *want* her to suffer for what she did to me."

"If you want to kill her slowly, be my guest. But now you have five seconds."

Jason heard the clock ticking in his head. He didn't think Pau was bluffing.

"As you wish," he said.

Déjà vu.

Bourne shot out his right arm like the blow of a hammer, striking Monika's chest below her throat and jolting her backward. She stumbled in surprise, losing her balance against the castle wall. He turned and advanced on her with his fists clenched, but he couldn't say anything. He couldn't tell her what he needed her to do.

Fight.

But she understood the game. Her eyes turned feline, hunter against hunter. Her teeth bared, and a menacing little growl purred from her throat. She lashed out with one leg aimed at his gut, and he staggered two steps back as if she'd kicked the air out of his lungs. She swung a hand, fingernails raking his face like claws, and this was no fake. He felt a sting as she drew blood, and the sight of the blood seemed to arouse her. She charged, and Bourne jabbed at her throat like a piston. He drew his fist back just as his knuckles connected with her windpipe, but she clutched her neck anyway and gagged. He aimed a blow at her chin, grazing it, and she snapped her head sideways as if dizzied by the impact. He took her by the shoulders and drove her backward, slamming her hard against the castle wall.

Below the wall, inches away, was a hundred feet of night air.

He bent her body at the waist until she cried out with pain. Her hair whipped around her face; her head and shoulders dangled over the edge. He grabbed her throat with one hand, squeezing it, cutting off her air. Her arms and legs flailed; her feet came off the ground. He kept pushing, farther back, farther back, her screams coming fast and wild as he forced her toward the point of no return.

The fall. The drop.

"Left shoulder," he whispered.

She knew what to do.

As Bourne choked her, as she kicked and struggled, her right hand slipped inside his jacket and drew his Sig Sauer from its holster.

Then she fired through his coat.

She fired again and again and again and again, exhausting every shot.

Bourne held her tightly as she emptied the Sig across the castle battery, and when he heard the crack of the eighteenth round, he swung her backward away from the wall, hoisting her into the air like a shot put toward whatever was behind them.

Then he finally twisted around. He had a split second to assess the situation as he dove for the ground. Two of the killers were down, dead of multiple gunshots. Pau lay on his back, twitching and skittering backward, a bullet in his shoulder. But the fourth man was still standing despite wounds to his arms and legs. The man swung his rifle toward Monika, who crawled along the battery floor toward one of the fallen guns. He fired, his aim off thanks to the bullet in the meat of his shoulder, but when he fired again, the next shot landed in Monika's thigh. She reared back with a shout of pain.

The killer fired again, barely missing Monika's head.

Bourne leaped for the nearest rifle, which lay in a pool of blood next to one of the killers, who had a bullet from his Sig in his forehead. He scooped it off the ground, rolled onto his back, and fired a tight burst toward the killer. The bullets sprayed over the castle wall into the night, but one found its mark in the man's stomach. The killer shuddered, then swiveled his weapon toward Bourne, still firing. Dirt and stone blew into Bourne's face, momentarily blinding him. By instinct, he rolled right, hard and fast, the frantic motion knocking the rifle out of his grasp. Bullets chased him, and a cutting pain burned across his shoulder. An inch to the left, and it would have tunneled into his ribs and sliced through his lungs.

A body blocked his path. For a terrible instant, he was a motionless target. He stiffened, expecting a kill shot, wondering if he would even feel the bullet hit him. But the shot never came. The blast of a handgun exploded from a new direction. His eyes cleared, and he saw Monika on her back six feet away, a Glock in her hand.

The killer pitched forward, one of his eyes gone where her bullet had entered his skull.

Bourne scrambled to his feet. A bloody slash made a line across his shoulder and arm. He helped Monika to her feet, the Glock still in her hand. They turned back to the castle wall, and she aimed the gun toward the bodies of the fallen men.

Toward Chrétien Pau.

But Pau wasn't there.

"Please put the pistol down, my dear," Pau said.

He stood halfway across the battery floor, one arm limp at his side where he'd been shot, but the other arm cradling one of the rifles.

Monika pointed the barrel of the Glock his way.

Pau managed a smile. "Brave. You're wounded, and all you have is a handgun. I don't honestly think your aim is good enough to take me out at this distance. Neither is mine, I confess, but with this weapon, it's quantity over quality."

"I guess we'll find out," she said.

"I guess so," he agreed. "Shall we?"

Pau fired.

So did Monika.

The one-handed recoil made him lurch off balance, and the bullet from the Glock missed him entirely. But his shot hit her forearm, went through and through, and the pistol dropped from her numb fingers. Pau took hold of the trigger, and his eyes burned with delight. He steadied himself and aimed at her again.

Then Pau's skull burst and brains erupted outward like candy from a piñata.

A giant wound opened up his forehead. Bone, blood, and brain sprayed onto the stone floor. He didn't even have time to look surprised; he was still enjoying his victory as he died. When his body collapsed, Bourne saw a woman standing right behind him, her arms outstretched with a suppressed Ruger rock-solid in her hands. She had one eye closed, one eye open as she aimed.

It was Johanna.

THE MAN ON THE RUG IN MONIKA'S COTTAGE WASN'T DEAD. HE WAS STILL alive, face down, but the volume of blood on the floor told Vandal that he wouldn't be alive for long. She ran forward and heaved the man's body over by his shoulder until he was on his back. The movement jerked him to consciousness, and his lungs gasped for air. She shined her penlight into his face, then hissed in surprise when she recognized him.

"Jesus! *Nash!*"

The Treadstone handler's eyes blinked open. His face, which was pale and drawn, contorted in pain. She ran the light over his body and saw two gunshot wounds, one in the meaty flesh of his side, the other an exit wound in his upper chest.

"There's a trauma kit in the attic," Vandal told him. "Don't die on me, okay? I'll be right back."

But Nash grabbed her wrist in a limp grip. *"Wait."*

"Nash, I need to stop the bleeding right now."

He struggled for words. "No, no, be careful, there's a shooter in the house. Vandal, someone shot me *here*. Handgun, suppressor. Someone saw me lying on the floor and shot me in the back."

"Nash, we're alone. No one is here but you and me. Unless—*shit!*"

"What?"

"Johanna must have grabbed a gun when we were in the attic. She thought you were one of them. So she shot you and ran."

At her feet, Nash inhaled sharply and bit down on his lip. "Who is Johanna?"

"Monika's sister."

"Her *sister*? Vandal, what the fuck are you talking about?"

"*Le Renouveau* traced Johanna to Salzburg. They tortured her to find out where Monika was, but she didn't know. So Johanna went looking for David Webb in Zurich. She's been trying to find her sister."

"Vandal, *Jesus!*" Nash spat the words back at her. His head lifted off the floor, and his grip tightened on her wrist with a burst of energy. "Don't you get it? Monika Roth is a Treadstone cover identity. It's not real. It was *never* real. We made up the legend for Shadow when we sent her to Europe. *There is no Monika.*"

40

BOURNE KNEW WITH A SINGLE GLANCE AT JOHANNA THAT HE'D BEEN fooled.

Chrétien Pau had played Monika. Johanna had played Jason.

He stared at the woman with the gun, and he didn't recognize her anymore. The vulnerability, the innocence, the flirting, the fear that had all been a part of Johanna's face was gone. She was now mature and hard, her firing stance in perfect balance, her gun as comfortable in her hands as her skin was on her body.

She was a professional. A killer.

But who was she?

Monika, leaning heavily against his shoulder, her forearm and leg leaching blood, pushed away from him and stood awkwardly on her own. Strangely, she didn't look surprised to see the woman in front of her.

"Storm," Monika said.

"Hello, Shadow," Johanna replied.

"I should have known it was you. I told Nash something else was going on, that we were missing a piece of the puzzle. But we thought you were dead."

"Yes, that was the idea. If you knew I was still alive, you would have sent people after me. It was much easier to hunt you as a corpse."

Monika shook her head with what looked like admiration. "Half a dozen witnesses saw you get on that boat in Cyprus. We found the gun on the deck. Blood. DNA. But no body. Our forensic people concluded you'd shot yourself and fallen overboard. You staged the scene well, but I'd expect that from you. Storm is nothing if not an expert at whatever she does. You even convinced Nash that the suicide was real. He's normally a cynic, but he told me not to worry. He was sure you'd really killed yourself."

"And you?"

"I wondered," Monika said with a cock of her head. "It seemed too easy. I was surprised you'd kill yourself with me still alive."

"You're right about that. I tried to kill you once, and you got lucky. The car bomb missed you. But I wasn't going to give up." Her voice rose higher, becoming sharp and shrill. "Not after what you put me through. Not after what you did to me, you *fucking monster*."

Shadow showed no response to the outburst.

Shadow. Not Monika Roth.

That was who she really was. Jason realized now what he should have guessed in the beginning. Monika had never existed at all. Everything about her, including her identity—including her *sister*—had been a lie.

Cain. Shadow. Storm.

All Treadstone.

Bourne took a step toward Johanna—he still thought of her as Johanna—but she instantly shifted the gun toward him. He found himself staring at the barrel of the Ruger from twenty feet away. Her aim and grip were solid. He was certain she wouldn't miss.

"Please don't move, Jason," she told him, her words clipped. "Please. I'm sorry about this. The last thing I want to do is hurt you, but if you get in my way, I'll kill you. Don't think for even a second that I'm bluffing. I'm not."

"I believe you," Jason replied.

"I'm not a liar, you know," she went on. "Not like *she* is. I meant the things I said. I really do feel something for you. Hell, I may even be in love with you. We're kindred spirits, you and me. We're both Treadstone, but neither one of us can turn off our emotions the way they want us to. We still *feel* things despite everything they've done to us. But that won't stop me from putting a bullet in your head if you get between me and Shadow."

"Do you think killing me will bring you peace?" Shadow asked in a calm monotone that barely rose above the wind.

Bourne watched Johanna's eyes burn to life like two fiery suns. "*Jesus!* After everything you've done, you're *still* trying to manipulate me. Get inside my head with your poison. Here's a little tip, you heartless goddamn robot. I'll never have peace, never again. You stole that from me. You messed up my mind forever. Now I have to live with that. The only thing that kept me half sane for the past year is the thought of getting revenge for what you did."

"Then shoot," Shadow said. "This is your moment. This is what you want."

Johanna's finger twitched on the trigger.

She was a fraction of a pound of pressure away from firing, but she held back, and she looked angry with herself for hesitating. Jason understood. He'd been there himself with the assassin known as Lennon.

It was hard to kill in cold blood. When a soldier was coming at you and killing meant survival, that was an act you could justify to yourself. But when your adversary was unarmed, helpless at the end of your barrel, you couldn't always bring yourself to take a life. Not even someone you hated.

Bourne put his body in front of Shadow, blocking her from Johanna's gun. This time, Johanna pulled the trigger without the slightest hesitation. She fired a bullet with perfect accuracy, the trajectory so close to his head that he felt the sting lace across his scalp.

"Get out of the way, Jason."

"Tell me what this is about," Bourne said.

"What is this *about*? Do you really need to ask me that? You know who Shadow is now. She's not your lover, not your fiancée, not the girl who got away. She's a predator. She's *Treadstone*. You know what she did to you ten years ago. My God, even as Monika, even in the midst of the mind games she was playing, she *cheated* on you. She betrayed you with this piece of shit on the ground. That's why I used *you* to help me hunt her. Because I wanted you to understand what kind of a devil she is. I wanted you to see how Treadstone destroys people like us."

"Johanna, what did she do to you?"

"Get out of the way, Jason," she said again.

"What did she do to you?"

"Goddamn it, move! Move! I will kill you!"

Behind him, he felt Shadow's hand on his shoulder. She limped around him, squarely back in the crosshairs of Johanna's gun.

"It's okay, David," she murmured. "You don't need to be a hero for me. Shall I be the one to tell him, Storm? Would you like to hear the story from my own mouth? Everything I did to you. All of my lies."

Bourne watched Johanna's finger on the trigger. He felt her

yearning to shoot. But Shadow knew her target well. A confession from her enemy was too tempting for Johanna to pass up.

"Tell him," she snapped. "Tell him everything."

"Okay. I'll say anything you want except to apologize. I never apologize."

"*Talk.* Tell him what you did to me. Show him who you are."

"Storm worked in Europe designing AI systems," Shadow said, keeping her focus on the girl and the gun. "That's what she was doing when I met her. We'd begun noticing artificial intelligence interfaces that were an order of magnitude more sophisticated than anything coming out of Big Tech yet. It was dark web stuff. Bad players—arms dealers, human traffickers—were already making use of the technology. So Treadstone went looking for the person behind it. I found this twentysomething girl in Salzburg. A tech genius, American expat, a loner. My mission was to kill her. But I saw potential in her, so I encouraged her to come work for us instead. She proved to be even better than I expected. She took to the physical and tradecraft training with an extraordinary skill. You know, I told Jason you were the best agent I'd worked with since I met him, Storm. That wasn't a lie. You were brilliant and capable. You had an unbelievable ability to put on a legend like it was a new set of clothes. I'm not surprised you were able to fool Cain with your story."

"Fuck the flattery," Johanna said. "Tell him what you *did.*"

"Fine. Like I said, you were good. Exceptional. But at the same time, I was worried that you were hiding something from me. That deep down you had a weakness that you were desperate to conceal. So I dove into your childhood, and I found some *incidents.* A classmate called you a name, and you beat her so badly you put her in the hospital. A cousin put a hand on your breast. You broke his arm. I began to realize you had a capacity for rage that I didn't think you could control. That was dangerous. That would wreck Treadstone if it came out at the wrong time or on the wrong mission. You hid it well, you hid it *so* well, but I got a taste of it when I observed you secretly."

"Observed," Johanna shot back. "That sounds so sterile. So innocent. You tracked my computers, my phones, my car. You had cameras on me everywhere I went. You watched me twenty-four seven."

"Yes, I did."

"Did you get off on it, Shadow? Is that the perverted fun for you, getting inside people's private lives like a voyeur? Watching me shower? Watching my boyfriend fuck me?"

"Interesting that you should mention your boyfriend," Shadow said, the monotone in her voice not changing at all. "That was the first time I witnessed what you were capable of. You see, David, Storm's boyfriend made the mistake of choking her in the midst of intercourse. He didn't stop when she struggled. A poor choice on his part. Perhaps he watched too much porn and thought she would like it. But you didn't like it, did you, Storm?"

"No."

"It made you angry."

"Yes."

"Do you want to tell Jason what you did?"

Johanna said nothing, but Bourne saw an explosion simmering in her face. Her hand tightened around the gun.

"She threw her boyfriend across the bedroom," Shadow went on, "and I watched her stab him one hundred and forty-six times."

Johanna fired.

She drilled a bullet into Shadow's leg in almost the exact place where she'd already been shot. The new wound forced out a long, keening wail of pain, and Shadow clung to Bourne as she collapsed to the stone floor of the battery, clutching her thigh, blood pulsing between her fingers.

"He *deserved* what I did to him!" Johanna shouted at the woman writhing on the ground, her voice rising to drown out the wind. "Nobody treats me like that! Nobody! But watching me kill him wasn't enough for you, was it? You couldn't just send me away. Fuck, you didn't even *care* what I'd done to my boyfriend. Murder wasn't disqualifying for Treadstone. I read all of your notes, remember? *I needed to discover what would happen if I forced Storm's unstable emotions to the surface in an operational context.* All that fucking shrink mumbo jumbo. The fact is, you were only concerned about what I would do on a mission."

She took a step closer. Bourne took note of the shrinking distance between them. A couple more steps, and she'd be close enough for him to bridge the gap with a well-timed leap. But he'd be jumping—weak and wounded—into the path of the Ruger, and he'd be up against an agent who was every bit as skilled as he was.

"What did she do?" he asked her.

"She sent me on a mission," Johanna said. "A *fake* mission. But I didn't know that. She used an AI-generated scenario. My own code. She used *my own code* to fuck with me. To trigger me. My instructions were to investigate a college professor in Berlin. He was suspected of producing and distributing child porn. I was supposed to gather evidence against him but take no action. Do nothing. Once I had enough evidence, they'd turn it over to Interpol to arrest and prosecute him. And I found evidence. *Jesus*, the evidence. It was all over his computers. Except I didn't know Treadstone had manufactured it. That it was all AI bullshit. That Shadow *wanted* me to find it. The man was completely innocent, and they set him up. They put a fucking target on his chest."

"Your instructions were to take no action," Shadow said from the ground.

"But you knew who I was!" Storm hissed, taking another step forward and aiming the Ruger at Shadow's head. "You knew my weakness! The whole scenario was designed to break me! That's what you wanted!"

"Yes. It was a test. You failed."

"I burned down his house!" Storm screamed. "I killed him *and his three kids*! The deep fakes you made, the evidence you made me find, included *his own kids*! What the fuck was I supposed to do?"

"Take no action," Shadow said again.

Bourne saw his one chance. Johanna's entire focus was on Shadow. Her body went taut, her muscles winding up like a spring, ready to uncoil. He tensed, timing his assault; he had a split second in which to shunt the gun aside and bring her down. But then it all changed. The violence washed over her like a wave and left calm water in its wake. She took a step back, and she actually laughed.

"God, look at you, you bitch, doing it to me again. Baiting me. Trying to give *Cain* an opening while I'm distracted." Her stare shifted to Bourne. "And you. I saw what you were planning. Quick thrust, grab the gun. Do you really think you can beat me, Jason? I'm good, I'm fast, I'm years younger than you are, and I'm not wounded. Don't make me hurt you. I don't want to."

Jason shook his head. "Why me, Johanna? Why this whole twisted plan?"

She shrugged. "I had to find out where Shadow was hiding, and I needed an ally to do that. I hacked into all of the Treadstone files before I staged my death. I read Shadow's bio and background, her notes, her reports on every agent she worked with, everything she did to them.

That's how I found out about you, Jason. When I read about what she'd done to you, how Treadstone had hidden the truth about your past, I knew you were the one to help me. I could bring *Monika Roth* back into your life, and you'd lead me to wherever she was. You see, whatever else she may be, Shadow is smart. She didn't have a whisper of her current identity anywhere in her files. But I was sure you could find her. Shadow's notes about you were very clear. You respond to danger. Danger toward someone you care about is your most powerful motivator. So I needed a threat. A real threat, nothing fake. You'd see right through that. But I had the answer right in front of me. Shadow's files told me what had happened in Switzerland, and I knew *Le Renouveau* was still looking for you."

"So you reached out to them," Jason concluded.

He heard Yanis Lorchaud in his head again. *You've been betrayed.*

"That's right. I gave them a tip about how to find you and Monika. The tip was me. I invented a legend for Monika's *sister*, someone who might know where she was. They came after me, like I knew they would. Then I came after you. I helped you remember how much you cared about Monika, because I knew you'd need to protect her." She stopped, and her face darkened. "But truly, I didn't plan for us to get together. That just happened. It was genuine. But I won't deny that the feelings between us helped my plan."

"Paris. La Villette. That was you in the woods. You went after Vandal, and then you tried to kill Monika."

"Yes."

"You told *Le Renouveau* about the island."

"Sure. And after you left the house, I texted them again to let them know you and Monika were both here. I needed them to keep coming after you. I needed you focused on the danger, not on me. You were beginning to suss out who Monika really was, and if you analyzed all of it, I knew you'd realize that her identity had to be fake. A cover. That would mean her sister was fake, too. So I had to keep you off balance."

"All to kill Shadow," he said.

"All to slay a *dragon*," Johanna replied.

"Except I can't let you do that."

Johanna shook her head. "You'd give up your life for her? After the way she betrayed both of us? Fuck, I almost told you the truth half a dozen times, because I figured you'd *help* me. Don't be a fool, Jason. Stand back and let me throw this piece of shit off the castle wall."

"Put down the gun, Johanna."

"No. I can't do that. I love you, but I'll kill you."

"If you don't put down the gun, you're going to die."

An arrogant confidence crept into her voice. "Really? How does that work? You think you can get the drop on me? You're unarmed, and you're way too far away."

"Yes, but Vandal's not," Jason said.

"What?"

"Vandal's in the doorway behind you. She's got an Astra pointed at your back. Even with a concussion, I don't think she's likely to miss."

Johanna shifted the gun and aimed at his forehead. "Seriously? That's weak, Jason. Is that really the best gambit you've got? Vandal's at the cottage, probably crying over Nash's dead body. That was a nice bonus, by the way, being able to shoot him, too. He's almost as much of a devil as Shadow. Now I'm going to count to five. I swear, if you're still standing there, I'll put a bullet in your head."

"Five," Vandal announced from behind Storm.

She fired.

She fired high, as Jason knew she would, not wanting to hit Bourne or Shadow with an errant shot. But the distraction worked. Johanna twisted with unbelievable speed; he had never seen an agent move so fast. She spun toward Vandal and let three bullets fly in the time it took Bourne to close the distance between them. But Vandal was already gone, taking cover behind the stone doorway at the castle steps.

Jason focused on the Ruger. He hammered Johanna's wrist as he collided with her body, and the pistol clattered away as they both tumbled to the ground. She struck back so fast he could barely react. Her elbow shot toward him, missing his windpipe by a couple of inches but hitting his upper chest with enough force to make him choke. She jumped—*jumped*—to her feet, and as he pushed himself off the ground, her knee connected with the underside of his chin and threw him backward. He tried to shake off the blow, but the sky over his head went into a crazy orbit. In those few seconds, Johanna scrambled across the battery floor and had her Ruger back in her hand.

From the doorway, Vandal fired again.

She aimed directly at Johanna this time and missed, but the sizzling round forced Johanna sideways. Bourne charged, and Johanna fired back at Vandal just as Jason wrapped an arm around her neck and clenched his fist around the hand that held the gun. The barrel of the Ruger went high; two bullets flew wild. Jason hung on. They wrestled in each other's arms. Johanna wriggled as he tried to contain her, and their bodies did a crazy dance, crashing into the castle wall. He had the strength, but she had the endurance, and he knew he was running out of time. With his shoulder, he threw all his weight into a single shove that drove her against the stone. Her head hit hard, and her body went limp for an instant. He used that moment to peel away the Ruger and stagger backward.

Bourne pointed the gun at her face from three feet away.

In front of him, Johanna's eyes focused again. She stared at the Ruger. "Nice. I knew you were good, but that was nice."

"Get on your knees," Bourne told her. "I'm going to tie you up and take you in."

"No. You're not. Kill me or let me go, Jason. There's no in-between."

"Get on your knees," Bourne told her again.

"I'm nobody's prisoner. If you want me, you have to shoot me. That's the choice. What's it going to be?"

Bourne tightened his grip on the Ruger.

"Vandal," he called sharply. "Check on Shadow. She needs help."

That was true. Shadow was losing blood fast. Slowly, the other Treadstone agent limped past them to tend to the woman on the ground. But now there was no one blocking the steps out of the upper battery. Johanna glanced that way, and he could see the calculations in her mind, doing what good agents did. Anticipating each of the next moves like a chess player. Figuring out how to get off the island.

If he let her go, she'd melt away. But he couldn't let her go.

Johanna studied the barrel of the gun with a strange curiosity. "Can you do it, Jason? I really wonder. Can you kill a woman you've made love to? Has that ever happened to you before?"

He knew he had to fire.

He didn't want to, but he had to fire. Johanna couldn't stay free and stay alive. This amazing woman, this irresistible girl who'd bewitched him and deceived him, had to die. He had no choice. It would be merciful and quick, a single shot as fast as suicide taking the life out of her pretty eyes.

"I have to do it," he told her.

"Yeah. I know."

"I'm sorry."

"It's okay, Jason. I still love you."

His finger curled around the trigger.

His mind took a photograph of Johanna's long blond hair, her blue eyes, her lips. He knew how those lips felt; he knew what it was like to kiss them. He could feel the warmth of her skin; he could feel her legs wrapped around him and remember everything about her body that was hard and soft.

"Goodbye, Johanna," Bourne said.

"Goodbye, Jason."

Then, accepting who he was, he cocked his arm and lowered the gun.

"Go," David Webb told her, and that was it. Like a deer bolting, Johanna was gone.

41

THE MEDICAL TEAM LOADED NASH ONTO THE TREADSTONE HELICOPTER. HE was going to make it. So was Shadow. They came for her next, but she waved them away before they could lift up the stretcher. The men backed off, leaving Bourne alone with her in the middle of the island field. It was still night, and the sea winds were cold and strong. Lindisfarne was on lockdown as American and British intelligence agencies sanitized the scene, hauling away bodies and guns and washing away the blood.

And, Bourne thought, preparing the lies they would tell. He knew how it would go.

Chrétien Pau would simply disappear. There would be no murder. No association with *Le Renouveau*. Maybe a plane crash while on a secret fundraising trip, a tragic end to such a promising career. The French election would be delayed, giving the establishment time to find a new mainstream candidate to run against *Le Roi Raymond*. In the meantime, Interpol would begin scouring the ranks of government, business, and media throughout Europe to root out the extremists hiding in plain sight.

The choice would be simple.

Resign or disappear.

On the stretcher, Shadow looked up at him. Dirt and blood on her face did nothing to dim her cool, elegant reserve. But he saw something approaching wistfulness in her expression, not for him, but for the island. Sarah Tedford would never return here. Her seaside cottage would go up for sale, and Shadow would disappear to some other part of the world. Every Treadstone agent faced that reality sooner or later, but it didn't make it any easier when it happened.

"I had to let her go," Jason said. "I'm sorry. I know that means you'll still be looking over your shoulder."

"If it's any consolation, I knew you couldn't kill her," Shadow replied. "That's who you are, David. What happened between us ten years ago may have been a lie, but I still know you better than anyone else. I'll always be in your head."

She made it sound like a curse. Maybe it was.

"Nash will take a long while to recover," Shadow went on. "It will be months before he's active in the field. He may never be up to the job again. In the meantime, I'd like to be your handler myself."

"Why would you want that?" Bourne asked.

"Because you're a superior asset," she replied, as if that were the only variable in play. "I'm going to be running operations at Treadstone, and I need someone who reports to me directly. There are missions that fall outside the normal chain of command. When that happens, I need someone I can trust."

"You mean someone you can manipulate," he said.

"No. That's over. You know exactly who I am now, David. *Jason.* I wouldn't try to control you again, and I wouldn't want to. You see, that's really why I wanted you to find me. Why I felt it was time you learned the truth about everything that happened ten years ago. Despite our past, I see an important future for the two of us."

"Aren't you afraid I'll fall in love with you all over again?" he asked harshly.

Shadow smiled. "I don't have enough ego to believe that. It doesn't even matter to me if you hate me. We can still work together."

"I don't hate you," Jason said.

"Good."

"But I'll never trust you."

"That's smart."

"If we do this, I choose which missions I accept," Jason told her.

"No, I choose the missions you do. Period."

He looked down at Shadow lying on the stretcher, on her back, her eyes blue and cold, and he had a brief, unsettling memory from the past of their naked bodies intertwined together. "This is going to be an interesting relationship."

"Yes, it is."

She waved at the medical team, and they approached and took hold of the stretcher from both sides. Bourne began to turn away as they loaded Shadow onto the helicopter, but then she called after him.

"One more thing, Jason. I wonder if you could do me a favor."

"What is it?"

"There's nothing personal in my cottage, of course. The cleaners will deal with my weapons and make sure they get back to me. But there's a small painting in the library I'd like to have for my new office. It's harmless, but I like it. Would you mind keeping it for me until we meet again?"

"Sure," he replied.

"Thank you, David."

He turned his back on Shadow and walked across the empty field, listening to the throb of the helicopter's engine as the machine rose up and veered toward the mainland. On the fringe of the field, waiting for him next to the Land Rover, he saw Vandal. She was supposed to be on the helicopter heading for the hospital, too, but in typical Vandal fashion, she'd refused the ride. She was going to be driving off the island with Jason as the waters cleared the causeway, and then he'd drop her at Heathrow in London.

From there, he didn't know where she'd go. Or what she'd do next.

"Ready to roll?" she asked.

"Almost. I need to make a last stop at Monika's."

"There is no Monika," Vandal reminded him.

Bourne said nothing, but he wondered if that was true. For him, in some part of his mind, Monika would always be real.

He got behind the wheel and drove across the fields. As they neared the empty village, they saw the lights of the cleaners at work, bringing Holy Island back to what it had been, no hint of the overnight violence. He stopped the SUV in front of the seaside cottage. Its door was still open. No one had gone inside yet.

"Wait here, okay?" Jason said. "I'll just be a minute."

He crossed through the garden and into the house, noting the blood that still trailed across the wooden floor. The cottage looked the same. It smelled the same. He imagined Shadow living in this remote getaway for years, the one part of the world in which she could be normal for a short while.

Was this where the real Shadow lived?

Or was this another false identity?

Bourne made his way to the house's old library. There were several paintings on the wall that he'd noted before, all of them ocean landscapes done in oil. He realized he had no idea which painting she wanted, and he didn't know how to decide which one to take. It was odd that she wouldn't have specified.

Then he took another look around the library, and he saw it.

It wasn't on the wall. It was on a small rolltop desk near the fireplace. The desk was otherwise almost empty. The six-inch-by-six-inch watercolor on the gold metal stand had been pushed behind an antique lamp so that it was nearly invisible unless someone looked for it. Jason went to the desk and took the small painting in his hand.

He could hear Shadow's voice in his head. *I wouldn't try to control you again, and I wouldn't want to.*

And yet he could already feel her tentacles wrapping themselves around him.

The painting was of Mont Saint-Michel.

FOUR WEEKS LATER, BOURNE SAT AT THE PARIS CAFÉ OUTSIDE THE PLACE de la Bastille, waiting for his *steak au poivre* and his bottle of 1664 beer. It was a sunny day, following stormy weeks. He noted the nearby Métro sign and saw no orange hashtag scrawled in chalk. Another day, another week, another month had gone by with no message from Abbey Laurent. He wondered if he would ever hear from her again, or if that relationship, like so many others in his past, had been buried for good.

He hadn't heard from Shadow, either. Rumors around the intelligence community had reached his ears that someone new was in charge of Treadstone operations. No one had a name. No one knew who he or she was. But Bourne was sure that Shadow had become the invisible hand pulling the levers of the organization.

That meant he was back in, too.

He had conflicted feelings about that. About *her*. There had been no request for a meeting, no rendezvous in the Tuileries to give him an assignment. But sooner or later, he would find himself staring at that face again.

Monika.

He glanced at the crowded plaza across the street, with its soaring column framed against the sun and the Génie de la Liberté glinting in gold as it raised its torch to the sky. Where there had been violent protesters a few weeks ago, now there were mostly tourists and children and locals eating sandwiches and drinking espresso. He saw a few old signs for *La Vraie* tied to the green railing around the Colonne de Juillet, but days of rain had washed most of them away. The riots had mysteriously vanished from the French cities as the instigators in the Guy Fawkes masks disappeared. Raymond Berland was dropping in the polls, and the mainstream candidate replacing Chrétien Pau—a sixty-eight-year-old doctor from a pro-European party in the National Assembly—seemed to have a lock on the presidency.

Le Renouveau hadn't gone away, he knew, but it had gone underground for now. It was pulling in its swords and strategizing for the future.

A young waitress emerged from the doors of the café with a silver tray balanced on one hand. She deposited his bottle of Kronenbourg on the table, and then she dug inside the pocket of her apron and put a cheap cell phone in front of him.

The power was on.

When he looked at her curiously, she shrugged and said, *"Pour vous, monsieur. D'une femme."*

For him.

From a woman.

As the waitress walked away, the phone began to ring. Bourne picked it up, answered the call, but said nothing.

"Hello, Jason," Johanna said.

He looked around the plaza. She had to be close by. It took him only a few seconds to find her, standing near a light post with traffic and bicycles coming and going in front of her. She wore black leggings and a red nylon jacket, with her hands in the pockets. No doubt she had her fingers curled around a gun. A wire led from a phone clipped to her waist to a microphone in her ear. She looked fresh and pretty, as she always did, her blond hair straight and parted in the middle, her blue eyes focusing on him at the café. She raised her hand and gave him a smile and a little wave.

"Why not come join me for a drink?" Jason asked.

"I would, but I figure you might have orders to kill me."

"I don't." He added, "Not yet."

"Well, smart girls take no chances."

He found himself wanting to cross the busy street toward her. To do what, he didn't know. But if he got close, he was sure she would run.

"What do you want, Johanna?"

"I don't know, Jason. I really don't. Maybe I wanted to see you again. Or maybe I thought we could declare a truce for the night and sleep together. Mostly, I guess I just wanted to say I'm sorry. Shadow manipulated me and lied to me, and it drove me insane. Then I went and did the same thing to you. I mean, in the beginning, I assumed you would be like all the others—like Vandal and Nash—killing without a cause and feeling nothing. So I didn't care. But then I realized you're different. I was drawn to you. I still am."

He said nothing. There was nothing to say. They could desire each other and not trust each other. They could want things they couldn't have.

"No message from Abbey?" Johanna asked with a nod toward the Métro sign.

"No."

"She's a fool."

"No, she's smart. Like you."

"Maybe. But she's still a fool."

They fell silent again. More traffic came and went between them on Boulevard Henri IV. The two of them simply stared at each other, wondering what to say next, but not wanting the moment between them to end. A car, a truck would go by, and he would lose her face for a moment, and then it would be back.

"What have you been doing for the last month?" she asked him.

"Recovering. What about you?"

"Planning."

His eyes narrowed with suspicion at what he heard in her voice. "Planning what, Johanna?"

She didn't answer him, but he saw a scary wildness in her eyes.

"Johanna?" he said again, with concern. "If you're thinking of going after Shadow, don't do it. She knows you're out there now. She'll be waiting for you, and she'll have a trap set for whatever you try. She won't show any mercy if she sees you. It won't be like you and me. She'll kill you."

"I know."

"I'm serious. She will take you out."

"Would you feel bad about that, Jason?"

"Of course I would. I don't want to see anything happen to you. Let it go, Johanna. You got her to admit what she did to you. That's enough. Go off and live your life."

"Uh-huh," she said.

Jason sighed. "You can't do that, can you?"

"No."

"I'll tell her you're coming. I'll warn her, and you won't get within a mile of Shadow. That's for your benefit, not hers. I want you alive."

"That's nice. I like it when you say that."

"It's true."

"Do you think we could ever be together again? You and me?"

"I don't know. Maybe. But it's hard to imagine, isn't it?"

"Yeah. I guess we'll see." She glanced at the plaza, looking small amid the bustle of Paris. "I should go."

"Johanna, I'm serious. *Don't* take on Shadow again."

"Oh, this isn't about Shadow anymore. I realized it's bigger than her. She's a symptom, she's not the disease."

"What are you planning?"

"I'm sorry, Jason, it's better you not know. If I tell you, then you'll try to stop me." Across the street, she made a little kiss at him with her lips. "Or who knows, maybe you'll realize you should help me."

"Help you do what?"

Johanna didn't answer immediately. He felt the heat of her eyes. Then she murmured into the phone, "Does she still have her hooks in you, Jason? Are you still part of them? Tell me the truth. Are you in or out?"

"Both. Neither. I don't know yet."

"You should be out," she said. "You should be with me."

"Johanna, what are you planning?" Bourne asked her again.

A white lorry paused on the street between them, stalled by traffic. He couldn't see her, and somehow he knew, whenever the truck passed, Johanna would be gone. But he still heard her voice on the phone.

"I'm going to destroy Treadstone," she told him. "I'm going to burn it all down until there's nothing left."